PRAISE FOR BLACK ARTS:

'I think it's a brilliant book, a great blend of action,
adventure, magic, horror and humour'
Charlie Higson

'Extremely impressive – this is a sparkling
and intelligent debut.'
Philip Ardagh, *The Guardian*

'Prentice and Weil do know how to spin a
thrilling yarn . . . devilish good fun.'
The Financial Times

'There are hints of Alex Rider and Indiana Jones
in the pickpocket hero of this exciting
adventure story . . . Full of dark magic
and a powerful sense of history.'
Booktrust

'Roistering and sweaty, full of magic and mischief
. . . The authors use of contemporary
slang is brilliant'
Literary Review

THE BOOKS OF PANDEMONIUM

BLACK ARTS

ANDREW PRENTICE AND JONATHAN WEIL

David Fickling Books

OXFORD · NEW YORK

31 Beaumont Street
Oxford OX1 2NP, UK

BLACK ARTS
A DAVID FICKLING BOOK 978 1 849 92132 9

First published in Great Britain by David Fickling Books,
a division of Random House Children's Publishers UK
A Random House Group Company

Hardback edition published 2012
Paperback edition published 2013

1 3 5 7 9 10 8 6 4 2

Text copyright © Andrew Prentice & Jonathan Weil, 2012
Jacket and illustrations copyright © Adam Brockbank 2012

The right of Andrew Prentice, Jonathan Weil and Adam Brockbank to be identified
as the authors and illustrator of this work has been asserted in accordance with the
Copyright, Designs and Patents Act 1988.

The Random House Group Limited supports the Forest Stewardship Council® (FSC®), the
leading international forest-certification organisation. Our books carrying the FSC label are
printed on FSC®-certified paper. FSC is the only forest-certification scheme supported by the
leading environmental organisations, including Greenpeace. Our paper procurement policy
can be found at www.randomhouse.co.uk/environment

MIX
Paper from
responsible sources
FSC® C016897

Set in Goudy

DAVID FICKLING BOOKS
31 Beaumont Street, Oxford, OX1 2NP

www.randomhousechildrens.co.uk
www.totallyrandombooks.co.uk
www.randomhouse.co.uk

Addresses for companies within The Random House Group Limited can be found at:
www.randomhouse.co.uk/offices.htm

THE RANDOM HOUSE GROUP Limited Reg. No. 954009

A CIP catalogue record for this book is available from the British Library.

Printed and bound in Great Britain by CPI Group (UK) Ltd, Croydon, CR0 4YY

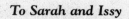
To Sarah and Issy

'Hell is empty
And all the devils are here.'

William Shakespeare, *The Tempest*

Prologue

The child died first. They hanged her from a willow tree. The others waited their turn in silence. It was cold that night, but they did not shiver.

This was how they said it had to be.

The tribe had spent long years searching for this place. They had roamed these forests for a time. Before that, they had crossed the grey sea. Before that was a dim age that no one was alive to remember.

The grove rose between two shallow hills on the north bank of the river. It was good ground. Clean springs bubbled from the wooded slopes. The river would give fish, and the hills would give protection.

Now, on the moon's sixth day, the child had to die, along with the others, in order to provide a different sort of protection. A blessing, of sorts.

Five men were evenly spaced in a circle around the

edges of the grove. They were dressed all in white, and the oldest of them carried a hazel rod looped with leaves made of bronze. Five fires burned at their feet. Eddies of smoke turned and gathered in the space inside their circle. Their people waited further back, beneath the trees. Together they had cut this clearing, pulled up all the stumps, stamped the dirt till it was flat and level.

In the centre of the space stood a dark lump of stone. It was smooth and black in the moonlight, except where a single seam of pure white gold cut through it. It was an unusual sort of stone to find. The old man had nodded over it in approval: a good-sized rock, hard and strong. It would last a long time.

The child died first, and eight others followed her, hoisted up to hang from the circle of trees around the clearing. As the ninth choked out the last of his life, a clatter of birds burst from the branches.

The old man threw more leaves on his fire.

It began as a trembling shimmer of light in the smoke-filled air above the stone. The men and women of the tribe stirred, uneasy. The priests' chant was soft. A rustling sound ran through the grove, like wind in dead reeds.

No one quite agreed on what happened next. Afterwards, most believed what the old man had seen, assuming that their own memories played them false.

In the old man's tale, a figure appeared quite suddenly beside the stone. It flickered and flexed, its form and face unclear. One moment it was no bigger than a man, the next it seemed to brush the stars. At last it decided on a single shape – a tall, stooped figure with the head of a raven, wrapped from chin to ankle in glossy furs.

It fixed the old man with its beady black eye, and croaked. He thought there were words, but he could not make them out. A tingling, prickling sensation scratched across his arms and neck.

A harsh cackle came from the wide black beak.

Again, the old man did not understand, but he knew the words he had to say.

'What is your name?'

Another croak, short and blunt. To the old man it sounded like 'Lud'.

'I bind you, Lud, to this stone,' he said. He gestured with his hazel stick to the black rock at the centre of the clearing. 'May it profit you. Let these hills be your hills. May it profit you. Let these people be your people. May it profit you.'

The raven's head cocked to one side. Its eyes turned pale gold. A gleaming darkness pulsed in the stone, and the raven was gone.

In the morning they cut the bodies down, cold and stiff, and buried them there, in the hard earth around the stone. They buried the child last of all.

The settlement on the hills by the river was named Lud, after the spirit that was bound to it. It began as a cluster of rough mud shelters, but soon there was a forge, and fields, and houses built of wood. It became a hamlet, then a village, then a kingdom. The tribe that had summoned the spirit was overrun by invaders in due course. The invaders were themselves overrun, and so on a few more times – but the place remained, and prospered and grew through it all.

The grove became old, then ancient. No bird built a nest in the trees, and no animal ever walked through the clearing. Sometimes the leaves shivered when no breeze stirred them; sometimes the branches were still when a storm raged all around.

When the trees were cut down, the black stone remained.

The settlement prospered, though its name changed to suit the tongue of the latest wave of conquerors. It gained and lost a few syllables here, a letter there, spiralling around its first form like a spinning top. It never changed by very much. Something slept here, and dreamed of the place as it had been and as it would be, and these dreams kept the place and its name centred around itself.

Its name was Lud.

Chapter 1

London, 1592

The day of the testing dawned cold and bright. Jack scrunched the top of his blanket up around his chin, huddling in the warmth. This was his favourite time of day. It belonged to him and nobody else, not even his ma.

He listened to her gentle snores, and watched a spot of light move slowly across the wall.

Jack had built the wall himself when the old one fell down, using an enormous slab of wood that he'd found washed up in the estuary mud. It had spent a long time underwater, and was crannied all over with dark fissures and tiny holes made by worms. You could still just make out a worn carving of a lion in the centre. Jack liked to imagine that it had once been part of a Spanish admiral's dining table. It had taken him a whole afternoon and two fist-fights to get it home safe.

The spot of light moved across the pitted wood, regular as a sundial. Right now it was crawling along a deep crack that ran from one corner to the centre, approaching the lion. When it reached it, his ma would stop snoring. A couple of minutes later, St Olave's bell would strike seven. Jack would have to come out of his blanket cocoon; it would be cold, and there would be things to do. Today there would be big things to do.

The delicious, warm, half-asleep feeling was ebbing away already. Jack pulled the blanket tighter, trying to hold it in.

His ma stopped snoring. Jack's eyes flicked back to the spot of light: there it was, right on the mark. He concentrated on feeling as warm and comfortable as possible.

The bell began to bong. His ma cleared her throat with an explosive *harrumph*.

'. . . five . . . six . . . seven, and up!'

Jack's ma had always been a brisk riser of a morning. She was a large woman, and she'd been slowed down in a lot of ways after her left foot was crushed under a stolen demi-cannon when Jack was eight. She'd had to quit her trade, but she'd never let the accident change her morning routine.

'Up, me lad! Up to greet the new day!' She seized the stick that lay on the floor beside her and heaved herself upright. She stretched, yawned and shuddered with pleasure.

'Cold one today. Get your blood flowing, Jack. Put some colour in those cheeks of yours. Tingle the yumours . . .'

Jack pulled his blanket up over his head.

Already she was clumping about, starting the morning's business. Her big, sturdy body was like an earthquake in the tiny room, pulling on clothes over her nightshirt, banging open the bread box for breakfast, jabbing at last night's fire to see if it had any life left in it. Jack heard a grunt of satisfaction, then a sucking sound as she lit her pipe.

Like the Spanish admiral's table, the tobacco in her pipe had come from the river – a cask washed up just east of Custom House Quay, trundled away by Jack before the stevedores could get it. It burned with a thick black smoke that smelled of mud and rotting winter leaves.

'Ah . . . what a tingle! Have a puff, Jack. Lord knows, you need as much tingle as you can get, today of all days.'

'Ma . . .'

'Yes, lad?'

'No.'

Jack stumbled to his feet, staggered into his trousers, wrapped the blanket round his shoulders and made a dash for the door. He'd got used to his ma's craze for tobacco smoking – mostly – but first thing in the morning it was still too much.

'Your loss, Jack!' Her laughter followed him out into the fresh air.

Jack's gaff was built up against the north wall of a small, grey, moss-eaten court. The court had no entrance apart from an ivy-choked opening in the west wall. Jack had found it two summers ago, while hunting for rats with a stray dog he'd made an alliance with. The dog had disappeared last winter, but the court remained. He had no idea what it was doing here, walled away in the middle of the Southwark Shambles. His best guess was that it still existed because no one else knew about it.

The court was empty apart from Jack's gaff and a canvas tent that sagged against the opposite wall. It had rained in the night, and pools of water gleamed in the tent's folds. The pile of firewood under the canvas was dry, Jack noted with satisfaction.

He pulled down one corner of the tent's roof. Clear, cold rainwater sloshed down over his head, making his scalp tingle. He rubbed his head dry with the blanket.

'How's the foot, Ma?'

'Oh, very bad . . . very bad . . .' She poked her head through the doorway, blew a smoke-ring, and winked at him. 'Never you mind the foot. You mind Sharkwell, boy. You worry about the testing.'

She was watching him, her strong, gypsy-queen brows

drawn together over her dark eyes. Most mornings, her eyes contained a spark of devilish laughter, just waiting for the right thing to set her off; but now they were serious.

She knocked out her pipe against the wall. 'Had your wash?'

'Yes, Ma.'

'Teeth?' She handed him the tooth stick, frayed at one end. Jack used the frayed end to poke half-heartedly at his teeth. His ma was smoothing down his hair, plastering it over his forehead.

'No practice this morning. You're ready, Jack. You stay sharp, and don't let Sharkwell put the fear on, and you'll be grand.'

Jack pulled a face, the stick still in his mouth. '*Rister* Harkwell.'

She stood back and appraised his hair, nodded in satisfaction, then pulled a small chunk of black bread out from her apron, bit off a corner, and started to chew.

'Yes,' she said after she had chomped at the bread for a while. '*Mr* Sharkwell. Don't forget it, Jack. You're going to have to pay mind to Mr Sharkwell from now on.'

'I know it, Ma.'

'He's a hard man, but—'

'But fair. I know.'

'You be sharp, Jack. Be sharp, and—'

'Don't cross him. I know.'

9

'And don't forget to mention my name when you speak to him . . . and steer clear of 'prentices.'

She passed him the loaf. The bread was tough and sour.

'They're only envious, you know . . .' She patted his cheek. 'You're sharper than the lot of 'em put together. Now, it's nearly time. Have you got your tools?'

'Yes, Ma.'

'Safe and ready?'

'Yes, Ma.'

'Show me, then.'

Jack rolled up the left sleeve of his shirt. There was a hidden pocket sewn onto the inside, and wedged into the pocket was a thin, tightly wrapped sausage of cloth.

'Good.' She patted his cheek again.

Jack scowled. 'Do you have to do that, Ma?'

'Course I do. I'm your ma.' She laughed, and for a moment the sparkle was back in her eyes. 'You go along now. Wouldn't do to be late.'

Jack walked slowly across the court. Already his heart was beginning to thud. He looked back as he was lifting the mat of ivy that hid the opening in the wall.

His ma was standing at the door, watching him.

'I'll be back before sundown, then,' said Jack.

'And what else?'

She said it every day, before letting him go. The answer came on its own, like a ritual.

'Watch my back.'

'Never forget it, Jack,' she said. 'Stay sharp. Stand the test, and don't be afraid.'

They were the last words she ever spoke to him.

Chapter 2

Jack wriggled out into a dark, narrow alleyway, glancing to either side to check that no one had noticed him. He liked having the court to himself, and he knew plenty of Southwark people who would be glad to take up some of the free space.

So far, no one had ever noticed him entering or leaving. Deep down, Jack wasn't surprised by this. Next to finding things, his biggest talent was not being noticed. The two went well together, especially if you were in Jack's line of work.

The problem with being in Jack's line of work was that it wasn't strictly lawful. Finding things was all very well, but sometimes the things he found belonged to other people. If he got caught taking them, he would be mutilated or killed.

Strangely enough, this wasn't something that Jack worried about very much. Perhaps it was because he was so good at not getting caught; or perhaps it was because the law was less worrying than Mr Sharkwell.

Sooner or later, if you lived in Southwark and broke the law, Sharkwell would notice you. Jack had always known this, and he hadn't been surprised when the summons came for the testing. When Sharkwell noticed you breaking the law, he didn't cut off your fingers or hang you up to die: he put you to work.

This was how life went in the city. No one worked alone, at least not for long. Clowns, carpenters, lawyers, cut-throats, apothecaries, puppet-masters, thieves – whatever it was you did, you had to be part of a company, know your place and follow the rules. If you didn't, you were in trouble. If you were a thief operating independent of Sharkwell, you were in bad trouble. Which was fair enough, Jack thought: the hard part was what happened if you failed him. Cutting off fingers was small beer compared to what happened then.

Fair enough, but hard as nails. That was Sharkwell.

Jack threaded his way through the alleyways, heading for Tooley Street. The mud from last night's rain squeezed cold between his toes with every step. He dodged round the worst of the puddles, and out into the early morning traffic.

On any other day, Jack would have been instantly on the hunt, eyes darting this way and that, sizing up prospects. This morning, he was in such a state that he didn't notice the wagon piled high with cabbages, or the dumpy baker's wife, too busy gossiping to watch her tray. Normally, a bun and a cabbage made breakfast and dinner, but today Jack wasn't hungry.

The wind oozed in from the river, whispering of rotting fish, damp and drains. It was the Southwark smell, as familiar to Jack as the sound of his ma's voice.

He was certain of one thing: if he failed, he wouldn't be smelling it much longer. Mr Sharkwell would see to that.

Just before the square tower of St Olave's, Jack made a right turn and cut down towards the bankside wharfs. He had never taken this particular turning before. No one ever did, unless they had good reason. The lane ended in a knot of low, sullen sheds, joined together with planks to make a wall. Beyond them rose the bulk of Mr Sharkwell's warehouse, and beyond that, Jack supposed, lay his infamous Privy Wharf.

The door looked heavy, its planks stained black with pitch and bound together by iron rivets. Jack hesitated. When he finally summoned up the nerve, the noise his knuckles made on the wood sounded feeble. He rapped again, harder this time. There was no sound or sign from inside.

Jack was just getting up the courage for a third knock when a hatch slid open in the door.

'Whaddyawant?'

A single disapproving blue eye glared out at him. There was a scarred, pink socket where its fellow had once been.

'Uh . . . I'm here for the testing . . .'

'Speakup! Can't hearya!'

'Here for the testing, y'r honour,' said Jack, a little louder.

'Y'r honour, issit? 'Nother lamb to the slaughter! Har har! What's the name?'

'Jack.'

There was the sound of heavy bolts being drawn back. The door was thrown open.

Jack took a step back.

The face leering down at him was shockingly hideous. Jack couldn't take his eyes off it. He wanted to, but he couldn't.

There was the missing eye, of course. Worse still, the tip of the nose was gone, sliced clean off. Something nasty had happened to the mouth, leaving it permanently twisted in a lopsided snarl. The bald scalp was crisscrossed with scars.

'And so? Yer here to see Mr Sharkwell, so get in, bigod!' The doorkeeper held the door open a little wider. 'Or trot off, 'tis all the same to me. What's it to be, boy?'

Jack had been summoned here by Sharkwell himself. He knew what would happen if he didn't show. It was enough to propel him inside. He ducked beneath the man's arm, and found himself in a long, dark passageway.

The doorkeeper stomped ahead, and Jack followed. They passed several closed doors. As well as the usual muggy reek of the river, Jack sniffed traces of spices, tobacco smoke and fatty cooking. Behind one of the doors he heard the unmistakable ping of a blacksmith hammering at his anvil.

'Wait here,' said the doorkeeper, before stepping through the archway at the end of the corridor. Jack peered after him, into a cavernous space packed with barrels and crates. A complicated system of ropes and pulleys hung from the ceiling. Men were working up there, calling to each other as they manoeuvred something that looked like a large cow through the air.

The cow mooed.

'Ho there! Jack, is it?'

A new man appeared in the archway. He was dressed like gentry, with a stiff white ruff, baggy pantaloons, and a rich-guarded jerkin. His boots were Spanish leather, and gleamed with oil. Not a stitch, not a seam was out of place.

'Yessir,' said Jack.

'Anne's grunting-cheat, ain'tchya?' For all his finery, the man's voice was pure Southwark. 'Sure you are – you have her blinkers, *sans questiownay*.'

'Yessir.'

The man beamed down at him over his ruff. 'Well, well, well. Anne's boy,' he said. 'Sharkwell's had his blinkers on you; crustier than a Pimlico Pudding Pie, you are. Chip 'n' block, apple 'n' tree – all that!'

'. . . um . . .'

'Right. I'm to be your queer-cuffin. See if you're rumpskuttle, or a pizzle-prancer, eh?'

Jack was impressed. Rumpskuttle was old cant – even his ma said rumpskuttle now – but he hadn't heard those others before. In fact he had no idea what the man was talking about.

'*Bene! Bene!* The name's Mr Smiles, by the by.'

'Pleased to meet you,' said Jack. 'So . . . I'm to see Mr Sharkwell?'

'Ho ho!' Mr Smiles slapped his thigh in amusement. 'You noddy. A rivelled margery-prater's got more chance of plucking a rose in Her Emjay's ruff-peck than you've of parlaying with Mr S! Got to clean your whistle first.'

Jack took that as a no.

Mr Smiles turned smartly, and strode into the warehouse, whistling a bouncy tune. Jack followed, wondering what came next. Mr Smiles was a little too bouncy to be trusted, he thought.

They skirted the outer ramparts of the vast pile of crates. The cow lowed mournfully as it swayed through the air above them. Jack tried not to look too wide-eyed.

'*Entray,*' said Mr Smiles, beckoning Jack through a door.

Jack found himself in a cobbled yard, walled in by old

damp brick. There was a window high up in the wall to his left. Opposite, at the very top of the right-hand wall, was a small brass bell.

Mr Smiles locked the door behind them. It took him some time, and a lot of rattling. He was careful to keep his motions hidden. When he'd finished he turned smartly about, and caught Jack watching him.

'Right chary one, ain't you?' He grinned. 'And you're right to be chary. This is the kennel of Trials, laddie boy! Three of them here, and there's a fourth if you wash clean. Curbing first, then a spot of wall-work, and thirdly Black Arts. You've been slapping on, I hope?'

'Yessir.' Jack was beginning to get the knack of conversing with Mr Smiles.

'Go to, then! Go to! Time's a wasting!'

'What – now?' said Jack.

Mr Smiles shook his head in amazement. 'What d'ye take me for? A Stepford rooster? You spy your instrument? You spy the finestra? Now go to't!'

Propped against the wall beneath the window was the curb – a long pole with a hooked claw at one end. Jack walked over and picked it up. He forced himself to take a deep breath.

'I need you to shift that shift, laddie boy. See it? No squeaks.'

Jack nodded. A white shirt was just visible through the whorled glass of the window. The curb was just long enough to reach. He held the base of it in his left hand, and used his right to guide the claw to the edge of the window frame. The slightest wobble made the tip swing wildly about.

By some happy chance, the claw gripped home at the first try. Jack tugged gently. The window swung open without a sound.

'Zooks! Nicely pinked,' murmured Mr Smiles.

The next part was the trickiest. A cord ran down the length of the curb, attached to a trigger at one end and the claw at the other. Jack had to grab the shirt's collar, and lift it clear of the window and away.

Silently he thanked his ma for all the endless practising she'd put him through.

'No tearings, either,' said Mr Smiles. ''Twould onsewer a fail.'

Jack edged the claw forward. Once, twice he made a grab for the collar and missed.

'The matron of the mansionard returns,' said Mr Smiles. 'You hear her stampers on the stairway! Swiftly, laddie boy! Swiftly! Look snappish!'

This time the tip of the claw nestled home. Jack squeezed the trigger and the claw gripped tight onto the collar. He inched the curb up. The shirt came free. Now it was easy: he backed away, bringing the shirt through the open window, and lowered it to the ground. Mr Smiles examined the collar. There were no tears.

'Hah! Yer Anne's boy bene-sewer! She always had a dab tab for the curb.' Mr Smiles dropped the shirt and pointed to the opposite wall.

'The Trial of Jack: Part the Second! See that clanger?'

Jack looked up at the bell, and nodded.

'Ring it.'

Jack approached the wall. There were some small gaps and cracks near the bottom that looked like good holds. Higher up, it got harder.

He put his hands to the first position. The damp brick-work was slippery under his fingers.

'Not scrumbled: I like it!' Mr Smiles beamed encouragingly.

Jack tensed and heaved, levering his body from one hold to another. He went up smooth, spidering his way, and in a couple of breaths he'd got himself exactly where he'd meant to.

Now came the hard bit. The next hold was a mossy, fingertip crack. It was further away than it had looked from the ground. Beyond it, the bell hung tantalizingly out of reach.

Jack's arms began to tremble.

He shoved off, stretching with his right hand for the crack. He rammed his fingers in and hugged tight to the wall. His foot scrabbled for purchase.

He couldn't find anywhere to put it.

Jack knew he was about to drop. The moss was slick.

The mortar was crumbling. He dug in with his nails, and tensed to reach for the bell. Just one more—

His foot slipped and his weight went with it. He fell.

He landed hard on the cobbles, with his elbow twisted under him. It hurt, but he hardly noticed: he knew with sickening certainty that he'd failed.

'A black day for you,' said Mr Smiles, hauling Jack to his feet. 'Mistress Fortune smiles not.'

Jack hung his head. He could already see the look on his ma's face.

'Hmm . . .' Mr Smiles bent over and picked up a shard of mortar that had tumbled down with Jack. He hefted it in his hand. 'You look game, laddie boy. And you're Anne's piglet . . .'

He leaned back, and threw the shard with unerring accuracy at the bell. It dinged.

'Let's agree that you clanged it, eh?' Smiles favoured Jack with a sly grin. 'But that's yer final chunter. Spoil again and you're out, faster than a weasel's neeze.'

Jack couldn't believe it. 'Thank y—'

'Say no more. Part the Third, and it's Black Arts. You brought your gilks and picks?'

Jack reached into his sleeve, and pulled out the cloth package.

Mr Smiles nodded approvingly. 'Sock it then, lad,' he chuckled. 'And mind – this one's *bene* tricky.'

Jack nodded. It was best just to get on with it.

The lock was a heavy iron box, set high up in the door. He peered into the keyhole. Just as he'd feared, it gave nothing away. There might be anything inside there: a tumbler, or a false chamber, or even a droplock.

He unrolled his package on the ground. All his picks lay in a neat line, tucked into little loops of cloth. His fingers danced above them, unable to make the selection.

In the end he took a Number Four Stroker, almost at random. He wet it on his tongue and pushed it carefully into the lock. He closed his eyes, and a grim little smile appeared on his face. All his concentration was in his fingers.

He could feel the fine tip brushing against the metal. He let his mind go blank. His nerves dropped away as the chamber of the lock began to grow in his mind. Everything depended on the shape, and finding a way.

There was always a way.

The Stroker wandered around the inside of the lock, probing for secrets. With each pass the shape got clearer and clearer. Mr Smiles hadn't lied, it was a tricky one: there were not one, but two false pinions. Jack could have wasted a lot of time there.

With a tiny snag, the Stroker caught against the tumblehome. The shape was complete. Jack knew what he had to do. He pulled out the Stroker, and replaced it with a Swivel Pick. That was all it needed. Now he pushed firmly, feeling for the tipping point. The lock gave a familiar, satisfying snick. He eased it round and pushed again. The door swung open.

'Bravissimo, laddie boy!' said Mr Smiles.

Jack turned round, and blinked. His mind returned slowly to the yard.

Mr Smiles was grinning down at him. '*Bene, bene, bene,* ladderoo! You've washed clean! Now to prove your pudding in the oven itself.'

'. . . oven?' said Jack.

'Crowdwork, lad – crowdwork. We proceed now to the plucking of the Rose.'

Chapter 3

The Rose Playhouse nestled in the heart of Southwark, a short ferry-ride across the river from the City of London. It was a grubby little theatre with a reputation for vicious entertainment. Nearby were the Bull Pit, and the Bear Pit, and the notorious Paris Gardens, where other, even more vicious entertainments were for sale.

It was said that all of London played in Southwark, and all of Southwark preyed on London; and nowhere was this more true than at the Rose. It was the perfect place for Jack's final test.

The afternoon had turned out sunny and warm, and the theatre was packed. The galleries up above were lined with sweaty, smelly gentry who'd paid fivepence to sit down. Mr Smiles had taken a seat here, and was watching the crowd with interest. Below him, the pit was heaving

24

with sweaty, smelly groundlings, who'd paid a penny to stand below the stage. Towering above everyone in the minstrels' gallery over the stage were sweaty, perfumed courtiers. They didn't have to worry about entrance fees. They paid for entire plays.

Plumb in the middle of these fabulous creatures was a small group that drew Mr Smiles' attention instantly. You didn't have to be an expert on what the well-dressed bravo was wearing (which Mr Smiles most decidedly was) to see they looked out of place. The seats to either side of them were empty, as if the courtiers feared some sort of infection.

They wore severe black robes, broad-brimmed hats and expressions of choking disapproval. They looked like Puritans, in fact, and this was the first strange thing about them: normally, the only time Puritans went anywhere near a theatre was to shout at everyone. Puritans, by and large, thought theatres were dens of vice and criminal activity. To be fair to the Puritans, this was usually true.

The second strange thing about them was their hands. Mostly they held them stiffly in their laps, but one or two were resting them on the handrail. Their right hands were stained a dark shade of red, ending sharply at the wrist like a lady's glove.

The third odd thing was their leader. There could be no doubt that he was their leader from the way they huddled in to catch his every word. He was dressed in a red doublet, red breeches, a red hat and a red cloak. His hand was stained red too, just like the others, only his stain looked quite different: older, and bone-deep – a birth-gift, Mr Smiles thought.

As the man spoke, his gaze roamed across the crowded pit.

On the stage, things were coming to a head. The King was about to lead his army into battle. 'I'll see blood flow before this day is out!' he cried.

The Wicked Duke Gonzago was standing just behind him. He produced a dagger from his sleeve. The crowd gasped. With a triumphant grimace, he stabbed the King in the back and plucked the crown from his head.

'The blood flows now! You see it? 'Tis your own!' Gonzago roared.

The crowd sighed as treacly pig's blood spilled across the stage. Even the Puritans were watching now – all except the man in red, who was still scanning the crowd.

'You're next, Gonzers!' cackled a man in the pit. The heckler was a sailor – staggering drunk, with gold earrings and a wine-red face.

There was a clash of steel from the stage, and everyone turned to watch as Gonzago and the Crown Prince went at each other with rapiers.

Mr Smiles tore his eyes from the action. He was here to watch the piglet make his play, and that wasn't going to happen on stage.

*　*　*

Jack inched his way deeper into the pit. Somewhere up in the gallery, Mr Smiles was watching. Jack knew that if he made a mistake, Smiles wouldn't miss it. He wouldn't come to help, either. Jack was on his own.

It took all his will to keep calm. He hadn't done anything risky, not yet. He was about to; but right now, everything was fine and level.

He glanced about him. He could hear his ma's voice in his head: *Nipping, Jackie boy, ain't just about quick fingers or a good eye. It's about not getting caught.*

It didn't seem so simple, now the moment had arrived. From where he was standing, Jack could watch his coney out of the corner of his eye. After studying the crowd for most of the third act, he'd fixed on the drunk sailor: not the richest-looking pigeon – though you never could tell with sailors – but he was alone, and engrossed in the action on stage. A plump purse was hanging from his belt, and he hadn't checked it in all the time that Jack had been watching.

Jack moved slowly towards him, slinking through the gaps like a stoat on the hunt. As usual, no one noticed him.

Without taking his eyes off the sailor, he reached into his sleeve pocket and pulled out a small curved blade. It was very bright and sharp, and instead of a handle it had three finger-sized hoops.

He slipped the index finger of his right hand through the hoops. No one noticed him do this, either.

'Run 'im through! Run 'im through!' shouted the heckling sailor. 'Cut 'is head off!'

Jack was about to move in when his eyes snagged on a man standing a little to one side of the sailor.

There was something odd about him. The hairs on the back of Jack's arms began to rise. He looked again.

The man had a brown face, white hair, and a slightly dazed look, as if he'd just been set down here from another world. His clothes were worn and dirty from travelling, but the cloth beneath the road dust was of good quality, and—

As Jack looked closer, he began to notice some very interesting details. The ring on the man's finger was set with a big red stone that looked like a ruby, and the ring itself was surely gold. He was wearing a sword beneath his travelling cloak – well hidden, but Jack could just see it peeking out, a fancy silver hilt bound with wine-coloured leather, and topped off with another big red jewel.

The more he saw, the surer he became. This man was no ordinary gull. This was a rich man, foreign – no business being down in the pit; he'd know that if he was from around here – and he had a gullish, coneyish look about him. As if he was thinking about something far away, not paying attention to his surroundings.

The man's purse was made of soft brown buckskin, with something foreign-looking etched on in gold. It called out to Jack: a well-travelled gent, with a well-travelled purse.

An interesting purse.

Jack trusted his instinct. He'd never really understood it, but somehow he always knew which was the meatiest pie, or the sweetest apple, or the best place to dab for eels. Now, the more he looked, the more he was sure that this purse was the plumpest prize here. Mr Sharkwell would be pleased if he brought him a good haul from his first job. His ma would be proud.

Jack licked his lips. He could almost smell the riches, bulging there at the foreigner's waist: the purse was heavy enough to make his belt sag to one side.

He looked up at the stage. The duel had turned into a pitched battle. Some of Gonzago's soldiers had just wheeled on a small cannon. Jack narrowed his eyes, glancing quickly over at the sailor and back up at the gun.

Jack had heard about this bit of the play. Apparently, the company had hired a magician for it. Jack had seen theatre-magic before, but this magician was supposed to be a real eye-popper – a pupil of Dr Dee, the Queen's Own Wizard, no less. Jack wasn't sure about that, but still – rumours got about for a reason. The Devil in Act Four was said to be a real spirit, summoned from the Seventh Circle of Hell; and this part coming up was done with genuine Greek fire, using a recipe passed down from the Titan Prometheus. Well, perhaps it was, perhaps it wasn't; but the rumours were there, and everyone in the pit was eyeing the cannon as the soldiers fussed around it.

Jack took another few sidling steps towards the foreigner, his eyes flicking between the purse and the action on stage.

One of the soldiers had produced a smouldering length of slow-match. He held it over the cannon's touch-hole at arm's length, shielding his face with his other hand. He gave the crowd an enormous wink – by now everyone was spellbound anyway – and pressed the slow-match to the hole. An ear-splitting shriek filled the theatre, and a torrent of bright blue and red sparks rushed out of the cannon's mouth, falling amongst the audience.

The crowd's eyes popped. Up in the fivepenny seats, someone screamed.

Jack made his move. He stepped forward and cupped the purse in his left hand, just enough to take the strain. The blade whispered across the purse-strings. In two quick strokes the strings parted, and the purse dropped into his fingers. It felt heavy.

Jack was already sidling off, forcing himself to move softly. At last, when he'd edged away six aching, endless paces, he allowed himself to glance back. The Greek fire was still gushing out from the cannon; the foreigner had never taken his eyes off it.

Something tickled the back of Jack's hand. He looked

down: it was a fly. It dipped its tongue, tasting his skin, then flew off.

Jack felt a prickling in his scalp, and his eye was drawn to a sudden movement above the stage. In the minstrels' gallery, a man dressed all in red had got to his feet.

He was surrounded by a bevy of men in black robes like crows or rooks. One of them pointed at Jack. His hand was stained with some sort of dye.

The man in red was staring straight at Jack. Their eyes locked. The man in red smiled.

Jack's fists clenched. He gasped as the blade on his finger bit into his palm, drawing blood. The pain brought him suddenly to life.

He ducked and ran.

Jack was good at crowds. He could always spot the gaps, and use them. In a packed pit, he thought he could outrun anyone – and by crouching and weaving in the right places he could pass unseen out of the theatre too.

In this second belief, however, Jack was wrong. Up in the minstrels' gallery, a narrowed pair of eyes followed his progress through the crowd. They widened a little at a bloody handprint he left on the whitewashed doorpost by the exit.

When the play ended, the man in red sauntered down to the pit. He paused in front of the doorpost, took out a handkerchief, and dabbed at the blood. A red spot blossomed on the white linen.

The man in red put the handkerchief to his lips. The tip of his tongue snaked out, and tasted the stain.

He smiled.

Chapter 4

'The Curse of the Nigromancers! The Magickal Torments! Posey-faced Eye-talianated sorcerer struck down through 'is own infernal transactions! What – another, you say? Another, I say! The first transformed into a slug! The second turned inside out! The third . . . A penny, sir, gets you the whole gory tale.'

The pamphleteer was at his usual spot opposite the theatre. The wall behind him was plastered with pictures of dismayed-looking wizards being menaced by horned, scaly-tailed demons. It had been the same story on every street corner for weeks now. London was in the grip of devil fever.

Jack waited there, hidden inside the clump of customers. His chest was still heaving, his breath whupping in and out in short gasps.

He watched the gates to the theatre.

There was no sign of the man in red. Jack didn't understand what had happened: the man had seen him, but he hadn't raised the hue and cry. He hadn't done anything.

'Eschew the paths of devils! Turn aside! Every penny you spend in Satan's pleasure pits you lay up in Hell's great bank! Repent and join the Elect! Follow sweet Nicholas, the demon's bane!'

A Puritan preacher, dressed all in black, was standing outside the theatre, bawling his lungs out. The passers-by ignored him.

With a start, Jack saw that the man's hand was stained red – just like the man who had pointed at him from the gallery. He turned to hide his face – and there was Mr Smiles, taking his elbow, giving him another start.

'Gandered the full drama!' whispered Smiles, steering him away from the theatre. 'As graceful a bit of nippage as I've seen!' He clapped Jack on the back. 'Come to! Come to! Let us make our divulgence to Mr S.'

They set off down the street, heading east. Every now and then Jack glanced back, half expecting to see a flash of red.

They took a different route this time, entering Sharkwell's warren through the back door of the Crooked Walnut tavern. Jack was as certain as he could be that no one had followed them.

He let the purse fall from his sleeve into his hand, and hefted it. It felt heavy. Jack imagined golden pieces of eight spilling out of it – or something even more precious. Diamonds and rubies. Giant black pearls from the Indies. He didn't know if pearls were heavy. He thought they probably weren't.

'Wait here,' said Mr Smiles. 'Don't open the jinglerig, mind you. Don't want Sharkwell misdoubting you, hey?' He passed through a door behind the bar.

The tavern was empty. It smelled of stale beer, woodsmoke, and the dirty rushes on the floor. Behind the bar, hundreds of empty purses hung in rows from rusty nails. Jack tucked his purse into his belt, wishing he could open it and find out what treasure it contained. Maybe they'd let him keep some. A single piece of eight, or one of the smaller pearls . . .

He heard a clobber of feet. The door behind the bar swung open.

'Well, well, well,' said a wheezy voice, and Southwark's worst nightmare stumped into the room.

Jack stood up straight. He'd heard a lot of talk about how hard Mr Sharkwell was, but until today he'd never seen it.

If you took a flaky old half-brick, gave it eyes and hair and dressed it in a fancy doublet, you'd get something that looked a lot like Mr Sharkwell. You might also realize that the same brick could be wrapped in a sock and used to smash your head in.

Sharkwell stopped at the bar, reached down and tapped off a mug of beer. Mr Smiles and the one-eyed, noseless doorkeeper came in behind, and took up positions to either side. Sharkwell took a long, slow drink. His eyes peered at Jack over the rim of his mug, travelling up and down his length.

He thumped the empty mug down.

'Scrunty, ill-nourished, and ragged. When I was a lad, I'd've broke you in half.' He grinned. 'Scrunty Jack. Hr hr hr.'

He had two teeth – one on top, one on the bottom. They were large, and brown like old wood.

'Sharkwell's the name. But you know that. Ain't that right, me little dearling?'

He paused, as if he expected an answer. None came, and he spat on the floor. 'Quiet little scrunt, ain't he, Meatface?' It was obvious who he was talking to.

'Aye,' said the doorkeeper. He had a pipe between his teeth, and smoke was leaking from the holes where his nose should be.

'No bad thing in a thief. It's a thief you want to be, o' course?'

'Yes, Mr Sharkwell,' said Jack.

'That's better.'

He didn't look like it was better. He looked like Jack was something nasty he'd just stepped in.

'Smiles here tells me you showed promise. That's fine.

We've standards here in Southwark. This Family's no rumpskuttle crew like that Turnball Street mob across the water. Every crony, hookman, jarkman, foister – yes, even poxy little nippers like yourself – if they're to work for Sharkwell, they're the best. Do-you-understand-me?'

'Yes, Mr Sharkwell.'

'Yes.' Sharkwell ambled out from behind the bar. 'Scrawny, ain't you?'

'Could do with some peckage,' said Mr Smiles.

Sharkwell snorted, and pinched Jack's arm. 'Show me yer teeth, boy.'

Jack opened his mouth.

'Not your swinish throat! Teeth! Give Sharkwell a grin.'

Jack bared his teeth as instructed, and Sharkwell leaned in for a closer look. His breath smelled like a tanner's vat. Jack forced himself not to flinch.

'Piece of advice, boy.' Mr Sharkwell leaned in a little closer. 'You've got a nice set of gnashers there. Take good care of 'em. They're your treasure. Don't want to end up like me, sucking soup for thirty year.'

'No, Mr Sharkwell.'

'Good boy. You're learning.' Sharkwell turned and walked back towards the counter. His hands were folded behind his back. 'Now,' he said in a loud, slow voice. 'How many laws do I 'ave, Meatface?'

'There's many laws, Mr Sharkwell.'

'Indeed. Many laws. But what's most important?'

'The First Law is this,' said Meatface. 'Sharkwell gets his shilling.'

'Right, my ugly lug.' Sharkwell bared his gums at Jack. 'Every penny you earn means a penny to me. Even simpler: Sharkwell takes half. You steal a groat, I want tuppence. You steal a goat, and I want 'alf a bleeding head, two legs, one horn and thirteen ribs delivered to my door. Simple enough?'

'Yes, Mr Sharkwell.'

'Aye . . . simple, ain't it, Smiles?'

'Plain as a thrice-trodden wicketspitch, Mr Sharkwell.'

'Aye.' Sharkwell nodded. 'But perhaps I should ill-luminate further – in case this unfortunate, tousle-headed urchin is *too-stupid-to-understand*.'

He reached inside his doublet, and pulled out the purse that Jack had stolen. Jack grunted with surprise. Sharkwell had plucked him clean.

Mr Sharkwell chuckled softly. 'Another lesson, right there: never trust a man what asks to see yer teeth.' He dumped the purse on the counter and loosened the strings.

Jack told himself to calm down. The thing itself was rumpskuttle, old leather gone soft with the years. The things inside would be rumpskuttle too. A twist of baccy; a pair of dice. Maybe some silver, if he was lucky.

He made himself picture it, but he didn't believe it for a second. He had known, in the theatre. Everything had fallen into place, like the snick when a lock tips over.

Sharkwell had it open now. He was poking around inside, looking puzzled.

He squinted up at Jack. 'Who'd you roll? A cunning-man? Got enough potions here to dose an army.'

'A foreign gent, Mr Sharkwell.'

'Foreign gent, eh? I stick to London coneys, meself. Never know where you are with a foreign gent . . .'

Sharkwell flicked his wrist over, turning the purse upside down on the bar lightning-quick, so that nothing spilled. He lifted it between two fingers, revealing its contents in a neat little heap.

A single lead ball toppled off and rolled across the bartop. It was perfectly round, and the size of a man's thumbnail. A pistol ball.

There were a couple more of those. There were three small gold coins of a type Jack had never seen before. Then there was a round brown thing like an oversized walnut; a tiny bottle filled with dark green liquid; a thick dark clot of what looked like hair; a clay pipe . . . other things, Jack didn't know what they were, but he was pretty sure it was rumpskuttle, all of it – apart from the gold of course.

Jack felt a strange frustration rising in his spine. There was as much money here as he'd ever seen in one place before. Sharkwell looked pleased, and his ma would be pleased – he should be pleased himself – but he wasn't. He'd been sure, back in the theatre. Even now, the smell of it lingered. Gold and jewels, and magical far-off lands . . .

'Don't know about this chink.' Sharkwell was turning one of the coins this way and that, holding it up to the light. 'D'you, Smiles?'

The coin was stamped with a crude image of a fly. Smiles squinted closely at the markings, and shook his head. 'Never scoppered such.'

'Gold, anyhow,' said Sharkwell. 'Good boy.'

He scooped two of the coins into his hand, and put the third into a sackcloth pouch that had appeared in his hand out of nowhere. 'Anything else here take your fancy?' he said, stirring the odd pile of objects with one finger. 'All trash to me, but we'll share and share alike . . .'

Jack thought of his ma, and pointed at the pipe. Sharkwell dropped it into the pouch. 'That'll do for a first job,' he said. 'Now, Meatface. What's Sharkwell's Second Law?'

Meatface cleared his throat. 'Sharkwell's Second Law is this: No crying beef to the Law.'

'That's right. That means no talking. No snitching. No blather. This is the most important law of all.'

Mr Sharkwell went over to Meatface, hugged him round the neck and pulled him over to stand before Jack.

'Allow me to make it simple.' Sharkwell hunkered

down, tugging Meatface with him till his ruined face was inches from Jack's.

'If yer stupid enough to get caught, I don't give a poxy twatling string what they do to you. They might 'ammer out your eyes. They might drop fat stones on your chest till all your ribs are broke. They might do worse. They do it for fun, you know. But still: no beefing.'

Jack gave a tiny nod.

'Look at Meatface 'ere. See how they ruined him?' Sharkwell patted the scarred scalp, stroked it gently. 'How'd they ruin you, Meatface?'

'Passing awful, Mr Sharkwell.'

'Passing awful,' Sharkwell rasped at Jack. 'Did he whisper a word? No. *Never-said-a-thing.*'

Meatface smiled grimly.

'Why didn't you squeal, Meatface?'

''Cos I was more scared of you, Mr Sharkwell.'

'That's right. This monster-rosity was more scared of me. Can you imagine what that means? Look at him. Have a good think. A good ponder.'

Sharkwell went quiet, giving Jack the chance to do just that. He reached out with his free hand and grabbed Jack close. Meatface, Sharkwell and Jack, hugged together in a triple clinch. Jack felt Sharkwell's breath on his ear.

'See, I understand little nippers,' said Sharkwell. 'You think you've had it rough. P'raps you reckon *you're* rough.

Life's been hard to you, and mean, and probably quite difficult.'

He pulled Jack closer, and whispered, 'But I'm harder, and meaner, and for *certes* more difficult than any other you will ever meet.'

Meatface chuckled slow and deep. Sharkwell grinned, and gave a twinkly wink.

Jack believed him.

Mr Sharkwell sprang upright, releasing his hold.

'So then. Yer Anne's boy. Curbing mod'rate, some very shabby wall-work, but a neat bit of nippage at the end. Though the haul was only middling. Oughter work on your eye, seems to me. Don't want to trifle with trifles.'

'No, Mr Sharkwell.'

'All in all, you're usable.'

Sharkwell spat on his hand and held it out to Jack. 'Scrunty Jack – will you be my man?'

'Yes, Mr Sharkwell.' Jack spat in his own hand, and they shook. Mr Smiles gave him a grin.

'I rate you Judicious Nipper. You work church and theatre to start. We'll see how you play out.'

'Yes, Mr Sharkwell.'

'You do learn fast.' Sharkwell looked down at Jack's bare feet. 'Smiles! Nail up the jinglerig! And see if you can't get the boy shod. Disgrace to the Fam'ly, him going round like that.'

With that, he turned and stomped from the room.

Mr Smiles took the purse and hung it from an empty nail in the rows behind the bar. There were dozens more hanging up there – hundreds, maybe – too many for Jack to count. He felt a thrill of pride, seeing his purse placed alongside all those others. Sharkwell's Family was the biggest in Southwark – some said the whole of London; and now he was part of it. A Judicious Nipper: he turned the sound of it over in his mind, and decided he liked it.

Jack looked down at his grubby toes. He felt as if they were floating a couple of inches off the floor.

Chapter 5

The shoes had once belonged to a lawyer's clerk who was hanged for being crooked, or so Mr Smiles said. The clerk, if he'd ever existed, must have been on the small side because the shoes fitted Jack perfectly. It was a strange feeling, having his steps cushioned by cool, cracked leather. The cracks pinched the soles of his feet now and again, but it was worth it. Jack stopped at the stone doorstep of St Olave's and jumped down on it as hard as he could. A loud smack cut across the bustle of traffic.

He was a Judicious Nipper.

He trotted along Tooley Street, clutching tightly onto his pouch of loot, thinking about what to spend the money on. The first thing to do was change it into English silver – no matter if the gold coin was from an unknown mint; gold was gold and the money-changers would be happy to have it. Then he could start buying things.

A jacket with a woollen lining.

A dagger, or a good knife at any rate.

New tobacco for his ma – something that didn't smell like river-dreck. It would go nicely with the clay pipe.

He took the pipe out of the pouch and stopped to examine it. It was a good pipe – long and slim, with a garland of roses sculpted round the base of the bowl. His ma would like that.

The stem was blocked up. That wasn't so good. Jack squatted down with his back to a wall, out of the traffic, shook out his tools from his sleeve and unrolled them on his lap. The Figging-wire should do it. He pushed it into the mouthpiece and wiggled it about, trying to get a sense of what the blockage was. Something came loose. He wormed the wire deeper into the stem, peered inside – and suddenly the wire slipped and a puff of powder came flying out of the pipe, straight into his eye.

The pain was immediate and savage, making him gasp. He screwed his eye shut and rubbed it with his finger, which turned out to be a very bad idea: the pain in his eye got worse, and his fingertip felt like he'd dipped it in molten lead. He doubled over, whimpering in the back of his throat. His tools clattered to the cobbles. Purple and green explosions bloomed behind his eyelids.

It felt like something very small and thin and sharp was

worming in through his eye, into his brains. It hurt so much he thought he might die of it.

The powder from the pipe could be poison. He had to get it out. He set his jaw against the pain and inched up his eyelid with his finger.

Hot tears streamed down his cheek. He hoped they were carrying the poison along with them.

Whatever it was in the pipe, it hadn't blinded him. He could still see through both eyes; but the vision in his right was changed. It was like looking at two worlds, one laid on top of the other.

His left eye still saw the old one – the usual traffic on Tooley Street; Young Tom the water-seller standing by a heavy-laden wagon, handing up a ladle to the driver; a dog scratching itself on the doorstep of the pie-shop opposite.

His right eye was seeing the same things. But it was seeing them differently. Everything was blurry and tinted red – but that wasn't the half of it. When Jack looked at the dog, its movements slid out of joint. Its leg scratched fast and jerky, while at the same time (and Jack knew this didn't make any sense) it was very, very slow. He closed his left eye, and immediately the effect was magnified. Jack felt like he was trapped in a jar of dark red honey; and the people around him were specks caught in the honey too. Young Tom was swimming down the street, his legs and arms moving at different speeds. The pie shop was pulsating slowly, its walls swelling and contracting like a living heart.

At the same time, the burning in Jack's finger was spreading – pulsing up his hand in time to the contractions of the pie shop.

Panicking, Jack switched eyes.

Something uncanny was happening to his finger. Starting at the tip, where he'd rubbed his eye, lines of dark, rusty red were crawling up it. The fingertip itself was pure red, and as he watched, the rest of the finger darkened to the same colour. The thin lines continued to spread across his hand like veins . . .

They were slowing down. They stopped halfway across his palm. The burning in his hand slowly died to a hot itch. Two of his fingers, his thumb, and half his palm were stained the colour of rust. The rest of his hand was a mottled web of red and pink.

Jack didn't know if he was poisoned or enchanted or what; the stabbing pain in his eye wasn't letting up, and now he was becoming really scared. He fumbled for his tools, scrabbled them up and put the roll in his sleeve. He saw the pipe lying on the ground. Another little trickle of powder had leaked out – it was the same dark rust colour as the stain on his hand.

After a moment's hesitation he picked up the pipe and dipped the end of the stem in the mud to seal it. He slipped it back into the pouch with the gold coin. Maybe he could take it to a cunning-man who would know about the powder, know the cure. Make him up a poultice. At least now he had money to pay with.

His bad eye twitched open. The scarlet mud writhed beneath his feet. Jack slapped his hand over his eye to shut it out.

As he hurried homeward, he found that his bad eye kept opening of its own accord, glazing the world over with red nightmare vision. Just before the turning into the alleys, Jack spied a washing line hung with damp stockings. He filched one and darted round the corner, then wrapped it tight around his head. The cool damp cloth pressed against his eyelid, sealing it shut.

The pain was still sharp. It made him slow and stupid. When he squeezed his way through the ivy and found the court empty, he blundered straight over to the shack. Later, he'd remember and curse himself: his ma should have been sitting outside, waiting for him, smoking her afternoon pipe. She was never inside at this time of day. He should have been on his guard.

It was dark inside the shack, but he could see his ma sitting against the opposite wall. She never usually sat there.

She didn't move or get up or say anything. Jack stepped through the doorway. The stain on his hand prickled. 'Ma?' he said.

She was propped up against the wall. Her eyes were closed, like she was asleep. A trickle of spit ran down her chin. A fat, shiny bluebottle was crawling across her lips.

'Jack, is it?' came a voice from behind him.

Jack stiffened. He turned, keeping the pouch clenched in his fist, wishing he had a weapon. 'Who wants to know?' he said.

'I do.'

It was the man from the theatre. Seeing him up close, Jack immediately thought that there was something very wrong about him. His eyes were so pale they almost looked transparent. His lips were cracked and parched, as though all the blood had been leached out of them long ago. His skin clung tight to his skull like shrunken parchment.

The man looked sick and starving. That was wrong too: his clothes were rich – velvet doublet, calfskin gloves, deep, dark red all over – and a jewelled rapier dangled from his left hip. No one rigged up like that should ever want for a meal.

His gaze darted over to Jack's ma, then back to Jack. 'Jack. I tried to have a conversation with your mother, but she wouldn't open herself to me. Perhaps you would oblige.' The man's mouth twitched, and one eyelid fluttered up and down. 'What did you steal today, Jack?'

The red man was blocking the door: there was no escape.

'She ain't my ma,' said Jack, stalling for time.

'Do *not* lie to me. You left something behind this afternoon.' The man produced a white handkerchief with a spot of dried blood on it – the same colour as his clothes.

'This is your blood, Jack. It led me here. To her.' He nodded down at Jack's ma. 'The same stuff flows in her veins, does it not? Now tell me. What did you steal today?'

Jack said nothing. The man's hands clasped together, the fingers of the left digging into the right like claws.

'A quiet one, eh? Let me help you, then. You stole a purse. In the theatre.' The man licked his lips. The tip of his tongue was sharp and purple. 'You will give it to me now.'

The pain in Jack's eye began to pulse harder. The stain was flaming up as well. He remembered Sharkwell telling him what happened to nippers that squealed. He tried to think, but the pain was making him stupid.

'I can't give it you now,' he said. 'I hid it. Back there.'

'Where?'

'I'll show you.'

'Tell me where!'

'It's complicated.' Jack's heart was pumping hard. He mustn't lose his nerve. 'Better if I show you.'

'If I find out you're lying to me, boy . . . If you've handed it over to the intelligencer . . .'

'Don't know what you mean,' said Jack. His heart thumped harder. Something was very wrong here.

'Don't you?' The man scratched his hand harder. 'We'll come to that in a moment, when you've shown me the purse. I trust that you will show me.' A faint smile hovered around his mouth, without ever reaching those washed-out eyes.

'I like being able to trust people,' he went on. 'It is good for the soul. It is also very easy, as long as you have a hostage. Something that is dear to them . . .

'In your case, I think' – the man's tongue flickered out again – 'your mother.'

'She ain't—' said Jack.

'Oh, but she is, Jack.'

The man raised his right hand, holding his palm out flat. The bluebottle buzzed over and landed on his fingers. 'I hold her life here.'

'What . . . ?' said Jack.

'That was your mother, Jack, but it might as well be any other bag of bones now.'

'Ma?' said Jack. He dashed across the room. She gave a low, burbling sigh. Jack shook her by the shoulders. 'Ma!'

'It's no use. She is here.' The black fly was crouched in the man's palm. It began to clean its hairy legs. 'Her life is in my hand.'

Jack leaped forward. The red man moved faster. Suddenly Jack's arm was twisted up behind his back and he was being marched out of the shack.

'Oh, I'll give her back,' the man chided, 'as soon as I have the purse. Where is it?'

'Wait,' said Jack. Somewhere, he couldn't tell where exactly, he had made a terrible mistake. 'I . . . I didn't hide it.'

51

'Oh really?'

'I lied. I've got a couple of things from it here, but—'

'Show me.' The red man let go of Jack, confident he couldn't run now.

Jack offered up the pouch. The man snatched it up, rummaging inside. His eyes lit up as he brought out the pipe. He sniffed hungrily at the bowl, then he snapped it off, clutched the stem to his mouth, and sucked his cheeks hollow.

A thin hissing sound escaped his nostrils. His eyes squeezed shut, his mouth lurched open, and the stem of the pipe dropped to the ground. For a moment he stood rigid.

The man was changing. As Jack watched, the cracks in his lips puckered and disappeared. His withered skin smoothed, and a dab of colour appeared in his cheeks. All his twitchiness drained away. His eyes opened. The whole thing was uncanny as Hell – but in that moment Jack took heart from the eyes. He'd never seen anyone look so roundly, joyfully at ease.

'My ma, then,' said Jack. 'You said . . .'

'Yes, I can let her go now, can't I?' For a moment the man observed the fly in his hand. Suddenly he closed his fist so tight that the knuckles went white. Jack thought he saw something glimmer there, shining red through the clenched fingers, then go out.

'There – gone.'

'What do you . . . ?'

The man dusted off his hands. The squashed remains of the bluebottle fell to the ground. 'And of course you must go too,' he said. 'You did well not to lie to me twice. Your end might have been much more terrible, but as it is . . .'

The red man drew a small, sharp knife from his belt, and stepped forward.

Chapter 6

Jack backed away. He didn't understand this. Somewhere in the course of this day he had signed his own death warrant. His ma's too.

He didn't understand, and it made the whole thing seem like something he was being told about, something that had happened to someone else. Dead flies and dead eyes and a knife getting closer. It was a wicked, murdering piece, with a runnel in the blade to let the blood flow. It was coming closer.

A cold, numb part of his mind was telling him that the thing to do now was run. The red man was between him and the way out, but he might be able to dodge round. But the idea of escape didn't seem any more real than the idea of his ma being dead, or the knife being about to cut his throat. All he could do was back away.

The pain in his eye was stabbing hard.

When he had backed halfway across the courtyard, Jack saw a ragged shape move in the shadows opposite, over by the ivy-choked entrance – a scabby old gutter-drunk, crooning over a jug in his lap. The same numb part of him wondered about this. Until today no one had ever found this place. Now – twice in one afternoon.

Then the drunk tottered to his feet. His jug slipped from his fingers and landed in the mud.

'Whatsh yer doin . . . wif th' boy.' The drunk's eyes peered blearily from beneath his hood.

The red man turned quickly and smoothly. He seemed to relax as he took in the figure of the drunk. 'Good day,' he said. Jack could hear the smile in his voice. He didn't bother to hide the knife.

'I needsh th'boy. M'jug – empty!' The drunk stumbled towards them.

The red man tossed the knife to his left hand. His right went to his sword hilt.

'M'jug. Th'boy . . . 's always fills 'em.' The drunk's mad stare was fixed on Jack, as if he wanted to drink him up. He was chewing on something. Dark, greenish-brown juice trickled from the corner of his mouth.

Jack was certain he had never seen him before, let alone filled his jug.

Then the bleary eyes snapped into focus, and winked at Jack.

The red man's sword flashed out – but the drunk wasn't

there. He ducked, rolling forwards. The sword whipped through the space where his throat should have been.

The drunk grabbed Jack's arm and whirled him across the courtyard. Jack splashed down in a puddle, and scrambled through the mud until he felt the wall at his back.

The red man glanced at him from the centre of the courtyard. 'Don't get any ideas, boy.'

The drunk pulled back his hood. He had long hair flecked with grey and a short, neatly trimmed beard. His whole face was changed – sharp and alert, like a fox tasting the air for scent. He seemed to have grown by several inches. The bleary chancer with the jug might never have existed.

'A pretty piece of theatre, intelligencer.' The red man cocked his head towards Jack. 'Employing urchins to do your dirty work now, are you?'

'No. In truth, his presence is . . . inconvenient. I'd half a mind to let you kill him . . .' The stranger chewed thoughtfully, then spat a stream of the brown juice onto the cobbles. 'Well, what's done's done. I think you'd best come with me now.'

He threw back his cloak. Beneath it, he was dressed in black velvet, with spotless white lace foaming at his collar and cuffs. A smallsword swung at his hip.

The red man sneered. 'Come with you? Would you like me to confess? To . . . what? Retrieving my property from a thief?' He laughed, a short high-pitched bark.

'You're cornered.' The stranger jerked his thumb over his shoulder. 'My companions are just behind me.'

'I think you're bluffing. I think you're alone and out of your depth.' The red man raised his rapier. The sword was very long, and needle-sharp.

The stranger stepped to the right, tugging his own sword from its sheath, his eyes fixed on the red man's.

'Aye. Well.' The red man side-stepped left, grinning wolfishly, keeping the distance between them. 'Your companions will find there isn't much left of you to scrape up.'

'Is that so.' The stranger's gaze didn't waver. He was grinning too now, baring his teeth, still chewing slowly – a killing gentleman, if ever Jack had seen one. They circled, taking little crab-like steps.

Jack pressed himself back against the wall. The courtyard was perhaps fifteen feet across, which meant that this was going to be ugly. In a few moments there would be very little space that wasn't filled with whirling, razor-sharp steel.

The red man flicked his wrist, and his sword flashed out.

'Ha!' cried the stranger. Their blades whispered together, then sprang apart.

The red man held his rapier straight out, pointing at the stranger's heart. He raised his left hand behind his ear, twitching the knife up and down.

'Hm! Elegant!' The stranger changed his stance. His free hand twirled high above his head, fingers waggling. He puckered his lips, and blew a kiss at his opponent. The red man frowned.

'Oho!' The stranger feinted, then attacked, his cloak swirling around his dancing feet. His sword spun delicate patterns, cut and thrust, faster than the eye could follow. The red man retreated, warding off the attacks. Jack squeezed into the corner as the fight swerved this way and that across the courtyard. He was trapped, as surely as if he'd fallen into a dog pit full of snarling, snapping mastiffs.

There was one consolation: this fight didn't look likely to last. The red man was competent, well-schooled, but he was no match for the stranger. There was very little in it – a split-second of speed, a sliver of cunning – but the stranger was always half a step ahead. The red man was starting to sweat. Soon he would make a mistake. If Jack kept his head down, he might still come out of this alive. As for what he would find in the shack . . . But he daren't think about that.

The red man retreated again, putting space between himself and the stranger. He lowered his sword, panting. 'Wait . . .' he said.

'You yield?' The stranger was panting too, his face glowing with triumph. 'Then put down your blades.'

The red man stooped, laying his rapier down – then his

left hand whipped out from behind his back. 'Seek blood,' he hissed, and flung his knife at the stranger.

It came with no warning, and murderous speed. The stranger parried; the knife hummed past his ear, swerved, and hung impossibly in mid-air.

Jack watched it float there, casting this way and that like an angry wasp. The stain on his hand was itching again, prickling like a nettle-rash. His mouth drifted open, but no sound came. This wasn't theatre trickery; this wasn't some mad-eyed conjuror touting charms in the market. This was . . . magic. Flat impossibility, right there in front of his eyes.

'Hm.' The stranger frowned, his eyes tracking the knife. The red man twitched his fingers, and it darted in. The stranger batted it away with a neat swipe. It glanced upwards, straining for his throat, but he twisted away and it flew past, already circling round for another attack.

The stranger grimaced and regained his stance. His eyes still followed the knife.

The red man skipped back. 'All I have to do now . . . is wait.' His fingers traced patterns in the air; the knife whirled and spun in response, probing for an opening.

The stranger was driven back to the wall beside Jack. His face was grim, totally intent on the knife. His sword flashed this way and that, cutting it to one side, driving it down into the cobbles, smacking it high in the air. Jack cowered down, covering his face, as it clattered off the wall an inch from his head.

The knife buzzed in again. The stranger twisted to one side, and it rebounded off the wall – another near miss for Jack – and hit the ground, quivering, its point embedded between two loose cobbles. Jack grabbed the handle without stopping to think. He could feel it wriggling in his fingers like an eel. There was a sharp, hot-metal smell coming off it – strong enough to make his head swim.

The stain in his hand was a burning, fizzing flame.

'Let it go, boy!' the red man snarled.

'No,' said Jack. He wasn't sure he could have let go, even if he'd wanted to.

The red man snapped his fingers. The knife strained to free itself, but Jack clung on, even though his hand was pure agony now. A bone-jangling buzz ran up his arm. The stain on his hand glowed for a second with a dark, coppery light. The red man's eyes widened. Then Jack felt a rushing hot wind all around him, and everything slowed down.

The red man snapped his fingers again. This time the knife didn't even stir.

The stranger leaped forward. Slower and slower. Jack thought the stranger would probably win now, but it didn't feel important. The dust from the pipe was important. It was the reason why the red man had come here.

He thought of his ma, and the last thing he felt was a slow lurch of dread in his stomach. Jack's own fault – he'd picked the wrong coney.

You never know where you are with a foreign gent.

Chapter 7

The eastern fringe of Sharkwell's demesne was pieced together from the buildings of an old Augustinian abbey. Sharkwell claimed he had won the property from Sir Anthony Sentlegar at dice (this was only true if you understood 'won' to mean 'stole' and 'dice' to mean 'knife-point').

Twenty years later, the herb garden was swamped beneath a slurry of new-built tenements and the friary was a whorehouse catering to the better sort of roger. The chapel had become a splendid kennel, where Sharkwell's champion mastiff, Billy Bearsbane, lived in considerable luxury.

The most unusual transformation of all had come over the abbey's beer-house – a brick building shaped like an enormous beehive. Its upper floor was stacked with breeches, bodices, partlets, girdles, doublets, gowns, cloaks, kirtles, rags and ruffs of every known colour and fabric. The ground floor, a single circular room, held Mr Smiles' collection of straw dummies dressed in exemplary costumes: the Gentleman Who Ought to Know Better, the Country Maid, the Lecherous Apothecary. There were dozens more. Mr Smiles had spent a long time making sure their outfits were correct down to the smallest detail. More outfits, in the livery of every guild and noble house, hung from the ceiling. One wall was covered with wax noses, fake beards and elaborate wigs.

In the middle of the room stood a girl in a tight linen cap. She wore a grimy apron over a plain woollen dress with a high-necked collar. She was carrying a basket of onions.

Mr Smiles knelt at her feet. He had a paintbrush in one hand, and a dish in the other. The dish was filled with blobs of mud: they ranged in colour from goose-turd green to a pale, nameless brown. He had already applied a thick foundation of filth to the girl's skirt and shoes. But he wasn't finished yet. He leaned back, took careful aim and flicked bright slashes of yellowish scum onto the hem.

'There's for the swine sheds athwart Long Southwark,' he muttered.

'Enough,' growled Sharkwell. He had already been kept waiting five minutes. 'She ain't one of your dollies, Smiles.'

'The lay must play: this onion-angel has tramped from Kent,' replied Mr Smiles. 'She must have the true road-muck, must she not?'

'Bah! Filth is filth.'

'Hush, Grampers,' said the girl. 'Mind the Fifth Law.'

'Mind? And whose law d'you think it is, Beth?'

'Yours, Grampers. That's why you should mind it.' The girl stared straight ahead. Her severe expression didn't change.

If Sharkwell was planning to resent his granddaughter's cheek, he didn't get the chance. Mr Smiles added a final flick of mud, and jumped to his feet.

'*Bene. Benissime.*' He took the girl's hand and led her across to the ornate mirror on the wall. Smiles had lifted it from the house of the Venetian ambassador himself. There was not a finer glass in all London.

The girl composed herself before the mirror. Pinched by the tight cap, her face was plain and stern.

'Now, Beth,' said Mr Smiles. 'Make your manner.'

Beth Sharkwell's face came alive. Her eyebrows creased together a fraction. Her nostrils seemed to change shape. Her eyes widened and her mouth spread in a broad grin. 'Onnnions!' she chanted. 'Oooo'll buy me fine ropes of hard onnnnions?'

It wasn't just her face that changed. She'd thrown up her chin, set her shoulders, taken up a swaggering stance.

She looked bold enough to stare down the Queen.

'Prime!' Mr Smiles was delighted. 'The coney will flop *sans peur*.'

A smile hovered at the corner of Sharkwell's mouth, like a rat poking its nose out of a hole.

There was a tentative knock at the door. Sharkwell's smile vanished. 'Who's there?'

Meatface poked his head into the room. 'Sorry to disturb, Mr Sharkwell. It's . . . There's . . . the boy Jack . . .'

'Who?'

'The nipper. Did his testing today.'

'The scrunt, is it? And so?'

'He— Oi! No, you can't go in—'

Jack twisted under Meatface's arm and stumbled into the room. He blinked. The room was full of straw men.

'Over here, Jack,' said Mr Smiles.

Jack saw them now: Smiles, looking anxious, Sharkwell looking furious, and a girl with a basket of onions. She looked him up and down and snorted. She appeared to be about his age, but the way she carried herself made her seem older. Her eyes were cool and grey, sharp as a knife. Jack wondered what she was doing here – not selling onions, that was clear.

'What you about, scrunt?' snapped Sharkwell.

The ice in Jack's heart had taken him this far: faced with his frozen determination, even Meatface had given way. Now, Jack felt the blood pounding in his head, pounding in his bad eye, and a choking pressure building in his chest.

'It's my ma, Mr Sharkwell,' he managed to say. 'She's . . .'

'Go on, out with it,' said Sharkwell. 'What's happened? You come in here into my private place with a wet stocking wrapped around yer head, I want an explanation.'

'She's murdered,' said Jack. Saying it was like throwing a stone into a well. It couldn't be taken back. *Never*, said a low, dull voice in Jack's head. *Never, never, never* . . .

'What, Annie the Curb, murdered?' said Sharkwell. 'Who'd want to do a thing like that?'

'Was on account of that pipe,' said Jack.

'Who did it?' asked Mr Smiles.

'Aye, who?' said Sharkwell. 'She was Family, was Anne. Good little worker in her day.'

'Was . . .' Jack glared at the ground. He wasn't going to cry. 'Was a man in red.'

Mr Smiles pricked up his ears at that. 'All in red?' he said.

Jack nodded.

'Eyes a-blenched, face like a lemon?'

'Aye.'

'Well! Leech me bloodless,' said Smiles. 'What would he . . . ?'

'What would who?' said Sharkwell.

'Nicholas Webb.' Smiles spoke very quietly, as if he were afraid someone might hear.

Sharkwell stiffened. His face went a darker shade of red. 'Webb? You sure?'

'Sure as shrouds. He was in the theatre, before. Wondered what he was doing there . . .'

'Aye, wonder's the word . . .' Sharkwell whistled softly. 'D'you know who you've tangled with, boy?'

Jack shook his head.

'That God-molester? Witch-finder Webb, the Bible-slapper, with his preachy army . . . ?'

'No.' Although now Jack thought on it – hadn't he, perhaps? From a preacher, or a balladeer, something half heard in passing . . . except that didn't make sense, for Webb to be a witch-finder. He was a sorcerer himself. Jack had seen it.

'Nicholas Webb, and Annie the Curb. I don't like this, Smiles. Not one peck of it.' Sharkwell shook his head. 'Tell it then, boy – start to finish.'

Jack tried to get the story out as straight as he could. He still didn't understand what had happened. It was hard to concentrate, with that word still repeating inside him. *Never, never, never, never . . .*

The straw figures all around them leaned in their heads as though they were listening too. Some of them had cloth faces with smiles and frowns painted on. Their eyes were all the same – black buttons, flat and empty.

At last he felt the end approaching. Somehow he had kept control over his voice.

'They were both gone when I woke up. Webb and the intelligencer. I went inside to see—'

He saw his ma lying face down on the floor. He saw himself walk up to her and turn her over. Her face . . .

Jack couldn't bring himself to really finish.

'You found her dead. Bleeding Christ . . .' Sharkwell spat on the ground. 'Nicholas Webb, the Lord High God-botherer himself, doing sorcery? I don't believe it.'

'Poison, more likely,' said the onion girl.

'Aye, Beth. Tell me, boy, what did Anne look like? Was there purple at the lips? Any froth?'

Jack shook his head. He didn't want to think about the way his ma's face had looked.

'What about her mouth? Closed tight? Or sort of stretched open?'

Jack nodded.

'Which one? Open or closed?'

'Open.'

'Like this?' Sharkwell twisted his mouth into a hideous grimace, so that the sinews in his neck stretched tight.

'Worse,' said Jack.

Her mouth had been straining wide, as if something very large had been forced down her throat. Her eyes had been stretched open in a look of atrocious horror. Jack knew what he'd seen, and there was no way it was poison.

He'd seen Webb suck up the powder from the pipe, seen his fist close around the fly – the light flaring between his clenched fingers – and then, afterwards, the knife. Webb was a sorcerer, and he had killed her by magic.

'Sounds like hebenon. Hmm. Fancy.' Sharkwell crossed his arms and glared down his nose at Jack. 'And he wanted the pipe. Probably some kind of poison in there too, I'd wager. Might be he's bringing even fancier stuff in from France. You did say the gent you nipped the purse off was foreign, didn't you?'

'Yes, Mr Sharkwell.'

Sharkwell leaned down and lifted the bandage from Jack's right eye. 'Ope it. Let's have a look-see.'

Jack forced his eye open a crack. The pain stabbed hard, and the strange darkling vision came again. Sharkwell's face bulged like something moulded out of animal fat, slurping slowly into a disgusted grimace.

'Blagh! You seen yourself, boy? Lookit this, Smiles – like raw tripe!'

Mr Smiles peered at Jack's eye. As he leaned in, his nose seemed to stretch out like a heron's beak. 'Blood-red, Mr S. Aconite, haply . . . Let me see the hand, Jack.'

Jack tugged the bandage back into place, and held out his hand. Sharkwell and Smiles examined it, Sharkwell turning it over like a steak he was thinking of buying. It tingled with pins and needles at his touch.

'Stains more like vitriol to me,' said Sharkwell. 'Scarlet

vitriol. You're a lucky boy, Jack.' He grinned. 'Any more of that foreign muck in you and you wouldn't be here, interrupting my business.'

Jack's eye was throbbing badly. He mustn't cry; if he did, he wouldn't be able to stop.

'And you're sure you didn't mention my name?' said Sharkwell.

'No.'

'P'raps we're out of it. He got what he wanted . . .' Sharkwell gnawed his lip. 'Lucky. Webb's a big fish.'

'What of the intelligencer?' said the girl.

'Who's to say with that shifty mob? Might be in-vestigatin' on Queen's business – might be lining his purse . . .'

'Both, mostwise,' said Mr Smiles.

One of the straw men's faces had slipped. The cloth was coming off. That was how she'd looked – like her face was falling off her skull.

'What'll we do then?' asked Jack. He was going to kill this Webb. He knew that all of a sudden.

He looked up. The girl was staring at him, scanning his face. She didn't seem to like what she saw.

'Law Eleven, Grampers,' she said.

'You reckon?' Sharkwell peered at Jack. 'Mayhap you're right, Beth.'

Jack realized who she was now – not an onion girl, not by a long shot, but Beth Sharkwell, Mr Sharkwell's granddaughter. *The* Beth Sharkwell: no wonder she looked haughty.

'You going to tell him or shall I?' she asked.

'Oh, I'll tell him,' said Sharkwell. 'Listen to me now, boy. This is the Eleventh Law, the Law of Fish. The rule is – big fish eat little ones.' He held up his forefinger and thumb half an inch apart. 'You are a tiny, tiny fish. A tiddler. Those men today . . . Nicholas Webb's king of the preachers, and a shiny man about Court these days, I hear. He's a proper sea-bastard – teeth bigger than your head, mouth like a Christmas cauldron. And that other, the *intelligencer* . . .' He scowled and spat. 'He's more of yer swarmy, coiling eel-fish – that's their way – lurk in the deep and drag a man down. That lot are worse villains than I am. So. Look-at-me-now, boy!'

Sharkwell's face glowered down at Jack, furnace-red. 'Look, and listen. I will say this once. The best, the *best* you can hope for is to scuttle down into the mud and pray your fishy heart out. Pray that those big fish don't come looking for you. Pray they think you're dead like your ma. 'Cos they will munch you up, boy, and I won't be able to protect you.'

'So he gets away with it.' Jack surprised himself by how angry he was. He surprised Sharkwell too, judging by his look, and the way he jerked his head back.

The girl snorted again.

'Hah!' said Sharkwell. 'Did you hear that, Mr Smiles?'

Jack glared up at them, from Sharkwell to Smiles. They were supposed to be his Family. His ma had worked for Sharkwell half her life. They were supposed to help him: everyone knew the Family took care of their own.

'I'm going to kill him,' said Jack.

Sharkwell's voice dropped almost to a whisper. 'If I'm not mistaken, Mr Smiles, that tiddler there has spoke back at me.'

'He's just lost his ma—' began Mr Smiles.

'I don't mind who's lost what. I mind that this nipper has spoke back. But I'm going to be generous. I'm going to assume that didn't just happen. Did it, Nipper?'

Sharkwell's eyes were black pools. A dangerous little spark danced in the centre of each pupil. Jack stared back at him.

'Did it? Mayhap it did, my little fishy,' said Sharkwell. His voice was soft now, deadly. 'Mayhap you want to find out what happens to tiddlers who talk back.'

Jack dropped his gaze. 'No.'

'No what?'

'No, Mr Sharkwell.'

'Right. And I'm sayin' this again, and you're going to listen, because it is *prime* advice. Do not go looking for either of those men. You will bring trouble on yourself. What's much worse, you will bring trouble on me. Lookit me, boy!'

Jack forced himself to look at Sharkwell, and clenched

his jaw even tighter. He didn't know why he'd come here.

'Are you going to be trouble?'

Except he *did* know, really. He'd come to Sharkwell because there was nowhere else.

'No, Mr Sharkwell.'

Sharkwell's little eyes flicked this way and that, sizing Jack up. 'Hmp. You know you've almost got me convinced, Nipper.' He turned and walked away. 'We'll bury your ma. Never let it be said we don't take care of our own. Meatface!'

'Yessir.' Meatface had been loitering at the door the whole time.

'Make the arrangements. Private coffin. Let's do her proud.'

After Jack and Meatface had gone out, Sharkwell, Beth and Mr Smiles turned back to shaping the lay they would make against Walter Calfe, the mercer, tomorrow.

They went through the plan three times. Sharkwell was only satisfied when Beth could walk the route from the merchant's kitchen to his counting house with her eyes shut. (This was in accordance with Sharkwell's Fifth Law: Hope for the best, allow for the worst.)

It was only afterwards that his thoughts returned to Jack.

'Did you mark the change in that nipper?' he said to Mr Smiles.

'Aye. Sorry business.'

'Scrunt got a bit of backbone all of a sudden. Could be the making of him.' Sharkwell smacked his lips. 'Course, he might turn awkward, have to be got rid of.'

'I don't think so,' said Beth.

'Oh!' Sharkwell grinned. 'Care to make a wager?'

'No,' said Beth.

'Right, so stash it then. You keep an eye on that nipper, Smiles. If he so much as farts in the wrong direction, I want to know.' Sharkwell clapped his hands together. 'Now let's have a drink. Those stinking dolls of yours are giving me the creeps.'

The mannequins' eyes stared blindly after them as they left the room.

Jack's ma was buried that evening in the cemetery of St Thomas's. The priest, roused from his supper by Meatface, gave her two prayers, a psalm and a short sermon, where he committed her soul to Heaven, and her bones to the dust. He remembered her name. He was scared enough of Sharkwell to give her that much, at least.

Jack wasn't the only mourner. Mr Smiles came too, with a sprig of rosemary pinned to his sleeve and another for Jack to wear. He brought five other thieves to help bear the coffin to the grave. Smiles stumbled as they set it down in the earth. She was a heavy woman.

They stood in silence, heads bowed, as the priest ran

through the service. He rattled off the final prayer, and left without another word.

Jack's tears started then, along with silent, thumping sobs in his chest. With every hollow thud of dirt on her coffin, he felt his ma going further and further away. The thuds grew muffled. Soon she would be gone for ever.

He bent double, trying to close the aching hole that had opened up inside him. He'd never felt anything like this before, not even when his pa died of the sweating fever. Jack had only been five and he hadn't understood. He could barely even remember his pa, but he'd always remembered what his ma had said:

It's just you and me now, Jack.

Except it wasn't – not any more. She was gone, and she was never coming back.

He felt Mr Smiles' hand on his shoulder. Smiles kept it there until the grave was filled. Then he stepped forward and handed the sexton a shilling to put up a stone.

'You'll gaff up with us,' Smiles said, turning to Jack. 'You're Family now. Come. She'll rest easy here.'

'Wait. Just a minute, on my own . . .' said Jack. Mr Smiles bowed his head and stepped back.

Jack knelt down and pressed his hands into the cold, damp earth. He had to say it now, while it was fresh.

'I'll get him, Ma,' he whispered. 'Kill him. I swear it.'

For a moment then he had the strangest feeling: something was watching him. Something right here, sitting on the grave in front of him. A crawling, prickling feeling flashed across his hand, where the rusty stain covered the skin. He looked up, half expecting to see his ma's ghost.

For the blink of an eye he *did* see something. Not his ma – he didn't have time to reckon what it was. It was gone in a blur of movement, a patter of footsteps fading behind him.

Jack turned from the grave. In the corner by the gate, something had kicked up the drift of dead leaves – but that couldn't have been the thing he'd seen. Nothing could move that fast.

'Smiles?'

Smiles was nowhere to be seen. Must be waiting out-side.

The wind. The wind had scattered the leaves, and Jack had seen – what, really? A blur, gone before he knew it. A fancy, a phantom of the eye.

There was nothing here but cold earth.

Chapter 8

The mornings were the worst. Each time Jack woke there was a moment of warm, sleepy forgetfulness. Then the sounds and smells of Sharkwell's warehouse would creep in – no snores from the other bed, no reek of tobacco, no spot of light on the wall – and he'd remember. Every morning he had to eat it raw. And then he had to swallow it for the rest of the day. He was a working nipper now, and there was to be no time for moping.

Sharkwell's granddaughter Beth made this very clear on Jack's first day as a resident of the warehouse. After the burial, Smiles had shown him a place to sleep amongst the stacks of empty crates in the darkest, mustiest corner of the main storeroom. Jack was threading his way towards breakfast the next morning when he had to stop. Just for a moment. He sat down, curled up over his knees and screwed his eyes shut.

He heard a snort. When he looked up, it took a moment to recognize her – no longer an onion girl, but a rich merchant's daughter with starched ruff, silver-wrought partlet and sleeves made of fine Dutch lace.

'Stopped for a sniffle, have we?' she said.

Jack shook his head. He couldn't trust himself to speak.

'Because there's no weeping here,' said Beth. 'Not over a dead ma, not over nothing.'

She still had the same haughty look – cool grey eyes sizing him up. Jack could feel snot dripping from his nose. He sniffed hard, and felt a sudden flare of hatred.

'"No moaning" is our law,' said Beth. 'Moany's next to coney, and coney gets caught.'

Jack nodded again. He wasn't going to speak till he could do it steady, show her he wasn't going to fold up under that look. Show her he didn't care whose grand-daughter she was.

'I know it ain't easy,' said Beth, a little more kindly. 'Why d'you think I live here with my grampers, and not my ma and pa?'

'Dunno.' Jack made his voice flat, like he didn't care either. 'They died, is that it?'

'Hanged,' said Beth calmly. 'I was seven, and I put in my morning's work. Twelfth Law: we work the crowd when one of us swings. Nine shillings I took that day. Now get up, look sharp – Smiles says you're to go see the cunning-man about that eye of yours. Eat first. Be back by ten o'clock. You've work to do, Nipper.'

Jack didn't want to leave the warehouse at all – Webb might still be about, or the intelligencer, looking for him – but his eye was hurting like murder. The pain would have driven him out, even without Beth showing him the door.

The Southwark cunning-man lived in a small rundown house on the edge of Paris Garden, next to the Swan Amphitheatre. To get there, Jack had to cross to the western end of Southwark, where the city edged uneasily into countryside.

He plunged into the morning commotion on Long Southwark. In the narrow stretch leading up to the bridge, two wagons had locked wheels. An axle had snapped and the churls were shouting at each other. Behind them, flocks of sheep waited patiently to cross into London and be slaughtered. To the right, the vats of Alfred's Tannery sent plumes of stinking steam into the air.

Jack tried to watch his back as he weaved through the crowds. He couldn't shake off the feeling that someone was following him. It shouldn't be possible in a crowd like this, but then it shouldn't have been possible for Webb to follow him yesterday, or kill his ma with a bluebottle, or send a knife flying through the air at his bidding. Seemed like lots of things shouldn't be possible but were.

So Jack watched his back, and tried every trick he

knew. He doubled back on himself and made unexpected turns; he went by narrow empty ways, then cut back into the thoroughfare; he ducked into a pile of hay and watched the street.

Nothing. He was imagining it, like yesterday at the graveside. Webb was too grand to sneak after a nipper anyway. If he wanted Jack, he'd collar him openly. Or would he? Webb was a sorcerer, and who knew what tricks and shadows a sorcerer might employ? And the other, the intelligencer – an intelligencer would stalk you for months to learn your secrets. You'd never know till it was too late, and you were trapped like a fly. But that made no sense either: what secrets did Jack have that an intelligencer would want to know?

No one was following him. Probably. Still, the itchy feeling at the back of his neck wouldn't go away, even when he shook all the straw from his shirt.

Jack arrived at the house at nine o'clock, jumpy and out of breath.

Nine o'clock in the morning was not a good time of day to be visiting the cunning-man. Jack's first few knocks went unanswered, so he started rapping on the window instead. This produced a smothered groan from inside, then a loud, clattering crash and a torrent of curses. Finally the door opened a crack, and a pair of bleary eyes peered out.

'A boy . . .' The cunning-man's voice was warped and

parched, like old, forgotten paper. 'What, just one? I thought I heard another . . .'

The cunning-man opened the door a little wider. He was wearing a robe that had once been a fine shade of midnight blue. It had a large, fresh-looking stain down the front, and when it flapped open Jack could see he was naked underneath. Pewter bracelets studded with bits of coloured glass dangled from his wrists, a silver vial hung on a pendant round his neck. His face was smeared with what looked like stage make-up.

'Where'd the other go?' The cunning-man peered over Jack's shoulder, then glared suspiciously into his face. 'What's the game, boy?'

'No game, sir. It's just me . . .' Only Jack couldn't help looking back over his shoulder too, to check. He saw the lane he'd just walked down – mud and filth, nothing else. 'I – I got something in my eye.' He pointed at the bandage. 'It was—'

'What's yer name?'

'Jack.'

'Well, Jack, I hain't got patience for boys playing games, specially not this time of the morning . . .'

'Wait.' Jack fumbled in his sleeve, and pulled out the coin from yesterday. 'I've gold.'

The cunning-man's eyes sharpened to two beady points, fixed on the coin. 'Come in, boy,' he wheezed hastily. 'Come in, Jack – too bright out here.'

Jack followed him into a dim, frowsty room with a narrow bed in one corner. The floor was covered with a chaotic jumble of papers, jars, dirty clothes and empty wineskins, topped off with a shattered jug that had soaked the whole lot in something that smelled of rotten apples.

'Forgive all this . . .' The cunning-man waved an arm at the pile. His bracelets jangled together. 'You choose an odd time to visit me, Jack-boy, I must say. Let's assay this gold, if you please.'

Jack produced the coin. The cunning-man weighed it in his hand, then bit it. 'Good, good . . .' He rummaged in the pile, picked up a clay jug and upended it. Dark liquid splashed across his robe. 'Pox,' he said.

In the end, he found the right jug under his bed: instead of wine, it produced a small shower of silver.

'I reckon this' – he fingered the gold coin and licked his teeth – 'is somewhat between an angel and an angelet, yes – say seven shillings, shall we? Usual fee is two, so . . .' He held out two silver coins. 'A crown will make up your balance, agreed?'

Jack took the coins, not really caring that he was being cheated.

Now that he'd been paid, a marked change came over the cunning-man. He cinched up the belt of his robe, and smoothed down its rumpled front. His movements were brisker; his gaze sharper. He reached up onto a shelf above his bed and placed a black velvet cap on his head, completing the transformation.

'To business,' he said. 'Raise the dressing off your eye.'

Jack did as he was told, keeping his eye tight shut. The cunning-man leaned forward, pressed gently against Jack's eyelid with his fingertip. Jack winced at the sudden stab of pain.

'Tender, is it?'

Jack nodded.

'So, so . . . Can you ope it?'

'It hurts worse when it's open.'

'Well, that won't kill you. Ope it now.'

Jack opened his eye. The cunning-man's face peering down seemed to bulge and stretch, like blown glass. The shadows in the corners of the room flickered and flowed like boiling water.

'Mmph. It certainly looks bad,' said the cunning-man. 'Can you see?'

Jack nodded. 'But different.'

'Different how?'

'All red and dark, and . . . stretchy. And there's things moving about.' Jack frowned. 'Something like visions – I don't know . . .'

The cunning-man squinted at him. 'Visions, is it?' He made a sound halfway between a laugh and a grunt. 'What did you say happened to this eye of yours?'

Jack hadn't said anything about it – the cunning-man

hadn't given him a chance – but he didn't bother pointing this out. Instead he told him about the pipe, and the powder, and Webb sucking it down. He left out the part about his ma, but not the flying knife: he wanted the cunning-man to know this was serious.

In this he failed. The cunning-man turned pale when Jack mentioned Webb's name, but then, when Jack came to the magic part, he burst out laughing.

'You are playing games, boy!' he said. 'Nicholas Webb a sorcerer – aye, and I'm Dr John Dee.'

'He was,' said Jack. 'I mean, he *is*. He made it fly. You're meant to know about magic: how'd he do that?'

'Threw it. If it were Preacher Webb you saw, which I doubt . . . No, boy, you've a fine poetical turn of mind, I'll grant, but I wouldn't go laying it on like that. Slander, you know. Nicholas Webb's pious as the day is long, and wants everyone to know it. Now about this powder . . .'

'Aye,' said Jack. 'I thought it was poison first, but now I reckon it's . . . sorcery. Look, it got my hand too.' He lifted his stained hand. The red had faded, gone deeper into the skin overnight – less angry than before, more like a birthmark.

The cunning-man barely spared it a glance. 'Forget sorcery, boy—'

'No,' said Jack. He'd gone over it in his mind last night again and again, and it always came out the same. He knew what he'd seen: not a trick, not his imagination, but black sorcery, and done by Webb. Never mind what Sharkwell had said about him being a witch-finder. Never mind what the cunning-man said, either. It made for a puzzle, for sure, but it wasn't true.

His eye was hurting worse than ever, his hand was itching, and he could feel his anger beginning to boil up again. 'I've paid you. I want what's due, so you look into it proper, or else.'

'Or else what?' The cunning-man stared at Jack for a moment, as if waiting for an answer. Jack glared back at him and said nothing.

'Heh. A wild little pup, ain't you? Very well.' The cunning-man returned to the back of the room, pulled out a wooden chest from under the bed, and rummaged inside. He came back over to Jack holding a dried-up twist of bone and fur attached to a string. 'Here you see my most powerful charm. If there's anything of magic about this eye of yours, we'll soon know.'

Jack looked at the charm. It was some sort of paw – a rabbit's, or a small dog's – very old and dusty, with a length of stripped-off shinbone protruding thin and naked. It didn't look much. 'What is it?'

'Why, a lucky cat's foot – ensorcelled by the mages of Egypt, and preserved by ancient arts.' The cunning-man grinned unpleasantly. 'That's the truth – though you'd never know the difference, would you? And now, if you'll untent your eye, we will all observe just how fantastical your story really is.'

The charm was dangling right in front of Jack's bad eye when he lifted his bandage, using his left hand. Then he lifted his right hand to force his eye open, and two things happened.

First, the charm swung violently away from him till it was straining horizontal against its string. Second, Jack saw something in the charm. Something trapped under the ancient fur, it looked like, twitching and squirming. For an instant it formed a screaming face, eyes stretched wide and fixed on Jack's hand – and then the string snapped, and the charm flew across the room and slid down the wall onto the cunning-man's bed.

The cunning-man leaped like a stung horse. He stood stock still for a moment, staring at Jack. Then, without saying a word, he went over to his bed, picked up the charm and put it back in the wooden chest. He went to the table. He snatched up a wineskin and started drinking. His throat wobbled like a chicken's wattle as he gulped, and his hand holding the skin trembled.

'Hey!' said Jack. 'What are you doing? What's wrong?'

'Naught wrong,' mumbled the cunning-man. He finished the skin and tossed it aside. He rummaged through the wreckage on the floor, tossing stuff about. 'Jesus! Naught wrong, no . . .'

He found a full jug and started sucking on that as well.

The trembling in his hand subsided as he drank.

'What're you going to do about it?' said Jack.

' 'Bout what?'

'My eye! What happened to the charm? What's the matter with it?'

'No . . . idea.' The cunning-man shook his head. He tilted back the jug and shook the last few drops of liquor into his mouth.

Then he went to work.

He worked steady for a man who'd just drunk a pint of strong liquor. First he dug up some herbs from his chest, laying them out on top of the bed. He mashed them together in a bowl, added a few drops of an evil-smelling potion and used his yellow fingernail to stir it all together with spit.

He paused for another drink, ignoring all Jack's questions, and set to work with a needle and thread. He was surprisingly handy with that as well. Soon he held up a neat little eye-patch with a damp poultice on the inside.

'This is for your pain. Keep her on for a spell – say six weeks,' he said, placing the patch over Jack's eye and tying it at the back of his head. 'Come back in a fortnight and I'll renew that poultice. The pain will pass. As for the visions, and . . .'

'The magic,' said Jack.

The cunning-man turned and settled heavily on the

bed. 'Aye. That.' He pulled off his hat and selected a jar of clear amber liquid from under the bed. 'That's beyond me, boy. Never seen the like. Not in thirty years of jobbing.' He unstoppered the jar and took a long slow swig.

'Listen close now, for this is my good, honest counsel. Don't speak of the visions, nor of what happened with the charm. Don't say a word. To anybody.'

Another swig and the jar was almost empty. The raspy smell of raw stingo filled the room, and now, at last, the cunning-man's voice began to slur.

'Lis'n . . . listen. There's evil being spoke about town when it comes to matters of witchery. More than usual. More'n ever. Preachers, red-hands . . . your Mr Webb's chief amongst 'em . . . Pious fright-mongers. They see e'en a . . . a tinge of devilcraft in a body . . .'

'But what is it?' said Jack. 'What happened there, with the cat's foot? I saw—'

'Don't – speak – of – it!'

'But if Webb's—'

'Speak of him not 't all!' The cunning-man swung round, eyes blazing. 'Too dang'rous. Even one such as I, a learned man, a doctor, a phil . . . philophoser . . . Aye, well.' He took a final drink from the jar, lay down in the bed, and turned over, facing the wall.

'Shut it on yer way out. An' keep that mouth shut too, and watch out for preachers. The red-hands. Aye, and that other, th'one followed you here . . .'

'There ain't no other.'

'No?' The cunning-man hiccupped. 'Have it your way then, boy, and be damned t'you. Cursed . . . Already cursed, comes here, nine o' th'clock, bigod . . .' Another hiccup. 'Have it any way he likes.'

Chapter 9

Mr Smiles was waiting for Jack at the corner of the lane leading to the warehouse. Standing beside him was a tall, stout boy with ruddy cheeks and blond hair.

'Well met by morning-light, Nipper,' said Smiles. 'Quite the piratical, circumnavigatory, mariner-wolfish facial furnishment you sport there.'

Jack fingered his eye-patch. It felt good on his face, and the poultice inside had moulded itself over his eyelid, cool, damp and soothing. The pain was less already, and if he tried hard he could resist the temptation to blurt out about the rest – the face under the fur, the charm flying across the room, the cunning-man's terror. Jack had already decided to follow the cunning-man's advice: he wasn't going to tell anyone about any of it.

'I saw the cunning-man, like you said . . .'

'. . . and he's tricked you up like a Drake, a Hawkins, a Frobisher.' Smiles beamed.

'Smiles likes mariners,' said the stout boy, with a grin. 'Shame he got seasick the one time he went to France, ain't it, Smiles?'

'The tragical event of my life,' said Smiles. 'Present yourself to Jack afore I pipe my eyes out.'

'Robin Butterbeak, Master Nudger, and we're well met, Jack. I heard about your . . . misfortune.' The boy was trying to look grave now. Jack didn't think it suited him. His cheeks flushed dark with the effort, and his blue eyes looked strained and slightly foolish.

'Rob will be your nudger,' said Smiles. 'That patch – memorable, Jack. Too memorable. You'll be impressed upon the peepers, bawled aloft by every balladeer in town. Notoriety . . .' He tapped the side of his nose. 'Shun it. You linger darksome in the shade; let 'em look Rob here in the eye.'

'I've the face for it,' said Rob.

Smiles chuckled. 'The face of a Saxon lummock . . . the gait of a hobbledy-cob . . . the lackwit gaze of a Cornish cousin's hedge-get.'

'Folks forget me,' said Rob. He ruffled his wiry blond hair down over his eyes, let his face go slack, and stared about, scratching his head. Jack couldn't stop a smile twisting up the corners of his mouth: Rob looked exactly like a country churl up for market, gaping at the sights.

'You smoke the lay?' said Smiles.

'I nudge, you nip,' said Rob. 'I palaver with 'em till you're away.'

Jack nodded.

'Sock it, then,' said Smiles. 'I'll be tarrying hawklike, dropping the eaves. A fresh duality is ever a joy to observe.'

They started with the market crowd in Tooley Street. Rob was good. He timed his nudges perfectly, blundering into the coneys just a second before Jack cut their purse-strings. Rob would apologize with a good-natured grin – long, awkward, rustic apologies – and finally request directions to St Paul's Cathedral. By the time the coney had finished explaining for the third time and fake comprehension was beginning to dawn on Rob's yokel face, Jack would be well away and watching from cover.

It was lucky Rob was so wily at the game, because Jack was finding it hard to concentrate. The cunning-man's final words haunted and confused him in equal dose. *Already cursed.* But a curse meant a spell, fancy words and twirling fingers, and that wasn't what had happened. A puff of powder from an old clay pipe – an accident. Poison made more sense than a curse. Except the powder wasn't poison. Webb had sucked it down like a drunkard on his jug, and looked all the better for it.

None of it explained what was wrong with Jack. And something *was* wrong with him, something very uncanny and weird. It was true the pain in his eye was subsiding as the poultice took effect – but still. He saw gargoyle faces appear in dusty old fur. He'd frightened the cunning-man speechless.

At least with a curse, there might be some way of lifting it; but an accident, a mystery . . . Jack tried not to think on it, tried to concentrate on the work at hand.

In the afternoon they moved on to the Rose Playhouse, first working the queues outside, then paying their way into the pit. In between nippings, Jack scanned the galleries for Webb or his Puritan friends. There was no sign of them. Jack knew this should be a relief, but it wasn't. A new, colder part of him – a part that hadn't existed before yesterday – wanted to meet Webb again as soon as possible. The blade on his Nipper's Claw could cut a throat as well as purse-strings.

He knew Webb was fast and strong – but how fast would he be, taken from his blind side while giving Rob directions to St Paul's? One quick swipe and it would be over.

It might not work, and even if it did, Jack wouldn't get away with it. They would hang him for sure. He knew what his ma would have said about such a plan.

But his ma was gone.

The days passed. Somehow Jack managed to avoid any more homilies from Beth about moping. Work made it easier. This was partly because Rob Butterbeak was cheerful company and partly because nipping required absolute concentration.

Mr Smiles worked them hard, a new trick every day and no supper till they'd mastered it. 'A nipper,' Smiles was fond of saying, 'is either quick, or dead.' There was no time to mope, or grieve, or worry about curses and sorcery and vengeance. Jack was rum-diving, practising the shoulder sham, unthimbling, bunging a nip and plying the dummee. The slightest blunder could cost him his neck.

Even so, his other thoughts had a way of breaking through at the worst moments. Several times a day, he still got the odd feeling he was being watched or followed – though he never caught anyone at it. It crept up like someone was stepping on his shadow, and the stain on his hand would set to itching. Usually the feeling came on sudden, though he began to notice that it happened every time he passed a few particular places: the south wall of the Clink Prison, the well at St Thomas's, the Southwark Cathedral boneyard, and a few other itchy spots besides.

Jack didn't know what to make of this, so he avoided such places as much as he could. Rob tolerated Jack's sudden changes of direction with his usual good cheer. He took to saying that Jack's itchiness was like a ratting-terrier's nose – a way of sniffing out the neatest score. Jack didn't set him right. At least Rob would talk to him about it; the other thieves his age had already made up their minds. His maimed hand and patched eye marked him out as uncanny – someone to be avoided.

Jack had no time for making friends anyway. There was too much to learn. It seemed that Sharkwell had a law for everything, and Jack soon discovered that not knowing the laws was no excuse for breaking them. On his second day he arrived back at the warehouse to a furious lecture from Beth. Word had got around that Jack had actually paid the cunning-man: this was in clear breach of the Nineteenth Law, which said that no one in the Family paid for anything in the Ward of Southwark. You stole from the straights, and the crooks gave out for free. The cunning-man was a crook, and low down on the scale. For a member of Sharkwell's Family to pay for his services was downright disgraceful.

The next day, as they were sharing a pint and a loaf before trying their luck with the bear-baiting crowd at the Swan, Jack asked Rob about the laws.

Rob laughed gloomily. 'Better ask Beth,' he said. 'I know up to thirty-seven, but there's plenty more. She's told me ones in the hundreds before now.'

Jack didn't ask Beth. Still, he tried to learn as much as he could. Every night he would lie in the small cave he'd carved out for himself, deep inside the mountain of dusty crates, flogging his brain to exhaustion.

When walking in the street, a nipper of Sharkwell's

Family must step aside for boys coming the other way if they were wearing the colours of any of the Livery Companies – except the Distillers and the Fanmakers. Both of these Companies had dealings with Sharkwell and must be made to know their place. You stepped aside for whores, unless they came from a house run by Sharkwell. When it came to actors, you stepped aside for the Chamberlain's Men, the Admiral's Men and the King's Men, but not Lord Strange's Men (Lord Strange owed Sharkwell money).

That was Law Twenty-three, the Law of Thoroughfare Precedence. Jack was well on the way to memorizing the first two dozen. It helped him get to sleep, kept him from thinking about his ma or worrying about whatever it was that might or might not be following him.

The question of the phantom follower always surfaced, though, bobbing up like jetsam from a sinking ship. If it existed at all it was something uncanny, he'd decided – but not sent by Webb. If Webb was following him so close, he would have acted by now. Which meant there might be something else interested in him. In him, or in the powder, or in the stain on his hand; there was no way of knowing, that was the torment.

It was much better to imagine what he was going to do to Webb. Thinking about Webb made him feel hard and bright, like red-hot steel straight from the forge. It was a good feeling, and Jack had imagined killing him in a thousand ways, but everyone knew the best and most likely way to kill a man was to cut his throat. For that, Jack kept his blades whetted wicked sharp. Time after time he imagined creeping up soft, choosing his spot, slashing out . . . And time after time that was where it went bad.

Jack didn't know the right place to cut. Did you go ear to ear? Or was it better to stab, narrow and deep? Sharkwell had forbidden him Webb, so he couldn't ask anyone in the Family for advice. Aggravating, because there were plenty of seasoned killers amongst the darksmen and the waterpads – men who'd blooded the lace a dozen times.

But even if someone had been willing to teach Jack the true miller's slash, there was an even bigger obstacle in his way: he had to get close enough to Webb to do the deed.

It was true that Webb was well-known, a big fish, like Sharkwell had said. But that didn't mean he was easy to find. Jack was trying. Usually he was good at finding things. Every spare moment, he burrowed through Southwark, nosing around after news of Webb. He spoke to all the scaly coves, the barnacles that leeched off the city. He rode with carters, gossiped with the gin-spinners and rolled dice with bargees.

No one knew much, and what scraps he picked up were outlandish. Webb must have got away from the intelligencer, because there was no word that he'd been arrested. Far from it: the rumour went that Webb was at large, and keeping busy. A Suffolk harper claimed that Webb had fought a duel with Beelzebub at Ipswich, and won. Lady Bunce's bed-maker said he had exorcized a ghost from the Tower of London, and was now often admitted at Court. Mary the Alsatian swore she'd seen Nicholas Webb arm-wrestle against the devil himself, left hand clutching his Bible, right hand sizzling in the infernal grip – but he'd won that contest too, she said, though fearful maimed for ever after.

All the stories agreed that the man was practically a saint – battling devils with one hand, toting his Bible with the other.

Jack didn't believe any of it. He was asking the wrong kind of people. The trouble was, the right kind of people would never talk to a scrunty little urchin from the Shambles.

It was now that being a member of the Family began to show its advantages.

The church of St Olave the Martyr was one of the itchy spots that Jack had been avoiding since the accident, so he loitered for the curate at the Gully Hole Ordinary instead. Even from there his hand was beginning to buzz by the time the curate arrived for his customary luncheon pie, and even then the man was too haughty at first to answer an urchin's questions.

That was before Jack mentioned Mr Sharkwell.

That same Mr Sharkwell who ran the bowling alley behind the theatre, the one with the pretty ladies. The one where the curate had lost all those wagers last week – he must remember all that money that hadn't been paid yet.

Jack got up to leave. The curate turned pale and scuttled after him, bearing a wedge of cold game pie, which he forced down Jack's throat, along with everything he knew of Webb.

Apparently, Webb really was a miracle man, said the curate: his vicar knew a verger at the cathedral who had seen him cast out a devil with his own eyes. Webb was a prophet, and he had formed a sort of clergy of his own, sworn to rid London of demons and magicians. They called themselves the Elect, dressed in Puritan black, and distinguished themselves by staining their right hands red. The priestly gossip ran that Webb and his Elect met in secret, at night, once a week.

That was all. Jack asked him where the meetings took place; he didn't know. He was only a curate. He was so terror-struck by the name of Sharkwell that Jack believed him, even though his story didn't make any more sense than the others.

Webb was no prophet – he was a sorcerer. Back before his ma's murder, and the stain on his hand, and the red vision in his eye, Jack would never have credited it. But he'd seen it. He didn't care if other people thought it was miracles, or holiness; to Jack, all that mattered was that it made him harder to kill.

Every night, Jack crouched in the darkness, running his Nipper's Claw backwards and forwards over his whetstone. It made a soothing, rhythmic rasp.

Secret meetings. Night-time meetings.

All it wanted was a dark alley, a sharp blade, and a chance. Webb would see how his miracles served him then.

Chapter 10

All London slumbered under a thick blanket of fog. In their gilded houses on Cheapside, the great merchants dreamed of galleons that groaned with gold and mountains made of silver. In mean Southwark shanties the moon-rakers snored out their liquor. They dreamed the same dream, their fortunes won.

The ravens in the Tower settled their feathers and clacked their beaks and dreamed of the stones buried deep underground.

And beneath the city, between roots and ruins and forgotten places, the stones dreamed too.

The fog muffled the night in velvet boots. The tide rolled hushed and smooth towards the sea; not a single wave lapped against the smoky boards of Privy Wharf; in the warehouse, all was silent and still.

Except Jack.

Jack, and some other thing.

There was a noise. It sounded like a footstep. It came from behind him, over by the stuffed bear and the barrel of pikestaffs.

Another. Closer this time.

Jack stopped and shivered and held his breath. There was no call for anyone to be there, not at this godforsaken time of night. The warehouse should be empty.

Lately he'd taken to creeping down to the wharf to watch the river. Night was the time when his worst thoughts came out to haunt him. Sneaking through the pitch-dark warehouse was good practice, and it kept him from picturing his ma's death face, all twisted up, the way he'd found her.

Sometimes there'd be men on the wharf – waterpads with drowned corpses from the river, darksmen bringing back booty from a house-breaking – but no Family was out in the fog tonight. Tonight he'd gone out late, and come in later. The first, faintest light of dawn was creeping soft across the river: it made the warehouse seem even darker.

Most people would have found it a creepy place. The warehouse was so big, so packed with strange stolen jumble and queer shadows and creaking rigging high above. Only Jack didn't find it so. In here he felt safe. For weeks he'd had the same itchy, followed feeling, coming and going, every time he went outside. But not in here. Not till now.

The noise came again. It sounded like a footstep right there, right beside him. A light footstep, such as a child might make.

'Hey!' Jack whispered.

He strained his ears against the dark. When the noise came again, it was on the other side of him. Near the gigger's casement-shop.

'What are you?' Jack's voice seemed fearful loud.

There was no answer. The silence went on so long that he started to hope he was spooking himself. But then the noise sounded again, and this time there was no mistaking it: light footsteps, scampering on the gantry overhead. A throb of pain shot through Jack's stained hand.

His fear sharpened. Whatever it was, it was small and fast, and it was everywhere. Maybe there were more than one. 'Stop it,' he hissed.

The footsteps stopped. The silence that fell was overwhelming. It stretched out until he heard something that sounded like a chuckle. It came from over by Lord Synge's greatcoach. Jack's heart was thumping so loud he nearly missed it.

The sneaking thing fancied itself a gamester. It was playing with him. Jack's anger rose up in a wave.

The chuckle came again – a raspy snickering, like a goat.

Swive it. Jack ran. The footsteps capered ahead of

him until he was out past the coach, ears straining . . .
Nothing.

Jack cursed. It was still there. The stain on his hand
was on fire.

Another chuckle, and he was running, through the
maze of casks, underneath a stretch of netting,
dodging between a lemon tree in a pot and a mound of
foreign silks.

His foot caught and he tumbled over. A booming crash
echoed through the warehouse.

The silence came down hard and Jack lay there, listening so fiercely that his ears popped. It was pitch black, and
he'd lost his bearings. He squinted up at the shadow above
him. With a jolt he realized it was the upturned face of the
Lively's figurehead. The rest of the stolen ship's prow
loomed over him in the darkness.

He was very near his sleeping place now.

'Where are you?' he whispered with mounting dread.

The chuckle answered from just where he'd expected it
– at the entrance to the tunnel he'd carved out amongst
the empty crates.

When he reached his sleeping place, there was nothing
to be seen but his blankets, his straw and his box of
provisions – his own private rat's-nest. Other people
didn't come here; but there was something here now.
If he reached out his arm, he might be able to touch
it. His hand was burning up. His eye behind the

patch felt hot and sticky. If he took off the patch . . .

Jack didn't move. He tried to speak, but his throat was closed up.

'Go away,' he croaked. 'Don't you come here more.'

Something brushed over his left side, ticklish, like a cloud of invisible cobwebs. His hair prickled up on his scalp, and settled. The *watched* feeling passed away – there was a creaking in the crates, a clatter from the roof – and silence.

It was gone. Jack had the strangest feeling that it had left because he told it to. It had heard him, and obeyed.

Which didn't make any sense, of course. What made sense was that the invisible watcher had gone to report to its master – whoever that might be.

Either way, Jack didn't think he'd be getting any sleep tonight.

'Come on, you lazy Taylor!'

Rob Butterbeak's face appeared at the entrance to Jack's sleeping place.

'My pa'll kill me if I miss the throw. Out! Up! Stop counting woolly-birds!' Rob began pulling the blankets off Jack.

Jack groaned.

'Come on!'

'Half a minute.'

Jack stuffed his feet into his shoes, and stumbled

blearily across to the pail of water in the corner. He splashed his face, and poked vigorously at his teeth with a frayed stick. He hadn't missed a day yet.

'Forget your teeth,' said Rob.

Jack didn't hear him. The ice-cold water had sluiced away his sleepiness, and now he remembered last night. He flexed his hand, but it wasn't playing up. He didn't feel anything watching him, either. In fact, he felt better than he had in days.

'Come on, Jack!' Rob's voice was hoarse with impatience.

Jack settled his patch in place, and took a deep breath. He'd never understood football.

His good feeling lasted as they crossed onto the bridge. Jack got the usual twinge in his stained hand that he felt every time he passed under the spiked heads on the south tower, but today it didn't bother him. The rotting, crow-poked faces all seemed to be grinning. Jack grinned back. As far as he could tell, nothing was following him. It was the first day in weeks that he hadn't felt watched.

North of the bridge, New Fish Street was unusually busy. The mob was eddying about Cornhill and they had to fight their way through. Rob kept pushing, shoving, muttering and swearing, anxious at the slightest delay. He didn't relax until they were safely perched high up on the churchyard wall of St Andrew's Undershaft.

'Right at the heart of it.' He cupped his hands round his mouth and bellowed across the street, 'Come on, you Bricks!'

Below them lay the broad muddy expanse of Cornhill. A wooden barricade had been erected along both sides of the street. Behind it, the crowd was packed five deep. All the shopkeepers had boarded up their windows the night before. Spots on balconies overlooking the road were going for as much as twenty shillings apiece.

Everyone around Jack, Rob included, was wearing something yellow. On the other side of the street, the crowd was a patchy sea of blue. Jack didn't have any colours, and it made him feel exposed: being part of a football crowd without making his allegiance clear was asking for trouble.

He leaned down and slowly eased a yellow feather from the cap of the man standing below him. He stuck it in the band of his eye-patch.

'Prime, Jack!' Rob thumped him on the back. 'Get the yellow on you!'

The hum of excitement grew louder. Chants were thrown back and forth across the street. 'WE'RE! ALL! The BRICK, BRICK WALL!' screamed Rob, along with a hundred others.

'We bought your clothes! We bought your clothes!' sang the Merchant Taylor supporters on the blue side of the street.

Jack looked over at Rob. 'I know,' shouted Rob. 'Spavined, ain't it?'

'What do they even mean?'

Rob shrugged, grinned, then joined in the next chant: 'OOH! TO! OOH TO BE! TO BE A BRICKLAYAH!'

Now Jack heard a rolling din approaching from both ends of Cornhill. The roars from the crowd surged, died down, and came back louder. Jack saw blue banners bobbing and swaying as they approached from the western end of the street. Yellow flags were advancing from the opposite direction.

The teams were coming.

'There's my pa!' shouted Rob.

It was easy to see who he was pointing to. Big Don Butterbeak was standing right at the centre of the Bricklayers' Company front maul. He had the same ruddy face as his son, though it was mostly hidden by a blond, haystack beard. He had fingers like sausages, and he was bellowing like a bull. Jack would not have stood in his way for a hundred pounds.

'He's playing bup today,' shouted Rob. 'Got moved up from guard under-quarter.'

For the past week, Rob had done nothing but talk about the match, and his pa. A year ago, a man of the Bricklayers had spotted Big Don's potential in a tavern brawl. Up till then Big Don had been an ordinary Southwark heavy-for-hire; but the Company teams were always on the lookout for new talent, and a company like the Bricklayers, low down in the pecking order, weren't too particular where it came from. Big Don's election into the Company had been quick – it had taken one week rather than the customary seven years. It had proved an inspired move: the Bricks had beaten their arch-rivals the Taylors in the last two matches, and Big Don had gained a reputation as a fearsome reducer.

The two teams came to a halt about twenty yards apart. In the crowd, the frenzy rose to a new peak.

A small man in a pointed white hat walked into the empty space between the teams. The Taylors and the Bricklayers flexed their arms, cracked their knuckles and glowered at each other. White Hat was talking, but no one stood a chance of hearing him.

'What's he on about?' asked Jack.

'He's saying no knives, nor biting, nor foul violence of any kind,' said Butterbeak.

'I thought that was the point.'

'Course not!' Rob looked shocked. 'This is football, Jack. English football. We ain't Spaniards.'

White Hat stopped talking. He checked that both teams were ready and lifted up a brown leather ball.

A kind of silence descended upon the street. Nobody moved.

White Hat threw the ball straight up in the air and ran like Hell.

He only just made it. As the ball went up, the Bricklayers and the Taylors charged. They met before the ball came down, with a ringing thwack of bone and sinew. Big Don was right in the thick of it, laying about with great sweeps of his arm. Everyone was howling.

The ball had vanished, swallowed up in the mêlée.

'Maul right! PUNCH HIM! BREAK HIS FACE!' Rob bounced up and down. 'We got possession!'

'How d'you tell that?' All Jack could see was a wild snarl of limbs.

'Spy the corners, there?' Rob pointed to a group of smaller men, looking furtive at the back. Now Jack saw the ball: somehow it had been passed back through the scrum.

'So they're going to score . . . a shy?' Jack was pleased to have remembered this bit of football cant.

'You mad? No one's scored on Cornhill since Fat Harry was King.'

No goal for forty years. The first bodies were being carried away from the ruck.

As far as Jack could work out, this football match was turning out like all the others he'd ever seen: a scrum of heaving, fighting men, and everyone else shouting. Rob was still in a frenzy of excitement, spouting nonsense about false pivots, rouges and furking.

'Right, I'm going to get started,' said Jack.

'Already? But what about the match?' said Rob. The

mass of footballers rolled forward a few paces. 'That's it! Heave! HEAVE!'

'You stay,' said Jack. 'I'll meet you after.'

'You're a diamond, Jack.' Rob dragged his eyes away from the football for a second. 'But don't you go nipping off any Bricklayers. Not today.'

'Right,' said Jack, and jumped down.

His eyes went on the hunt, sizing up the coneys. It had been a good idea of Rob's to come here, even if he had no intention of working himself: everyone in the crowd was distracted, easy nips. On the other hand, everyone round here was wearing Bricklayers' yellow.

Jack cast about, trying to find anyone who wasn't a bricklayer. He spotted a pair of journeyman wax-chandlers dressed in their company's pale blue livery; but they wouldn't answer. His ma had always said it was unlucky to nip off bee-keepers. He eyed up a gentry sot leaning against the church wall, sucking the dregs from an empty wineskin; but when the toper let the sack fall, Jack saw that he had a filthy yellow scarf at his throat.

Perhaps he should just ignore Rob . . .

Then he heard the voice – a nasty rasping sort of voice.

'Repent, footballers, of your sins! Hereof grow envy, malice, rancour, choler, hatred, displeasure, enmity, and what not else?'

It didn't sound like a bricklayer.

All at once his hand began to throb. It was a different feeling to the itchy spots or the tingle of being followed – a cool throbbing from his fingertips to the root of his thumb. It was faint, hardly there, like a ghost's handshake.

'Is this murdering play, now? This mayhem exercise on the Sabbath Day? No! 'Tis devilry plain!'

The voice was coming from around the corner of the church. Jack saw an eddy in the crowd and dived through. The feeling in his hand gripped a little harder and warmer, tugging him gently towards the voice. It was not unpleasant, and when Jack flexed his fingers they felt strong and capable.

'Sometime your necks are broken!'

Jack squeezed a little further and saw the speaker. He was a preacher, dressed in black. His eyes were rolled up to Heaven and his arms were outstretched.

'Sometime your backs, sometime your legs,' he bawled. 'Sometime your arms . . .'

Jack stopped breathing.

Outlined clear against the whitewashed wall behind him, the preacher's right hand was stained dark red.

The murder in Jack's heart came rushing out. He'd nursed it for weeks, and now without thinking he slipped the Nipper's Claw onto his finger. One quick slash to the throat . . .

Jack pushed the thought away, frightened at himself.

Murder, in broad daylight, and the wrong man at that. He might as well throw himself in the river to drown.

'Sometime one part is thrust out of joint and sometime another; sometime your noses gush out with blood, sometime your eyes start out!'

With a bright, wolfish eye, Jack settled back against the wall to consider. His hand was still throbbing, blood-warm, but it was working just fine. He ignored it. The thing to do, he decided, would be to wait for the preacher's nonsense to stop, then follow him wherever he went next. This might be the man to lead him straight to Webb. Today. The thought made him smile.

'The devils are here, here, very here!' shouted the preacher, slapping his red hand against the wall. 'They are bound in these stones, my brothers! And with this accursed sport you do feed them in blood! Blood . . . and unholy injury!'

The crowd ignored the ranting and watched the game. The preacher was oblivious, drunk on his own righteousness. Jack was the only one listening as his howling peaked.

'One man can lead this city to salvation. Hear him! He will cast out the devils – from the wells, and the walls, from the very stones themselves! He will purify our souls, our city! His name is Nicholas Webb, my brothers. He is your brother too!'

The man held up a sheaf of handbills. ''Tis all writ here.

Read! Read your salvation! The city's salvation! The Reckoning arrives soon!'

The preacher stepped forward, and thrust the pamphlets into people's faces. It wasn't very wise, thought Jack, provoking a football crowd like that. Could get you hurt, even if you were meant to be holy.

As the preacher turned, Jack noticed the purse hanging from his girdle. A heavy purse. His pulse quickened, and the feeling gripped his hand again, gentle but very warm now, tugging him towards the purse.

Webb's man; so in a way it was Webb's money. It was no true revenge, but it would be something – some small measure . . .

He certainly wasn't a bricklayer, either.

As if it was the most natural thing the world, Jack sidled up beside him. His right hand was hot. Mr Smiles had taught him Fingle's Feint last week, and this seemed the perfect chance to try it out.

'Repent, and join with the Elect, my brothers! Repent, for the Reckoning is at hand!'

'Here, preacher,' said Jack.

The preacher looked down at him. 'Do you wish to learn the Truth, boy?'

'Sumthin' like that,' said Jack. 'Give us a sheet, then.'

The preacher held out one of his pamphlets. As Jack reached forward, he fumbled it, and the paper dropped to the ground.

He bent over to pick it up, bumping into the preacher as he did so. His right hand was burning hot now, but a *good* hot, and he'd never nipped so deft or so sure. With a snap of finger and wrist, Jack cut the preacher's purse-strings, and was away.

Smiles himself couldn't have done it sweeter.

Chapter 11

'Who'd you pluck then, Jack?' asked Sharkwell. 'The Three Wise Men?' He let one of the coins go tumbling over his knuckles.

There were at least two dozen gold coins piled on the bartop of the Crooked Walnut. They lay there, glinting.

While Rob shouted the Bricklayers to victory, Jack had robbed the red-handed preachers. He couldn't believe it: after weeks of scuttling in their burrows, it seemed the Elect were back on the streets in force. His hand led him to them, like a game: warm, warmer, hot – and here's another preacher. Jack trotted out every one-man dodge Smiles had taught him, from Gelding the Gimblet to the Crossbitten Bung. Before the end-of-match surge carried him away, he'd taken five fat purses.

It was a good morning's work. Each purse was heavy with gold – but that wasn't the half of it. Jack had almost blurted something out when he saw the cheat rolled out in front of Sharkwell. They were the same coins that he'd taken in his Trial at the Rose – the strange foreign coins with the fly stamp.

Sharkwell held one up, with the fly facing towards Jack. He could still feel the tug of the gold.

'The reason I ask who, me young scrunt, is that I cannot help but see this here marking.'

Jack stayed quiet. He was mighty curious about the fly stamp; but the prime business for now was to hide his excitement from Sharkwell.

'So I ask you again, who'd you sconce? For your own scrunty little sake I hope you tell me it weren't no big fishes.'

'It was a Merchant Taylor, Mr Sharkwell,' said Jack, looking him straight in the eye. 'Might've been a big fish, I s'pose. He was dressed like one.'

'That's right!' Rob laughed. His pa had knocked out three men and the Bricklayers had triumphed; his day couldn't have gone much better.

'And what were you doing, oaf-face?' said Sharkwell.

'He was nudging for me,' said Jack. 'He picked the coney out, Mr Sharkwell.'

'I didn't ask you, scrunt.'

'I was nudging, Mr Sharkwell, like Jack said.'

'And you took this here gold off of' – Sharkwell turned over the coin in his fingers, considering it – 'a Merchant Taylor. Heh.'

'It's true,' said Rob.

'Hmf. Well then, you're owed your due.' Sharkwell flicked one coin to Jack, and one coin to Rob. He kept the other twenty-odd for himself.

The coin felt warm in Jack's hand, as if it was happy to be there.

'I'm keeping these safe, for your betterment,' said Sharkwell. 'Can't have nippers running around like earls, now, can we?'

Jack and Rob didn't argue the point.

'Get out.'

In the street, Jack clapped Rob on the shoulder. 'Thanks for shielding, mate,' he said. 'Thought he had me scrumbled, there.'

''S all right. You're the one did all the work.'

'Old Sharktooth took more than his shilling, didn't he?'

'Pff. We got enough. What you going to spend yours on? I'm for a yellow hat, Bricklayer-fashion.'

Jack was thinking he might go back to the cunning-man – or a better cunning-man. Get some proper answers about his weird eye, the stain on his hand, the thing in the warehouse last night . . . And suddenly, almost as if thinking about it had summoned it up, the watched feeling twisted hard at his back.

He whipped round. A trickle of mortar rolled down the slope of the tavern roof.

'Pox on it,' he muttered. It was back, then. After last night he'd almost dared to hope he'd got rid of it.

Rob was staring at him. 'What?' said Jack. 'Don't you ever get that?'

'Get what?' said Rob. 'You look like you just seen a ghost.'

'No, not . . . You know that feeling like someone's watching you. Following you, might be. Itchy sort of feeling.'

'Sometimes,' said Rob doubtfully. 'At night, maybe . . . Not like what you just—' He stopped; frowned. 'Might be it's that third eye.'

That stopped Jack in his tracks. 'What? I never . . .' He'd taken the cunning-man's advice: he hadn't told anyone about his weird eye, not even Rob. 'What third eye?'

'It's nothing.' Rob's ears went bright red. He was a very bad liar, Jack thought.

'Ballocks it's nothing, Rob,' he said. 'Tell me. Come on.'

'It's nothing, only . . . I mean, I don't believe in it.' Then it all came out in a rush.

The other thieves were talking behind Jack's back. Different rumours – some just thought he was strange, too quiet, a loner – but others went further.

119

'I don't believe any of it,' Rob assured him. 'They're just jealous 'cos we're a good team.'

'What're they saying?'

'They say . . .' Rob wouldn't meet Jack's eye. 'You're bad luck. Uncanny-like. Marked for trouble.' He looked up. 'But that's only 'cos they don't know you, Jack. I know you're straight, I know you'd never put me in trouble . . .'

'No, course not,' said Jack.

'So it's all right,' said Rob. 'Who cares about soft-head stories, right?'

'Right.'

This time it was Jack who couldn't look Rob in the eye. He did care about the stories: the stories frightened him. They were too close to the truth, or at least the truth as Jack saw it.

Cursed, the cunning-man had said. And *bad luck*, *uncanny* – they weren't so different.

Something was wrong with him. Maybe from even before meeting Webb; maybe the bad luck ran deeper. He'd got his ma killed, he'd got himself fouled, and now something uncanny and invisible was following him.

Either that, or it was Jack who was the soft-head.

Soft-headed or not, over the next month Jack and Rob stole more money than any other pair of nippers had ever taken in a year.

They went after the preachers of the Elect. After their

first success, they began to pick on them, Jack using his hand to hunt them down. It wasn't hard, once he'd learned to recognize the grip that drew him to them – warm; warmer; hot – and anyway, more preachers seemed to be pimpling up every day, bursting out their dire warnings to the street. As if London had caught a bad case of preacher-pox.

At first they were ignored, just like at the football match. Sometimes it seemed to Jack that he was the only one listening. Their sermons fitted with what he'd heard already – all about devils, evil spirits summoned up by sorcerers haunting the city, and Nicholas Webb, the Man of Faith whose mission it was to cast them out. They even gave accounts of the meetings where Webb cast out the devils with his own hands. But still there was no sign of the man himself, and his preachers never gave out where and when the meetings took place.

The preachers all had red stains on their hands – but when he looked close, Jack could tell it was just pretend, not the same as his bone-deep, rusty-blood markings at all. Jack reckoned the Elect probably used beetroot. He still didn't understand his own stain, and the different ways it itched.

There was the warm-warmer grip that led him to the gold. Then there was the scratchy feeling he got from being followed, and then again there were the itchy spots. The first two were all right – useful, even – but the itchy spots really did feel like a curse. There were places where his hand flared up so badly he could barely move it. Sometimes his eye would start to throb as well. Jack didn't know what it all meant, but it must mean something.

Then the Outrages began, and Jack had new things to worry about.

In fact, the first Outrages had happened weeks ago. According to the preachers, the one that happened the week after the football was the seventh. Only this time the story was so horrible that people began to take notice, especially with the Elect screaming it from every street corner. What was more, Jack knew it was true. He'd heard it first from a watchman who'd actually been inside the house. Jack had gone there himself, thinking of taking a look, but before he was within twenty yards of the place, his hand and eye had begun to hurt so fiercely, he was forced to turn back.

An entire family had been found dead at their dining table in Wapping. The youngest child was on the table, carved into four neat portions. The ceiling of the room was covered in footprints. They lived next door to a wealthy old man with an interest in ancient books, who was called a magician by some. He was also found dead, his jaw stretched wide open as if something had crawled down his throat to tear at his innards. The charred remains of a leather-bound book were found clutched in his hand: all the pages were burned, but the title on the cover was still just visible. The book was called *The Diabolon*.

After that, the Elect started to attract an audience. London was terrified and thrilled, and the red-hand preachers gave the fear a name – devils. Devils, summoned up by magicians. London must be washed clean, they said. The devils must be exorcized, the magicians driven out. And Nicholas Webb was the man to do it: the strength of his faith was enough to protect him from even the strongest of Hell's legion.

More Horrors followed as the weeks went by, each one more gruesome than the last, and always there was a dead magician lying in the wings, with a burned *Diabolon*-book somewhere nearby. The preachers' sermons grew frenzied, and their audiences swelled by the day. Now Webb's name was on everyone's lips – and still Jack could not catch sight of him. In the daytime he trailed the preachers through the streets. In the evenings he followed them back to their stronghold at Bygott House – a hulking, hunchbacked building overlooking Paul's Wharf. Watching them come and go, Jack figured out why they carried all that money about. Wherever the preachers went, they handed out gold to beggars, doxies, scrubs and shabaroons – all the scum of the street. It worked out well for them: there wasn't a pauper in London who didn't support Webb now.

There was one other curious thing that Jack gleaned from watching Bygott House. Mostly the preachers came and went quite openly, dressed in their black robes and proudly displaying their red hands for all to see. A couple of times, though, Jack saw a particular preacher arrive muffled up in a dark green cloak and hat, with gloves covering his hands. Never leaving – only arriving. The strangest thing about it was that this preacher, who went by the name of Wrath-of-the-Righteous Jonson, was usually the most public in his devotion to Webb; in fact he was something of a leader amongst the Elect. Jack would have given a lot to know where he went in his disguise, and what he did.

Still there was no sign of Webb. There was plenty of talk, but the more Jack hung about Bygott House, the more he was convinced that Webb never went there. He was said to spend most of his time at Court, behind closed doors and high palace walls. Jack had about as much chance of cutting his throat there as on the moon.

His only chance was the secret night-time meetings; but so far he'd never got close to sniffing one out. He even slipped out a couple of nights to watch Bygott House; he saw nothing. The only way would be to know in advance which night a meeting was to take place; and even then they'd probably travel to it by secret ways, and be hard to follow.

All in all, after three weeks of following the Elect around, Jack felt he'd hit a sort of wall and didn't see any way over it. There was one consolation: he was making more money than he'd ever dreamed of.

He and Rob had honed their system down to a fine art.

They'd wait until a sermon was over, then Rob lumbered forward and asked the preacher a stupid question.

'Whurrs yis divvels?' he'd say in his thickest accent. 'I en't seen nowt.'

The preachers would try to explain. Devils were everywhere, they said: locked in the stones, hiding underground – except for the times they came out, released by the wickedness of the magicians to feed on good Christian folk.

'Yer wha'?' said Rob.

The preacher would sigh and try again.

By then, Jack was already away with the purse and the money. It felt good: each time was another little revenge.

Jack's only disappointment was that Sharkwell kept all but a fraction of the takings. He claimed he was keeping it safe. Jack and Rob didn't believe him. But it didn't really matter. They still made enough money to feast like kings every night. Rob fitted himself out with a complete gentleman's wardrobe in Bricklayers' yellow. They paid for good seats at the theatre, and the bear-baiting and the cockfighting. They gambled. They smoked. They drank wine with their dinner.

None of this went unnoticed by the other thieves. The more money Jack brought in, the more the Family talked. They'd always thought him uncanny, but now, with the new anti-magical mood about town, their talk grew more pointed. The word on the wharf was that Jack's luck wasn't just luck. He fought a nipper who said his ma had been a witch. He won the fight, but that didn't stop the rumours.

It all came to a head on a day when Jack had duty hauling crates in the warehouse. Rob was out with Smiles on another job, so when Black Pod the waterpad came for Jack, he had no one watching his back.

All day he'd been wrestling with the familiar sense that something was following him. He'd jumped at shadows and squeaks a dozen times already.

Jack was on edge, but Black Pod was a master waterpad: there was no hearing the man as he came up behind, soft and subtle and spindly. The first Jack knew was the thin knife-blade in his ear, and the cold fingers gripping his throat.

'Lucky Jack Patch – where d'yer get yer luck from?' Jack felt the knife-point stroking his ear, and the man's grizzly stubble scratching his cheek. 'Tell Black Pod. Tell 'im what yer charm is. Is it 'neath here?'

The knife edged in under Jack's eye-patch and flipped it up.

Jack shut his eye.

'Ope it, boy, or I'll ope it for you.'

Jack believed him. He opened his eye. The knife was an inch away.

'Funny how yer luck runs out with a dirk in your face.' Black Pod drew the knife away a fraction, and leaned in. 'What you scry?'

Black Pod was a dim, wavering outline. Beyond him was a red mist, except for a bright spot high above. It kept changing shape. It was too small for Jack to make out what the shapes were. It was moving about amongst the ropes and rigging up there.

Before Jack could answer, there was a whipcrack snap, and one of the pulley blocks plummeted from the heights, shedding rope and tackle as it dropped. It seemed to Jack that it fell very slowly but with absolute certainty.

Black Pod must have seen something in Jack's eye, or else years on the river had sharpened his instincts. He looked up just in time. The block missed his head, and caught him a glancing blow on the shoulder.

He dropped the knife, and Jack sprang away.

Black Pod grunted a curse through gritted teeth. His arm was hanging at an unnatural angle. 'What are you? A witchling?'

Jack could see the fright and pain in his eyes. His voice was trembling.

'Don't you curse me, boy.' Black Pod backed away, fingering a charm around his neck. It looked like a pike's tooth. 'The river still protects her own. Don't you come for more.'

After that, no one tried to find out his secrets. When people saw him, they spat on the ground, or made the horns to ward off the evil eye. They whispered that Jack had a ghost who followed him around and told him where the gold was.

Jack didn't know what to believe. Something had been following him, it was true; and now, for the first time, he might've actually seen it. He had no idea what it was. He didn't believe in friendly ghosts, or guardian angels. That block could just as easily have been meant for him.

Chapter 12

Jack and Rob's luck changed the day they went to St Paul's Cathedral.

It was Jack's idea: Wrath-of-the-Righteous Jonson, foremost preacher of the Elect, was going to address a large audience from Old Pol's Cross, in the cathedral yard. The streets were humming with talk – word was there was going to be an exorcism, and a burning of evil, ensorcelled books; others claimed that a gang of magicians were planning to disrupt the sermon with their Hell-kissed charms. Jack wanted to be there. He was certain that Webb had to show this time.

Rob wasn't so sure. Not about Webb, because Jack didn't talk to him about that, but about St Paul's. He was right as well, because the churchyard wasn't the safest place to go greasing. You found all sorts there: what looked like a plump sheep might easily turn out to be a wolf. Only an experienced eye would know the difference. It took a whole afternoon of arguing, and the purchase of Rob's favourite tripe and trotter pudding for Jack to talk him into going.

In the end he had to promise that he wasn't going to steal from any preachers, or liverymen, or sharps. They'd only tweak from the dew-eyed chuffers in the crowd. Jack didn't mind that: after a month of stealing from preachers he'd got a pile of gold, but no closer to Webb.

Rob whistled snatches of 'O Parson, Your Parsnip' as they fought their way through the traffic on the bridge. Ahead, over the river, Jack could already see the cathedral: even half ruined as it was, the steeple rose high above all the surrounding buildings.

On the north bank they hurried past the Fishmongers' Hall and on to the turning down Thames Street. The air was rank with the smell of mouldering fish-guts from the wharf beneath the bridge.

They stuck to the street's edges. A train of wagons crushed its way through the mud in the middle of the road. On either side, vendors were setting up their stalls. Fishwives, scrap-lads and a Puritan preacher – not one of the Elect, just an ordinary fanatic – hawked fish, tin and salvation.

'Bessst plaice . . .'

'Scrapped yesterday, no rust . . .'

'. . . from the eternal fires of damnation!'

The river wind wormed its way upstream, slithered over mudbanks and crept under Jack's shirt to jab icy needles into his skin. He barely noticed – all he could think of was Webb, and what he would do if he saw him. He imagined throwing Webb from the top of the steeple of St Paul's, seeing him fall straight down to Hell.

The thought made Jack feel good and warm inside.

A right turn up Dowgate, and the crowd thinned out as the streets grew broader. The houses were big and well-appointed. Some of them had gleaming coats of arms mounted over their doors in painted plaster. Rob was talking about jobs the Family had pulled off in this nobbish part of town – legendary jobs, great merchants stripped of their life's work, fortunes lifted in a single evening.

One thing all the stories had in common, or at least all the recent ones, was Beth. Jack was only lately beginning to realize that her place in the Family wasn't just a matter of being Sharkwell's granddaughter. More than once he'd seen her arrive back at the Crooked Walnut with a basket full of money. However many times it happened, Jack didn't realize it was her till she plonked down her takings and said something like 'Hah! The Destroying Angel strikes again!' Until she did that, she looked like whatever part she'd been playing on the job – onion-seller or noble lady, it didn't seem to matter to her.

She'd started looking at Jack differently since his

success with the preachers. She wasn't like the other nippers, whispering behind his back; nor was she the dagger-eyed shrew she'd been at first. She just watched him calmly, sizing him up. Jack didn't know what to make of her. He couldn't tell what she made of him, either, which was part of the problem.

'Beth Sharkwell,' said Rob, a dreamy look in his eye. 'Wouldn't you like to know how she does it? She reads books, you know. Studies it all up . . . She could walk up to any lord in the land, I swear, and he'd be bowing to her, kissing her fingers like they do – writing her poems before he knew it. Last year she hooked one just that way. The Strand Palace Triple Slam . . .'

'Why don't you write her a poem yourself?' said Jack. This was another recent discovery – the best and most entertaining way to make Rob shut up about the Legend That Was Beth. 'O *Sharkwell, Beth Sharkwell . . . You torment my heart well . . . You are a Harsh Mistress . . . You're making me wristless . . .* Right, that was terrible . . . *With your beauteous bubbies—* No, no, no!' Jack dodged as Rob, flushing darkly, aimed a punch at his arm. 'You want her maiden favours. You—'

They covered the rest of the way to St Paul's at a sprint, Jack cackling wildly. Rob caught him at the end of Watling Street and bowled him over into the dust.

'Yield!'

'Ballocks to that!'

Jack found his face being squashed beneath the considerable weight of Rob's buttocks.

'I think I'm about to guff,' said Rob. 'Tripe and trotters, remember, Jack?'

'All right, I yield,' said Jack. 'Come on, let's find this Wrath-of-the-Cocksmen . . .'

'Jonson.' Rob got up, and they passed through the gates into the cathedral yard.

The yard itself covered twelve and a half acres, but the frowning bulk of the cathedral dominated it easily, blotting out half the sky. The walls of the precinct were lined with shops, and everywhere people were buying, selling, haggling, plotting, shouting at and over each other. It was a madhouse, just like always, only this time Jack was instantly aware that something felt different.

He stopped dead in the middle of the road. The stain on his hand was flaring up hot. He winced. Ever since his accident he'd avoided coming to St Paul's – he'd had a feeling it would be bad like this. The cathedral was an old place, and those were usually the worst. He felt his good mood beginning to slip.

'Itchy-town?' said Rob, looking back at him. This was a word they'd come up with recently. It was partly Jack's feeling of being watched, but there was more to it than that. It was something about the whole town – the devils out murdering, the red-hand maniacs on every corner, the tension rising. As if London was an enormous, flea-bitten beast with a clutch of welts its paws couldn't reach. Slowly going mad over it. Building towards a scream.

'Itchy-city,' said Jack.

It was writ plain on the faces all around him. They were angry, flushed, expecting violence. It was more than the usual cathedral-yard buzz of gossip and slander, carping and cozening. Running underneath was a restless, uneasy mutter, as if the air itself was a-grumble. Jack noticed that some of the ordinary folk had dyed their hands red, like the preachers. He hadn't seen that before.

Rob raised an eyebrow at him. 'You sure you want to do this?'

Jack thought of Webb, shook himself, and grunted yes.

'Right,' said Rob. 'Fine. There's your man.' He pointed to a spot in the corner of the yard where the crowd was even thicker than elsewhere. Jack could see the narrow covered pulpit of Pol's Cross sticking up above the sea of heads. The pulpit looked empty, but even from this distance he could hear one voice raised above the rest.

Rob shoved his way through the crowd, Jack slipping along in his wake. He looked about, trying to see if he could spot Webb, but he kept getting distracted. Something strange was happening as they got closer to the cross. He should be feeling the grip by now, leading him in, warmer and warmer to the preacher's gold, but instead something else was happening. Beneath his patch, white fire was pulsing through his eye in a series of slow explosions. The pain there was back and growing worse, and the stain on his hand was burning and tingling like a nettle-rash.

'Rob, maybe we should—'

'There,' said Rob. 'There he is.'

Wrath-of-the-Righteous Jonson was standing on a wooden stool, facing slightly away from the crowd and towards the pulpit. His lips were pale and flecked with foam; his hair was pale too, somewhere between grey and whitish-blond, hanging down on either side of his gaunt white face. He had hardly any eyebrows and no eyelashes. His whole face writhed as he talked, as if he had a family of eels trapped beneath his skin.

He was talking to the pulpit: 'St Paul's Cross. Do we bow down before you – a Popish saint? Even that, even that would be . . . Oh, but nay . . .' His eyelids twitched rapidly two or three times. He smote the pulpit with the flat of his hand.

Jack felt every blow as a stinging buzz in his hand. Like the feeling it got around an itchy spot, only much stronger.

This was something new.

Thwack, went Jonson's hand against the pulpit.

'"Old Pol" is what we call you, for we know . . . you are no cross but *Old Pol's Stump*, brothers – *Pol* not for Paul but for *Apollyon!*'

He let up smacking the pulpit for a quick writhe. The

wasp-stings in Jack's hand stopped, leaving behind a nasty itch.

'The churchmen preach from atop a stone soaked in damnation! Devils all around us, bound to this city like sinews to the bone! And we wonder when the Reckoning comes due . . . We wonder, though in our hearts we know, in our blood we know, in our sinful, tainted blood . . .'

Rob tweaked Jack's arm. 'Same old rubbish.'

Jack nodded. As far as he could tell there was no sign of Webb. There was no gallery, no cluster of red-hands as he'd hoped. He wondered if he should ask Rob to look for him. He hadn't told Rob the whole reason for coming here, but Rob knew there was something more to it than money. In fact he had probably guessed everything by now – he was quick when it came to people and their inner workings.

Before Jack could make up his mind, Rob jogged his arm.

'Hah! I've spotted a good one over there, when you're ready,' he said, pointing out a shiny-faced, gaping fat man with a wooden jug in one hand and a gold chain round his neck. Jack couldn't mark where his purse was under his furred robe, but it looked like it would be a plump one, and an easy take.

'Right. Good pick.' They'd catch this coney, and then he'd ask for Rob's help. If it was a good cheat they wouldn't need to steal anything else today.

Jack began to edge himself into position, on the other side of the coney from Rob. He couldn't help keeping half an ear on what the preacher was saying. Jonson had a voice like a whip.

'Every night, those who call themselves scholars, cunning-men, magicians – they summon them up with their vile book, their *Diabolon*. Every night! And we wonder that they do us mischief? When did Hell do other? When did the devil not claim his due? And in blood? Who amongst us has not seen the Horror?'

'I have!' shouted a woman on the opposite side of the crowd. 'I seen my sister dead of one o' them bastard wizards! A divvil come and suck out her soul!'

A murmur ran through the crowd. Jack slipped the Nipper's Claw onto his right hand, and glanced down at the red stain running over it like a birthmark. It was tingling and buzzing worse than ever. Again he felt a prickle of danger – but now he could see the bulge where the coney's purse was, and this was going to be easy. Rob would knock him off balance, the loose robes would flap out, the man would be looking the wrong way. Easy. He edged into position. Rob was moving up on the other side, making no effort to conceal himself: he looked like he was trying to shoulder his way to the front of the crowd.

'A devil came and sucked out her soul.' The preacher's voice had dropped to little more than a whisper. Somehow it was still audible over the general clamour. 'And how did she look? How did her face look?'

'Like—' the woman began to answer.

'Oops!' Rob collided hard with the fat man, who staggered into Jack. Jack let himself be borne along, slipping his hand under the robes, cupping the purse and slicing through the strings all in the one moment before—

'*The devil!*' Jonson screamed, and smote the pulpit as hard as he could.

Jack's hand seized up, clutched in a grip of needles and knives. His weird eye stabbed with pain, and for a moment he was blind.

He jerked away.

The purse didn't come. One string still held it.

The fat man felt the tug and grabbed Jack by the hair, ripping off his patch. The poultice flopped off his eye. Jack screwed it shut, and twisted and wriggled out of the fat man's grasp.

'Stop thief!' shouted the man. Another hand grabbed at Jack, missed. He ducked, weaved, went down and scooted along the ground a little way, then popped up again; no one grabbed at him this time. He was almost at the front, and everyone here was more interested in the preacher. He clutched his right hand to him; it was still burning, and his vision was – misty. His right eye had popped open, all by itself. It was so swollen it wouldn't quite close properly. He must look a sight.

138

Almost clear now. Round the back of Old Pol's Cross, or whatever it was supposed to be, then to the gates. The sooner he was outside the precinct, the better.

His eye twitched.

The world lit up blood-red, and –

Time stopped.

Jack was looking at Old Pol's Stump. Not the pulpit: the wooden structure with its little lead roof, the preacher and his audience were just faintly visible through the redness, like a gathering of feeble, washed-out ghosts. He wasn't looking at them – could barely see them.

The stump. It lay beneath the pulpit, beneath the earth, underground, but Jack could see it quite clearly. It was more real than everything else. An ancient stump of blackened stone, with a single vein of white gold running through it like a lightning strike. There was something else too, inside the stone.

But he couldn't see that, not yet.

What he saw first was things that had happened here, at the stump. He knew this the way he sometimes knew things in dreams – without reason or explanation.

He saw a king standing before a crowd of people, holding a sword high over his head. There was no cross in this vision – just the black stump, and the young king standing beside it, sword in hand.

He saw a temple with the stump at its centre. Priestesses rising and falling in worship. Herbs burning in clay pots – he could smell their acrid, pungent scent.

He watched. He knew it was forbidden, but he wasn't afraid. They didn't know he was there.

They prayed to the stump. There was some sort of statue set on top of it, but it was the stump they worshipped. In front of it was a table, laid for a feast. As Jack watched, the food shrivelled and rotted. The plates rusted. The statue crumbled to dust.

There was a flaw, a scribble across his sight, and the vision changed once more: now the stump was below ground again, and a new cross rose above it on a marble column. In the background the cathedral was changed too, to a massive, solemn building of grey stone with a white domed roof and sad-eyed statues gazing down. Smoke rose on all sides, pillars of smoke from some vast, unimaginable fire; in the sky above, strange black crosses flew in rows. A droning, tooth-rattling hum filled the air.

He was standing in flames, but they didn't burn him. He was breathing ashes, but did not choke. Still no fear: he felt that he couldn't be harmed here, that nothing could touch him . . .

Another scribble of confusion, and here was the black stump in a woodland clearing, with a ring of people gathered round. In front of them stood five white-robed men. Bodies dangled from the trees. Dead. One of them was a little girl, about eight years old.

And now he felt fear.

Something was watching him. The thing inside the stone. It was there with the dead girl, but it was here now too. It was here, and it could see him. A figure with the shape of a man, though taller than any man Jack had ever seen. It was a perfect black all over, like a man-shaped hole leading into ultimate night. It had its back to him. It began to turn, and Jack had time to see that its face was not the face of a man; no, not at all—

And then he was thrown off his feet, and the breath knocked out of him.

'Got you, you little trug!'

Jack sprawled. His head was all fuddled. It felt like he'd been looking at the stump for hours, and now . . .

Something heavy was on top of him – something puffing and wheezing. The fat man. Only seconds had passed.

Jack shut his right eye. Too late. He could see clearly as the man slammed his great fat fist down into his face.

A white light exploded in his skull, but he wasn't knocked out. The fat man had him pinned. In the background he saw a ring of shocked faces. Was that the preacher's voice, shouting? He was hauled to his feet, strong hands holding him by both arms.

The shouting came again. It wasn't the preacher; it was coming from behind him, from the crowd of onlookers.

Rob Butterbeak broke through the crowd like a boat shooting the London Bridge rapids. He came at the fat man low and hard, shoulder first. The man went down like

141

a skittle. Rob turned and swung at the man on Jack's other side. The man lost his hold on Jack. Jack threw himself clear as they both went down, tangled together.

'Get out, Nipper!' shouted Rob. He was on top of the man now, scrambling to his feet. 'That way!'

There was no time to think. Angry faces and grasping hands were coming at Jack from all sides. He turned and ran, squirming and dodging, somehow avoiding the hands.

Rob was a fast runner. Rob would get clear. It was better to split the pursuit, find their separate ways out of here. Jack didn't look back till he was safe in the press of people around the Watling Street gate.

No pursuit. He'd got away.

The area around the cross was a heaving scrimmage. He saw four sergeants dive into it, clearing a path with their cudgels. The cudgels rose and fell. He couldn't see . . .

Then he could. The sergeants were emerging from the scrum victorious. Two of them were dragging a battered, bloody figure. Rob's heels trailed along the ground behind him. The fat man was bringing up the rear in triumph.

Rob was taken.

Chapter 13

Time stood still. Or at least it seemed that way to Jack. He'd thought, since his ma's death, that he'd learned all about grief. Now he found he knew nothing. If you mixed in a whole barrelful of shame, it was much, much worse.

There was a legend at Newgate, where Rob was now. Everyone knew it – the story of the huge, spectral hound that haunted the prison. It came to you as soon as you went inside, and made sure you didn't escape. It was called the Black Dog, and Jack felt as if it was with him too – a cold black guardian keeping watch over him the whole time, keeping him locked up, alone with his guilt.

Mr Smiles was so worried that he took Jack off his nipping duties, and then Jack really *was* alone, holed up in his nest amongst the empty crates. Sometimes Smiles came to visit. 'Five partners o' mine have danced the hempen jig,' he said. 'You'll learn to carry it.'

Smiles couldn't help, though, because deep down it wasn't guilt that sent Jack's head spinning in circles. It was fear. If he tried to explain it, he wouldn't be allowed to stay in the warehouse. He knew that Sharkwell would pack him off to Bedlam with the other moon-lickers and be done with him.

Jack was scared. Either he'd lost his mind, or what he'd seen at the stump was real. If that was true, then there were even bigger, scarier monsters out there than Webb. And Jack had an idea what they were.

Devils. Just like the preachers were always saying.

The devil at Pol's Stump had seen him. It knew who he was now.

The only time he ventured out was to visit the cunning-man to get a new poultice made up. He found the house in Long Southwark boarded up. Someone had scrawled *Neckromansser* across the door in red chalk. There was no answer when Jack knocked.

Time passed. Except sometimes it didn't. Sometimes it stood still.

They all turned out for the big day: foisters, whiddlers, the bawkers and the beggars, nippers, rufflers and the water-sneaks. There must have been at least a hundred villains of every shape, size and criminal persuasion assembled on

Sharkwell's wharf that morning. Jack had no idea that the Family was quite so big.

There were two barges waiting to carry them across the river. In the centre of the larger one stood a covered wagon. A colourful picture of a steaming pie was painted onto the side of it.

Sharkwell clambered, a little stiffly, into the prow of the boat. 'Lads and ladies . . . a word now.' He held his hands up for silence.

It was an unnecessary gesture: it was early still, and while the mood on the wharf was cheerful, no one was talking.

'Rob Butterbeak was one of us. He was a prime nudger. And he didn't squeal,' said Sharkwell. 'Now he's walking west, Black Dog by his side. So before he dances, we'll do him proud.'

There were mutters of agreement from the crowd.

'What is my Twelfth?'

The Family seemed to be expecting this: their response came quick and regular, like prayers in a church.

'We clean out the crowd when one of us swings,' they all said together.

'It could be you, it could be me,' said Sharkwell. 'But it ain't. So sock it to 'em.'

Sharkwell's Family boarded the barges in good order. Today was a Hanging Day, and they were going to Tyburn.

Jack had never been on a barge before, but he barely

145

noticed that they'd slipped the mooring and started for the opposite bank. He kept his head down, trying not to think about anything. He'd made himself a new patch out of rags. So far it seemed to be working, though his eye throbbed worse than it had in weeks. He'd promised himself he'd never take it off. All he wanted was not to see anything like what he'd seen at the stump ever again.

They disembarked at the Savoy Steps, and he plodded along numbly, following the feet of the nipper in front. The Family headed north and west towards the crossroads and the hanging grounds. They marched in a pack, like a small army.

Jack only lifted his head when they paused in the open country past Holborn. Flagons of beer were passed around. It was one of those days in early spring which remind a body that summer might actually exist. The thieves sent up a cheery babble as they lounged on the close-cropped pasture and warmed their backs in the sun.

Sharkwell had set up his command post in the hot-pie wagon. He divided his men into smaller groups and gave them their instructions. Jack and the other nippers came last and were given over to Beth. They were to work around the Tree.

'Right where it's thickest!' said Sharkwell. 'That's where I want to see you scuttlin'.'

Beth led them across the fields. The crowd was already too dense along the road, waiting for the carts from

Newgate gaol. From the faint cheers sounding from the east they knew that the condemned procession had already set out.

Jack wasn't ready for the Tyburn Tree. They came around a hedgerow, and there it was, dark and unholy against the blue sky. It always looked bigger than you expected. The nooses were already hanging down, empty.

There were five ropes. One of them should've been his.

They were walking downhill past families sitting out on blankets, vendors strolling with their trays and children playing catch-the-thief. Everyone seemed cheerful to be out of the city on a fine sunny day. The continual cries of ale-sellers and eelmen clashed with the songs of the death hunters, Tyburn's special breed of balladeer. All their songs were about some magician who was due to hang today.

> 'The devil was his one true Lord
> And so the noose is his reward.
> Such mayhem writ on every page
> The Bible of the evil mage
> The Diaboliad!'

There was no ballad for Rob Butterbeak.

Most of the crowd was already drunk. As they got into the thick of the mob, the air was heavy with the stink of cheap beer and sweat. Worse, there was a frenzied excitement building by the moment, and an unceasing, eager murmuring all around. The cheering from the east was getting louder and louder.

'We split here,' said Beth. 'Work your way in. Be wise to your coney. And remember: shave it to the second as Rob drops – 'cos not even a soddin' goldsmith is paying mind to his purses then. Take the jinglerigs to the hot-pie wagon. He's set up over there.' She pointed back the way they'd come: Jack saw Sharkwell leaning out of the wagon's open front, doing a brisk and surprisingly honest trade in meat pies.

'Right,' said Beth. 'Sock it to 'em. Do Rob proud.'

The other nippers slipped away into the crowd. Jack was glad to be alone. He didn't want to get any closer to the Tree, though.

After a few steps the feeling that he was being watched came on strong and itchy.

He glanced over his shoulder. Standing behind him was a girl with a gormless, slackwit face, picking her nose. Not watching him at all.

Then the face shifted, and Jack saw it was Beth. It was uncanny, the way she could do that.

'What?' he said.

'Can't you guess, Jack Patch?' said Beth. 'I've been watching you – you've got sniffles on again. Couldn't be a sorrier sight if you tried. What's Law Seventeen?'

'No moaning.'

'Ah, so you do know it,' Beth said. 'What about Law Six?'

Law Six was one of the important ones, and until Rob was taken, Jack would have said he agreed with it. He didn't know what to think any more. Rob had saved his life, and because of that, Rob would hang.

And he was meant to be happy about it.

'Save your own skin,' said Jack.

'Right, and Rob Butterbeak forgot the law. He made a mistake.'

Jack saw Rob being dragged away by the sergeants. For the last three days he'd seen that struggle play out in his mind's eye over and over again. Each time he didn't do anything to help. He just stood there and watched.

Beth didn't seem satisfied. 'Would you save me?' she said.

'No.'

'Good. So you're learning. You have to mind yourself.' Beth snorted. 'If you don't, sure as hellfire I won't come and save you.'

'You sound just like your grandpa,' said Jack.

'Who better?'

A rattle of drums and a shrill howl thrummed from the east.

'Here they come!' someone cried, and the crowd surged ahead, jostling Jack and Beth forward. Women shrieked and laughed. Men stamped and cheered.

'Time to work,' said Beth. 'Mind your face.'

She stuck her finger back up her nose, and let her chin hang loose. She was still watching Jack, seeing if he understood.

Jack turned away, looking from face to face in the crowd.

He hated them all. He hated the comfortable guildsman, tricked up in his finest clothes. He hated the man's plump pigeon wife, clinging to his arm, all giddy. He hated the apprentice boys, daring each other closer to the gallows.

'Face. Mind it.' Beth gave him a loose-lipped grin and wandered off. Jack hated her too, the way she managed to look like all the rest – eager and excited. Hungry for the show.

The drums were a rolling, rattling roar, drowning out everything else.

'Hats down! Hats down!' came an excited shout. Some people started taking their hats off, but others refused loudly.

'Doff my cap for the devil's minion, is it?' shouted a shrill Welsh voice.

'I'll doff you, Taffy!'

'Bloody wizard-lover!'

A tussle started up. Jack could have had at least one purse out of it, but he didn't move.

He could see the death-wagons now.

There were three wagons, carrying five figures. The

first man was travelling in a cart all by himself. He cowered and dodged as the mob pelted him with whatever came to hand. He must be the magician, Jack guessed; but the crowd's mood had changed for the worse, and all five were getting their share. Jeers, rotten vegetables splattering in their faces.

Rob was the last. He passed close. A clod of earth hit him hard in the temple, making him reel. Jack looked away: he didn't want Rob to recognize him.

The drums and the shouts and the thrill coursed through the crowd, knitting it together. The feverish din grew to one animal roar as the wagons drew up beneath the Tyburn Tree.

Jack saw Big Don Butterbeak bellowing near the front. He was fighting, trying to get through to his son. The crowd stood against him.

The thought occurred dimly to Jack that at least his ma would never see him like this.

There was a hangman for each of the prisoners. Now they came forward. The magician was hauled up first of all. The crowd booed and jeered him so much that they didn't have any breath for the others.

Rob Butterbeak looked very small beneath the giant pillars of the Tree. The rope was already hanging above him. His hands were tied together. Rob tested the bonds, flapping his hands helplessly. Jack could see that he was shaking.

The hangman slipped a black cloth over Rob's head, and settled the noose around his neck. He jerked the knot tight with a professional tug.

At the gallows the magician was trying to make a final speech, but no one could hear him because the frenzy had gripped hard now. All Jack felt was a rising tide of shame and horror, running through every bone in his body. The drums began their final surge. The screeching of the mob came together into one awful jangling shriek.

Rob dropped.

Jack forced himself to watch. Five bodies fell, and jarred – as if every part of them broke at the same time. Rob's legs kicked once, twitched and were still.

A dreadful sigh rolled through the crowd, everyone breathing out all at once. For a moment there was quiet, and then the hubbub started up again.

'A good one, that,' said the guildsman. He sounded pleased with himself, as if he'd succeeded in some difficult task.

'Wasn't it awful,' agreed his wife. Her eyes were still shining with excitement.

'Diddle diddle dumplings ho!' The cries of the food men and the beer-sellers rang out loud again.

Jack stared at Rob's body. It was swaying slightly, a dead weight on the end of its rope.

It should have been him.

'Some say that thieves are cowards, and I would not disagree . . .'

Jack recognized the voice immediately. He saw its owner a second later – a swirl of white hair, and a red right hand raised to the sky.

'But there are worse sorts of vermin. You see one hanging before you.' Wrath-of-the-Righteous Jonson must have been preaching for a long time. His voice was scratchy and hoarse.

Jack's pent-up anger burned through him. He felt it as a tightness, as if he couldn't breathe. He started pushing, shoving, ripping his way through the crowd.

He slipped his Nipper's Claw onto his finger.

'That sorcerer breathes his last! Never again will he scan the foul pages of his accursed book. Never again will he summon the foul names listed therein: Lucifuge, Sargatanas, Behemoth . . .'

Jack burst through the small circle that surrounded the preacher.

'What?' For the briefest instant their eyes met. Wrath-of-the-Righteous looked astonished.

'Bastard,' said Jack. In one smooth, perfect movement he slashed the preacher's purse-strings, and caught the jinglerig. He rolled under someone's arm and through their legs, and was away into the safety of the crowd.

A few breathless moments later he was standing in the lee of an oyster tub, tugging at the strings. The purse was loaded with more gold than any he'd taken yet. And right at the bottom, something else: an Elect pamphlet, torn in half and folded in four, with several lines of writing scrawled on the back.

He'd keep that. Jack slipped it into his sleeve, and looked up.

Beth was standing not ten yards away, watching him. Their eyes met. She turned on her heel, and vanished into the crowd.

Chapter 14

The ceiling of the kennels had been painted once. Now the saints' faces were cracked and peeling, and the deep blue of the sky behind them had faded to a grim, damp-spattered grey. But not everything about the chapel was ruined: the monks had shaped the space to echo and redouble their chants and psalms, and that still worked. Jack could hear the roaring din inside from halfway across the yard.

Mostly he could hear Billy Bearsbane. The hound was in a frenzy as he waited on his daily pound of horseflesh. But between the barks and the sound of chewing, Jack could make out voices. Arguing voices.

'I don't care if he's robbed the Mint—'

'. . . all this gingerbread? He's lucky.'

'It's against Law Twen—' That was Beth, for sure.

The barking drowned out whatever else she said.

Jack loitered outside, cursing himself. He'd been summoned here for three o'clock, and he wasn't going in till he'd heard the bells strike. The longer he could put off having to explain himself, the better. That shave with Jonson had been sheer duncery – and Beth had seen it all.

Thinking on it made his guts twist up, like standing over a long, sheer drop. With a rope around his neck. He'd stolen from preachers before, of course – but the only person who knew that was Rob, and he trusted Rob.

Had trusted. Jack felt a fresh stab of pain at the thought, and the sudden image of Rob dangling, dead. He forced it away. He could feel the scrap of pamphlet scratching in his sleeve.

He tried to stay hopeful.

If Sharkwell didn't feed him to Billy, he'd take the pamphlet to a scrivener, get the writing read, see if it was anything important. The way Jack's luck was running at the moment, it would probably turn out to be a shopping list, or Bible verses, or something equally useless.

That would have to wait, anyway: the bells of St Olave were striking three.

Jack went in, walking slowly between the stalls where the lesser dogs resided. Billy Bearsbane lived at the top, where the altar had once stood. Beth and Sharkwell were standing inside his pen. They were the only two people the mastiff would let near him. Smiles was keeping his distance, and holding the lantern.

Jack's approach set Billy growling. It sounded much worse than the barks.

'Hush, there,' said Beth. 'It's just a nipper.' She scratched the dog behind the ears.

'Oh, but that's where you're wrong, my dovey.' Sharkwell rubbed his hands together. 'What we have here is no longer a mere nipper.'

Beth sniffed. Jack wondered what he meant.

'The arch-rogue hisself,' said Mr Smiles.

'Too right,' said Sharkwell. 'This one's *impressed* me. Know that you did that mooncalf Butterbeak proud today. He swings, you nip a whole buzzard. Takes a right cold one to do that.'

Jack wanted to say that there'd been nothing cold about it, but he held his tongue.

'Gives me a chill just thinkin' on it,' continued Sharkwell. 'So. I've decided to give you a step up.'

A step up? And no mention of the Jonson shave? Surely he wasn't going to get away with it?

'How'd you like to be a darksman, Lucky Jack?'

Jack was so surprised he forgot to speak.

'Well?'

'I – I'd like it fine, Mr Sharkwell.' Jack wasn't going to be fed to Billy after all. He couldn't quite believe it.

'Gramper, he's not right for—' said Beth.

'Stash it! You mind the laws and mind who's your captain. Else I show you what's right, Beth Sharkwell.'

Beth stared hard at Sharkwell for a moment, then nodded.

Sharkwell gave her a gummy grin before turning back to Jack. 'Right. Now tell me, Lucky Jack: you ever heard tell of a mincing wizard, goes by the name of Udolpho?'

'No, Mr Sharkwell.'

'Gentry cove, friend to all the best kind of folk. Reads them their stars and the like. Must be a rich sort of cozening lay for Udo, for he's rich as the Pope, they say. Anyway, where we come in is this: what with all this magical blather going round, all his servants have left. Can't find any new ones. So me and Smiles thought we'd help him out.'

They wanted to do a wizard. Jack didn't think that was a very good idea at all. Sharkwell tossed a chunk of horse to Billy, who snapped it out of the air.

'Now I don't believe in the stories going about. You know the ones – devils and demons, wizards killing their neighbours and themselves . . . No. Such stories is spread by villains for their own purposes, as a villain like me knows very well.'

'Trash for gulls to swallow,' said Beth, and sniffed again.

'That's right, girl. Tell me, Lucky Jack. Do you believe in magic?'

Sharkwell was smiling. That was when he was most dangerous.

'No, Mr Sharkwell.'

'All right,' Sharkwell's gimlet eyes didn't swerve. ''Cos I remember you saying some guff about your ma and sorcery. I remember telling you to pay no more mind to the matter. To stay away from a certain kind of fish.'

He knows, thought Jack. *He knows*. He kept his face still.

'I don't believe in that guff, Mr Sharkwell. I swear it.'

'So you'll raise no objections to this here job, then,' said Sharkwell. 'You'll jump at the chance, won't you?'

'Yes, Mr Sharkwell.'

Jack's heart sank. He wasn't just worried about the wizard. Darksmen worked houses, not the street, which would make it difficult to keep after Webb. Still, when Sharkwell thought he was doing you a favour it was best to look grateful.

Beth was staring at him with narrowed eyes. She shook her head. 'I tell you: he's not right.'

'Stash it, girl . . .' Sharkwell spoke slow and quiet. 'My goat but you have a tongue on you.' He took Beth by the arm and pulled her out of Billy's pen. Not roughly, just firm.

'You see, here in my Family we don't believe in magic, but we *do* believe in luck.'

Now he grabbed Jack with his other hand, and pulled him close.

'And that's why I'm putting my luckiest nipper . . . and my best girl . . . together.' Sharkwell hugged them both

tight enough that Jack could smell the pies on his breath.
'You and Beth are going to do this one. Smiles will fill you
in on the particulars.'

A wizard. Jack felt his heart begin to thump. He'd been
lying like a Spaniard. He believed the stories. Of course he
believed in magic: he'd seen it with his own eyes. It was
too late to argue now, though. Sharkwell had trapped him,
good and tight.

'Off you trot.' Sharkwell pushed them away.

Jack saw Beth think about arguing for a heartbeat. He
prayed silently that she'd protest again, and make
Sharkwell give the plan up; but then she ducked her head
and walked away. After a few steps she turned sharply, and
looked him up and down, from his shoes to his scalp
and back again. Jack had the impression that she didn't see
one thing she liked.

'Better start now, Smiles,' she said. 'We'll need every
bit of your magic to make this nipper disappear.'

Mr Smiles only had one day to prepare them. It was a rush
job, and he did his best, but neither he nor Beth was
satisfied.

Beth was still drilling Jack on their story as they walked
to the magician's house.

'Dress?'

The dress had been selected with great care by Mr
Smiles. It was bottle-green velvet, very threadbare, with

most of the lace missing from the collar and sleeves. Smiles had added in a few tears with a blunt knife for good measure.

'Belonged to our mother,' said Jack. 'Her favourite. You salvaged it . . .'

'When did she wear it?'

'Um . . . when she was playing with us . . . in the garden?'

'When she was playing wickets. Her wickets dress. Right . . . This?' Beth pointed to a plain silver pendant around her neck.

'Locket. Father gave it to Mother when they were betrothed. Got a picture of him in it.'

'Good.'

Jack had never seen Beth like this. The scornful act she usually played was gone. Not that she was treating him as an equal, exactly; she was just too obsessed with getting everything right to treat him in any particular way at all.

'Who are you?'

'I'm your long-lost brother. You rescued me.'

'That's right. We're insep'rable. I'm the only family you've got . . . So act it. Like this.'

Beth stopped, took Jack's hand and fixed him with a look of tender affection.

Jack blushed. It was one thing to do it in front of Mr Smiles, quite another in the middle of the street.

'No! Remember, I rescued you. Try to look grateful.'

Jack was trying his best, but it felt stupid. He looked stupid too – he could see it in Beth's eye.

'Just remember.' She twitched the lace of her collar, disarranging it just so. 'You play it shy. I'm yer long-lost sister you hardly know, and now you're in this fancy house, fine gentleman . . . you're shy. You look stupid and stare at the floor. Think you can manage that?'

'I can stare at the floor,' said Jack.

'Huh. Funny.' Jack thought he saw the corner of her mouth twitch. 'Well, we're here – corner of Addle Hill.'

Jack took a deep breath.

The magician's house teetered up above them, leaning out over the street. It looked like any other house, Jack told himself. But so had the house in Wapping where the dead family were found. All manner of strange business might be lurking inside.

At least the stain on his hand wasn't playing up, nor his eye. That was one thing to be glad of.

Beth took Jack's hand, and altered her face. Afterwards she was no longer Beth, preparing for the job; she was someone else. An image of Rob flashed into Jack's mind – Rob on the way to St Paul's, chatting about the Family's past triumphs.

Beth Sharkwell – wouldn't you like to know how she does it?

They walked hand in hand to the door of the house. Beth

knocked, and stood back. Jack found himself trembling slightly. He felt strangled by the unfamiliar tightness of the lace ruff around his neck.

Beth gave his hand a quick squeeze. 'I'll do the talking,' she whispered. 'You're the quiet one. Shy. You'll be fine.'

The door opened. A moment later, Jack fixed his eyes on the step at his feet – it was the only way to stop himself bolting like a frighted horse.

There was no one there. The entrance hall was empty. A bulging round mirror opposite the door reflected him and Beth, wildly distorted – Beth in the centre of the mirror looking like a warped giant, Jack in the corner like a bent dwarf. To one side of the mirror, a staircase led up into shadows.

'Good afternoon,' said a voice.

Beth spoke out in a completely new voice. 'Dr Udolpho? Your pardon, sir, but . . . my name is Elizabeth Monfort. This is my brother, Jack. We've come about the positions. The servants' positions – we saw them at St Paul's . . . at the Si Quis door . . .' She sounded a little hesitant, a little scared even; but her grip on Jack's hand was firm and her palm was cool and dry.

'Aha! You have come in answer to my petition? Then come in – come in, don't hesitate.'

'Pardon, sir – your door, opening like that. It's given me a little fright.' Beth edged across the threshold, pulling Jack close against her side.

Beth was putting it on, but Jack didn't need to. He was afraid. He found himself huddling closer against Beth, and it was no act. He half expected the door to slam shut behind them, and the Horrors to begin there and then.

The door did not slam. Instead, a slight, well-dressed man appeared at the head of the stairs.

He didn't look like a wizard. He looked like a courtier, or like an actor playing the part of a courtier – neat little beard, thin moustache, doublet slashed with flame-coloured silk. He pranced like a courtier too, as if coming downstairs was some sort of complicated dance.

Jack found himself feeling both relieved and oddly disappointed. The wizard, if wizard he was, stopped at the bottom of the staircase and examined them.

'You certainly appear satisfactory,' he decided. 'Boy and girl, as requested, right sort of age . . .' He smiled encouragingly at Beth. 'Tell me about yourself.'

Beth and Mr Smiles had spent half yesterday working out the story, arguing over every little detail. Now Beth brought it out polished and perfect, with just the right mix of sorrow, bravery and hesitation – the wreck of her family's fortune, the death of her parents, her brother's kidnapping by Barbary pirates and the heroic sacrifices she'd made to get him back. The story even explained his maimed hand and eye – cruel heathen tortures, punishments for his attempts to escape. Jack had thought the story was over the top, but that had been Beth Sharkwell

164

telling it. Hearing it from Elizabeth Monfort, he found himself hanging on every word.

She was good. Too good for Udolpho. Jack could see the way he looked at her, going along with it, feeling the story. Wizard or no, he was lolloping in like a good little coney.

'A tragical tale,' said Udolpho. 'You are a remarkable young lady.' His eyes rested on her face, all soft and misty. Jack noticed Beth's eyes widen for a moment, then she looked modestly down at her feet.

'Ahem. Let me show you the nature of the job, then you will decide if you want the work . . .'

'Thank you, sir,' murmured Beth, all demure.

'I do hope it suits.'

When the magician turned his back to lead them from the room, Beth's mask slipped. She elbowed Jack in the ribs, grinning in triumph. Jack had never seen her look so happy. Fair enough, he thought; she deserved it. *You will decide!* Five minutes in the house, and the man was eating out of her hand.

Still, Jack told himself to stay chary. They were into the house, very well: this was not the end of the danger, but the beginning. A magician's house . . .

Udolpho ushered them into a room beyond the hall, saying something about how rare it was to find maids of gentle birth.

Jack had to smother a gasp as they entered the next

165

room. It was astonishing – a dining room with silver on the table, paintings on the walls, and a huge open fireplace with still more silver mounted above it. Everything was flooded with golden evening light. Jack had never realized you could have this much light in a house without being cold. It was obvious when you thought about it – that was what glass windows were for – but in that first moment it looked like glorious, mighty magic. He'd seen glass windows before, of course, but only from the outside.

'You have a beautiful house, sir,' said Beth. 'It reminds me of happier days.' Her eyes were shining. Jack saw the effect they had on the magician as he led them on into the stone-flagged kitchen. He kept stealing little glances at her face when she wasn't looking. He seemed almost embarrassed at the idea of having such a girl as his servant.

'Your first duty would be to cook, my dear,' he said, waving an arm to indicate the rows of copper pans hanging above an even bigger fireplace.

There was a stale half-loaf of bread on the table, surrounded by scraps of dried-up salted meat, and a pan covered in rancid grease. A heavy fall of soot from the chimney had covered the floor in front of the fireplace. Jack wondered just how long the magician had been without servants – and then found himself wondering what exactly had driven the previous ones away.

'I trust you can manage . . .' said Udolpho.

'Oh yes,' said Beth. 'I have been obliged to manage, sir.'

She raised her chin slightly. She looked fragile but determined, pretty in a way that Jack had never noticed. She was putting it on, of course. She even managed to make a little flush of colour appear high up on each cheekbone.

'Well,' said Udolpho, 'I must say you seem a very brave, very capable . . . young . . . lady.'

'You are too kind, sir. I am sure my brother and I will be very happy here. For him to be residing in a respectable house – and such a house as this . . .' The shine in her eyes went up a couple of notches; a single tear gleamed on her lashes, catching the light to full advantage.

'I will show you the sleeping quarters,' said Udolpho, leading them up the back stairs, and out into a narrow corridor with further doors leading off it. The plaster on the wall was dyed a deep, rich blue, with golden stars and moons sprinkled across it.

'Were you to take the position, the first floor would be your concern, Jack,' said Udolpho. 'It is the domain of my philosophical investigations: you will assist me as I delve into the realms of the spirit, ha ha.'

Jack maintained his silence, though his ears pricked up at the mention of spirits. Udolpho paused and looked him up and down. It was the first time he'd managed to tear his eyes from Beth.

'You are quiet, Jack. And small – even better!' Udolpho

gave Jack's head a pat. 'Both are necessary to be my assistant, as you'll see. Now – upwards!'

He led them up a further flight of stairs, and through a smaller, shabbier door.

'You must, please, forgive the . . . the bleakness of the chamber, Elizabeth; my previous servants were not of your . . . quality.'

The attic was a little less other-worldly – bare boards on the floor, yellowing plaster on the walls, a bed and a chair in one corner.

'You will not mind sharing with your brother, I hope,' said Udolpho, indicating the bed.

'Of course not.'

Jack thought he saw Beth's expression falter for the slightest instant, but then he was looking for it. Udolpho, he was sure, hadn't noticed.

'It is so much more than I could have hoped . . . even yesterday . . .'

'You will take the position?'

'Yes, sir! Oh thank you! Thank you, sir!'

'Now, now. It is settled. Your wages will be . . .' Jack saw a quick calculation going on behind Udolpho's eyes. 'Say a shilling a day?' He swept his arm about the room. 'Your new home. I trust it is to your liking?'

'Very comfortable, sir.'

'And you can begin your duties tomorrow?'

'First thing.'

Udolpho didn't seem to know how to leave the room. Jack saw him start to bow, then quickly change it to a simpering sort of nod. Beth curtsied low.

Once the door was shut she relaxed and turned to Jack, snorting with laughter. *'I trust it is to your liking?'* she mimicked. 'But mark that he didn't give us any food. Pompous little coxcomb. Nice house, though . . .'

'I was trying not to . . . you know, stare about,' said Jack.

'Aye, Udo and me both noticed that,' said Beth. 'Don't worry – it was perfect. You're meant to have spent the last six years in a heathen sod-house. Of course you'd stare. You were fine.' She sat down on the bed. 'Oh, you'd better go now before I forget.'

'Go where?'

'See about getting an extra blanket.'

'But there's already two . . . on the bed . . .' The expression on Beth's face made Jack trail off.

She snorted again. 'We ain't sharing this bed, Lucky Jack. You're sleeping on the floor.'

Chapter 15

Beth snored. It was a gentle, girlish snore, but still definitely a snore. There was something funny about the idea of Beth Sharkwell snoring, Jack thought as he lay awake on the floor.

The boards were hard and cold, and his hand had started to itch again after being quiet all day. He couldn't sleep. He missed his nice straw nest at home – at Sharkwell's. Strange that he thought it home now.

Jack wondered what Rob would have said if he heard he was sharing a room with Beth Sharkwell. Probably nothing: Jack would have said something, something outrageous, and Rob would have punched him. That's how it would have gone.

He felt his face go hot when he remembered what he'd said about the two blankets. He hadn't meant anything by it; she'd taken it the wrong way, calling him 'Lucky Jack' like that. Or maybe just pretended to, in order to put him down. That was the sort of thing she'd do, for sure. She'd been acting kindly enough, but that was because she was pleased with herself, the job she'd done. First thing tomorrow, she'd be back to squashing him every chance she got.

Beth didn't trust him, either. With her watching, there'd be no freelancing after Webb, no more following red-hands in the street, trying to sniff out their meetings.

His thoughts tumbled away, chasing each other down guilt-worn grooves: Webb's meetings. Webb, who'd killed his ma. Webb, whose followers were always going on about devils – devils all around us, hidden in the stones.

The powder in his eye. The thing in Old Pol's Stump. Devils . . .

Jack shivered. He turned over on the floor, snuggling tight in his blanket.

Maybe Udolpho was a real magician; maybe he'd teach Jack. But then again, maybe they'd all end up dead, bloody footprints on the ceiling and mouths stretched wide in horror. Jack didn't want to think about that.

As he began to drift off, Jack heard a scuffling sound in the wall. The itch in his hand stabbed harder for a moment, then both it and the scuffling went away.

The last thing he thought before he fell asleep was that rats were like devils, they got everywhere.

All around us . . .

* * *

Beth was already up and gone when Jack awoke the next morning. He wondered how long he'd slept in. It was hard to tell – the house was so quiet; maybe all gentry houses were quiet, the noises of the world outside shut out along with the cold.

Anyway, it wasn't a noise that had woken him; it was a smell. A good smell.

Jack opened the door to the stairway, and a waft of savoury air made his mouth water. Now he could hear noises coming from below – sizzling, and busy sounds of work being done in the kitchen. He hurried downstairs.

Beth was standing with her back to him, stirring a pan over the fire. The soot on the floor was gone, as well as the mess on the table. The smell was overpowering: bacon frying, and something else, something almost better than bacon . . .

'Morning, Nipper,' said Beth without turning round. 'Had your maiden slumbers?'

Jack yawned, putting a bit of show into it. 'I thought your grandpa said I was a darksman now.'

'Huh. First, he might be Grampers to me but he's Mr Sharkwell to you. Second, you're no more a darksman than I'm an apple-squire.' Beth opened the oven door, and the other smell identified itself as freshly baked bread.

'If, Nipper, you manage not to queer my lay here, then, Nipper, you'll be some way along to being a darksman. For now' – she wrapped her hands in her apron, pulled out a tray with a steaming golden loaf and turned to lay it down on the table – 'you're Jack the Nipper. Now slice this up. Our lord and master awaits his breakfast.'

Beth took the slices of bread and fried them in the pan with the bacon. Jack wondered if it was all for Udolpho. All that meat – and for breakfast, not even lunch or dinner . . .

'Stop staring,' said Beth. 'It ain't seemly.' She tossed over a piece of fried bread. 'You'd better have that. Don't want you drooling all over Udo's peckage, do we? You're serving him. Up in the magical rooms.'

'Right,' Jack mumbled, gulping down his mouthful. Suddenly he didn't feel so hungry any more.

'Wipe your mouth. Good. Now before you go up, I've got a job for you.' A cunning gleam appeared in Beth's eyes. 'Smiles said you shaped nice at Black Arts.'

Jack nodded.

'Take a gander at this.' She led Jack to the door at the back of the room.

'Two ways into this house,' she said. 'Front door, on a latch-bolt; this one leads out to a side alley. This one's locked, and doubtless Udo'll give us the keys when he remembers; but we're going to do better.'

'What – you want me to crack it?'

'That'll be the start. By the end of this day I'll have every key in this house in my pocket.'

'How's that?'

'Ope the door, and you'll see . . . later.'

Jack reached into his sleeve and pulled out the roll of tools. It crackled oddly as he opened it up. Of course – the pamphlet from Jonson's purse, the one with the hand-written note on it. Maybe he could get Beth to read it for him later.

For now, he took a quick peek at the lock and selected a Number Four Stroker. Feeling inside, he didn't think this would be a hard one. No: it was simple. The Mizzen Gilk would do it.

A few twists and pokes and he had it open. 'Not bad,' said Beth, pulling it shut again. 'Could be faster, mind – simple job like that.' She gave Jack a grudging nod.

Upstairs, a bell started clanging. Beth grabbed a plate, arranged the bacon and bread and thrust it all at Jack. 'Take this up. And mind – we're playing for his trust, super-subtle. You're the shy one, so keep it quiet and mod-est, understand?'

'Enter,' said a low, echoing voice.

Quiet and modest. Jack pushed the door open.

The first thing he saw was a monstrous creature hanging from the ceiling right in front of him: it looked like a dragon without the wings, covered in greenish-brown scales, its enormous jaws grinning, showing rows of curved teeth.

It didn't make a move. Jack stared into its red eyes.

There was a desk opposite the door. Light streamed in through two large windows in the wall to the right. No sign of Udolpho.

The hair on Jack's neck began to prickle.

'Sir?'

With a silent rush, the curtains drew themselves shut.

The room was plunged into complete darkness. The door slammed behind Jack, leaving him blind. All at once the fear was upon him, thick and choking.

'Welcome, Jack!' said the low voice.

'Jack! Jack! Jack!' A high squeaky voice echoed the first, from the other side of the room.

Jack took a step back. His hand scrabbled for the door handle. He couldn't find it.

With a hissing flash a skull appeared in the darkness. It was flaming, lit up by a rain of sparks that fizzed from its empty eye-sockets.

Jack opened his mouth to scream. It came out as a wheezy gasp. His back was pressed against the door. He couldn't move.

The skull vanished. At the far end of the room, the curtains drew back, flooding the room with daylight.

Jack found himself crouched against the door, clutching the plate like a drowning man.

'You didn't drop my bacon.' Udolpho was sitting at the desk, grinning like a cat. 'Smart work for a one-eyed boy! Bring it here.'

Jack looked about in a daze. There was no sign of the skull. Had his eye-patch slipped? No – it was still there. His arms and legs were trembling uncontrollably.

'Come, come!' Udolpho beckoned.

Jack walked unsteadily towards him. On the desk was a wolf's skull, a burning candle, and an hourglass filled with what looked like powdered gold. Beside it was a crystal ball the size of a man's head. The wall behind the desk was covered in bookshelves, the other covered in charts with lots of curving lines and crooked symbols.

The monster hanging from the ceiling watched him with its red eyes. Glass eyes, as Jack now realized.

He set the plate down with a sketchy bow.

Udolpho skewered a forkful of bacon and bread, chewed and swallowed. 'Mmm – delicious. You did well to save it. Remarkable. But then you have had a remarkable life, have you not?'

'Yes, sir,' said Jack.

'And your sister is a remarkable young lady,' said Udolpho, selecting another piece of bacon.

'Yes.' Jack tried to put his disordered thoughts together. 'She saved me. She's like a ma to me . . .'

'Quite so.' Udolpho set down his fork and looked up at Jack with his head to one side. 'Tell me, Jack. Have you ever encountered the Other World?'

'Um . . .'

176

'Manifestations of the spirits – voices from the stars – things of that sort?'

'Magical things, sir?' said Jack.

'Indeed.' Udolpho smiled roguishly.

Quiet and modest, Jack remembered. It took an effort – he was still feeling scared. 'Pardon, sir, as I don't know nothing 'bout stars and spirits, but was that magic before, as I came in?'

'What do you think?'

'I s'pose, sir.'

'As well you might.' Udolpho smiled, and pointed to the cupboard next to his desk. 'Have a look in there.'

The cupboard door was open. Inside were rows of books – only as Jack looked closer he realized they weren't books at all; they were painted leather spines, no more. He could see a small keyhole hiding in one of them.

'Push,' prompted Udolpho.

The second, false door swung inward. It opened onto a narrow passage, very dark and musty. Jack imagined a ravening devil trapped inside there, just waiting to spring. He took a deep breath.

'Here. Go on, take a look.' Udolpho handed Jack the candle from his desk. Jack ducked his head and stepped into the passage.

Now he could see that the passage was more of a cubbyhole, no more than six feet from end to end. No devils. Different-coloured ropes hung from the ceiling.

One wall bristled with small pipes like stretched-out trumpets.

'Pull on that red rope there, next to the door.'

'This?' Jack's hand hesitated.

'Don't fear, boy. Pull.'

Jack reached inside and pulled. He heard a soft sound behind him, and turned.

In the main room, a wooden skull had dropped into view from a hatch in the ceiling. Grey ash tumbled from its eyes. It looked rather pathetic now, dangling on a rope.

Jack felt stupid, remembering how terrified he'd been. Stupid and angry.

Udolpho chuckled.

For the rest of the morning, Udolpho instructed Jack in the tricks of his unlikely trade. There was a rope to make the crystal ball light up, one to open and close the curtains, another that made creaking footsteps sound across the floor. Each of the speaking trumpets produced a different spectral voice in a different part of the house. Jack learned to impersonate spirits, heathen gods, ghosts, angels and devils.

In the afternoon they put those lessons into practice. By then Jack wasn't angry any more, and he was convinced of two things: first, Udolpho was no sorcerer. Second, he was as handy a rogue as any in Sharkwell's Family.

The first coney was called Lady Marchland – a fat,

solid-looking matron wearing a triple rope of the biggest pearls Jack had ever seen. She was in London to get her daughter married, and that was why she'd come to see Udolpho; but Jack, watching from the cubbyhole, reckoned he knew what she really wanted.

From the moment she came in, Udolpho was toying with her. He flattered her with words and with his touch, pressing her hands, stroking her arms, grasping her bodice as he placed her in her chair just so. It was all mixed up with his magician's blather – but Jack saw the way she blushed and simpered, and he saw that Udolpho saw it too.

Within a few minutes, her pearls were laid out in a circle on Udolpho's desk. The Tears of Cupid, he called them – they were meant to be an offering, to help summon some sort of spirit. Right on cue, Jack produced some whispering sighs and light pattering feet.

Lady Marchland gave a little scream. Udolpho muttered something about Cupid's fires. When Jack turned back to the keyhole, Udolpho was standing by the desk with a moaning, trembling Lady Marchland clinched tight in his arms. He was kissing her stout red neck. Jack could see his face, contorted in a look of furious concentration.

The pearls were gone from the table.

There were three more fine ladies that first day. The end result was always the same – Udolpho munching at a scaly old neck, having just swept up the cheat into his sleeve. Watching it made Jack feel slightly sick. It was a queasy way to make your living – but what a living! Golden sovereigns, precious stones, cunningly wrought jewels – all got by a few fancy words and a little bit of nuzzling. Jack never saw what became of the goods. One moment they would be laid out on the table; the next they would be gone, sleeved by Udolpho too quick to see. The man was obviously a dab quilter, which was worrying: anyone who could hide a fortune in his clothes might be able to spot Jack's own sleeve-pocket, with his roll of gilks and picks hidden inside. Jack resolved to plant them in the attic. He wouldn't be needing them any time soon anyway.

'What think you of magic now, lad?' said Udolpho as Jack emerged from the cupboard after the last of the ladies had left. 'Hey-hey?' He winked, took Jack's hand and hauled him to his feet. As Udolpho let go of his hand, Jack felt something pressed into it. When he opened his palm, a single small pearl glimmered there.

'For you, for a fruitful beginning,' said Udolpho. 'Lady Marchland's daughter is as ugly as she is: I doubt not but she will be back. Rubies next time, for she has a famous jewel-box, and I think she enjoys being kissed.'

Jack held up the pearl to study. Udolpho chuckled to himself. He was just bending down to close the false door to the cubbyhole when they heard the first scream.

It came from the kitchen. It could only be Beth.

Udolpho was up and running in an instant. He bolted down the stairs; Jack only caught up with him at the kitchen door, where Udolpho had pulled up sharp.

Beth was standing in front of the fireplace, hair torn loose from its neat bun, brandishing a copper saucepan and screaming her head off. Round the other side of the table from her was a thief. Jack recognized him from Sharkwell's wharf – Salty Silas, a barnyard-cuffin who specialized in scrobbling live pigs. He was circling crab-wise round the table, twitching a butcher's cleaver left, right, left in front of his shiny red nose.

Jack felt a horse-laugh rising. He smothered it with a cough.

'Give it up, my lass, give-it-up give-it-up give-it-up . . .' Silas was muttering, licking his lips, eyes glaring crazily at Beth.

He was playing his part to perfection, but Beth was even better. She turned to Udolpho, screamed, 'Do something! Help me!' and the appeal was so strong that Jack found himself half stepping forward. Silas turned, seemed to size up the magician, then laughed and lunged across the table at Beth with the cleaver. Beth swiped back at him with the saucepan.

'S-stop!' Udolpho took a tiny, hesitant step into the room. 'I say, stop!'

Silas snarled and brandished his cleaver. Udolpho retreated fast, backing right into Jack. Beth socked Silas with the saucepan, and he turned tail, banging out through the door.

Udolpho looked like he was going to collapse with relief – but Beth beat him to it. She began to totter and sway, slowly enough so that Udolpho had time to step in and catch her under the arms.

Udolpho now . . . Jack had to smother another laugh. All afternoon he'd been pawing at ladies' bodices, kneading them to his will like warm dough – and now here he was, lowering Beth into a chair as if her touch might burn his hands. Still, he couldn't seem to take them away. His face had gone bright red.

'What happened, Elizabeth? Please, tell me – you're safe now. He's gone . . .'

She took him there and then – took him with her eyes, as soon as she opened them.

It started off like a rescued princess gazing up at her hero, then changed slowly, as she seemed to realize it wasn't her hero after all. The best thing about it was how she made it seem accidental; a moment later she was pulling herself together, staring hard at the table in front of her.

'Thank you for your help, sir,' she said.

'I?' Udolpho laughed, a choked-off sound in his throat. 'You were the one . . . I mean, of course, I—' He stopped, seemed to realize where his hands were, and snatched them away. 'Ahem. What happened?'

'The door was unlocked,' she said. 'He tried to make me . . .' Her top lip juddered. She bit it shut, took a deep breath. 'The door was unlocked.'

'But that's impossible!'

Udolpho ran to the door that Jack had picked. It was open. He frowned. 'I don't understand.'

Beth fingered a bruise under her eye, and winced. 'I'm afraid Jack and I will have to leave at once. I swore to protect him—'

'And I swear to protect you!' said Udolpho, getting agitated now. 'Both of you.'

'You could not protect me today,' said Beth. 'I do not blame you, sir. Anyone can forget to lock up. You must understand – I have my particular reasons, after what happened . . . my parents murdered, my brother taken . . .' She was sobbing now, tears streaming down her cheeks. 'I cannot abide an unlocked door!'

Udolpho squirmed like a stricken beetle. 'Please, Elizabeth!' he said. 'F-forgive me!'

He turned and ran up the stairs, taking them two at a time.

'He's in a hurry,' said Jack.

Beth kept on sobbing.

'You've got him, haven't you?'

Beth ignored him.

A moment later Udolpho was back with the bunch of keys from his study. 'You must take charge of this.' He held out the bunch of keys to Beth. 'I see I cannot trust my own memory in these matters, but you . . . I can trust you . . . And I pray you . . . I mean, I hope you will stay. For your own good . . . and mine.'

Beth made a little sound between a sob and a laugh. Udolpho was still holding out the keys. Beth let them stay there, looking up past them at Udolpho's face. Her eyes cleared, her cheeks still wet with tears began to glow – and then she threw her arms around Udolpho's waist and pressed her face to his chest.

'I will stay, sir!' she said, her voice muffled. 'To be trusted . . . I am sorry I spoke so . . . To be trusted like this . . .' She stood back suddenly, pulling herself together again. Her face flushed bright red. 'Beg pardon, sir.'

'Hrmph,' said Udolpho. He was standing stiff like a wooden man, his arm still holding the keys out in front of him.

'Beg pardon for I am behaving disgracefully,' said Beth, staring at the floor. 'I am all awhirl. To meet such trust, such kindness in a stranger . . .'

Udolpho's face softened, and he licked his lips. Jack saw his eyes dart up and down Beth's body, quick and creepy as a lizard's tongue. 'But you must not think of me as a stranger, Elizabeth.'

'No, sir.' She took the keys then. 'You are my good and kind master.'

* * *

Sometime during the day, Beth had rigged up an old sheet as a curtain, dividing the attic in two. On her side was the bed, the chair, and most of the floor. Jack was left with the corner nearest the door. There was a chill draught coming in tonight. Jack huddled up in his blankets while Beth got undressed behind the curtain, whistling snatches of different tunes.

'Um . . . Beth?'

'Good day today, Nipper. There's a bit of supper for you . . . wait.' A hunk of bread and a thick slice of ham came sliding out under the curtain. 'Now tell me all about Udo.'

Between mouthfuls, Jack told her what he'd seen and done, looking around for a good hiding place for his tools at the same time.

'So you don't know where he puts the cheat,' she said when he'd finished.

'No. I mean he sleeves it off the table, must do . . . But after – I don't know.'

'Huh. Well, keep a sharp eye. We've time yet.'

That was when Jack took out his roll, thinking he'd pass it through to Beth to hide under the mattress. The roll crackled, and he remembered the pamphlet inside, and how he'd meant to ask Beth to read it for him. She seemed pretty cheery at the moment, so Jack decided he might as well risk it.

'Beth?' he said.

'What?'

'You read books, right?'

'What of it, Nipper?' Beth's face poked up from under the curtain. She was wearing a long red woollen nightcap. 'You want me to read you a bedtime story? How about this.' Her right hand came out, jingling Udolpho's bunch of keys. 'It's a short one, but the ending's happy. Man falls for Beth Sharkwell's wicked wiles. Man gives her his keys. Beth Sharkwell takes all his money. With a little help from Lucky Jack Patch. The End!'

'He's wily himself,' said Jack. 'Leads his ladies by the nose, he does.'

'All the better,' said Beth. 'He leads them – they lead their husbands, get all that money in the first place – and right at the front, there's me, leading the leaders.'

'Because you're Beth Sharkwell.'

'Tricky as a bale of fullams, me.' She laughed. 'Way of the world, Nipper. Coneys piled upon coneys, and me sitting on top, nice and soft. Now what d'you want me to read?'

Jack handed her the pamphlet. She scanned it quickly. Her face changed as she read: the cheerful glow disappeared, and suddenly she was her usual pale, severe self. A narrow crease appeared between her eyes.

'Where'd you find this?'

'Off a coney,' said Jack.

'What sort of coney?'

'One of the crowd – at the hanging. Can't remember which,' said Jack. 'I was just curious . . .'

Beth shot him a sharp look. 'So you don't have no idea what this is about.'

'No.'

'Funny. 'Cos what it's about is your man Webb. Man my grampers forbade you from going after, you recall? Big Fish Webb. Which you was robbing one of his preachers there at the hanging, as I recall . . .'

Jack tried to look surprised. Beth didn't seem convinced.

'What d'you want with this stuff, Jack? Sainted Uncle Webb going round the city, banishing devils with his Bible . . . ? Gull-bait, the lot of it.'

'What about that?' said Jack, pointing to the handwritten note.

'Nothing, I dunno, just . . .' She squinted over it. 'Bloody Hell, script like an inky woodlouse, this. Says . . . *Vixen's Hole, first of May, midnight.*' She looked back up at Jack, and frowned.

Jack was trying so hard not to blink that he froze like a rabbit.

Vixen's Hole. First of May. Midnight.

Three weeks away – and he knew the Vixen's Hole: it was notorious, the fanciest whorehouse in town. As for what the Elect would be doing at a place like that . . . there could only be one explanation.

The secret meetings.

He could feel Beth's eyes on him like loaded pistols.

'I probably shouldn't have told you that, should I?'

He answered too fast – so fast he ended up tripping over the words. 'Wadye . . . What d'you mean?'

'Stop doing the innocent with me, Jack, I invented that play. You're poking your fishy little nose in places you shouldn't, ain't you?'

'So—'

'So I won't have it, not on my watch. You're a good worker, Jack. Get on with life, make money, forget this . . .' She flapped the pamphlet at him.

Jack didn't say anything.

'What're you planning – go down the Hole and . . . what? Bring a knife, hope Uncle Webb shows up?' She snorted.

It was too much. 'You don't understand,' Jack blurted out. 'He killed my ma, did her in with sorcery, and—'

'Sorcery?' Beth practically spat the word, anger mixed in with the contempt now. 'You ain't still off on that, are you? After all you've seen today, you still think . . .'

'It was different,' Jack muttered. 'It wasn't like what Udolpho does.'

'. . . and you think you're the one to tell the difference? Jack the darksman, Jack the sorcerer . . .' She sucked her teeth, a scornful kissing noise. 'You know the best way to skin a coney? It's to make them think they're wiser than they are. You start getting ideas above your state . . . You know what the difference is, then, between you and a coney?'

'What?' said Jack quietly.

'Coneys end up losing their purses. You – you step false, you end up dead.'

'Maybe,' said Jack. He didn't want to argue any more.

'There's work to do here, now. All right? And when Udo's plucked, there'll be something else. Work, like you're duty bound to do. Not chasing after big-fish sorcerer-preacher murdering gents. You need your blood cooling.'

Vixen's Hole. First of May. Midnight.

Webb would be there. Jack was sure of it. This was his chance.

'Stop plotting,' said Beth. 'Give me those tools – I won't have you sneaking off in the night.'

There was no use fighting. He passed over his roll of gilks and picks.

'That's better. Now you keep your mind on the job. Quickest way to do any job is do it right, simple, first time.'

'All right,' said Jack – thinking, she was right in a way. The First of May was three weeks away still, but three weeks wasn't for ever. The sooner they finished here, the better.

Chapter 16

It didn't take long for Beth to take complete charge of Udolpho. She never flirted or played the wanton. If anything, her play was the opposite – little darting glances that never quite met Udolpho's eye; little blushes that she could call up at will; long brooding silences.

It made Udolpho crazy, hooked him even more firmly than he'd hooked his ladies. He trusted Beth in everything. There was a money-box in the dining room, hidden behind the fireplace, and she took from it whenever she needed to. She was paying tradesmen, even placing new orders for things around the house.

Money was a form of magic, Jack realized. With money, life could be transformed into something beautiful, ordered, harmonious. He'd always thought you just used it to buy things, and of course that was what Beth was doing – buying things and paying people to bring them to the house; but by organizing the combinations of things and people in the right way she had created a sort of stage, where Udolpho could play the part of a king. Everything was clean, everything smelled good, nothing ever ran out. Beth took care of it all, and Udolpho loved her all the better for it.

The days passed quickly, bringing a steady stream of gifts to Cupid, Venus, or whatever other spirits Jack was impersonating. Sometimes Jack caught the moment when Udolpho palmed the cheat, sometimes not; but he never saw what he did with it. Udolpho would take the offering while the lady wasn't looking, then keep it hidden in his clothes till later, when he was alone in his study. Only then would he lock his treasures away.

'Fine sort of darksman you are,' Beth told him one night as they sat in front of the embers of the kitchen fire. 'You're supposed to be scoping him.'

'You could sneak in,' Jack suggested. 'Search the study. Maybe you'd find it better than me.'

'Oh, I could, could I?' said Beth. 'With Udo sleeping in the next room? What happens when he wakes up, finds me there?'

'What do you mean?' said Jack.

'Yesterday he tried to kiss me on the stairs. He finds me tiptoeing about his private chambers, he'll think it's his lucky night.' She shuddered. 'I'd have to play along too. Only way.'

'That's rank.'

'That's why I ain't going to chance it.'

'It's rank anyway . . . kissing him on the stairs. It's like what he does with his ladies, only . . .' Jack stared into the embers, not even sure what he was driving at.

'You think I enjoy it?'

'Well, yes. The play-acting. Don't you? You're good enough at it.'

'Aye, too good,' Beth muttered, shaking her head. 'Udo's a lecher, natural born; another month of this and he'll want me in his bed.'

Jack drew up his top lip as far as it would go, stretched out his tongue to touch his chin and croaked. It was his Vomiting Frog face – he'd developed it watching Udolpho with his matrons.

'Right,' said Beth. 'Don't bear thinking on, does it? Catch up, Jack. Don't do anything stupid, mind, just . . . if you see a chance, take it.'

'Never fear,' said Jack. He thought of Udolpho pawing Beth like he did his ladies. It was enough to make him squirm. Not that he'd needed any more reason to hurry; but still, it added a new twist. In his bed . . . No, there was no way . . .

'Never fear,' he repeated. 'I'll take it all right.'

In his dreams he crept up behind Webb. He saw the white of the man's throat. He cut, and watched the blood flow.

Vixen's Hole. First of May. Midnight.

* * *

Jack got his chance three days later. None too soon: it was nearly the end of April. He only had a week left.

Udolpho had been acting strangely all day, rushing through his appointments as if there was something more important in store, something he was waiting for. He kept glancing at the clock, and when the hands reached five he practically threw Lady Parrey out of the front door. Jack was just squeezing out of the cubbyhole when he returned.

'That will be all, Jack,' he said. 'Tell your sister I will be eating in here tonight.'

There was a knock at the front door. Udolpho flinched, and hurried from the room.

Jack waited till he heard his footsteps in the hall, then ran as fast as he could down the kitchen stairs. Beth turned, startled, as he burst into the room.

'Cover me,' he said. 'I'll be hid in the study. Say I've gone out or something. Oh, and Udo's eating at his desk tonight.'

'Wait . . .' said Beth, but Jack was already hurling himself back up the stairs, along the painted corridor and into the study.

He paused at the entrance, listening: voices came up from the hall below. He just had time . . . Risky, but Jack reckoned the odds were favourable. He tiptoed quickly across the room and into the cubbyhole, pulling the false door closed behind him.

He was committed now. He could feel his heartbeats thudding in his chest as he listened to the footsteps coming up the stairs. He took a couple of slow, deep breaths.

Two men's voices – Udolpho, and another, a voice that sounded strangely familiar. The door opened and they came in.

Through the keyhole, Jack watched them cross the room from the door towards the window. They stopped in front of the desk. Udolpho was a step behind the other man, and looking more nervous than ever. The visitor was wearing a dark green cloak with the hood pulled down low over his eyes.

'You have the money?' he said, turning to face Udolpho. Jack caught a glimpse of pale features beneath the hood.

'Y-yes. If you will accept part payment in . . . pearls?'

'Show me.'

Udolpho bent over the chair behind the desk and lifted the leather cushion. Jack stiffened. Udolpho was fishing up a key from around his neck, fitting it to a hole in the seat. The seat swung up. Inside was a gleaming tangle of treasure – all the takings from Udolpho's ladies.

The magician turned to his visitor with a handful of gold and another of pearls. 'We can weigh them, if you want. There are scales in the cupboard.'

Jack felt his heart start to sprint. The cupboard . . .

Which cupboard? He'd never seen any scales in this one, but . . .

'Here,' said the visitor, holding out his left hand. 'Just one of them.' Udolpho handed him a pearl and he held it up in front of his face. 'Good. These will suffice. No need for scales.'

'You are kind,' said Udolpho, pouring the rest of the pearls into the man's hand. He licked his lips. 'And so . . . the book?'

The man's right hand came out from beneath his cloak, holding a plain wooden box with an iron clasp.

Jack's own right hand started to itch. Behind its patch, his bad eye was throbbing.

The man was wearing gloves, but his right sleeve had pulled up and Jack could see a narrow stretch of skin around the wrist.

The skin was stained dark red.

'In here,' the man was saying. 'The true *Diabolon*. Look, if you want.'

Jack's hand was itching harder now – harder than at any time since he'd arrived at Udolpho's. *Diabolon*. The devil book. And a red hand.

It didn't figure. It didn't figure at all.

Udolpho took the box, laid it on the floor and opened it, moving with a feverish haste that Jack had never seen in him. The visitor stood still, watching Udolpho scuffle through the pages. Jack couldn't see the book itself because the magician's body was in the way. The visitor moved across the room, rolling his eyes impatiently – and that was when Jack saw his face.

Of course he knew the voice. He hadn't recognized it because both times he'd heard it before it had been shouting, hoarse. But the face – there could be no mistake about the face. Gaunt, white, with the yellow-grey hair hanging down to either side, the mad eyes, the writhing movements beneath the skin.

It was Webb's champion preacher. The one who'd been at St Paul's, and at Rob's hanging. The one Jack had seen entering Bygott House, dressed in green. Just as he was now.

Wrath-of-the-Righteous Jonson.

What was he doing here? It didn't figure . . .

At least now Jack knew what Jonson had been up to, going about in disguise all those other times.

He was selling the devil books.

It didn't figure at all.

Udolpho was still muttering over *The Diabolon* when the preacher ran out of patience.

'You are satisfied?' he said. 'The book – you like it?'

'Oh yes . . .' Udolpho breathed; then he started to his feet. 'Yes, of course,' he said in a normal voice. 'You will want . . .'

'To be gone,' said Jonson. 'You will keep the book well hidden, of course. There's true magic there, not for the eyes of the world.'

'Of course, of course,' said Udolpho; he could barely tear his eyes from the pages.

'And you will be *careful*, won't you?'

'Yes, yes . . .' Udolpho murmured.

With a final lustful glance he replaced the book in its box, and locked it away inside the armchair. The two men walked over to the door and down the stairs. Jack sat where he was for a good half-minute, his thoughts hammering, before he remembered to get out of there.

They could steal everything. He'd seen the hiding place. They could take the treasure and go, tonight.

Jack pushed open the cupboard and padded across the room. As he passed the armchair, the stain in his hand twitched again.

Chapter 17

'We wait,' said Beth. 'Give it some more time, let him fill up his treasure chest.'

They were in the attic. She was sitting on the edge of the bed, the curtain drawn back. Jack was already wrapped in his blankets on the floor.

Best not to argue, Jack thought. They still had a week, and arguing would only make her suspect he wanted to be out before the first. Which was true, after all.

'What was he doing when you gave him his supper?' said Jack.

'Sitting at his desk, looking in his book.' Beth smirked. 'He shut it double-quick when I come up to him with the food. Probably got lewd pictures in it, the old goat.'

'Aye, probably.' Jack hadn't told her everything about the book, and he hadn't said a word about

Wrath-of-the-Righteous Jonson. It would only set her off.

'Anyway, you did well today. Risky, but worth it. I was starting to worry, but now . . . Aye, we can wait. Let the coney fatten.'

Jack didn't like the sound of that at all.

'Good work, Jack.' Beth drew the curtain. 'You sleep well now.'

The darkness began to gather that same night. Jack knew Udolpho was still awake downstairs, looking at *The Diabolon*, muttering as he read through the pages. Jack could hear the words in his head, or at least imagined he could. Strange, sibilant words coiling their way through the house.

The scratching in the walls started up around midnight. Jack had heard something like it a few times since they'd been here, but now it was louder and quicker, as if the rats were trying to escape from something – some slinking horror of the night, in there with them in the forgotten spaces of the house.

Jack started to spook himself, imagining that whatever was in there would come out, gnaw its way up through the floorboards and bite him while he slept. He imagined the feeling of it – a weight on his chest, cold, naked paws on his face, the prickle of claws, then tearing pain as it went for him – his eyes, his nose, his tongue . . .

He might have drifted in and out of sleep in the small hours, but he was awake for the watery grey dawn.

When Jack brought him his breakfast, Udolpho was still reading. His eyes were red and strained. He snapped *The Diabolon* shut as Jack came in, and sent him away immediately with instructions to let no one into the house. If any of his ladies came, they were to be told he was not at home.

Just standing near the book made Jack feel uneasy. His hand itched – and his eye flared up whenever he glanced at the desk. It made him wonder what he'd see if he lifted his patch.

The idea set ants crawling all over his skin. He remembered the stories of the Horrors. Dead bodies and bloody footprints. And every time, a magician somewhere nearby. A magician, and *The Diabolon*.

The itching in his hand subsided once he was out of the door, away from the book – it was the book that was doing it.

The book that Jonson had brought.

The more he thought it through, the less sense it made.

Again he wondered about raising his patch. He could look through the keyhole, scope out the book—

Jack jumped as the bell rang just above his head. He waited a moment before going in – didn't want Udolpho wondering why he was standing there just outside the study door.

Udolpho was sitting bent over his desk, reading. 'What?' he said, covering the page with his arm.

'You rang the bell. What d'you want, sir?'

'The bell?' Udolpho looked confused and irritated in equal parts.

'You rang it.'

'No I didn't. I told you I'm not to be disturbed. So don't disturb me. Tell your sister I don't want lunch today either. Go, go!'

The rest of the day was idle, but not peaceful. Jack was sure there was something new in the house – real magic now, not like before. Of course he couldn't talk to Beth about it.

For her part, Beth was annoyed that Udolpho wasn't seeing any of his ladies. The way she saw it, each one he turned away shrank the cheat. Still, she wanted to wait. Jack began to suspect she was deliberately drawing the job out, making sure they'd still be here on the first. Not that there was any real chance of finishing it anyway, with Udolpho locked up in his study and showing no signs of shifting.

The next day Udolpho ordered up a jug of wine with breakfast. Again he stayed in his study all day, and again no one was admitted to the house. The bell rang four times – once because Udolpho wanted his jug refilled, once to

cancel lunch, and twice for no reason at all. He was looking worse – Jack was sure he hadn't slept, and his neat
moustache was beginning to blur as stubble sprouted on
his cheeks. His eyes were red and jumpy. In the afternoon, sitting in the kitchen with Beth, Jack heard footsteps
from the floor above, pacing back and forth – Udolpho's
heavy tread, and then a second set of footsteps behind
him, like the ones Jack had made pretending to be Cupid,
softly creaking across the boards.

'It's only his tricks,' said Beth when Jack pointed this
out. 'He's been drinking – he's probably practising something, getting his ropes tangled. That's why the bell keeps
going off too.'

'You think?'

'What do you think? He's got this book – he must be
working up to something, reading about some new play for
his ladies.'

'I don't like it.'

'Neither do I, Jack. He was doing fine for us before,
putting up treasure every day . . . Whatever this is he's
planning, it had best be good.' She shook her head. 'Least
he's stopped his pawing . . .'

It was true: Udolpho had lost interest in Beth along
with everything else.

On the third day, he started sending them out to buy
things. Beth had always been the one to do this before, but

now he insisted they both go. They had to range far across the city to find what he wanted – an odd list every time: hare's fat, rose vinegar, a long hazel stick, white leather shoes; then other things that Jack had never heard of, alchemical ingredients with exotic names – gum Arabic, Roman vitriol, gall-nut.

That evening was when Jack finally got up the nerve to lift his patch. He turned the matter over in his mind all day. He'd sworn after Pol's Stump that he'd never look out at the world through his bad eye again, but now, with the growing certainty that there was something in the house, something that couldn't be seen with ordinary sight ... If there was, it was better to know it than not.

It still took every scrap of courage he had.

He tried it outside the study in the painted corridor. First he peeled up the patch, and then he opened his right eye a crack – it stung after being covered for so long – and looked about.

Redness, at first; red clouds that cleared to reveal – nothing. Or nothing like what he'd seen at Old Pol's Stump, but not quite nothing at all. There were shadows where there shouldn't be, and they were flowing into each other in a weird, unsettling way. Like the way water begins to stir before it boils.

He flipped the patch into place and ran down to the kitchen.

That was the first time he asked Beth straight out to lift the cheat now, any way they could. She refused, like he'd known she would.

On the fifth day, Udolpho sent them out to get a yard of white linen. It had to be spun that very afternoon, between three and five o'clock, while they watched. That evening, when Jack brought Udolpho his supper (along with his fourth jug of wine), there was a cat in the study. It didn't look happy to be there – it had scratched jagged streaks all over the floorboards and furniture, and when Jack came in it made a dash for the door. It was brought up short by a string leash around its neck, attached to one of the legs on the armchair. Jack hurried past it, set the food down and got out, trying not to breathe. The room smelled strongly of cat's piss.

'He's losing his wits,' Jack said to Beth in the kitchen afterwards. 'We have to leave before something happens.'

'Right, right, the scary devils are coming. We ain't leaving till I give the word. So stop trying.'

'I'm not trying anything, I swear. Listen! He doesn't even bother closing the book any more . . . He's like a madman, one of the really bad ones, you know – the alley screamers. I tell you—'

'You tell me?' Beth frowned. 'I think you've forgot who's master here, Nipper.'

'But . . .' She hadn't called him that for days. 'Look, don't you feel it too? Something's going to happen. Something bad.'

Beth got the broom from the corner and started sweeping the floor around the fireplace. She didn't say anything for a minute.

'Beth?'

She kept sweeping, biting her lip. 'All right,' she said finally. 'I see Udo losing his wits. I don't see this bad thing happening, 'cos I think what you're scared of is sorcery. And there ain't no such thing. And I ain't going to lose money on account of your being gull-frighted.'

'I ain't—'

'Wait. I also know you want out of here, because of a certain date at a certain Hole. So listen straight: we ain't leaving without the cheat. All of it. And there's no taking the cheat, long as Udo's sat in his room all day. So we stay.'

'But—'

'No. I ain't asking, I'm telling. That's how it's going to be.'

The first of May was two days away now. That wasn't even the worst of it, not any more. Jack had looked about the house with his patch off a few more times, and the shadows were thickening, flowing down the walls like pig's blood. The noises in the walls at night were quickening, becoming frantic.

Something was coming. Soon.

He remembered the ballads he'd heard in the streets. He remembered the look on his ma's face when he'd found her body.

If they didn't get out tonight, Jack thought there was a good chance they might never leave the house alive.

Chapter 18

I t was nearly time for bed when the bell started ringing upstairs.

'Get it,' said Beth, without looking up from her sweeping. 'I'll do the fire.'

The bell kept on ringing.

'Hop along,' she said. 'His lordship's anxious.'

'All right, all right.' Jack got to his feet.

He hesitated with his foot on the first step. The daylight was long dead, and blackness had swallowed the stairway above. He looked back. The kitchen was bright and warm. Beth was humming to herself as she damped down the fire.

The bell was still ringing.

For a moment Jack thought of going back for a candle – but if he did, Beth would sneer and call him a tender coney, gull-frighted. He shook his head. What was he?

Scared of the dark? This was no worse than a Southwark alley on a moonless night.

He took a step. Then another. He kept one hand against the wall to feel his way. The bell was clanging away fit to raise the dead.

He was almost at the top of the stairs when the ringing stopped. The silence that followed was much worse.

Jack heard a noise behind him. He whipped round, reaching blindly with his hands. 'Beth?'

There was nothing there.

'Beth? You playing tricks?'

A cold prickle ran through him – and he heard the sound again. It was above him now. A rustling, like heavy cloth dragging across the floor.

Jack stood still and held his breath. His heart was pounding, his right eye and hand were itching like fury, but everything else was quiet. He wanted more than anything to be back in the kitchen, whatever Beth might say. He should have brought that candle, at least. Even the littlest light would make all the difference – but Udolpho's study was a lot closer now, and he could see a glow seeping under the door.

Jack ran for the light. He reached the door and knocked. There was no answer. He put his ear to the keyhole and listened. He heard nothing – and then, behind him, the heavy, soft sound came again.

Jack threw himself against the door. To his intense

relief it wasn't locked. He stumbled through into Udolpho's study.

Inside was a strong smell of vinegar, and scented, burning wood. The room was dim, the air thick with smoke. Udolpho was standing over a low, bright light, with his back to Jack. He was dressed in the long linen shift. He was wearing the white leather shoes, and a cone-shaped hat made out of paper. The devil book was open on a lectern beside him.

The magician hadn't noticed Jack bursting in. He couldn't have rung the bell, either. The pullcord was tied up in the other corner of the room.

All Udolpho's attention was fixed on the floor in front of him.

'Um . . . sir?' said Jack. He took another step into the room.

Udolpho didn't reply. He was swaying from side to side.

Then Jack saw what he was looking at, on the floor, and had to bite into his knuckle to stop himself from crying out.

The cat had been divided into four neat pieces – body carved in two, head and tail removed. The pieces were spaced evenly around a circle that Udolpho had drawn on the floor in its blood. More symbols were scratched into the wood or traced along the circle's edge in coloured chalk. The white light was shining up straight out of the floor, in the centre of the circle.

Udolpho drew a shape in the air with his hazel stick. In the corners of the room, the shadows slid together. The light shivered, and rose up off the floor.

It was getting brighter. Jack couldn't work out what it was. It wasn't a candle, or a lamp; it was *flat*, and it was now hovering in mid-air, about a foot off the ground.

A little shining circle of light, and whichever way he turned his head it was still . . . flat. He could feel something building in the air around him – and now he could hear that sound again, a rustling of heavy cloth, getting louder.

Something was coming.

Jack was filled with the overwhelming desire to run as far and as fast as he could.

He dashed back to the door, and through it. He almost crashed into something coming up the stairs. He threw himself away from it, into the wall.

'Oi! Mind yourself!' said Beth. 'And the candle!' She shielded the flame with her hands, so that it grew strong again, casting dancing shadows on the wall.

Jack was so relieved to see her he couldn't speak.

'Why're you chucking yourself about?' Beth laughed. 'You're not still scared, are you? It's a bit dark, but—'

Jack took a deep breath. 'He's—'

'What's he want?'

'Nothing! He wasn't ringing the bell. There's something else doing it!'

'Really.' Beth pursed her lips.

'We need to leave,' said Jack. 'He's not got his ropes tangled. This is real.'

'I told you, we're leaving when we've lifted the cheat, and not before. Weren't you listening?'

'No, you listen to me.' Jack grabbed her by the wrist. 'We need to go now.'

Beth looked down at his hand on her wrist. Lit up by the candle, her face glowed like a cold-hearted angel.

'Stow it, Jack Patch,' she said. 'Stow your guff and take your hand off me.'

'No! You listen! He's killed the cat . . . Just look inside there, you'll see!'

'Stop.' Beth wrenched her hand free and jabbed Jack in the chest with her finger. 'You know, I said this would happen. Happens all the time with green nippers: first proper dark job and you ain't got the stomach for it.'

She sniffed contemptuously, and walked upstairs. 'I'm going to sleep now. If you want to go on babbling, you can do it to the shadows. I ain't listening to it.'

Jack didn't see any choice but to follow her. It was that or be left alone in the dark.

He tried again, up in the attic, but it only made her angry. She wouldn't listen. Well, so be it: if Beth was angry, Jack was furious. Furious, and terrified, but he still had wits enough to know talking wouldn't do any good now.

211

He listened to Beth's breathing. As soon as she was asleep, he would leave. She could stay if she liked. She could find out for herself . . .

She still sounded like she was awake.

He imagined Beth lying up here as the screams started downstairs. Somehow he knew there would be screaming. Would she admit Jack was right then? Or would she only believe him when the thing from behind the light came rustling up the stairs?

Sure as hellfire I won't come and save you . . .

Law Six: Save your own skin.

That would serve her right; but how would he explain it to Sharkwell? The thought froze him. If he turned up at the wharf without Beth, and without the cheat, Sharkwell would not be gentle. It might be worse than the shadows, and that light, and whatever was coming from beyond it.

No. Nothing could be worse than that.

Jack twisted the blanket between his fingers. He was pinned and caught, and the worst of it was that he knew what he had to do now.

It was what he'd been brought up to do. Jack the thief. Anne's boy. Scrunty Jack with the magic fingers.

He couldn't leave without Beth. He was going to have to force her.

Beth's breathing was low and even. Jack was so close he could smell her.

He reached forward, sliding his hand under the pillow. Beth snorted in her sleep, and shifted to a more comfortable position. Jack took the chance and slid his hand another inch. He could almost touch the prize now.

Beth's eyelids fluttered.

Jack froze. After an eternity, he managed to nudge his fingers forward. They settled on the keys.

Beth smiled, muttered something, and shuffled deeper into the pillow.

Fighting down the urge to breathe, Jack reached further. There – just beyond the bunch of keys – there it was. The familiar thickness of his roll of tools felt good in his hand. Snagging a spare finger around the keys, he began to inch his hand out. Beth grunted again. Jack forced himself not to hurry.

The tools and the keys came free of the pillow. Jack backed away from the bed, and crept softly out of the room.

It was a blessing that the first part of his plan needed all his concentration. It meant he hadn't had to think too much about what came next.

He moved down the stairs. He had no candle and the darkness was thick about him. Step by awful step, and each one was harder than the last. The light was brighter beneath Udolpho's door. And Jack could hear the magician's voice.

'*Veni celeriter iubeo . . . Veni . . . celeriter . . . iubeo . . .*'

Jack summoned up all his courage, and walked in.

The room was brighter because the light had grown. It was now a foot-long hole, a torn place in the air. It was still flat – as if it didn't exist in the same space as everything else. Jack wanted to look away from it at once.

There was a new smell in the air – a sharp, hot, metallic smell, like the old vats at Abe's Tannery. It was growing stronger.

'*Veni celeriter iubeo* . . . I summon you, Duke Agares. Obey me, by the name thou knowest.'

Udolpho was kneeling before the blood-drenched circle, still dressed in his ludicrous robes. He did not look round as Jack stole past him. He didn't look as if he would notice anything except what was going on in the circle.

Jack was good at sneaking, but he'd never tried to move more quietly than this. *You're not here*, he thought. *You're no one.*

Please . . .

It wasn't for Udolpho's benefit. Jack was sure he could have marched up behind him and set off a cannon without the man noticing. No. Jack was terrified of the other thing in the room. The thing that was coming.

Most of all, he didn't want that thing to notice him.

It took a lifetime before he was kneeling at the chair. He lifted the cushion and found the keyhole. He spread out his roll of tools. For a dreadful moment he couldn't see the right one. Couldn't even begin to decide.

He'd never be able to pick the lock anyway. His hands were shaking too much.

Simple, he told himself. The lock was simple, the sort of thing his ma had had him cracking when he was six. As long as he concentrated on the lock and nothing else, he could do this. He didn't even have to think about it.

He let his eye and fingers choose by themselves. The Number One Gilk. Nice and simple. He teased its end into the lock, felt the length of the pin – just one pin, and here was the place to grip, and—

Snik.

The lock turned over. Jack lifted the lid. It came up soundlessly on oiled hinges.

The cloth-sliding noise came again, the light blazed brighter, and Jack saw his shadow printed clear against the wall. He couldn't help but glance round, shielding his eye.

'Ah!' Udolpho whispered. 'Am I a god?' In the brilliant light Jack saw the magician's face very clearly – runnels of sweat on his forehead, a streak of blood on his cheek. His face was shining.

'Everything is . . . so clear.'

The light.

The flat light was brightening, brightening, as the hole in the air widened.

'I summon you now, Agares! I conjure you to come! *Veni celeriter iubeo! Veni celeriter iubeo! Veni . . . ce . . .*

215

ler . . .' Udolpho's voice faltered and died. He sank down, kneeling before the light.

Jack lifted his patch, and the room grew suddenly dim and red, as if a cloud of blood had passed across the sun. He could see clearly now. He immediately wished he couldn't.

Something was coming. It was pushing its way through. The hole in the air was widening because it was being pulled apart by long thin fingers – fingers as twitchy and hooked as spider's legs. Behind the fingers was a dim, quivering shape that seemed to change every time Jack tried to look at it.

It had eyes – that was all he knew for sure. Big, round, silver eyes.

Jack couldn't have moved now if he'd wanted to: every muscle was frozen with terror.

'I, Udolpho, conjure thee, spirit!' The magician's voice rose in triumph. 'Come, thou, then, Duke Agares! Come, thou; come, come and do my will!'

It was coming. The hole in the air stretched wider. The light split into shards, and shattered. The fingers scrabbled, gripped the edges of the hole, and pulled.

Jack grabbed Udolpho's jewels and ran.

When he woke Beth, it was amazing how quickly she understood. She took one look at the bag of jewels in Jack's hand, and her eyes shrank to tiny black pills of anger.

She didn't say anything, but the next moment she was out of bed. And the next she was pulling her dress over her head and propelling Jack ahead of her down the stairs – she didn't even put on her shoes. She passed Udolpho's door without a glance. In the kitchen she grabbed a sack, and in the dining room she filled it with Udolpho's silver plates.

They were out of the house and walking in five minutes.

Jack had to fight the urge to caper. The relief of escaping was too great to shut in. He had to keep hugging himself to stay quiet. He had to force himself to stay alert. After curfew the Watch would arrest common folk just for being out on the street. And even worse than the Watch were the other curfew breakers. Pimps, punks, shavers and murderers – and, of course, thieves. Any of them would kill for what Jack and Beth were carrying. It would be very stupid to escape from a devil only to go and get his throat cut.

Right now, though, Jack was more worried about Beth than the entire criminal population of London. She really did look like a destroying angel, striding along, her face set like stone. Jack kept expecting her to say something, but she stayed silent. She didn't even look at him. She went fast down Addle Hill towards the river. It was only when they were in sight of the water that she spoke.

'Can't take the bridge after dark,' she said. She was

keeping her voice low, but Jack could hear the anger trembling beneath. 'There'll be watermen at the wharf. Take us across to Paris Garden stairs.'

Jack could see Puddle Wharf up ahead now, a single torch flickering reflections over the water. Soft voices and a rattle of dice came from one of the boats drawn up against the jetty.

'Now.' Beth stopped. She spoke fast, still not looking at him. 'Before we get on the boat, you'll hear me.'

'Beth—'

'No. You listen to me now. You bolted back there. Craven child, you are. Worse, you broke the Laws. We report to Grampers tonight or tomorrow, and if I tell him what you did he'll have your life.'

She was right, Jack realized. Back in the house he'd only worried about getting out and delivering Beth back to Sharkwell alive. He'd never imagined the price would be Beth crying beef to Sharkwell's Law, watching him suffer Sharkwell's justice. But she was a Sharkwell herself, after all; and she looked angry enough to do it.

'You can't do that,' he said. 'You don't understand – we had to get out of there!' He felt his earlier anger rising again. 'I could've left you. Then you'd have seen.'

'Stow it,' Beth hissed. 'Shut up, craven, and hear me out.' She took a breath, and went on. 'When we report, I do the talking. Whatever I say, back it up.'

'Like what?'

'Never you mind. Do it, that's all.' She started on for the wharf.

Jack didn't move.

After a few steps she stopped and turned. 'Come on!'

'What, and then you peach me to Grampers?' Jack shook his head.

Beth surprised him then. She was on him, a knife out of her skirts and at his throat before he could move. 'Run from me, Nipper?' she said, looking straight into his face now. Her teeth were bared in a wicked grin. 'You don't see, do you? We're here. We're going home tonight, against my orders. You think I want it known a frighted craven kid got the better of me?' She shook her head. 'You don't need to worry, Jack Patch. You'll live, with no one but me to know what you really are. I'll know, and I'll make sure you never get a chance to foul up anyone else's job. That I *can* do.' She lowered the knife, and turned again for the wharf. 'But you'll live. Long as you back up my report.'

The bells were striking two as they reached the river. Two o'clock in the morning, on the first of May.

Chapter 19

The Crooked Walnut was heaving with its lunchtime custom, food and drinks being carried hither and thither through a cloud of smoke and chatter, a stink of frying fat, mouldy rushes and stale tobacco.

The owner of the tavern sat in a corner booth, eating his own midday meal – a stew of soft lamb's kidneys swimming in greasy broth. He sucked it up from a large spoon, mashing the kidneys against the roof of his mouth with his tongue.

Jack and Beth sat opposite Mr Sharkwell. Jack was feeling nervous. Beth had a dangerous glint in her eye.

They'd handed in the cheat to Meatface last night – Sharkwell was asleep when they arrived – and Jack had awaited the summons all morning, his nerves getting sharper with every hour that passed. The delay could only be bad news. Beth must already be shaping her vengeance with Sharkwell.

Jack only hoped she wouldn't interfere with tonight. In the terror of those last few days, he'd almost given up on the meeting at the Vixen's Hole. He felt guilty about that. It was craven, forgetting his promise to his ma just because he was scared. Now Beth was out to get him disgraced: what were the chances he'd be free to slip away this evening?

Sharkwell slurped up a last spoonful, mashed the meat to a paste and swallowed. Then he looked up and grinned, showing both his teeth.

'Well, me little dearlings.' He wiped his mouth. 'Smiles and me told over your cheat this morning, first thing. My, my . . . Beth Sharkwell and Lucky Jack the Darksman.' He reached below the table, produced two bulging cloth bags and pushed them across, one in front of Jack and one in front of Beth.

To Jack's surprise, the two bags were the same size. If anything, his was slightly bigger. If it was gold in there . . . even if it was silver, this was more than he'd ever got for a single job before. Much more. Which surely meant he wasn't in trouble. *Not yet*, he reminded himself: Beth had still to make her report.

'Grampers, before you warrant him darksman . . .' Beth began.

'Aye? Something I need to know, is there?' Sharkwell

raised his eyebrows in mock curiosity, as if he knew what was coming. Maybe she'd already spoken to him.

Here it comes, thought Jack.

'I don't think he should be a darksman, Grampers,' said Beth. 'See, we didn't stick to the plan. Couldn't, because of what he did. Happened just before we scarpered—'

'Ha!' Sharkwell slapped his left hand down on the table. 'I knew it!'

Beth shut her mouth, looking blankly at Sharkwell.

'Your face!' Sharkwell cackled. 'Don't you worry, girl, I know all about it. Heard tell this morning. You've won me a wager. My girl Beth's a thief without peer, I said to Smiles, but she ain't no killer.' He turned to Jack. 'So it was Jack Patch, was it? Knew you were a hard boy, but I never smoked you for murderings.'

Jack glanced sideways at Beth. She was keeping her face blank. He tried to keep his own face still, but his mind was racing. He couldn't tell if she was as surprised as he was, or if maybe this was part of a plan to get back at him – except Sharkwell was pleased, that was obvious . . .

'A killer,' Sharkwell snorted in admiration. 'And none of your pissy cut-throats neither but a poisoner, a gruesome gutwrack villain. What'd you use, henbane? Word goes the look on his face was something awful. Course, the balladeers say it was a demon or some such – one more dead spell-pusher; who's going to think otherwise? – but you and me know better, eh? Eh?' He leaned across the

222

table and clapped Jack on the shoulder. 'We're going to have to watch this one, Beth.'

Beth was looking at Jack now, and when she spoke she'd composed her voice perfectly. She was quick, Jack knew that already, but it was uncanny how fast she took in what had happened.

'It was well thought out, I'll give him that . . . but he could stand watching, Grampers, and I still don't like making him a darksman. He went against the plan. Perfectly good plan, it was. No call for murdering the magician.'

Sharkwell winked at Jack. 'Aye, but what you don't see, my girl, is the only reason there weren't no murders in the plan was that I knew you wasn't capable of it, and I never knew Jackie-boy was. Dead men tell no tales, dead men don't spy you in the street by chance, like, and cry beef . . . No, this way's better.' He gave the side of Jack's head a playful slap. 'Never had him down as a killer, did you, girl?'

'No.' For a second Beth's eyes were fixed on Jack's. They flickered thoughtfully across his face, then she looked away. 'I didn't.'

'So, Jack Patch: you're a darksman now, and not just an ordinary darksman but a Blooded Darksman,' said Sharkwell. 'You've deserved honours, boy. Arms of the trade. Haven't had a poisoner in the Family for nigh on five years – not since Dutch Abe did himself in.' He reached under the table again. When his hand came out it was holding a dagger – an ugly old thing with a broad six-inch blade, made for punching under the ribs to a man's heart. He slid it across the table. 'Here's your blade, boy. Not even Beth here gets one of these.'

Jack stared at the dagger. The letter S was burned into the pommel.

'Well, what do you say, boy? Look at him, Beth girl, he's forgotten his courtesies.'

Jack pulled himself together. 'Thank you, Mr Sharkwell,' he said.

Jack's relief was short-lived. As soon as they left the Walnut, Beth grabbed him by the collar and pushed him hard against the wall.

'Don't you ever try that again.'

'Try what? You shaped out all right. I backed you, like you asked.'

Beth pulled back her fist.

Jack bit his lip. He hadn't fought with a girl since he was seven. Beth was taller than him, and angrier.

'What did you think, *Poison Jack*?' Beth was staring at him, studying his face as if he'd come out in pox. 'Thought you could play me like that, did you?'

'Play you . . .?'

'Aye – get rid of Udo in time for your outing tonight . . . hah, and you expect me to believe it was the devil come for him, I suppose, just like you said it would? Jack the magician . . .'

'What, you think I did it?' Jack could feel his own anger welling up to meet hers. 'Really? You think I'd do that – kill someone, what, so you'd *believe* me?'

'Aye, but I don't. I don't believe in devils, nor sprites, nor none of your gull-bait chatter. I'd settle for that – Jack's a gull, what of it, only the man's dead.' Beth's voice was dangerously level. 'What are you really, Jack?'

'Nothing. I never killed—'

'That's right,' said Beth. 'No, that's enough. Nothing. That'll do. You stay that way to me, Jack. You keep out of my sight.'

Jack went back to the warehouse alone. He met Mr Smiles coming out.

'Holloa, Jack,' he said – but for once, Smiles wasn't smiling. At first he wouldn't even meet Jack's eye. 'Felix-itations are the order of the day, I hear? A Blooded Darksman . . .' Now he looked at Jack, and *he* was doing it too, the same as Beth – searching his face, like for some foul mark – only where Beth had looked angry, Smiles looked sad. Disappointed more than anything, and again Jack wanted to say it: *It's not true, I never killed him, I never killed anyone.*

Except it would be true before long.

Jack said nothing. Smiles shook his hand, seemed about to say something, then swallowed it.

225

As Jack passed into the warehouse, he saw shadows moving overhead.

'Don't hex me!' called a voice in the rigging. 'Have a care, boys! Here's ol' Sir Nigromance hisself!'

The rope-jacks jeered and hooted him all the way back to his sleeping place, but none dared clamber close enough to show their faces. As he looked over his tools, Jack felt a bleak twinge of mirth. Poison Jack, Sir Nigromance, the Blooded Darksman . . . except he hadn't done any of it – not yet – not quite.

He wasn't a nigromancer, though last night he'd seen a devil.

He wasn't a killer, though tonight he planned to kill.

Jack wasn't anything. Not yet. Not quite. The dagger in his hand felt heavy, brutal. It would do.

What are you really, Jack?

He was scrunty Jack. He was his ma's son.

He was going to murder Webb.

The Vixen's Hole wasn't much to look at from the outside – a grubby old building in Soper's Lane, south of Cheapside. There had been other buildings on the same plot before this one. Some had burned down. Some were washed away when the river flooded. One or two had been razed by conquering armies. Every time, a new building grew up from the ruins of the old. And every time, the same ancient trade flourished here – like a weed with deep roots that would always spring up again no matter how many times it was plucked.

The sign outside was old too, its paint flaking so that Jack could only just make out the design of a slim fox silhouetted against the moon. Two torches burned in front of the doors. Without them, the Hole would have looked like any other low tavern, shut up for the night.

Other than the torches, the only thing that set the Hole apart was the sorts of people who were coming and going through the doors. From his hiding place, Jack had seen guildsmen in rich fur-trimmed cloaks; drunken gallants with jewelled rapiers at their hips; nervous, furtive young lords dressed in gleaming silks and black velvet masks. As each visitor reached the doors, Jack saw gold spin – to be snatched out of the air by the doorman, who was surprisingly quick behind his great slab of belly.

Hidden in the shadows of an alleyway across the street, Jack was close enough to see their faces. He'd been watching for the best part of an hour, and he'd seen a lot of gold change hands. What he hadn't seen was anyone who looked like they might be going to a devil-casting. These gentles were hot for whores, not hellfire.

Jack shouldn't have arrived so early. When he'd first settled in he'd been ready – teeth set, sinews stiffened, spirits bent up to their full murderous height – just like all the times he'd imagined. But the longer he waited, the less ready he felt.

To kill a man. That was no small thing. He'd sworn to do it, and he wanted to do it – but still. There was no taking it back. A killer he'd be, for good and all. Smiles and Beth would look askance at him, and there'd be nothing he could say. He would deserve the looks. He would deserve the Blooded Man's blade that he carried.

If he could do it. He'd never killed anything bigger than a chicken before. He imagined the scrape of the blade slicing through gristle and sinew, the warm blood flowing out across his hand. The mess.

If he could do it.

Jack eased his Blooded Man's blade from its sheath, tested the edge with his thumb, and scowled out across the street. It was nearing midnight. Maybe there was no meeting after all. Jack felt a little glimmer of hope, and immediately hated himself for it. He'd sworn an oath on his ma's grave.

Somewhere away down Cheapside, he heard a bell toll, and the voice of a watchman sing out: 'Twelve o' the clock, and all's well!'

Closer at hand, footsteps turned the corner of Soper's Lane. Footsteps in a hurry. Jack shrank into the shadows of the alley, and watched the man pass.

The man was striding down the middle of the lane. He wore a dark green cloak with the hood thrown back. His face was pale and set, dirty-white hair flowing out behind. He didn't look awkward or ashamed; he looked angry.

It was Wrath-of-the-Righteous Jonson.

Jack shuddered. The fear was stronger than ever, now the point was reached; but there couldn't be any more doubt. If he wanted to see this through, he had to move now.

Jonson tossed the doorman a coin and shouldered past him without a word.

'Ha' mercy,' Jack muttered, and touched his dagger for luck.

Before he could change his mind, he hurried across the street to the Vixen's Hole.

Chapter 20

The doorman slid across the door to block Jack's path. 'What's this, rascal?'

Jack forced his voice to sound easy. 'Here.' He pulled a coin from his purse and sent it spinning.

The doorman's chubby fingers plucked the gold out of the air. He gave a greasy leer and stepped aside. 'May the vixens please you.' He ushered Jack inside.

Beyond was a curtained doorway. Two girls in bright taffeta gowns stood on either side like painted posts. From their eyes Jack knew they'd seen the coin.

'Here's a young, golden gentleman,' said the one in red.

'Young, but I'll wager from waist down he's a centaur!' giggled her companion. She had sleepy eyes and tumbled hair. Both girls wore heavy powder, and bright blue ruffs of the broadest kind. They had long fox tails sewn onto the backs of their dresses, just below the waist.

Jack tried to walk past them as if he knew what he was doing. They weren't having it, though: they fell in to either side of him, each taking one of his arms.

'What's your pleasure, darling?' said the girl in red. She stroked his cheek.

'You want to come with us, golden boy.'

The curtains parted, and Jack found himself being drawn into a large, dim chamber filled with silks and cushions. The girls still kept hold of him, one to each arm. He looked about, searching for Jonson. Everywhere there were girls, all dressed (or undressed) differently, save for the bushy fox tails sashaying on their rumps. Jack could feel himself flush at the sight, and at the warm soft flesh of the two girls pressing into him from either side.

Jonson. Jack hadn't seen him at first, but there he was, just slipping through a door at the far end of the room. Jack tried to pull away from the girls, but their grip was firm. They were steering him in the wrong direction.

'Don't we please you?' the rumpled girl pouted.

'We will please you, golden boy,' said the other, pulling Jack close.

'No,' said Jack. 'I'm not—'

A fly landed on the red-dressed girl's cheek. She blinked and waved it away, relaxing her grip. It was enough: Jack twisted clear and ran. He was vaguely aware of bumping into someone, voices raised behind him – and then he was through the door and into a short corridor.

Doors led off to either side. There was no sign of Jonson.

The corridor ended in a low arch, and the first steps of a winding stairway, leading underground. The boards squealed beneath Jack's feet. He stopped, and listened: from below came a faint grumble of footsteps, descending. Was that Jonson? If Jack could hear that, then Jonson might hear him.

He followed a few breaths later, going slow, treading on the outer edges where the steps complained less. His hand had begun to itch, deep inside. There was no light. He tried not to think what might be waiting at the bottom.

The stairway seemed to last for ever. It felt to Jack like he was circling down and down into the roots of London. Twice, to the side, he felt passages leading off into blackness, but he ignored them. Always, below, came the sound of footsteps hurrying down, and with every step Jack took, the irritation in his hand got worse. Whatever was waiting at the bottom, this was an itchy spot he was entering.

Finally there was a glimmer of light ahead, and Jack could see his hands in front of him. The light grew brighter as he descended. Jack heard the sound of a door closing. He waited and poked his head round the last corner.

The room was empty. Paintings covered the walls, crowded across the low ceiling, flickering in candlelight. Old, fading paintings of naked men and women, rutting together like beasts.

There was a door in the opposite wall.

Jack went over and tried the door, but it was locked. He put his ear to the wood, and heard nothing.

A draught blew cold on the back of his neck. Jack stared round at the staircase. For a moment he thought he heard more footsteps, very close at hand, and his heart leaped in terror. The draught blew again, then passed away. There were no more footsteps.

It would be easy to make his way back up and out into the night. Easy, and safe – and craven. Jack touched his dagger again, turned to the keyhole and shook out his tools from his sleeve.

He stroked up the innards of the lock. It was no more than a pig-latch – no doubt he could lift it – but if someone was waiting on the other side . . .

Jack unscrewed the Brogger's Cup that formed the base of his tool-roll. The cup was a brass bowl, with a short blunt bud attached to the bottom. Jack placed the bowl against the door, and stuck the bud end in his ear.

He heard the soft thunder of blood in his head, a deep scrape as the bowl shifted against the door – and from beyond the door a faint murmur of voices. Voices some way off – but who was to say there wasn't a silent guard right there on the other side of the door?

There was only one way to find out. Nothing else for it, either. Jack pulled out his Swine Gilk, slid it inside the lock with a practised shimmy, and twisted. The lock lifted without a sound.

Slowly Jack nudged the door – one inch, two inches open. He put his eye to the gap.

There was no one guarding the door. Jack was peeking in on a hollow, firelit space, much bigger than he expected. The part he could see was just a fraction of it – a long wall to his left, with a walkway running alongside bordered by a row of crumbling columns on the right. The columns were many times the height of a man. Their shadows were black as ink. The firelight was coming from somewhere beyond, in the part of the room that was hidden by the door. That was where the murmuring voices were coming from too.

Jack gathered up his tools and inched the door open till he could slip through. Moving as quickly as he dared, he crept over to the nearest column and plastered himself behind it.

He waited for the count of five. No one came. An oniony, eye-watering smoke hung thick in the air.

Slowly, trying to ignore the creeping feeling of eyes watching him, Jack peeked round the side of the column.

Looking to his left, Jack saw a long central aisle running the entire length of the space. The columns flanked it to either side, soaring overhead like frozen trees, their tops lost in shadow. A small crowd of people, all of them cloaked and muffled, was gathered at the far end, around a shattered block of marble. Jonson had just joined them, and they were standing talking softly together.

Jack's hand was itching hard now, and his eye throbbed. Through the smoke, the wall behind the people shimmered. Light from a pair of flaming braziers struck sparks from chips of coloured stone, thousands and thousands of them, glittering in the half-light. They made up a patchy, glowing mosaic: a woman, half turned away. She was combing her hair, stretching it out tight in long black tresses. Round the edges were other figures, very crumbled; they might have been more women, or men, or even animals.

As Jack looked at the picture, a strange prickly heat ran through him. Behind its patch his bad eye began to pulse with blooms of lurid pinkish light.

There was something there. Something in the wall. Jack knew it, just like he'd known about the thing at Udolpho's.

The smoky air felt dense and heavy.

A man stepped forward towards the wall. He was dressed in the long cloak and round hat of the Elect; only, where their clothes were black, his was a dull brownish red. In his left hand was a Bible.

The man turned to face his audience. Jack's hand closed on the dagger at his side.

'Welcome, my brothers,' said Nicholas Webb.

Jack could see the smile on Webb's thin lips, but for a moment he couldn't hear him. Angry blood pounded in his skull. Something was buzzing around his head – a fly.

He waved it away. All his fears shrank to a single sharp point.

What are you really, Jack?

Away in the light, Webb was talking quietly:

'. . . long have we waited. Our time is coming. For too long this city has wallowed in sin. The Reckoning is long overdue. But it comes soon, my brothers. In three days our Reckoning arrives.'

Webb cast his eyes down to the ground, as if he was unworthy of the task he spoke of. His voice was so gentle, it was hard for Jack to recognize the man who had crushed the life out of his ma.

'I am not your master in this, I am your *brother* in a holy fight. Together we shall drive the devils from this city and make it new.'

Slowly Webb raised his head and looked his audience in the eye. 'After the Reckoning we will build the city of God on Earth.'

His eyes burned with a pale, fanatical fire. Jack recognized him then. Those pale eyes. The way he'd smiled . . .

The fly landed on Jack's cheek, tickling him. He brushed it away. Webb was stepping up onto the broken block of marble. He raised his right hand. It was covered with a tight black glove. He stretched it out towards the picture on the wall.

A bolt of pain shot through Jack's hand like a pine log

crackling on a fire. He had a sudden urge to run to the foot of the marble block.

Altar, a woman's voice whispered. *My altar, yes, come worship*—

Jack could feel her words tugging at him, making him move.

Come, golden boy, COME to me—

Webb was still speaking, but Jack couldn't concentrate. The other, silent words gripped like a tide, dragging him into the light. Could Jonson feel this? Could the others?

Jack tried to freeze, clinging to the column.

No! Look at me, worship me. LOOK—

Jack's hand snapped into a claw-like fist. It moved slowly upwards, against his will. He watched his fingers coming towards his face. He wanted to stop it, but he couldn't.

His hand lifted the patch from his right eye.

He looked. He couldn't help it.

The picture was alive. The little flecks of stone flowed together, tendrils of colour throbbing through the wall. Jack saw bodies writhe up out of the patterns – a warrior, a smith with his hammer, a man with the body of a stallion. All of them were bowing down to the woman. As Jack watched, she turned towards him.

Her body was like a young girl's, but her eyes were old, dark and old, heavy-lidded, looking straight at him . . .

Golden boy.

This time Jack stepped out from behind his column before he knew what he was doing.

Golden boy. You can save me.

Webb's hand stroked the wall, and a fire blazed forth, brighter than the sun, so bright that Jack was sure it must blind him—

The spell was broken. Jack threw himself back behind the column, pressing his cheek against the cold stone.

No one had seen him.

Gasping, he flicked his patch back into place. He risked a peek round the column. The wall was just a wall. The girl was ragged stone, nothing more.

Except that his hand was still burning, and his eye behind the patch was flooded with blazing light.

Webb had started speaking again.

'For many a long age, a succubus has lain here, a she-devil bound to these ancient stones,' he said. 'She has poisoned this place, and poisoned the minds of men. You saw their shame upstairs. You saw how they worship at her temple.' He pointed to the ceiling, towards the Vixen's Hole.

'Lust for sale; and your soul lost in the bargain. That is how she sucks her power. That is how she feeds. Our Lady Midnight.'

Slowly Webb raised his right hand, and began to peel off his black glove, one finger at a time.

'She will be the next of the ancient ones to be cast out of London. Purged by our faith, my brothers. Purged by the fire of our faith!'

The glove fell to the ground. Webb held his hand aloft. It was red – not the beetroot-red of the preachers, but rusty, like dried blood, and deep, rooted in the veins of the hand. It was a bigger, darker version of Jack's own stain.

On the wall behind him the patterns stirred. Jack's patch was down, but he could still see it. Judging by the gasps, so could Webb's audience.

Webb held his red hand aloft, fingers spread. The chamber filled with a familiar scorching, metallic reek. Jack knew it now: the stench of sorcery.

'This is the sign of my agony.'

In his left hand Webb raised his Bible. 'This is the sign of my faith.'

Jack shook his head. He needed to keep his wits. This was real, Lady Midnight was real, and something big was happening – sorcery, not faith. Sorcery enough to scramble his head. He staggered, clutching at the column.

A cry went up from the audience. On the wall the patterns eddied and crashed together like water in a mill run. The girl appeared again, turning to face the audience, naked for all to see. She was no longer a picture made of stone, but a woman with silken skin and softly curved flesh, a goddess . . .

Worship me.

'Do you mark her?' cried Webb. 'Behold Lady Midnight – Handmaiden of Brid – the girl who drew the moon down in her hair.'

With your body, worship me.

Every man in the room must have heard that silent, silvery voice this time. A shiver went through the crowd, and again someone cried out.

She was beautiful and proud. No man could resist her, and she knew it. She tilted her head to one side and smiled at Webb.

Webb stood firm. 'Would you tempt me, lady? Do you not know me?'

He opened his arms to her. All at once he seemed to stand an inch or two taller; and the girl's smile froze.

You.

'So now you know.' Webb smiled, and pushed his right hand closer to the wall. The hot-metal smell was something solid now – a long flexible blade, sliding up into Jack's brain.

NO, with your BODY you WORSHIP.

Jack felt a hot tingling flush run through him. He blinked tears away. Somewhere, someone sobbed.

'The power of faith is my shield! I name you, Lady Midnight – Ulla, Pearl of the Sea – and by the power of the Holy Gospel, I cast you out! Out! Out!'

Webb pumped his Bible in the air with each shout. At the same time he thrust his right hand against the girl's

Now was the time. Now he must try, or die in the attempt.

He drew his dagger, slowly, silently. A fly settled on his cheek. He brushed it away. The Elect were all gone. Only Webb remained.

Jack crept round the side of the column. Webb was kneeling with his back to him, facing the ruined altar. Chips of coloured stone were scattered on the floor around him.

Jack padded closer. He could feel his pulse jumping in his throat. Where was the best place to stab? He'd heard someone say that a knife in the belly gave a long, slow death; but that would mean reaching round. Better to stab him in the back, at least at first . . .

Webb was close now – three more paces. He knelt perfectly still, head bowed, almost as if he were asleep.

The back. The back first, a good punching blow, then the belly.

Something was crawling over the back of Jack's neck. The same fly, its legs tickling him as it crawled.

Another fly landed on his face. A big fat bluebottle with a swollen body. This time when he brushed at it, it didn't go away.

'You didn't think I hadn't noticed you, boy?' said Webb.

Jack lunged, but Webb was turning and rising to his feet, quick as a lizard; and now Jack's face was covered in flies – climbing in his nostrils, crawling into his eyes and mouth. He scrubbed them away from his eyes, and punched forward with the knife.

'Hah! Quite the little brawler, aren't you?' Webb laughed, dancing back out of reach.

The flies began to bite. A thousand tiny fires went up all over Jack's skin. He opened his mouth to scream, and the flies flowed in, a solid swarming mass. He tried to spit them out, tried to breathe – breathed in flies. He was gagging, choking . . .

'Did you know I've been looking for you? We have unfinished business, you and I. You will tell me many things, before the end.'

Webb stepped forward, raising his hand. Through the buzzing veil of flies Jack saw the brazier to the left side of the altar begin to topple over, very slowly at first and then with gathering speed – and Webb hadn't seen it; Webb was still reaching out for him: it was none of Webb's doing, Jack realized with a last flare of hope.

The brazier crashed to the ground. Burning logs and coals scattered everywhere, showering sparks all over Webb, and suddenly Jack could see quite clearly because the flies were gone. Gone from his throat, gone from his face, their crawling touch gone from his body.

Jack ran. He ran down the aisle, dodged past the columns and wrenched the door open. He stumbled through the room full of paintings and threw himself up the winding stairs. Step after step after step. He didn't feel the weight of his legs, or the burning in his lungs: terror was at his back, and it blotted out everything else.

There was the top of the staircase. And there was the door to the Vixen's Hole. He burst into the crowded room. He heard angry voices behind him, but he carried on running. He was nearly away.

'Where do you think you're going?' The hand came down hard on his shoulder. It was stained red to the wrist. Jack writhed and twisted, trying to escape, but the grip was unshakeable. It stopped him dead in his tracks. He tried to turn.

Chapter 21

The red hand gripped harder, pinching Jack's neck. 'Do as I say. Go up, quickly.'

Jack allowed himself to be hurried up a staircase, out of the crowded main room. Slowly, slyly, he reached for his dagger. His fingers found only an empty scabbard.

'Oh no.' A dry chuckle.

Jack knew he'd heard the voice before, but his thoughts were all tangled up. He'd failed. Webb was still alive.

And now the red-hands were going to kill him.

Jack kicked back with his heel, and missed. The hand squeezed tighter, choking him. The corridor at the top of the stairs was empty. Jack was pushed, still struggling, past five bright-painted doors – red orange yellow green blue.

The man shouldered the blue door open, and threw

Jack inside. Jack stumbled forward – towards a large four-poster bed and an olive-skinned girl in a scrap of blue silk. She looked up, angry, but Jack was already spinning away, twisting, to face the red-hand.

He blinked.

The man striding towards him had a long, foxy face and a mocking half-smile. He was shrugging off his black Elect robe: Jack saw fancy silks and velvets, and a small-sword.

The intelligencer. The man who'd fought Webb.

'What is this boy?' screeched the girl. 'Kit! *Basta!* This is my hour of free.'

'Hush!' said the man.

Jack heard shouts and commotion in the corridor outside.

The intelligencer grabbed Jack by the shoulder. 'Don't lollygag!' He kicked Jack's legs out from under him. 'Hide, damn you!' He gave Jack another kick to bundle him under the bed. With his other hand he dragged the girl to her feet.

'As for you, Cat, my nublet of joy . . .' The intelligencer smothered her protests with a kiss.

There was a thunder of feet outside. Jack shrank back into the shadows under the bed. The intelligencer had folded the girl in his arms, blocking the doorway.

The door banged open and a hatchet-faced preacher stormed in. Others followed, tumbling into the room. Jack saw no flies, apart from an ordinary dead one in the dust under the bed.

There was no way out.

The preacher cleared his throat. The lovers ignored him.

'Excuse me!' The man reached forward.

The intelligencer broke off his kiss with a loud wet smack. ''Sblud, priest! Can't you see I'm occupied?'

'Have you seen a boy? He may have entered this room—'

'A boy? I prefer girls. As you can see.'

'Then you will let us look for ourselves.'

'Hell's teeth, man!' the intelligencer roared. His voice had changed: he sounded very grand all of a sudden. 'Do you know who I am?'

'I do not care who you are. I demand—'

'You demand nothing of Lord Burleigh's natural son! Come between me and my wenching, and I will have your head! Now begone, you jumped-up little God-bothering son of a jackanape!'

The intelligencer returned his complete attention to the girl. The Elect might have been fleas for all the notice he took of them.

He was carrying off his high-gentry act, Jack thought. It helped that he looked gentry, with his long hair, his gold earring and well-trimmed beard. The piratical look, as was the fashion; but he wore the clothes better than most men

248

of fashion – as if he might be an actual pirate. His sleeves and breeches were crusted with tiny pearls, but they fit close. He would have no trouble drawing the sword that hung at his waist. No trouble swinging it, either.

He started to lick the girl's neck. The Elect stood there, ...red-faced. They didn't know where to put their ... retreated outside. The intelligencer ... was ...the wench aside. ...nt to perfection.'

...intelligencer gave a ...bodice.

...was peering at Jack under the bed.

...den at your service. That's twice I've saved you.'

'M'thanks,' Jack muttered. The man *had* saved him, after all. After a fashion. Jack wasn't sure he was out of danger yet.

The man Morely took a handful of tiny seeds from a pouch at his belt, popped them into his mouth, chewed, and spat the juice on the floor. Jack smelled the spicy scent again. The juice was a dark greenish-brown.

'Well?' said Morely.

Jack remembered every bad story he'd heard about intelligencers. You only heard bad stories.

'You're afraid, aren't you?'

Jack said nothing. He needed to think of a way to escape. Morely was fast – he'd seen that when he fought Webb.

'Kit, you like *zimarra*?'

'Brava Carlotta! So quick!' She was holding out a grey silk gown.

'They looking for boy, no?' Carlotta giggled. 'What did 'e do?'

'Some...

one side...

five. Then I le...

'One . . . two . . .

Jack crawled out from

the dress was down over his he

The next moment Morely was stuffing stockings down Jack's bust, and the girl was brandishing something that looked like a dead cat. She rammed it down over Jack's head.

'A fine russet *parrucca*,' said Morely, mulching Jack's breasts into place with both hands, 'is the very thing for your sallow complexion. Don't you agree, Carlotta?'

''E no sallow.' Carlotta leaned in and started dabbing at Jack's lips with a brush. 'Is nice boy.'

'Nearly there,' said Morely, giving Jack's cloth teats a final pat. He tilted his head back and examined the effect. 'A neat little strumpet. But we should do something about this.' He grabbed Jack's right hand and slipped a lacy white glove over it. Jack noticed him look close at the stain as he did so.

Jack yanked his hand away. Morely winked.

'Stay still,' Carlotta hissed. She was still busy, fluffing at Jack's cheekbones with a rabbit's foot. 'You want I make something with this?' She plucked at his eye-patch.

'Don't touch that!' said Jack.

'Leave it, my dear. Best not to know what's under there, eh, Jack?' Morely came forward, and began pulling at the wig. Carlotta was pinning a vixen's tail to the back of the dress. 'We can just tug a few locks . . . down . . . and . . . There!'

The two of them stepped back.

'*Bello*,' said Carlotta as she turned Jack towards the mirror on the wall.

It was a cracked, yellowing old glass, and maybe that helped; but Jack saw a tidy little moll with red lips and pretty pink cheeks staring back at him. The tumbling tress of hair hiding his patch was an advantage, if anything – made him look right wanton.

He turned – left, right. The vixen's tail swayed whenever he moved.

'You are pretty, boy,' said Carlotta.

'As are you, my sweet.' Morely grabbed Carlotta round the waist. 'But we've no time for compliments. Jack, please don't look so worried. It won't answer. Look lewd. Now.'

Morely wrapped his other arm around Jack's shoulders, squeezed Carlotta close, and hustled them out through the door.

Even from up here, Jack could tell that something was amiss. The main room below was in uproar – men shouting, women screaming, objects being smashed.

At the top of the stairs Morely stopped and looked over Jack's disguise one last time. 'Head down,' he said. 'Simper. You're a pair of vixens. Jack?'

Jack nodded.

Morely took a couple of deep breaths, and Jack saw something shift in his face. Carlotta had seen it too: she leaned away from him and frowned.

His eyes were dulled. His cheeks turned blotchy. It was the sort of uncanny trick Beth might pull – but Jack didn't think Beth could ever look so raddled and fouled as Kit Morely did now.

There was a roar and a crash from the room downstairs.

'To battle then, my pretties.' Morely's voice slurred. He stumbled a little as he drew them down the stairs into the madhouse.

At least three different fights were going on in various parts of the room. Broken furniture lay on the floor; half-dressed figures were charging about; in one corner a man lay sprawled against the wall with a woman standing over him, sobbing.

Worse, Jack saw red-hands in amongst the confusion. They were grabbing people, examining faces, shouting questions.

Jack's shoes clattered on the stairs as Morely pulled him along. He didn't want to die in a dress. He tried to take small, mincing steps.

'Steady, Jack,' murmured Morely. Suddenly he began to sing in a quavering voice:

'*Now is the month of Maying,*
When merry lads a-are playing, fa la . . .'

A man was lying unconscious at the bottom of the stairs. They stepped over him. A red-hand strode past, ignoring them.

'*Each with his bonny lass*
Upon the gre-eny grass, fa la.'

A jug smashed into the wall just above their heads,

showering them in wine. Morely took no notice. He kept them weaving towards the door. His song slurred, but his grip around Jack's waist was iron-strong.

'*And to the bagpipe's sound*
The n-nymphs tread out their ground, fa la!'

They were only five steps from the door when Jack saw something that made his blood run cold.

Wrath-of-the-Righteous Jonson was guarding the door, inspecting the faces of everyone who went by. The doorman lay at his feet. His throat was cut.

Jack felt one of his stocking-breasts beginning to sag. His wig was working loose. There was no time to think, no time to waver.

What would Beth do now?

Play it brazen. There was no time for anything else.

'*Stay, dainty nymphs, and speak . . .*'

Morely was still singing. Jack saw Jonson's pinched white face looming closer and closer, like something in a dream.

'*Shall we play at barley-break, fa la?*'

'Stop,' said Jonson, stepping in front of them.

'Oh nnnoshir!' Morely slurred. 'These pretty fillies are mine. I've paid, s'now we're off. Off somewhere a mite more peaceful.' He tried to shove past.

'Wait.' Jonson's gaze slid over Carlotta. Morely shuffled another step towards the door.

Jonson turned to look at Jack.

Brazen.

'Maybe this gentleman wants to come with us, my lord?' Jack giggled, reached out and put his hand on Jonson's leg, high up. 'He's welcome, long as he pays.'

He squeezed.

The preacher's face wrinkled up like he'd just bitten a lemon in half. 'Get out!' he snarled.

They were out into the night. Morely kept up his stumbling, weaving gait till they reached the end of Soper's Lane. They left Carlotta there, but Morely wouldn't let go of Jack's waist. He wouldn't let him take the dress off, either.

Cheapside was empty, and dark. Morely hummed the tune he'd been singing as he pulled Jack along.

'What a bawdy boy you are, Jack. *Come with us*, indeed! You're a true-born trollop!'

Jack could hardly believe they'd escaped. His legs felt like water. Morely's arm round his waist was the only thing holding him up.

All of a sudden, Jack remembered Sharkwell's Second Law. He saw the gaping scar where Meatface's nose should have been. Heard the man's voice: *I was more scared of you, Mr Sharkwell.*

'You better let me go, and you better make sure no one ever knows I talked to you.' Jack had thought he'd spent all his fears down under the Hole, but now here was a new one at his throat. 'Please! If they find out—'

'Let you go?' said Morely. 'I'm afraid there's no question of that.' Jack wriggled, but he was weak and the man's grip was strong. 'What happened to Udolpho, Jack?'

In the darkness, Jack couldn't see Morely's face.

'Are you afraid, Jack?'

'Yes. You let me go free now.'

'I said no. You are far too interesting, and besides, I don't think you're nearly afraid enough. After what you've seen tonight . . . What were you doing down there, Jack?'

'I can't—' Jack began.

'Don't you think Webb will find you, if I let you go free?'

Jack didn't know what to say. Morely was talking sense, so it seemed. That was what intelligencers did, though: everyone knew they spoke fair till they had you well and truly netted, and then . . .

Then what? Could it be any worse than the flies?

'Come with me now. There is a doctor who keeps a house nearby. A very safe house; and perhaps he can help you. It is that, or face Webb on your own. Is that what you want?'

'I can't. I—' Jack stopped.

The familiar itchy feeling was buzzing in his fingers. It crawled all over his hand. He felt a tingling of unseen eyes between his shoulder blades.

He twisted round, looking blindly into the black street. He wondered if he should raise his patch.

'What is it?' asked Morely.

'Nothing,' said Jack, but he was lying.

Something was following. Something was watching from the shadows.

Maybe it was a fly.

Suddenly all Jack wanted was to be out of the dark.

'Where's this house then?' he said.

The doctor's place was not far – Milk Lane, just off Cheapside. They walked fast now, no longer speaking. Jack still felt the eyes on his back, and the itch in his hand. It was a relief when Morely steered him over to the doorway of a large, dark, shuttered-up house.

The door was locked, but Morely had a key. He led Jack through the pitch darkness inside, and Jack thought he must have been here many times before to know his way so well. They arrived in a back room where a little moonlight leaked in through window shutters.

Once Morely had got a candle lit, Jack saw that he was in a library – bookshelves lining two walls, more books and papers on the tables and the floor. One wall was painted black, scribbled all over with chalk.

It was a funny kind of room. Jack felt his fear pressing in again. Morely had locked the front door behind them, and Jack had seen the key. It had more twists and turns in it than any he'd ever heard of.

'Who is he, anyway?' said Jack.

'Who?'

'This doctor.'

'I suppose I can tell you now,' said Morely. 'His name is John Dee.'

'What?' Jack snorted. '*The* John Dee?' That had to be a lie, surely, or Morely's idea of a joke. Dr Dee was the Royal Magician. He had conjured the storm that sank the Spanish Armada. He talked to angels, and did the Queen's horoscope.

'God's truth, lad.' Morely reached into a cupboard and slid out a thin straw pallet. He cleared a space by gently easing aside a pile of books. 'This is for you. As your senior and your better I will take the bed upstairs. *The* John Dee's bed, in fact.'

Morely turned to leave. 'You should rest. He'll have questions come the morning.'

'No more questions,' said Jack. 'You said you'd let me go.'

'I said nothing of the kind,' said Morely, and he was gone before Jack could say any more. A bolt slid shut on the other side of the door.

Jack pulled off the wig and gown and sat down on the pallet. All of a sudden he felt dizzy, and very tired. The silence of the strange house stretched out around him.

He was locked in. He'd started off with his dagger and his stupid plan, and now here he was, prisoner of Morely the Intelligencer – or prisoner of the Queen's Magician, if Morely spoke true. Disarmed, locked in and scared, like a small animal in a trap.

At least he was alive.

Everything was confused, and he was too tired to work it out. The thin layer of straw felt softer than goose-down.

All he could think of was a rhyme his ma used to sing to him when he was little.

Dr Dee commands the sea.
See? The Spanish flee.
Clever Dr Dee!

The rhyme carried on rolling round his head till he drifted down into numb, exhausted sleep.

Chapter 22

The room was silent now. Something had woken him, though. Some noise ... It had only just stopped, Jack was sure. He could almost recall the sound of it, but the memory fell apart like wet paper in his grasp.

He heaved himself up, blinking the sleep out of his eyes. A strange room. Books everywhere. Moonlight streaming in through a lead-paned window. One wall painted black, covered in chalk markings.

It all came tumbling back: he was at Dr Dee's house. And last night – only it was still night, still the same night, and ...

There it was again. A scrabbling, like little claws, coming up the outside of the house.

Jack scrambled to his feet. The window was shut and bolted. There was nothing there, but then the scrabbling came again, and with it the familiar scratchy feeling in his hand. Jack stood still, his heart thudding.

Something scraped against the window. There was nothing there, nothing visible, but he felt sure that if he uncovered his eye he would see . . . what?

A face, looking in at him.

It was Webb. He was here, or he had sent something here. Jack knew he had to act but his arms wouldn't obey him, wouldn't move to lift the patch.

'Crukmuk.'

The voice was inside the room with him. The window was shut and unbroken, but it had got in anyway. It was there on the windowsill.

'Crukmuk ferdamptem wizward!'

The voice was low, but trembling with anger. Jack's fingers were clumsy with panic, but he got the patch up somehow.

'*Gishishishishish!*'

Daubed on the windowsill was a five-pointed star set inside a circle. It gleamed with light. And inside the circle—

'Flankit-it-*iti*! O, O, quetzen ickben *lost* verit-lick . . .'

The creature looked like a very ugly child, perhaps two foot tall. It was dressed in battered plate armour, smeared with mud and blood; dressed down to the waist, that is.

Below the waist, the creature had the shaggy, diseased, stick-thin legs of a street-dog. One of its legs was trapped inside the light.

Jack gulped.

The dog-boy-soldier thing looked up at him. It shook a tiny fist, and swore. Jack didn't understand half the words it spoke.

'Crukmuk spentchild! *Your fault*, this! *Uuurp!*'

The light inside the star was the same flat white light he'd seen at Udolpho's; and it was sucking the creature in. Leg first. The creature was struggling, but as Jack watched, its other leg brushed against the light. The light flowed up it, and gulped it in, and the creature screeched and sank deeper.

It was trapped. Surely Webb wouldn't have sent something like this – except whatever *was* this? Jack tried to speak, and realized his mouth was hanging open like a door off its hinges.

'Uh . . .' he said.

The creature punched itself in the head a couple of times. It was bald in patches, like a mangy cat, and Jack noticed a thin red line like a seam running all the way across its scalp, across its face and on down its throat under the armour. Its skin was ridged and scabbed to either side of the line, as if its entire body had been squashed and pinched together very tightly.

'See me, do you now? Cretin! You unbinding: now see what follows!'

'What . . . ?' said Jack.

'You make unbinding from Master Webb . . . Now you must bind, Master Gape-gob! Bind *now*, before I slither—'

'Wait – wait,' said Jack, with an icy jolt of fear. 'Master Webb? You serve *Webb*?'

'Not more, no . . .' It shook its head again. 'Not wait! Magic boy-master can do it. Bind me. Back into knife, I care not— *Oooh! Oh Zdeck!*'

The light strained and swelled, and another two inches of the creature's dog-legs disappeared into it.

'Please you, magic boy! Bindings! *Graark!*'

Jack saw the creature's agony and fear, plain. Whatever else it was, it was helpless.

'Help, please you!' it begged.

'Right,' said Jack. 'Here. Let me . . .' He leaned over the windowsill, grabbed hold of the creature's arm, and hauled.

'Nononononono!' the creature screeched at him; but Jack could feel it coming loose, dragging free of the light that held it. He was on the point of pulling it out – he thought – when he looked down at the place where its legs met the light.

The legs had been calf-deep. Now they were buried in the light up to their furry haunches. It didn't make sense: Jack had been pulling it out – he'd felt it.

'Spundle-boy! Hell is opposites, wit you nothing? Must *binding*!'

'What's binding?' said Jack. He could feel the panic rising again now. 'Listen, I want to help, but—'

'Ahem,' said a voice from behind him. 'May I ask . . . what is going on here?'

The intelligencer was standing a single pace behind him, holding a candle. The man must move like a weasel: Jack hadn't heard a thing.

Morely leaned over to look at the creature. It froze, scowling up at him with a look of intense suspicion; but Morely seemed to look straight through it.

'There's . . . You can't see it,' said Jack.

'I see a windowsill, and a pentagram,' said Morely. 'A trap of the doctor's, to protect the house from loose devils. As to what *you* see . . . Hm. I note with interest that you have raised your eye-patch, Jack.'

Morely shut his eyes and put his fingers to his temples.

Loose devils, thought Jack. Which meant . . .

'CHI CHI CHI CHI CHI!' said Morely.

'What?' said Jack.

'Ti ti ti ti ti . . .' he said, very softly, tapping his temples in time to the words. 'Poh-poh-poh-poh-*paah* . . . CHI!' He opened his eyes, and looked down at the creature on the windowsill.

'Stone me alive,' he said. 'An imp.'

'Flacktet!' The imp cursed as another portion of its legs disappeared into the light. 'Yes imp, very clever lokmok man! You know bindings?'

'I might . . .' said Morely. He glanced sideways at Jack, then back at the imp. 'If you can explain yourself. What are you doing here?'

'No time . . .' the imp growled.

'Best be quick then, Imp.'

The imp swelled up, as if it was about to explode with rage; then it sank another inch into the light. It made a choking sound.

Morely raised an eyebrow.

'Lokmok!'

The imp started gabbling away in such a rush that Jack couldn't make out the words. Morely seemed to be following it, though.

'So that was you, nearly killed me?' he said when the creature came to a spluttering, squalling stop.

'Yaai!' the imp whimpered.

Morely turned and looked at Jack. He waited.

'What?'

Morely narrowed his eyes. 'You are a strange boy. You can see the thing, but you can't understand it, can you?'

'No,' said Jack. 'What's it saying?'

'You remember Webb's flying knife?'

Jack nodded. He wasn't likely ever to forget it.

'This imp was bound inside it. Spellbound, as you

might say. The imp made it fly, in fact. You really didn't know . . . ?'

'What? So it *is* Webb's servant, then,' said Jack.

'*Was*. You released it. With that strange right hand of yours. And apparently without knowing you were doing so.' Morely spoke softly. 'Ever have the feeling something's been following you, of late?'

'No,' said Jack, looking away.

'Chik-chik-chik! Must *binding*, lokmok!' The imp's eyes rolled up in its head. It slid deeper into the light; it was up to its waist now.

'You're a very bad liar, Jack,' said Morely. 'Every time, you look down and to the left. Never varies.'

The imp screeched a long string of furious, un-intelligible words.

'Apologies,' said Morely. 'The imp points out that it is trapped, and is being dragged back to Hell.' He cocked his head at the flat white light. 'Also that it has saved your miserable life more than once, and you owe it your help.'

'What?'

'Something about a bucket full of fire . . .'

Jack remembered the brazier toppling over, the fire spilling out, sparks shooting up over Webb. At the time he'd hardly wondered about it; he'd been too busy running. He knew that Morely was watching him, trying to read his face.

'There was – there's been something . . .' He didn't know how to talk about it. 'It's true. I think it's telling the truth.'

'It's really up to you.' Morely sprang to his feet and hurried over to the nearest bookshelf. He started rifling through the books, holding them up to the moonlight, tossing them aside one by one. 'The only way we can keep the imp here, in our world, instead of there, in Hell, is by binding it to your service. It claims it belongs to you. Now you must take care of it. That is, if you believe it is telling the truth?'

Jack looked down at the imp. It was clinging with both hands to the edge of the windowsill, pale and sweating. The bright red weal down the centre of its face stood out, and so did the livid, pinched skin on either side. The whole face was distorted – as if it had been crammed into a very narrow, very sharp space.

The imp squeezed its eyes tight shut, then opened one of them a crack. Jack could see a sliver of pupil looking up at him.

'Magic boy . . .'

Jack supposed that meant him. 'What, Imp?'

'Is truth, truth I tell. Servant, I follow to you. Save from Nickless, break arm Black Waterman. But . . . when binding . . . not knife, please? Knife, very pinching. Real body. Arms, legs.'

Very pinching.

The memories fell into place, one by one. The knife going dead in his hands. The brazier tipping over. The block plummeting down to hit Black Pod.

And the imp was in real agony – close to death, or something worse than death.

'All right,' said Jack, 'but—'

He heard Morely take a hissing breath behind him.

'Should have warned you,' said Morely. He was whipping through the pages of a small black-bound book, speaking as he read. 'Demonic bargain: takes effect instantly. Now we have to rouse out a body . . . something with arms and legs, dammit . . .'

'A rat?' Jack suggested.

'Do you have one to hand?'

'Something like . . . a spider?'

'Magnificent,' said Morely. 'A spider, or . . .' His eyes gleamed. 'Yes, I think we can do better than that.'

He raced over to a desk on the far side of the room, and flung open a narrow drawer near the bottom. He returned carrying the entire drawer. 'Look here,' he said. 'Plenty of bodies.'

The drawer was full of beetles, ranging from a tiny lady-bird to a monster the size of a man's fist. Their wing-cases were dusty jewels, green and gold, red and silver and blue.

The imp's eyelids fluttered, and it moaned. The Hell-light was licking up around its belly.

'Don't gape,' said Morely. 'Pick one – quickly now!'

Jack ran his eye along the glittering rows. He alighted on a giant stag-beetle with green wing-cases over a golden body, and bulging eyes that sparkled blue as sapphires. Its jaws stuck out to either side of its face, sharp and jagged. Its horn was like an enormous misplaced nose, sprouting out of its forehead above the eyes. 'That one,' he said.

'Right, set it down here.'

Morely was reading from the book again. The page he'd chosen teemed with dense, cramped handwriting. Near the top was a crude drawing of a five-pointed star with a circle round it. Jack didn't like the look of it – nor the way Morely's eyes were roving greedily across the page, drinking in all those words. It reminded him of Udolpho.

Suddenly he was afraid again. 'What is binding, anyway?' he said.

'You saw what Webb did to poor old Lady Midnight?'

Jack nodded.

'Well, binding is the opposite. Webb *unbound* her from her place, the picture in the wall, in order to cast her back to Hell. We will rescue your imp from Hell by *re*binding it. Specifically, to this beetle here. In return, the imp becomes your servant. A rare chance, boy. Could come in mighty useful in this game we're in . . .'

'And you've . . . done this before?' said Jack.

'Never,' said Morely. 'This is *The Diabolon*, not some common— What?'

Jack tried to master his face, but he knew he was failing.

The Diabolon: the same book that Jonson had sold to Udolpho. The book that had driven the magician mad, got him killed, almost got Jack killed along with him.

'What is it, Jack? What's ailing you?'

'Nothing.'

'You're lying again. You know it's no use, Jack. This won't go away. You're part of it now.'

Jack turned away from Morely's hungry eyes, back to the imp. The light was flowing, seething around its battered breastplate. *Feeding*, Jack thought. The imp's poor ugly face writhed in agony, stretching into unnatural shapes. Like his ma's face after Webb took her.

The imp was there because of Jack. He didn't understand about bindings, or servants, or what Morely wanted, but he understood that much.

He swallowed. His throat felt very dry.

'What do we do?'

First they had to spit in each other's faces three times, and rub in the spittle with a silken cloth. Next, Morely scraped at the insides of the giant beetle with the point of his dagger. He worked fast but carefully, cursing to himself under his breath. When it was done, he mixed the beetle-innards with a handful of green powder.

'Eat it,' said Morely.

'What?'

'Eat it – you heard. Mixed with the squill, you won't taste a thing.'

The squill was bitter, impossibly bitter – even worse than dried beetle-innards – though Jack could taste them too, a musty, earthy sort of taste that made him gag. As he swallowed them down, there was another flare of light from the pentagram. The imp cried out, head thrashing, fists drumming against the windowsill.

'Hellfire,' said Morely. The imp was sunk up to its chest now. 'Quickly, Jack: the Goez must say the words of bidding.'

'What's the Goez?'

'You are, fool! Repeat after me: *Atherouor aoio. Maial-ario aoria iaio.*'

Jack tried his best to imitate the strange sounds. He was sure he got some wrong, but Morely didn't stop. He glanced down at the book, took up his dagger and sliced open his palm. The blood flowed down his hand in a thick dark stream. He ran his finger round the edges of the pentagram, leaving a circular smear. 'Come on, come on!' he muttered.

'Ack! On!' the imp screeched. It was up to its neck in the light now. Its fingernails dug into the windowsill, clutching, splintering the wood.

'Quickly, Jack!' Morely's eyes raced across the page.

'You take the beetle in your hand – your *right* hand, damn you . . . Now turn in a circle, seven times clockwise then thirteen times widdershins, and hiss!'

'Sss . . . sss . . .' Jack began.

'No. Wait—' Morely looked down at the book, frowning. 'It must be one continuous hiss, one breath the whole way. Hurry now!'

Jack turned, and hissed. Seven times clockwise, then thirteen the other way – dizzy and light-headed, running out of breath.

'There!' said Morely. 'Done!'

Jack looked down at the pentagram.

The imp was gone. The light stirred once, and Jack could almost have sworn it bubbled, like a belch; then it went out.

The cold darkness closed in around them. 'Oh,' said Morely. His voice sounded small and sad. He was staring at the book.

'What?' said Jack.

'I am a fool,' said the intelligencer. 'A fool.' He read aloud: '*Seven times clockwise, thirteen widdershins, from the devil's direction . . .*' He buried his head in his hands. When he looked up there was blood all over one side of his face.

'What? What's it mean?'

'From the devil's direction, don't you see? From inside the pentagram looking out! We did it the wrong way round.'

Jack slumped, exhaustion and disappointment settling over him . . .

. . . and a pulse of heat shot through his right hand, following the lines of the powder stain.

'Wait,' he said. 'Mr Morely, wait – I think . . .'

In his palm, something stirred. His eyes were still adjusting to the darkness, so he couldn't see it; but he could feel it – the beetle with a new weight to it now, moving weakly in his palm.

'Imp?' he said. He held it up to catch the moonlight from the window. Its eyes gleamed, and its great horns waved feebly up and down. The beetle seemed to sigh – a dry, scratchy sound.

'Magic boy,' it chirped. One of its forelegs twitched, then it slowly clambered up till it was standing on tiptoe on Jack's hand. It flexed its wings. 'Ah, wings! I thinking you kill lokmok man, give me meat-cloak.' One of its eyes winked out for a second, then reappeared, twinkling. 'Joke! Good intelligencer help, wise lokmok, I kentit! Wings, and—' It stopped, and suddenly its eyes went bright, ten times brighter than before, lighting up the room. 'Reverse bind!'

With a sudden whirr and rattle of wing-cases, the imp took off and flew in a circle around Jack's head. Its entire body was shining now, blinding bright.

'Reverse bind! Reverse bind! Kreefel! Enklessent! Most excellent skifflemoot!'

Morely was staring stupidly at the spinning, chirruping blaze of light.

'What's it talking about?' said Jack.

Morely looked at him, eyes dazed. 'I've absolutely no idea.'

Chapter 23

The imp snored much louder than Beth ever had.

One moment it was circling Jack's head, flashing and babbling; the next it had landed on his hand and fallen into a deep slumber. Its antennae twitched as if it was dreaming, but its shell was dark.

Grey fingers of daylight were creeping around the edges of the shutters. There was no question of Jack sleeping.

'Can I go now, Mr Morely?' he said.

The intelligencer was moving restlessly around the room, chewing at his spice-seeds, spitting in the corners. 'Aye,' he said. 'I've helped you acquire a demonic servant to go with your other uncanny powers. Now of course I'll let you go and wreak still more havoc about town. Why not?' He spat, and laughed. 'And for God's sake call me Kit, boy. After such a night as this . . .'

'All right. Can I go now, *Kit*.'

'No.'

In the pale dimness, Jack squatted down and tried to feel less like a bubble that was about to burst. He couldn't believe that any of this was actually happening. None of it: it felt easier that way.

Intelligencers didn't rescue thieves.

Demons weren't servants.

Beetles didn't talk.

The only thing that felt real was that he was a prisoner, and therefore must escape. He was starting to wonder how he was ever going to explain the whole mess to Sharkwell, when the imp stirred in his hand.

'Krrt! In is coming!' The imp's wings whirred, and it flew up to perch on Jack's shoulder.

Jack heard the front door slam, and a stomping in the corridor. The door crashed open. A man came in backwards, holding a candle and a pipe.

'Hmph!' he said, fiddling with the pipe. 'Damned thing . . .'

His face was gaunt and deathly white, except where broken veins reddened his cheeks and the tip of his long bony nose. His eyes were black pools of fury, hooded in their sockets.

'Light, you! Dammit! Dammit! And blast Nicholas Webb!' The man's beard bristled silver. Jack took a little shuffling step back.

The pipe caught. The man set off pacing around the room, as if he had no time for standing still.

'Hear this, Kit! A sad night's work. Our cause confounded. Our enemy triumphant.'

'Perhaps, Doctor—' Kit began.

'Stuff!' said the man as he pounded past them and began another circuit. The smoke from his pipe pulsed and jagged in time with his steps. His black robes flowed out behind him like storm-clouds. Jack had no doubt that this was Dr Dee himself. *The* Dr Dee.

'A busiest man,' whispered the imp in Jack's ear.

Again, Jack found it helped to think that none of this was happening.

'We are overthrown, and Webb has command of the field.' The doctor accelerated. 'I retreat, dog-whipped, from Hampton. Such hellish impudence. He has the foaming gall to come after me! And prospers with it! The smooth-chopped puppy!'

'I think you might—' Kit tried again.

'Must you blabber, Kit? Can't you see I'm thinking?'

As the doctor sped about the room, he left a comet-tail of pipe-smoke behind him. He walked so fast that the puffs still hung in the air when he came around again. Soon there was a circular trail of smoke to mark his route.

'Another fool-wizard destroyed – *The Diabolon* found charred amongst the wreckage – where do they get it from, I ask you! The news arrived just in time for Webb to ambush me with it in Council. I thought we might count on Robert Cecil, and certainly Essex's party, but last night they would not even hear me out. Me, Kit!'

The smoke puffed particularly thick at that. Kit opened his mouth to speak, then seemed to think better of it. His eyes wandered over to Jack, and his brows twitched, just a fraction.

'. . . then Her Majesty would not admit me after Council. Too busy talking to Webb! I saw him sliding in, the serpent. I was left outside.'

Dee hadn't even noticed Jack yet. This was no act – he really hated Webb. Jack didn't think he'd ever seen anyone look so angry.

'Tcha! Outside, Kit! It has not happened these twenty years and more!'

The doctor came to an abrupt halt in front of Kit. 'Well? And what news from the Hole? Another banishment, or . . . ?' His black eyes flicked over to Jack. 'Who is this . . . girl? Boy? I must say, Kit, even for you, this is playing the bawd a mite high.'

Kit grinned like a cat. 'From the Hole – yes, another banishment. Webb still speaks of his Day of Reckoning. Three days off, now. And the boy is called Jack. He is the cutpurse I told you of – the one whose mother . . .'

'Oh. The one we've been watching, eh?' The magician's gaze returned to Jack, and stayed fixed this time. 'But come, Kit,' he muttered, still staring at Jack. 'Why the rouge?'

Jack had forgotten all about the make-up. The old man seemed embarrassed at the sight of him, and no wonder, him looking like such a peculiar. He wiped furiously at his face.

'A necessary ruse,' answered Kit smoothly. 'He was blundering about the Hole. He is a danger to himself. I trugged him up to save his life, and bring him here to you.'

The doctor leaned in, gnawing on the stem of his pipe. 'Perhaps he is a danger to us. Did you think of that?'

'Oh yes,' said Kit. 'I also thought you'd want to see him.'

'What are you, boy?' said Dee.

Jack felt his deep black eyes boring into him. Suddenly he was afraid. They'd been to dark places, those eyes.

'We fly, or make havoc?' The imp dug its claws into Jack's shoulder.

Dee blinked. 'Kit! Is that my Goliath beetle?'

'Give word, master, and I vengewrack!' The imp growled, and its eyes pulsed silver at the doctor. 'You cruel trapman, nei?' It clacked its jaws together and gathered its legs to spring.

'Halt!' The doctor's hand darted to his neck, where a tight knot of black wire hung from a chain.

Jack felt something stir in the air between them, and the imp quivered and settled back onto his shoulder. 'Snarrkly tripst-magics.'

'Hm.' Dee eyed the beetle. 'I see the imp is bound to his service.'

'Aye,' said Kit, 'and he could see it, with that eye he keeps covered, and—'

'The hand, I can see, yes.'

Jack hid his hand in a fist – too late. They were both looking at him now. A scheming intelligencer, and the Queen's Own Conjuror. They looked like they wanted to eat him up.

'So. Here you are at last. Fresh from the Hole . . .' Dee shook his head. 'And before that, Udolpho's. You take some explaining, boy.'

'Kit said you'd let me go,' said Jack.

'Did I? I don't recall . . . Well, if I did I must have been lying.' Kit smirked. The man had at least seventeen different smiles, and Jack didn't trust a single one of them. 'There's more to you than meets the eye, isn't there, Jack?'

'I never—'

The doctor shook his head. 'Come, boy. You are a magician; you are found at the very heart of dark happenings – I am the Queen's Wizard – you must make divulgence to me. How did you come by that stain on your hand, for instance?' His eyes narrowed, weighing Jack up. 'Did Webb give it you?'

'He never gave me nothing,' said Jack. 'Ask Kit – he knows.'

'Does he now?' The doctor laughed softly. 'Very well then.'

His hand went to the twist of wire at his throat, and he glanced around the room, checking the windows, the door, even the ceiling. Once he'd inspected every corner, he nodded, satisfied.

'Kit? Follow me. We have much to discuss.'

'Wait,' said Jack. 'What about me?'

'This room will hold you, I trust. Think on your situation, boy. I hope to find you more amenable when we return. Come, Kit.'

The two men left the room, bolting the door behind them.

Beth was eating salted radish on the wharf when Meatface came with the summons.

'Himself wants you, miss,' he said. 'You and Poison Jack Patch, in the Dice Room.'

'Poison Jack Patch, is it now?' she said, scowling over her radish.

'There's some calls him that.' Meatface grinned. 'Black Pod's named him the Nigromancer, saying he whistled up a devil to murk up the conjuror.'

'Black Pod's a blathering old wifey,' said Beth.

'Her her her.' Meatface laughed slowly and hideously. A snuffling sound came from the crater of his nose between chuckles. 'There's not many would say that to his face, miss.'

'Not many?' Beth snorted. 'There's only one of me. What's Grampers want, anyway?'

'Not fer me to say,' said Meatface, turning pious.

Beth dabbed the last of the salt, crunched up her radish, and went to find Jack. It was aggravating, having to go trailing after the last person she wanted to see – Jack the Nigromancer, forsooth – but the orders came from her grampers and she must obey.

Half an hour later, she knocked at the Dice Room door, alone and more aggravated than ever. She'd searched the warehouse, the old abbey buildings, the Walnut and the wharf, and asked around: no one had seen Jack since early last night.

She might have known this would happen. Last night was the first of May. *Midnight, first of May, the Vixen's Hole*. She should never have read him that damn parchment.

The Dice Room at the Crooked Walnut had a large window right behind Sharkwell's seat, so that anyone playing against him would have the sun in his eyes. On a fine May morning like this, it made him into a black shape, cut out against the light. He was picking dried snot from his nose with a dagger when Beth entered. The table in front of him was scattered over with ledgers, and different kinds of false dice – High Men and Low Men, Gourds, Fullams, Bristles and Langrets.

'Where's Poison Jack?' he said, as soon as she came in. 'Where's my Blooded Man, girl?'

'Gone,' said Beth.

'Gone?' He laid down his dagger with a clunk.

'Looked everywhere,' said Beth. 'No sign since last night.'

'Ain't that a pity,' Sharkwell sighed. 'I had such a hoyting lay for you two. Such a lay of bawkers and barnacles . . . Gone where, d'you think?'

Beth glanced up at the ceiling as she shaped her answer. A fat bluebottle was turning lazy circles overhead.

She felt a new twinge of annoyance. Jack hadn't taken that parchment by chance: he'd broken the Law of Fish, along with a round dozen others. She should tell out everything – but then that would have to include her own blunder, reading Jack the parchment in the first place. Besides, it felt a lot like crying beef.

'Come on, girl, I can see you've something to say – out with it.'

She cursed silently. Grampers was the only one who could read her face true.

'He . . . when we was at the magician's, he was still poking after Webb. Harping on vengeance. Maybe now he's blooded . . .'

'Oh dear,' said Sharkwell. 'Oh, what a pity. Such plans I had for the two of you, such pretty plans. You're a good girl, Beth, but you've always wanted the killing touch.' He chuckled. 'With Poison Jack Patch at your side – well, but now he's gone . . .'

He cocked his head to one side, looking at her. She wished she could see his face. 'Is that a little smudge of tenderness I see? From my Destroying Angel?' He smacked his gums together. 'Who'd have thought it?'

'Who'd have thought what?' Beth set her face hard. 'I wouldn't piss on that one if he was afire. He was a . . . He was too hot in the head, I always said so.'

'And now he's off on the mad lurch, like to get himself killed. And we both know the Sixth Law, don't we, girl?'

'Course.' He was right: Jack had brought this on himself. Why should she care? 'Let him lurch. We look after our own skins.'

'Good girl. Shame, though . . . Never as much gold off a nipper as I 'ad off of him. Anne's son, he was, no doubt of that.'

He was. Not 'is': was. Beth had a sudden mad urge to go to the Vixen's Hole and see what she could see. Jack might not have been taken; he might have got away . . . Though if he had, surely he'd be back by now.

'He was never one of us,' she heard herself say. 'Too hot in the head to be a thief, a real thief.'

She knew it was true.

It only made her more angry.

* * *

284

For a little while after Beth left, there was silence in the Dice Room, only broken by the senseless bumbling of a fly about the windowpanes. Sharkwell was thinking.

After a while he settled over his main ledger, fingering out the accounts. But now the fly had given up on the window. Every time he tried to make a tally, it buzzed low over his head and settled on the page. It licked its smug little fly legs like a bacon-fed gloaker. It was aggravating. It made him lose count. Each time it landed he swiped at it, and each time he missed.

After this had happened for the sixth time, Sharkwell's face grew murderous smooth. He rose to his feet, pulled off his slipper, and crept sinister towards the fly.

'I'll squash you, my pretty,' he whispered. 'I'll squash you up . . .'

The fly settled against the wall.

'That's it, my pretty . . . Thaa . . . There!' Sharkwell brought the slipper down short, sharp and true. The Darksman's Jab: he'd invented it himself. The same stroke had killed men in the darkest of places – in grime-racked, moon-parched alleys; in sinking ships and burning cities. It had never failed.

Only this time – where there had been one smug fly, there were two.

'Sodomites!' Sharkwell struck again, one-two, quick as murder.

Now there were four flies.

'I'll squish you ... turn you to mess ... swiving ... little— AAACH!'

Sharkwell slashed out with the slipper again and again, and with each stroke he hit true, and with each stroke came more and more flies. The air turned black, and he couldn't see. He was swiping blind, and the black buzzing filled his ears, and he was stumbling, weeping, clutching at his throat.

Something came spinning across the floor to rest at his feet. Suddenly the flies were gone. Sharkwell blinked, tears running down his cheeks.

The thing on the floor was a Blooded Man's blade.

A cold, nerveless voice spoke up from the corner: 'I believe this is yours, Mr Sharkwell.'

Chapter 24

Jack heard the second bolt slide home with a heavy *shunk*.

'Skeezchurl villains!' The imp whirred up, flashing an angry red.

'Shh . . .' Jack pressed his ear to the door and listened. He heard Dee and Kit walk deeper into the house; a door open and close; silence.

He heaved all his weight against the door. Jack reached into his shirt-sleeve for his tools, unrolled them and laid them out.

His hand hovered for a moment, weary, but it wasn't a difficult choice: the Grappling Spoon or nothing. He jimmied it into the crack between the door-frame and the door. He worked the thin metal up to grip the bolt. It was hard getting it into place; and once it was there, the bolt wouldn't shift. The door was perfectly fitted to its frame, and the bolt to its housing. Brute force might have done it. Maybe, if he'd had the Blooded Man's blade – but he'd lost the dagger underground last night.

It really was hopeless.

Jack wondered why he was even trying. He felt dizzy and sick. It was more, he knew, than tiredness.

He slumped back against the unworkable door and looked first at the windows, which were barred with two-inch iron, then at the solid stone flags on the floor.

There was no way out. And even if he could escape, what then? Outside was Webb, and devils, and flies. Outside was Sharkwell, and Beth, and great, swingeing lies to explain where he'd been all this time.

What Jack really wanted was a hole he could crawl into; darkness; a place he could sleep easy. He closed his eyes. He was too tired to cry.

'Ho!' Jack heard a whirring and felt a wind on his face. He didn't open his eyes. 'Ho! Hitzh! Magic boy!'

'What d'you want?'

'Want steely glint vengewracker! Want mad-lad killerboy! Not this sniveller! Tcha!'

Jack didn't say anything. He could hear the imp's wings fizzing about his head.

'I spy-kreep this boy, time and betimes. I being

follower. I spy magic boy with his grisly doings, his sneaky-steal acts. I watch his murder-hunt for Nickless. I want also! I follow!'

Jack looked up. The beetle was spinning six feet above his head, flashing colours and spitting words like a nightmare squib. It sounded furious.

'I never spy magic boy mingeing like a flerkrippelt boggrat! Sniveldrip like mingey-mousy. Snein!'

If Jack had it right – and he wasn't sure that he did – it seemed like the imp was trying to stiffen him up.

'Now! Says word and we make skapings, eh, magic boy? Then killings, vengewrack begins. Now! Now! Your command I await!'

The imp shot down and landed on Jack's wrist. It jumped up and down a couple of times. It pulsed through every colour Jack had ever seen, then several more that he'd never even imagined.

'Huh.' Despite everything, Jack was impressed. He was talking to a magical flying beetle which said it was his servant. Everything else might be goose-pissed to Hell, but a magical servant – Jack found he was smiling at the thought.

He lifted the creature up and turned it this way and that. Seen in daylight, the beetle was even weirder than he'd thought. Rainbows of colour ribboned across the hard shell. Tiny lights glowed deep inside it.

'So you do whatever I say, then?'

'Your command, I make true. Even when hope is croaked. I am servant bound.'

'Jump, then,' said Jack.

The beetle did a little hop.

'What's your name?'

'Apexdrumcorporal Arcathonn Tufrac Anael-kra Calzas Baraborat Mecktic – *Eie Eia* – of the Sixth Circle, Wegrizkov sigil, Awkwardest Legion, Grand Duchy of Samaz.' The beetle drew itself up and tossed its horn in a jaunty fashion. It looked to Jack like a military salute.

'I think I'll just call you Imp.'

'The wise choice, magic boy.'

Magic boy. 'My name's Jack.'

'Dumbnix! I-ware namings, magic boy.'

'And you're a devil,' said Jack. 'You're from – Hell.'

'Hell – is word. Devil is word. Devil, imp, nixie, djinn . . . All are words of me. Mattering smattering. No matter. Actions I serve! I fly and bite and fight!'

The imp spun into the air and hovered in front of Jack's face. He squinted at its jaws: they looked murderous sharp.

'Right.' Jack got to his feet. 'Show me then, Imp: chew us a way out.'

The imp went to work with a will. It flew from window to window, floor to ceiling, wall to door. Just as Jack had commanded, it bit into the wall plaster, the thick door, the wood of the window-frame; it even had a crack at a flagstone.

The plaster crumbled to dust. The wood curled into shavings. The stone screamed and shattered. For a while. But each time, after a while, bright, flinty sparks flew up and the imp was thrown back.

It buzzed all around the room, chittering with frustration. 'Wizward make too much sealing. Ferwitsig hairychin! All in and no out!'

After it had bounced away from the door for the third time, it gave a howl of rage and attacked a large oak bench. This time the end was quick: the imp buzzed through the bench like a demented weevil. In moments the oak was reduced to a few sticks of kindling, then wood-chips, then a pile of sawdust.

'Kraa!' The imp emerged from the wreckage, glowing bright red with rage. 'You viz sealings! See? Wizward truggery! No way through!'

Jack couldn't see any sealings, whatever they were supposed to be – talking to the imp was worse than chatting with Mr Smiles after a few glasses of stingo. He made out two words in every five, and even the part he understood was confusing.

But it was clear they wouldn't be chewing their way out any time soon.

'Can't you do something else?' said Jack. 'Something – I dunno – magic?'

'Magic!' The imp sounded insulted. 'Pif-paf! I reverse-bind now! Go back-forth, place-to-place, anywhere I please! I go into door – door obeys.' It flashed purple, and did a little flourish in mid-air.

'Um . . .' Jack frowned. 'Why didn't you say that before?'

'Ferkruppelt boyfool ask for chew. So: imp chewing.'

It shouldn't be possible, but the beetle was definitely shrugging.

'Stupid, but I enacts. Am bound to follow command – even if stinkdrop.'

'Right.' Jack scowled, and pinched his nose in frustration. They'd wasted so much time. 'Next time, Imp, I order you to tell me if I'm giving you a stupid command, or if you can think of a better way. Now do your magic. Get us out.'

'Endly you say right! Clever I think not, magic boyfool. And so.'

The imp flew across to the door and settled on it. It crawled around, running its feelers over the wood. Eventually it found a place it liked, and crouched down. Its shell pulsed a low, dull blue.

'What are you doing?' said Jack.

'Hsst. Work uneasy, need shushub.'

The glow on the imp's shell gradually faded, until there was only a faint, winking light deep inside it. Then that went out as well. The imp's body clattered to the floor, unmoving.

'Imp?'

Jack bent and picked up the beetle. All the light had gone out of it, except for its original sheen: it looked just like it had in the drawer, before they'd bound the imp into it. Beautiful, shiny – and dead.

'Imp!' Jack hissed. 'Wake up!'

No response. Jack began to curse himself. It was his fault – he'd given the imp some impossible command; he'd killed it . . .

And then he froze, listening.

Very faintly, on the other side of the door, he heard the whisper of bolts sliding back. First the top one, then the bottom.

'Imp?'

The voice that answered was old and creaky, and it seemed to be coming from inside the door itself.

'Puuush . . .'

Jack pushed the door. It swung open without a sound. He snatched up his tools and sneaked his head out.

The corridor beyond was empty.

'Hoooold . . . on . . .'

Jack jumped. The imp was talking to him again, talking from inside the door. However that worked.

'Hold . . . shell to . . . woodgrain. Now. Quick . . .'

Jack touched the beetle's body against the door. He felt a fizzing in his fingertips, and his weird eye twitched.

The door gave a soft sigh. Ever so slowly, like stars

293

coming out at night, lights began twinkling deep within the shell – first one, then another, and then whole constellations, winking in the dark.

'Now. Take me up. No flizzing for now,' breathed the imp. Its legs waggled feebly. 'Tired.'

'Are you hurt?' said Jack.

'Tired only. Breathdrain. You finish make skapings, now.'

'Right,' said Jack. The imp curled up its legs, and the lights faded deep inside its shell till he could barely see them. 'Right, all right, I finish . . .'

Cradling the beetle in his palm, he crept down the hallway. He remembered the twisty front door key from the night before: he hoped the door wasn't locked.

The imp started snoring, softly this time.

The door was locked.

Jack put his eye to the keyhole. The innards were curved and twisted like a nest of half-moons. Jack had never seen anything like it.

There was no time for Feelers or Strokers. Jack rolled out his tools and pulled out a Number Two Figging-wire. He pushed it into the knuckle of the lock and twisted.

The wire slipped, and bent out of shape. When he tried to pull it out, it slid deeper into the workings, then stuck fast.

'Wake up, Imp!' Jack whispered. 'Do it again: reverse-bind it – open the door!'

The beetle didn't stir.

Jack pulled out another wire, but as he did so, footsteps sounded in the corridor.

He turned.

Dr Dee had his head cocked to one side, like a magpie that's caught sight of something shiny. He didn't look angry. He looked curious.

'How the devil did you get out of my library?'

The air was filled with gulls, screaming and squabbling over the enormous, half-butchered carcass of the blubb-cheat. Its blood was spilled across the wharf, and slicked out across the river.

All the Family was here – as fuddle-frowsted a collection of waterpads, broggers, versers and setters as had ever been seen on the Privy Wharf. Stripping the blubb-cheat was a frowsty chore, and most of them had been at it all night. The rest looked fuddled because they'd been sleeping off their May Day revels until just a moment ago. They gagged at the stench, and scratched their heads, and tried to figure why they'd been roused. The Family was only mustered like this for special occasions – hangings and such.

The blubb-cheat had washed up in the estuary on yesterday evening's tide. The lawyers said it was a Fish Royal, and forfeit to the Crown. The waterpads didn't care: they'd ripped it off in the dark before dawn and towed it up the river. And all morning, all hands had hacked away, touting every imaginable kind of tool – pikes, spades, cleavers, axes, and a couple of billhooks dripping with fresh blood.

Most of the blubber had been stripped off now, unwrapped like a giant scarf in yard-wide strips that glistened in the morning light. Standing on top of the carcass, cleaning his nails with a dagger and apparently oblivious to the death-stench that filled the air, was Sharkwell.

'Hear me close now,' he said. 'Ill news. Poison Jack Patch is gone.'

A low mutter went through the crowd. Near the back, Black Pod piped up: 'Good riddance!'

'Stow it, you tufty prat!' Sharkwell scowled. 'There's more to be said. This ain't no ordinary nipper or nudger. This is a Blooded Darksman, what's brought in more gold than the rest of you sorry lot together.'

Another mutter. Again, Black Pod wanted to be heard. 'What of it? If he's taken, he's taken. Sixth Law. Why's the Nigromancer any different?'

Behind Black Pod, right at the back of the crowd, Beth was wondering the same thing. The mutterings were growing louder, and with good reason: the Law was the Law.

'What of it?' said Sharkwell, his voice rising. 'I'll judge what, Black Pod. Are you a clerk, to be quoting Laws to me? Did I say he was taken, either? He might be, sure. If he is, then I want to know it. If he ain't – I want him back. Either way I want to know.'

Sharkwell's gaze roamed across his audience. His bloodiest, scariest gaze. Beth was the only one who saw the glimmer of something else. Something like fear, she thought . . .

But she thought it with only half her wits. The other half was pondering the fact that Sharkwell had changed his mind. It was less than an hour since he'd ordered her to let Jack well alone – and now here he was, mustering the whole Family to go out searching. And that when there was a mountain of stinking whale-fat to cut up and render before it rotted.

It was strange. It didn't reckon up.

Sharkwell never changed his mind.

'What about the blubb-cheat?' someone shouted.

'I'll give you blubber, you speevilling turd-merchant!' Sharkwell's face was white as bone, except for the two livid spots of rage high on his cheeks. 'Forget the pissing whale. It can stay right here mouldering away till its guts grow gardens. I want to be satisfied. I want answers. I want you to find Jack Patch, who he's with, and report back to me – understand?'

The crowd was silent now.

'Do you understand?' said Sharkwell.

There was a low hum of 'Yes, Mr Sharkwell.' But from

where she stood, right at the back, Beth could hear other things – things said too quietly for her grampers to hear.

'Sneaky little nigromancer,' said one of Black Pod's 'prentice waterpads.

'Sharkie's golden goose,' said another. 'I bet he has turned traitor.'

'Surest way is find him, and kill him where he stands,' Black Pod muttered. Those nearest him nodded agreement.

Beth didn't stick around to hear any more. She hurried out into the streets, heading north.

Chapter 25

'I didn't,' said Jack, springing to his feet. 'I mean . . .'

There was no point trying to run. Kit had eased into the corridor behind Dee. The door was locked fast. The imp was asleep.

'I doubt Webb himself could have broken through my sealings.' Dee's eyes gleamed like wet black stones. 'You are an interesting fellow, Jack.'

'I ain't.' Jack didn't like the way Dee was looking at him. 'It was the imp that did it.'

'Your imp.' Dee gave a short laugh. It sounded like two dry walnuts rubbing together. 'Would you come with me, now?'

There was no escaping it. Dee took Jack's arm and steered him into the library. He sat down at the desk, while Kit took up position by the door. They weren't leaving anything to chance.

They weren't offering Jack a seat either, so he stayed standing before the desk. Kit was behind him, watching, and Jack couldn't watch him back. He tried to glare at Dee, but somehow he couldn't face up to those deep black eyes. They made him feel small, and alone, and in the wrong.

He wished the imp would wake up.

'Well,' said Dee, 'we have spoken, Kit and I, and he has convinced me of one thing at least. I do not believe you know how much danger you are in.'

'I told you—'

'Soft, boy!' Dee held up a bony old hand. 'You tried to escape. Do you really think yourself safer outside?'

'I didn't try . . .'

Dee raised his eyebrows. Jack stammered to a halt, his words swallowed up by the old man's silence.

Behind him, Kit chuckled softly. But Jack wasn't watching Kit. He was watching Dee. He couldn't help it: somehow his eyes were held in place.

Dee wasn't laughing. Dee was shaking his head. He looked grave.

'What happened at Udolpho's, Jack?'

The question came up sneakily from behind, from Kit. Jack jumped. It wasn't what he'd been expecting, and it took him a gulp too long to answer. Udolpho again – Kit had asked about him in the street last night too.

'Don't . . . know about that,' he said. Then, as an afterthought, 'Who's Udolpho? Friend of yours?'

'No friend,' said Dee. 'I knew of him, of course – a fool, a weak man . . . and a dead man, Jack.' He left a long pause. 'We know you were there.'

'And the day after he caggs out, damn me if you're not toting a Blooded Man's blade,' said Kit. 'Would you care to explain that, perhaps?'

'No.'

'If you won't, I'm certain the City Recorder would be most interested,' Kit mused. 'Boy magician mixed up in the Horrors, along with his demonic familiar, an imp of Satan no less . . .'

Jack clenched the imp in his fist, and tried to swallow his fear.

'Tell us what happened, Jack.'

'Nothing.'

'We know very well that—'

Then Dee raised a finger, and Kit stopped.

The silence stretched out. Dee watched Jack, not bothering to contradict the lie. Jack wanted to look down at the floor, but his eyes were still held by the doctor's. They were very deep, and very dark, and very old; and as he stood there under their gaze, Jack felt something happening to him.

It was a strange feeling – nothing like the tingling itch he'd got when the imp was scoping him, and nothing at all like the hot, crawly touch of Webb's magic – but Jack was pretty sure it was magic, all the same. He was pretty sure Dee could find out anything about him if he wanted to. His ma used to have a way of looking at him that wasn't so different. She'd only use it when something was important, but when she did there was no way he could lie to her.

'It hurts to remember her, doesn't it?' said Dee. His voice was soft.

Jack gulped, and nodded.

'You . . . swore to avenge her.'

'Yes.'

'And you never harmed Udolpho.'

Dee nodded, and the spell was broken. Jack stumbled against the desk as if he'd been suspended an inch above the floor, and just now been dropped.

'We have common cause, then, you and I. Yes . . .' Dee was still nodding, as if he was listening to a voice that no one else could hear.

'What d'you mean, common cause?' said Jack. He was trying to stay chary, but there was a strange excitement thrumming through him.

'Webb is set against me and all my kind,' said Dee. 'He has hounded friends of mine to death, and would do the same to me if he could. And he is succeeding. With every new Horror, he gains ground.' He gestured past Jack towards Kit. 'That is why I have had to employ this skulking villain.'

Kit snorted.

'And that is why I would dearly love to know the truth behind these Horrors.'

Dee's eyes returned to Jack, but this time there was no spell in them. They looked old, and worried, and tired. 'Kit is right, you know: if you quit this place, you become Webb's prey. You fall under suspicion for Udolpho's murder. You may fall foul of Sharkwell. Are you so sure . . . ?'

'You ought to know the doctor pays handsome,' Kit added. 'If you bring him good intelligence . . .'

'I can protect you,' said Dee. 'If we vanquish Webb, I can indeed pay you handsome. And I can give you what you want.'

'What's that?' said Jack.

'Revenge. Webb's death. A life beyond, free of it.'

Jack thought about that for a long time.

The truth behind these Horrors. And what happened at Udolpho's. Could it be they really didn't know about Jonson selling the books? Jack could help with that. Maybe with other things too.

It would be a treachery to Sharkwell, and to Beth, and to the Family. He'd lose his place. He'd never work in London again. In fact he'd have to quit London: Sharkwell would come after him, after his blood . . .

But what if these men could hurt Webb and he didn't help them do it? That would be breaking his promise, made to his ma on the cold earth of her grave.

He looked up. 'You said you pay handsome . . .'

Dee eased back in his seat. Jack felt something relax in the room – like the tension that breaks with the beginning of a thunderstorm.

'You are with us, then,' the doctor said.

'Maybe. If you can—'

'Pay handsome, yes. I think I can do that. Depending . . .'

'No,' said Jack. 'No depending. I talk to you, I'm marked. Can't work here any more, can't stay in London.'

'I can promise you one hundred pounds,' said Dee. 'Beyond that, we shall see.'

Jack felt like he was falling, falling so fast that his stomach caught in his throat.

One hundred pounds – an incredible amount: he mustn't let it dazzle him. This wasn't payment for a job, or a piece of information. He remembered Sharkwell's Second Law, and Meatface. *I was more scared of you, Mr Sharkwell* . . .

He mustn't sell himself short. 'See what?' he said.

Behind him, he heard Kit spit.

'Shrewd little devil, ain't you?' said the intelligencer.

'Yes, well,' said Dee, and Jack thought he saw the ghost of a smile on the old man's face. 'I seem to recall you driving a hard bargain yourself, Kit.'

'I asked only the intelligencer's due,' said Kit. 'You'd

get nothing less from anyone, doing the job I do.'

'Quite right,' said Dee. 'But now that we have a second intelligencer in our midst . . .' He was looking at Jack now.

'He's no intelligencer,' said Kit quickly. 'Doctor, I—'

'I am so,' said Jack – even though at any other time or place, he'd have agreed with Kit straight away. 'Just as much as you are. You don't have a sniff at the moment, do you?'

Kit scowled.

'I mean, you've been chasing him around, and going to his meetings and all, but you can't prove anything. He's winning . . . Don't mistake, I want you to win, I want to see him die.'

'Of course,' said Kit, rolling his eyes. 'So why don't you help us?'

Jack took a deep breath. He'd made up his mind to this as soon as he started bargaining, or at least that was what he'd told himself; but now the moment was here, and it felt like he was standing in a high place, about to take a dive. Black water below, and he didn't know the depth.

He stepped out into thin air.

'I will,' he said. 'I'll tell you everything I know, and I'll do whatever I can to help. For half.'

Dee chuckled. Kit let out a low whistle of disbelief.

'Half whatever he gets' – Jack tilted his head at Kit – 'and if Webb's to die, I want to be there and see it, I want to be part of it . . . and . . .' His mind raced. There was something more, surely – if he was throwing his lot in with a scurvy intelligencer and a half-crazed wizard, there must be something more. 'Aye, and the doctor to cure my hand and eye, if you can, Doctor, or at least explain what's happened to it, and . . .' He nodded. 'Aye. That's it.'

'Is that all?' said Kit. He sucked his teeth, twisting up his face like he'd just bitten into something bitter.

'That's all.'

'As for your hand, and eye.' Dee's eyes flicked down to Jack's right hand, and roved over its stained and mottled surface. Two spots of colour had appeared, high up on his cheeks. 'That hand is as like to Webb's as two quills. And Webb can do things – aye, well. I'd be a fool not to delve deep . . . And as for your share – you must understand, the intelligencer's due refers to any pickings to be had when Webb is toppled . . .' He was so excited about the hands, he could hardly get his words out in order. 'Kit? I say let's not spoil the stew for want of a penn'orth . . .'

'It's a damned sight more than that, Doctor. Webb has a goodly lot of pennies hidden away, we know that much.' Kit sighed, and shook his head. 'If the intelligence is sound. I don't know, *half*? To a rumpskuttle alley-rat . . .'

'And a thief,' said Jack. Now he was committed, he felt a strange, mad boldness taking him over. 'Don't forget that, if it's stealing you're about.'

'When the man is condemned, we call it confiscation,'

said Kit. 'Of course, we try to do it quiet, without unnecessary . . . procedures.'

'Right,' said Jack, 'so I'll help you get him condemned,
and we can confiscate it, after. Quiet-like.'

'A deal, then?' said Dee.

Kit slouched over from his place by the door, shaking
his head gloomily. 'Aye, a deal, damn it.' He spat on his
palm and held it out to Jack. 'Half and half, though I call
it villainy.'

Jack spat, and shook.

'So.' Dee leaned forward, grinning like a dog over a
steak. 'What happened at Udolpho's, Jack?'

Beth found the Vixen's Hole scattered all over the street.

She'd been here once before, when she was twelve and
starting to shape womanly. She and Smiles had dreamed
up a sweet lay of pretending to sell her as a punk. The
apple-squire who ran the Hole paid Smiles six golden
angels for an intact girl child. Beth stole away the next
morning, still intact, and with twenty more angels hidden
inside her smallclothes.

Beth thought punks were sorry creatures; but she'd had
to grant there was something fine about the Hole. On the
inside, it felt like some great king's palace – not in
England, but somewhere foreign and wicked – so much so
that she'd even wondered if whoring might not be such a
bad life, if you did it somewhere like this.

The place looked different now. All the doors and windows were smashed open, and the insides of the bawdy-house were spilled onto the street like guts from a butchered pig. Punks and their trumpery, mirrors and carpets and cushions, trampled in the mud. Beth was surprised by how cheap it looked. All the magic had left the place.

'Morning,' she said, sidling up to the nearest girl, a dark-haired lass in a red dress. The punk looked round at her and grunted. 'Trouble at the Hole?'

'Trouble?' The punk laughed, short and mirthless. 'More'n that – ain't no more Hole, and ain't no more vixens, what it amounts to.'

'Oh aye?' said Beth. 'What happened?'

'What happened?' The punk rolled her eyes. 'Everything happened. Starting with them prickless preachers – but then, tcha! All our bad luck come at once. We never had no trouble with the rogers befores. Then last night? Two killings – killings – one a girl and one a roger. Watch called in, house broke up – and now where are we to go, I ask you?'

'Preachers were those red-hands, weren't they? Elect, as they call 'emselves.'

The punk frowned. 'Might be they were,' she said. 'How'd you know that?'

'I know enough,' said Beth. She made a silver shilling appear in her hand, the way Smiles had taught her, and danced it over her fingers.

The punk watched the shilling. Beth watched her eyes as they followed it across her knuckles. She waited till the girl was about to speak, then interrupted, keeping her off-balance. 'Might be there was a boy here last night too. Raggedy-looking boy, but he had gold to spend. Might be you saw him, or someone else did . . .' She flicked the coin high in the air, and made it disappear.

The punk was looking at her now, half scared, half hungry, and Beth knew she'd caught her.

'There was a boy,' said the punk. 'Aye, there was, a pretty golden boy, but he didn't want a sacking – ran off, he did . . .'

'Where?' said Beth.

'I don't know, honest. Couldn't tell you. Nice-looking boy, he was, mistress.'

Mistress. Beth had to laugh at that. She flipped the shilling over. The punk fumbled the coin, bent down to pluck it from the mud.

Jack had come here, and so had the preachers. Nicholas Webb's men. Stupid nipper, lurching after the big fish.

Beth was still angry with Jack, but she didn't want him to swing. She'd known that from the moment her grampers set everyone to searching for him – before, even.

She trotted away from the carnage around the Vixen's Hole, making purposefully for St Paul's. She felt pleased with her morning's work.

The prickless preachers. The red-hands.

It was a start.

Dee asked him to start at the beginning, leaving out no detail no matter how shrimpish it seemed: so Jack told them about the dusty foreign gent at the theatre, and his accident with the pipe, and how Webb had sucked the poison powder down.

He could see that Dee was interested in the powder: his cheeks coloured up, just like they had at the sight of Jack's hand. Maybe he'd ask more about that later, but for now Jack had to press on, because the best of it – the best intelligence, as they called it – was still to come. *The Diabolon* – Dee sat up a little straighter at that – and how it had scrumbled Udolpho's wits, led him on to his destruction . . . the night it had arrived, the night he'd watched the cloaked and hooded stranger deliver it.

'Only it weren't no stranger, 'cos I knew him; when he looked my way I knew him.' Jack paused, and looked at the two men. They were like puppets on a tight string, all knotted up on his words. He held the pause, enjoying it.

Kit was the first to break. 'Well? Tell us and be done, and then we'll see if you merit your half.'

'It was Jonson.'

Silence, for a space. Neither man moved.

'Webb's Jonson?' said Kit. It came out in a strangled sort of whisper.

'Aye, Wrath-of-the-Righteous Bleeding Jonson.'

At first Jack thought the doctor was having a fit. His chair shrieked back across the floor. He came to his feet in a sort of convulsion. His bone-pale face went pink all over.

Jack was about to step forward and take the old man's arm, when he realized he was laughing. It started as a rumbling roar deep in his belly, ran through a stage of hacking coughs, and ended as a wheezing, high-pitched giggle. The doctor finished bent double, completely overcome.

'Lord above!' he gasped. 'The shameless— Oh, Jack. I was hoping you might help us. But this! This . . .'

'He's diabolical,' said Kit. 'Webb – let me straighten this – he spreads the Horrors himself, and then offers himself as the saviour . . .' He looked wildly over at Dee. 'Why, but the man's a marvel! A prodigy! We knew he was a villain, but this – this is so . . . so ripe!'

'Aye, and ripe to fall, Kit—'

Dee stopped suddenly, and the colour drained from his face. 'But of course we shall need proof. The word of a thief – pardon, Jack – and unsupported? No.'

'But – if you tell them . . .'

'Oh no, Jack, no – in my position?' Dee snorted. 'Webb has the Council, Webb has the Queen's ear. No. You did not think that giving me this one piece of intelligence would resolve all, did you?'

Jack was silent. Actually, that was exactly what he'd thought, even if he hadn't realized it before.

'No, no,' said Dee. 'The dice are all a-spin, and it is for us to see that they land aright. Jack, you said you want to be part of this?'

'Aye,' he said.

'Good!' Dee sprang to his feet, and began pacing the floor in a tight circle. 'Three days till the Reckoning. We will need . . . Kit! What will we need?'

'The books,' said Kit. 'Find where they're kept, and then we need to put Webb in the same place.' He thought for a moment. 'Trail Jonson.'

'Right,' said Dee. 'That's for you and Jack, then. And I shall begin fulfilling my side, Jack.' He stopped his pacing, right in front of Jack. 'This *foreign gent* of yours . . . Yes, I think I shall begin there. Kit, find the boy some clothes. You must begin your search immediately.'

Chapter 26

K it was still picking bits of their hasty breakfast out of his teeth as they set out from Milk Street.

'What d'ye think,' he said as they jostled their way into the crowds. 'How much does Sharkwell care about stray nippers? Will he trouble to search for you . . .?'

A fly buzzed through the air in front of them.

'Because I know Webb will be looking. Webb, Sharkwell, you, me . . . One can never tell who's hunting who, in these affairs . . .' Kit sounded quite cheerful about the idea.

Jack felt queasy. There was a thick, plaguey heat to the morning, and flies were creeping in the gutters, clambering over the dung-cruft, buzzing in packs through the air. He'd never noticed how many flies there were in London.

It didn't help that he was walking down Cheapside in

broad daylight, dressed in the clownish robes of a lawyer's clerk.

'See anything, Imp?' he said, for the third time.

The imp claimed it would be able to recognize any flies that belonged to Webb. Right now, though, it seemed to have other things on its mind. A low snicker rustled up from its hiding place in the folds of Jack's ruff.

'Lookenzee rump on yind sow-pig, heh heh . . .'

'What's that?' said Jack.

'Gescrumpft! Wobbling, jobbling, jorky porky.'

A large pie-lady swayed by, her tray resting on her belly. The imp chuckled nastily.

'Stop smirking, Jack.' Kit sucked his teeth, and spat. 'Spoils the effect. Try and raise the nose. Lofty does it. You're an articled clerk, snottier than a lord.'

Jack put his head back, thrust his chest out and swaggered. The ruff was too tight and scratched his neck. The hat was too big, and the brim flopped low over his eyes. At least it would hide his patch.

Kit had given himself a proper disguise – a grimy smock and a heavily stained apron. He looked like a tanner's diptom, or a butcher's mate, just one among thousands of lowly Londoners. All primped up in his prating-boy rig, Jack felt much more exposed; but as they walked on, he realized that Kit had made a spry choice. London was rotten with lawyers: no one much cared for the glib-tongued crew, specially when even their boy apprentices held themselves aloof. One glimpse of his robes and people either scowled or looked right through him. Either way, it was the robes and the nose in the air that they saw, not Jack.

Swaggering came a mite easier then – especially with the imp still passing filthy comments on every man, woman and animal that passed. It was a mite easier, but he still felt queasy, and it wasn't just the heat or the clothes, or even the flies. It was the glazing in Kit's eye behind the brave words; the tremble in Dee's fingers when he fumbled with his pipe; that thing he'd said about dice spinning.

Jack had a nose for fear – you had to, growing up in Southwark, the same way an old mariner might have a nose for tempests. He hadn't caught it at first because he'd been too scared himself, but it had been there all along. When he'd told them about Jonson and the books, it went away for a moment. But only for a moment.

The fear. He'd thought he was throwing in with a couple of deadly-sharp gents, big toothy sea-bastards. Maybe they were, at that. Maybe there was always a bigger fish ready to eat you, however big you grew; maybe everyone was afraid.

Dee and Kit certainly were.

Dee and Kit were afraid they were going to fail.

Jack was so distracted that he didn't spot the knappers until it was almost too late.

They were loitering in a doorway, scanning the crowd

– Long Jane and Ram Cat Peprah, two of Sharkwell's finest.

Jack stumbled, turning his face away. Kit took him by the elbow. 'If y' please, young master?' he said. 'It's this way.'

Jack's heart was pounding. He could feel Ram Cat looking him over. He tried to pull up his chin and sneer.

'Insult me,' Kit breathed. 'Do it – now, play the scene.'

Jack curled his lip. 'I know my way, villain,' he said, shaking Kit off. His voice was trembling. He forced himself to speak loud, braying like a real lawyer. 'How dare you put your hand on me!'

'Sorry, master.'

Jack swaggered off into the crowd, with Kit grovelling along beside him. He forced himself not to look back. There was no hand on his shoulder, no dagger at his back.

'Bravely done,' said Kit in a low voice as they turned the corner. 'You make a nice disdainful little clerk. Sharkwell's, weren't they?'

Jack nodded.

Kit ducked into an alley between two houses, pulling Jack in with him. They watched the foot traffic pass for a few moments.

'I think we've shaken them off,' whispered Kit.

Jack shook his head. 'They're master knappers.

They could be watching us right now – we wouldn't know.'

Or just Ram Cat watching, he thought. Ram Cat to stick to them, Long Jane to report back to Sharkwell – that was how they'd play it. *I was more scared of you, Mr Sharkwell.*

'Do you think they saw you?' asked Kit.

Jack shrugged.

'Well, if they've turned this corner they've done it by magic,' said Kit. 'Come on, we don't want to miss the sermon.'

St Paul's was the usual stew, all of London boiling merrily together within the precinct walls. From inside the cathedral came the buzz that gave the building its other name, the Beehive. It was the soft roar of money moving; the whispers of a thousand brokers, scriveners, merchants, usurers – even a priest or two.

In the churchyard the din was even louder. There were beating hammers, cries for drink and meat, a vicious snarling row between a heavily pregnant sow and a stray dog. It was the endless, perpetual shout of the city.

Wrath-of-the-Righteous Jonson's voice carried over them all. He was preaching from Old Pol's Cross again, and he'd drawn the crowds like bees to a rose-bed.

'There's our man,' said Kit.

The preacher's words rang out overhead as they strolled through the crowd. He spoke of the Reckoning that was coming. The city would be cleansed, made anew through the power of the true faith. First, though, there were going to be more Horrors, because some people wouldn't give up their wicked ways until they were forced to.

The crowd lapped it up, especially the details about how the forcing was to be done. Jack and Kit loitered at one of the stalls at the back, pretending to look at the goods on sale – used pewter, blunt knives, a pair of boots looking out of place.

'What happens now?' whispered Jack.

'We stick to him.' Kit's voice was thin as November ice. 'Don't let him out of our sight till he leads us to the books.'

'How do you know he'll do that?'

'Because in three days' time there's the Reckoning, and the books are going to be a part of it. Hear what he's saying now . . .'

Jack listened.

'The abomination will wax fouler before the end, my brothers,' said Jonson. 'Darkest before the morn, aye, and Albion shall weep blood for her deliverance. Only thus shall you know your saviour when He comes!'

'That sounds like they're planning more Horrors, don't you think?' said Kit. 'And more Horrors means more *Diabolons*, we think, and so . . .'

'We stick to him,' said Jack. He felt a tremor of excitement, now that the prey was in sight.

They waited for the sermon to end. Jack was listening

more closely now – Jonson might give something else away without meaning to – but he'd finished up about the Reckoning, and was concentrating on his old devils-and-magicians talk. Old Pol, and Demogorgon and the rest of it. Jack recognized some parts from the last time he'd been here – and before he could help it he was seeing Rob. Rob, plunging through the crowd to his rescue. Rob, dragged away by the sergeants. Rob, hanging from Tyburn Tree.

He wondered what Rob would say if he could see him now, a turncoat dressed up in fancy livery, keeping company with an intelligencer.

'No need to look so sad, boy. You're going up in the world. A demon-servant, a gallant blade for a partner . . .' Kit examined his reflection in a polished plate, twitched up a corner of his moustache.

'We ain't partners,' said Jack.

'No?' Kit pretended to be insulted. 'I save your life – twice . . . you're lurching into half my gains? That makes us partners, no?'

Rob had been his partner. Rob saved his life, and died for it. Kit had saved his life too, but only to serve his own turn. Still, it was Jack's turn too – they were going evens on the cheat, half and half, and they'd spat and shaken . . . What did that make Jack, splitting words with a fancy-spoken, half-gentle villain, stealing through the streets in disguise, rousing up treasons for the Queen's Wizard?

'Not even,' said Jack, but he wasn't as sure as he sounded.

'Phaugh . . .' Kit shook his head. 'You walk a lonely road, Jack.'

'Maybe,' said Jack. 'Maybe not.'

Kit frowned, squinting at the reflection in the plate. 'Jonson's moving on. I'll take this,' he said, pressing a coin into the stall-keeper's hand.

Beth nearly missed them. She'd marked the clerkish livery when the boy arrived, and like a fool she hadn't looked past it. She should have done better; she knew the power a costume held.

Her heart was sinking as the preacher finished his noise. There would be other Elect in the streets, but she'd felt strangely sure of this one – the loudest, best-known of the lot.

Then she saw the movement – the lawyer-boy slipping out into the crowd ahead of the preacher. The boy was with a tradesman, and something about the way they both moved made her pause, then dart forward, skirting round till she could see their faces.

Jack. Different, with his broad-brimmed shappo pulled low, and looking worried and unhappy – but then he always looked worried and unhappy.

The man didn't look like a tradesman – he might fool some but not Beth, and besides, what would Jack be doing with a butcher's mate? No, he was bigger than that. Beth felt a vague dread growing, as she remembered that first time she'd met Jack, and Grampers telling him the Law of Fish.

What had he gone and got himself into?

Too late, she thought to herself as she followed them out of the yard. She'd found him too late.

A mocking, preening gimblet he might have been, but all the same, as the day wore on, Jack realized he could learn some tricks from Kit Morely. The business with the plate was good. Kit called it 'front-boxing'. Jonson was always looking over his shoulder, but by watching him in the reflection they could stay ahead of him. They front-boxed Jonson all over London, staying so close that he didn't utter a word they didn't hear.

The only problem was, he didn't say a single word that was useful.

When the preacher went into the Mercers' Guild, they walked straight in ahead of him without being challenged – and listened to a long bartering session about Investments in Conduits. When the preacher ate his lunch at a stewshop in Newgate Market, Kit sat down next to him, bold as brass. Jonson didn't so much as look his way; but neither did he reveal anything except a taste for bread dumplings. The imp kept watch for spectral flies, demon messengers and the like, but saw nothing.

After the stewshop, they stayed with the preacher out through Newgate, where they passed out of the City beneath the prison walls. The pitch-caulked heads of traitors bared their teeth from the spikes above the gate.

Jonson headed west and north up Holborn Hill. Now the road was less crowded, they had to let him pass and follow at a distance, scurrying in and out of inn yards and gardens.

When they lost sight of him, they didn't worry: Jack and the imp had made a plan.

'Up you go,' said Jack. 'Flash the way, like we said.'

'Up, tup,' said the imp. 'Green for go.' It buzzed into the sky. A small, blinking green light appeared high in the west.

The imp kept up its station overhead. Jack and Kit followed it away from London, out into the country. It looked like a tiny flashing star, very faint; if you weren't looking for it you'd never notice.

Much the same thing could be said of the small, silent figure that had been following them ever since they left St Paul's. At first it looked like a poor but respectable girl on an errand for her mother; then a beggar on the lookout for scraps; and now it was a butcher's boy leading a pig.

Jack wasn't looking for any of those things, and he never noticed.

* * *

They saw the building site from a quarter of a mile away. It was a huge job of work, covering the whole expanse of Red Lion Fields. The air rang with the beating of hammers, the sawing of wood, and the cries of workmen as they put up stands and stalls. It looked like they were building a fairground, or a tourney field. Thick, choking dust filled the air. The sun boiled down. Jack's head was aching.

The imp buzzed back down and landed on his shoulder. 'Screech-mouth, there over.' It prodded Jack around with its gnashers until he saw Jonson, talking to a nervous-looking man with an enormous, much-folded piece of paper.

Jack and Kit had no trouble staying close as the preacher inspected the works. There were hundreds of carpenters on the job, hammering, sawing, hurrying from one task to the next. Jack had shed his robes halfway up Holborn Hill, and both he and Kit were sweaty and frowsted with road dust and bits of hedgerow. No one took any notice of two more grimy wretches.

Whenever Jonson stopped to talk to someone, he asked the same question: 'Will it be ready?'

'It will be ready, brother,' came the answer, the same every time. 'Ready for the Reckoning.'

The preacher spent a long time looking at a raised stage in the middle of the field. He was particularly concerned about the positioning of five smaller platforms set around it, and kept on checking them against something on the foreman's piece of paper. Jack wished he could see what was drawn there, but the man held it too close for him to spy.

Finally Jonson tutted and pointed to one of the platforms. 'That's out by a full cloth yard. The symmetry must be exact, do you understand? All five evenly placed.'

His orders were instantly obeyed, though it meant tearing the structure down and building it afresh.

'Do you mark that, Jack?' murmured Kit as Jonson walked on. He nodded at the wooden frame that rose above the stage – two massive posts, joined in the middle by a heavy cross-brace.

'What?'

'Another Tree is growing.'

Jack saw it then. He'd been too busy looking at the five platforms – there was something there too, he was sure, but it couldn't be as bad as what Kit was pointing out. Because the big thing in the middle wasn't a stage. It was a scaffold – a hanging tree, even bigger than the one at Tyburn.

'You could drop two dozen from there. Neat. All lined up in a row.' Kit pursed his lips.

Jack remembered the magician who had died with Rob. But it didn't make any sense: hanging all the magicians in London wouldn't get rid of any devils.

'So in three days—' Jack began.

'Two now,' said Kit. He sounded tired.

'And what is it? What does it mean, a Reckoning?'

Kit didn't answer. He was still looking at the scaffold.

'What?' Jack insisted.

'You heard Jonson.' Kit spat in the dust. 'Something terrible is going to happen, it will be blamed on magicians – and whoever else Nicholas Webb's taken a dislike to – and then he will have a free hand.'

'Aye, but to do what?'

'Whatever he likes,' said Kit. 'Starting with a bit of ropy-ropy, throaty-necky, choky-deathy . . .' He glanced back up at the scaffold. 'I wouldn't be surprised if one of those spots is reserved for you – aye, and nor am I out of it.' His voice was light, but Jack was watching his face. For the first time since Jack had met him, Kit's face was completely empty of expression.

'*Krrk, krrk!*' The imp flew down and interrupted them. 'Screechyman homewards, and you chit-chatter!'

With the sun sinking behind them, they skulked after Jonson as he made his way back to London. He walked fast, hurrying to make the gate before it shut.

They both felt the fading sun as a curse. A whole day gone, and only two more before – what? Jack still didn't understand about the Reckoning. He wasn't sure he wanted to, either.

Jonson went straight back to Bygott House without stopping or talking to anyone. Jack heard heavy bolts thud into place after the door was closed. The house crouched hunchbacked over Thames Street, crabbed and sinister with age. The windows were small, barred and shuttered. Jack wondered what was inside. Maybe everything – the books, the gold, all Webb's secrets.

'Can you break in there, Imp?'

'Big bindage there.' The imp rattled its wing-case. 'Kohrot-Shuk. Can eat me up krumple-krimp, if insides. Make mens and boys mad also. Maybe possible. But danger very much.'

'What's a . . . Kohrot-Shuk?' asked Jack.

'Devil you would say it,' said the imp. 'Big bad devil.'

Jack nodded. Somehow, it didn't surprise him. He wondered what Bygott House would look like if he lifted his patch.

'So we wait for him here.'

'You can if you like.' Kit shook his head. 'I have other business to attend to. The imp can keep watch. You should return to Milk Street – try to sleep now, while you can. When this begins again, it will move quickly.'

'Where are you going?'

'A personal matter. Our business is done for the day, and done ill, I fear. Go – sleep. Speak to the doctor. Let us hope he has done better.'

'I ain't moving till you tell me what's up.'

Kit chewed, and spat out a mangled spice-seed. 'Very

well then, I wish you good luck.' And he turned and marched off down the hill.

Kit God-save-us Morely, the man who knew it all. He was well ahead now, disappearing round a corner. Jack watched him go.

'Imp, can you keep watch?'

'If Master commands,' said the imp.

'Aye. If Jonson leaves, come fetch me.'

Jack started after Kit. After a few paces he broke into a jog.

Jack soon realized that tailing *with* an intelligencer went down sleeker than soup compared to tailing *after* an intelligencer. Kit employed every foxy trick there was: he made sudden turnings and back-doubles; in Rometown he jumped three fences; by Billingsgate he scuttled into Thatcher's Tavern and left by the back door.

It was blind luck that Jack kept up for as long as he did.

On the approaches to Smart's Quay, Kit stopped to drink at a fountain. Jack ducked behind the corner to hide. When he peered back a moment later, Kit had vanished as surely as if he'd melted into the mud.

Beyond the maze of chandlers, coopers and shipping offices, the masts of a dozen Brittany fly-boats creaked overhead.

Jack slipped away – there was no point blundering in any further. He walked back to the doctor's house wrapped up in silence, still trying to fathom what business Kit might have with French mariners.

He had no idea that he was still being followed.

Peeking round the corner of Milk Street, Beth watched Jack walk up to the house. She thought she'd never seen him look so low as he did now.

She waited until she saw the windows light up inside, then streaked away into the gloaming.

Chapter 27

A raspy smell of burned feathers lingered in the hallway. Through the library door, Jack heard Dee's voice, low and excited. There might have been another voice too, or perhaps more than one – it was hard to say.

Jack knocked. He heard a mewing squeal and a thud from inside.

'Begone!' shouted Dee.

'Begone where?' said Jack.

'Not you!' Another squeal, then a sound of rushing wind. 'Yes – now. Wait, Jack, I'll be some time here . . .'

Jack was hungry: there'd been nothing to eat since breakfast. He scrounged in the larder and found some stale bread and musty dripping. He banked up the kitchen fire, drew his chair in close, and collapsed.

He was worn out. His feet ached. He couldn't

remember how many days it was since he'd last had a proper sleep. He closed his eyes, but it did no good. Sometimes you could be too tired to sleep.

They were no closer to Webb. He'd thought – it was stupid, but deep down he'd hoped that by sacrificing the Laws, and his safety, and his old life, he was purchasing his revenge. After he turned traitor, Kit and the doctor would sort out the rest.

That was the stupidest idea he'd ever had. You paid for things with work and time and trickery, not by hoping someone else would do it all for you.

What was Dee up to in there? Why was Kit visiting Frenchies? The way his face had drained empty as he gazed up at the scaffold – Kit was up to something. Jack wished he knew what it was.

He wondered what Smiles was doing, and Beth. He wondered if he'd ever see them again. He probably never would – not that Beth wanted to see him anyway. She'd said so, plain enough. Jack was surprised by how sad that made him feel.

He watched the fire, and tried not to wonder any more, until the flames and his fears began to bleed into each other, like watered-down paint. When he drifted off to sleep, he had a horrible dream. His ma was in it, trying to tell him something, but he couldn't hear her over the buzzing of the flies.

* * *

'There you are!'

Jack blinked himself awake. The fire had died down to embers. Kit was back, sitting in front of the fire beside him; by the look of him, he'd been sleeping too. It was Dee who had spoken, from over by the kitchen door.

'Well?' he said, looking at their faces. 'No?'

'Jonson . . . wasn't helpful,' said Kit, yawning and stretching. 'No visits to magicians; no visits to Webb; no sign of any cursed books – just . . . a building site.'

'Disappointing,' muttered Dee.

'Worse. They are building a sort of fairground in Red Lion Fields.' Kit got to his feet and stretched again. 'And they're framing up a monstrous great scaffold right in the middle.'

'And whom do they plan to hang, I wonder?' The doctor lit a candle at the fire's embers. Boiling wax dripped on his hand, and he swore. 'Damnation! Where is he now?'

'Bygott House, with the imp standing watch,' said Kit. 'He stirs, we'll know it.'

'Good, good,' said Dee. 'I too have had a day of frustrations . . . though not entirely without interest, no, no . . .' He raised the candle high, and turned from the fire – and Jack was surprised to find that the doctor was looking at him, not Kit. 'Come, Jack,' he said. 'This bears upon you more than any of us.'

Dee led the way to the library. When he opened

the door, Kit and Jack both stopped and stared.

'Don't be afraid!' said the doctor, without glancing back.

'I'm not.' Jack wasn't quite sure if this was true. Even Kit looked spooked.

The room was a wreck. The furniture had been shoved to the corners, there were broken bowls and burned feathers scattered all over the floor, and other things mixed up in them – hazel rods, a silver sword, a ram's-horn trumpet. The only clear space was in the centre of the room: two or three bare flagstones scribbled over with chalk markings, with the scrunched-up corpses of five white mice placed neatly in a circle round the edges.

It was Kit who stepped into the room first. He stopped near the mice, stiffened, and sniffed the air. 'My God, what is that smell?'

The room did smell awful: burned feathers, blood, and something else hot and metallic underneath – just like what Jack had smelled in Udolpho's study. Jack wondered what he would see if he raised his patch.

'It's certainly not your God,' said Dee.

'Aha. Funny. So it was— Wait, let me guess, I love riddles. Not my God, but . . . my . . . dog?'

Dee squinted down his nose at Kit. 'As it happens, the Lesser Scrying-Demon Machiel is known to his friends as the Stinkpup, and one of his three heads is that of a whippet. And I did summon Machiel earlier. Among others.'

'You summoned *devils?*' said Jack, peering into the corners. His hand was itching. 'Are they . . . still here?'

'Oh no,' said Dee.

'But ain't that . . . that's what made the Horrors, ain't it?'

'Not with Dee wielding the chalk,' said the doctor. 'No, no. Summoning is a trifle. A deadly trifle if it goes wrong, sure, and it demands a sacrifice . . .' He waved a hand over the shrunken mouse carcasses.

'Udolpho killed a cat,' Jack remembered.

'That would have called up something a little more . . . toothy,' said Dee. 'For what I was after today, mice suffice.'

'Small fry,' said Kit. 'Nothing to what we did last night, Jack.'

Dee cocked his head to one side. 'As you say, Kit. Petty devils, and usually most willing to help . . . You *can* come in, Jack.'

The candlelight didn't help. Every shadow in the room looked like it was alive. Jack didn't budge.

'My dear boy!' Dee laughed. 'I swear there's no devil here, not now.'

'All right.' Cautiously Jack stepped over the threshold. He picked his way through the debris and sat down on the windowsill, as far from the dead mice as possible.

'Good,' said Dee. 'Here's my frustration: Machiel and his roostmates were not their usual talkative selves. I've been asking and asking—'

'Wait,' said Jack. 'You talk to them?'

'But of course! Why else would I summon them? It is not for their good manners, I can assure you; and I do not require another bound servant at present . . .'

'You just . . . talk to them.'

'That's right. I asked first about the books: sadly, the creatures only gave me hints. Nothing definite – Machiel claimed that the books were held near running water . . .'

'So – anywhere in London then,' said Kit sourly. 'What a great help.'

'Quite.' Dee nodded. 'Unless you know the right question, these interviews with devils are often little more than blather.'

'Oh aye, and you expect me to believe you spent all day blathering?' said Kit. 'What did you hear?'

Dee shook his head. 'Nothing.'

'But . . .' Jack frowned. 'You said . . .'

'*Nothing* can be just as interesting as *something*, Jack.' Dee glanced down at the chaos on the floor. 'Especially when speaking to those, like Machiel, who are usually most happy to talk. I asked about this red powder – and your hand, your eye. I asked and asked, and not one devil would speak of it. More: many of them refused to have any more words with me at all, on any subject. A most unusual silence. Almost as if they were afraid.'

'Afraid of what?' asked Jack.

'Now that is the question.' With the candlelight reflected in his eyes, Dee looked like an old, mad hawk. 'If only we could ask your foreign gent. We know that *some-one* sent the powder. And you say Webb sucked it down like mother's milk—' He stopped short. 'Well, I suppose even the most outlandish stories begin to seem plausible . . .' His voice trailed off, and his long white index finger wandered across the dribbles of candlewax on the table, as if tracing out a map.

'I wonder . . .' Dee looked up at Jack, and the lines shifted in his face. The light in his eyes seemed to recede until they had no surface at all. 'It is strange, how you have stumbled into these matters, Jack. Strange, but perhaps not . . .' He trailed off once more.

Jack wanted to ask him, *Perhaps not what?* And what were *these matters*, and why was it *strange*? But before he could speak, a loud knocking echoed through the house.

Dee's head swung up to face the door. 'Expecting visitors, Kit?'

'No.' Kit was in the library doorway already, hand on his sword-hilt.

'Nor I.' Dee scowled. 'But soft, soft. Let's not greet them with naked steel.'

There was another flurry of loud knocks.

'Be ready now, Kit.' Dee rose to his feet and stalked out into the hall. Kit stepped aside to let him pass, then readied himself, standing against the wall just inside the library. His hand was still on his sword-hilt as Dee opened the front door.

'Good evening, good Sir Magus.'

It was Beth's voice.

'Good – ah – good evening, child.' Dee sounded puzzled but relieved.

Jack wanted to run, or to slam the library door. Either way would mean showing himself. He made a frantic door-shutting gesture at Kit.

Kit shook his head, laid his finger to his lips and eased his sword an inch from its sheath.

'What do you want with me at this hour?' said Dee.

'Well, if it please y'r honour . . . Come now, show yourself to the doctor.' Beth had changed her voice, made it more gentle – not so gentle as her Elizabeth Monfort voice, but still gentler than Beth Sharkwell, the Destroying Angel.

'Stay a moment,' said Dee, 'I am not . . . ah . . . oh.'

'It's me teeth,' said a second voice.

Sharkwell's voice.

Jack wished the floor would open up and swallow him.

'I 'eard you could make 'em grow back new. They 'urt like sodomy.' Sharkwell's voice was louder. Jack could picture him edging his way across the threshold, into the house.

How had they found him?

'Only a moment, Doctor. All we ask is that you look . . .' Beth was inside the hall now.

'Yes, I see, but I am not . . .' Dee sounded flustered. 'No. No! Not in there – I will—'

It was too late. Beth was in the doorway. She looked Jack up and down, taking in his new clothes.

She sniffed. For a single second Jack felt all his terror fold up into pure embarrassment. Then Sharkwell was there, and the terror was back, along with an absurd urge to laugh.

Sharkwell, with his jaw bound up in a dirty off-white handkerchief, tied on his head in a rabbit's-ear knot. Carrying something wrapped in sackcloth. He grinned at Jack and stepped through the door, pushing Beth to one side.

Kit came away from the wall, his sword out and levelled at Sharkwell's throat in a single motion. 'Softly now,' he said. 'Softly, man, and no one bleeds.'

Jack took a step back. He had to hand it to Sharkwell: the man had ice in his veins. A sword-point at his throat, and he hadn't even blinked.

'Well, well, well,' said Sharkwell, still looking at Jack. 'The bleedin' prodigal.' He flapped a hand at Kit's blade. 'Put up the skewer, mate. I ain't here to hurt.'

Kit's eyes darted sideways to Jack, then back to Sharkwell. His sword never wavered.

'See, if I was here to hurt, you'd be hurting.' Sharkwell turned his blue eyes on Kit, twinkling sweet and cheery. 'I've twenty blooded men outside if it comes to that . . . But see how I come, unarmed, with only a tiny little girl for company? Fine gent like you would stain your honour doing me harm, wouldn't you, Kit Morely?'

'I've no more honour than you, Cedric Sharkwell,' said Kit.

'Keep it to Mr, and we'll all be easier . . .' Sharkwell's gummy grin flashed out like a billhook. 'Last man called me Cedric lost his tongue. Now put up the blade, and we can talk, gentle-like.'

'Do it, Kit,' said Dee.

Kit raised his sword so it was pointing at the ceiling instead of Sharkwell's throat.

Sharkwell took another step forward, and now Jack could see Dee standing in the hall. There was a whirring behind him, and Dee was turning, startled – something flashed through the air past Sharkwell's shoulder . . .

The imp swerved. '*Balkutt Yayn!*' it screeched, flashing crimson.

'Holy Mother!' said Sharkwell.

'Stop!' said Jack, at the same instant.

The imp stopped. One moment it was plunging towards Sharkwell's face, the next it was still. Its jaws trembled an inch from Sharkwell's eye.

338

'What swining trick . . . ?' Sharkwell grimaced, edging back.

Beth was frozen, staring at the imp with eyes like wagon-wheels. She opened her mouth to speak, but nothing came out. Jack's fear receded just enough that he could enjoy the spectacle: Beth Sharkwell at a loss for words.

'Come here, Imp,' he said.

The imp perched on his shoulder, glowing a dangerous red. 'No man to hurt Master,' it muttered.

When the imp spoke, Beth gave an audible gulp.

'Where'd you come from?' said Jack. The imp was supposed to be several streets away, watching for Jonson. Not that he was tempted to send it back: if it came to violence, he felt a lot better having it here.

'I feel dangewrack. Perils in Master, all shiverlick. I come. Bound to you, nei?'

Slowly, like a lizard sizing up its next meal, Sharkwell turned his stare on Jack. For someone who claimed not to believe in magic, he seemed very little flustered. Beth was still gaping, all at sea.

'Seems Black Pod was right,' he said. 'Jack the Nigromancer. Damn me if you ain't the darkest darksman ever served this Family. What you doing, talking to a beetle, eh?'

'It is his familiar,' said Dee, coming in from the hall. 'An imp, bound to his service.' He pushed Kit's sword aside, and placed himself in front of Sharkwell. 'Perhaps we ought to sit and talk like friends, at table. Mr – Sharkwell, is it?'

'Aye, and you must be the wizard.' For a moment Sharkwell kept his eye on Jack; then, with a tiny nod that Jack didn't understand, he followed Dee to the table and eased himself into a seat. He laid down his bundle, grinning daggers at the doctor. Jack was amazed how quickly he'd recovered. 'Bound to his service, is it? Just like scrunty Jack here is bound to me, Doctor.'

'What?' Beth shook herself, tore her eyes away from the imp. 'But – he's going about with an intelligencer . . .' She glanced over at Kit with a flash of pure loathing.

Jack felt his ears go hot. If he'd been wondering what she thought of him, now he had an answer – though it didn't help with the much sharper question, the same question Beth was asking: Why hadn't Sharkwell come in heavy, armed and backed up – come in to gut him like a fish?

'Well, my girl,' said Sharkwell, leaning back in his chair. 'But has he turned his back on the Family? Has he betrayed us, broke our Laws? What'll we do with him, eh? Seems to me there's only one man who gets to decide that.'

'But—'

'See, I ain't told you all I know about this here caper of Jackie-boy's.' He looked from face to face – Jack, Kit, Dee and Beth – and clapped his hands together.

'Enlighten us,' said Dee.

'Yes,' said Kit. 'Let us in on the joke.'

'Gold,' said Sharkwell. 'Lots and lots of gold coins with little flies on 'em. Belonging to a certain Mr Nichol-arse Webb.' He flashed Jack a sticky grin. 'I don't blame you for going after it, lad – you're a Blooded Man now, and don't have to come to me for every little thing.'

He nodded to Kit and Dee in turn. 'Don't blame you for working with them as can get the job done, neither. Many a crooked intelligencer's brought profit to the Family before now – ain't that so, Mr Morely?'

Kit nodded. He picked a seed from between his teeth, rolled it onto his tongue and started to chew. 'It's so.'

'So,' said Sharkwell, 'seems to me the only Law you might have broke is the first.' He smacked his lips at Jack. 'You ain't forgotten that, have you, Darksman?'

Jack didn't know what to say. Beth was right: he'd betrayed the Family, known he was doing it at the time, and now he'd been caught. Surely Sharkwell knew that. Surely, surely there could be no forgiveness.

'Hr hr hr,' Sharkwell chuckled. 'All them gold coins you brought in, all with the same mark . . . You didn't think I hadn't twigged, did you, boy? I been watching your Mr Webb for months. Him and his preachers both, their comings and goings, their funny books . . .'

Dee started forward in his seat. 'What do you know about the books?'

'Tickled you there, didn't I?' said Sharkwell. 'Course, I

marked Mr Webb as being far too big a fish to rob blind. I'd have to break him first. Kill off his influence. No small task, for an 'umble thief like me . . .' He gave a slow, crusty wink. 'But not for the Queen's Magician, eh? Aye, Jack was right to come to you.'

'I sense you have a proposition, Mr Sharkwell.' Dee's expression was very still.

Sharkwell stared straight back at him. 'Ain't no proposition. Best be plain, Doctor: this is how it'll be. I'll give you Webb. I'll give you his devil books. You will see that he swings.'

Dee blinked. 'How do you know all this?'

'You doubt me? Did I not sniff out your burrow, and track you down, and that in less than a day? There's not a sparrow farts in this city that I don't know. Still, if it's proof you're wanting' – Sharkwell shook out his bundle; a pile of small black-bound books tumbled out onto the table – 'here it is.'

'*The Diabolon*,' said Dee.

Jack felt his right hand throb, deep and hot. These were devil-books, he was sure.

'But how did you find them?' The doctor frowned. 'How could you possibly . . . ?'

Jack was watching Beth. She'd got her face back – was playing it steady as a mask. Only he saw her nostrils twitch ever so slightly, and the little sideways glance she gave her grampers, just as Dee asked his question.

He would have bet a hundred angels that she didn't know the answer – and a hundred more that she was awful keen to find out.

Beth turned and caught him looking. She flared her eyes at him, in a way that might have been angry or might have been something else. Something he didn't understand. Jack looked away, suddenly ashamed again.

'Never you mind the hows and whys.' Sharkwell tapped the side of his nose with his finger. 'These are straight from Webb's secret store, what I've seen with mine own eyes, and that's all that matters to you. Now – do we have a bargain?'

'What about the gold?' said Kit, frowning.

'Tell him, Jack.' Sharkwell smiled at him, all innocent. 'Tell him about our First Law.'

The silence came down heavy, tautening like a gut string. Sharkwell's smile never wavered. Jack didn't trust it. Dangerous to trust a smile like that, but then what if he turned it down? He imagined the way Beth would look at him, and then he imagined the vengeance Sharkwell would surely take. It didn't bear thinking about.

Besides, if Sharkwell really knew how to see Webb hanged, Jack needed him. Trust didn't come into it.

'Sharkwell . . .' Jack licked his lips. 'Sharkwell gets his shilling.'

'Wise lad.' Sharkwell slapped the table, and beamed.

'We can all be friends, take Webb for all he's got, and split it half and half.'

'Three ways,' said Kit quickly.

'No.' Sharkwell's smile blinked out. 'You're using my people, you play by my Laws. Half for me, the rest you split as you see fit.'

'I don't think so,' began Kit. 'We've—'

'Done,' Dee interrupted. 'We agree to your terms.'

Kit started in astonishment, and glared at him.

'Right then,' said Sharkwell. 'That's a nice tidy piece of business.' He spat on his hand and held it out to Dee.

Dee spat on his own palm, and shook on it.

The rest was planning, and it went by fast. Sharkwell had most of it worked out already.

Webb kept his secret hoard at a little house by the river, out West. The gold was stored in a disused kiln at the bottom of the garden. Webb was sleeping at the house tonight, which would suit their purposes very well. Almost too well – but Jack was keeping his doubts for later. For now, the plan was being made. They could question it afterwards, when Sharkwell was gone.

The timing was the most important part. Kit and Jack would meet the boat at Savoy Steps, at the dark of the moon. The Liberty of the Savoy was a good place to meet, a safe haven from City Law; and the steps were only a short stretch downstream from Webb's house. The robbery would take place an hour before dawn, the gold carried off in one of Sharkwell's boats. In its place, Kit and Jack would leave behind the incriminating books, to be discovered later.

'For you can be sure he'll never go anywhere near 'em otherwise,' said Sharkwell. 'You command the boat party, Beth. See the takings safe back to Privy Wharf. Make sure Jack here don't swive it up with his hot-head ways. Partners once more, hr hr hr.'

Beth looked over at Jack, and nodded. Her face was still set tight.

'Be good to work together again,' said Jack, testing her out.

Her lips might have narrowed by another fraction. She didn't look pleased, that was for sure. She didn't look much of anything.

'How's Smiles?'

'Last I saw, he was searchin' after you.' Beth's voice gave him nothing, either. She looked away.

'Now for your part, Doctor,' said Sharkwell. 'I was thinking dawn, while he's still blinking the crust from his eyes. You hammer down the door with a few lordly witnesses . . . Once they see his store of devil-books, no one's going to listen to any whining about missing gold, are they?'

'No.' Dee grunted. 'A good plan, Mr Sharkwell. If all this plays out as you say, Webb will most assuredly hang.'

'Course he will.' Sharkwell rose to his feet. 'Now, gentles – just remember, now we're on a thieving lay together, who is the King Thief. Who is the King Thief, Jack?'

'You are, Mr Sharkwell.'

'That's right. Come along, Beth.' He stopped at the doorway, and leered back at Jack. 'See you at the wharf, Darksman.'

Chapter 28

Above the city, the full moon was riding clear through the cloud-wrack. Down on Milk Street it cast a narrow strip of light between the overhanging rooftops. The shadows crept near on either side as Beth and Sharkwell made their way towards the river – close and dark and thick, full of questions.

'I don't . . .' Beth broke the silence. 'This lay, with Jack and the wizard – when did you figure it, Grampers? This morning you said—'

'Never mind that,' said Sharkwell. 'I have my ways, Beth. You don't need to know 'em. Or have you forgotten your Laws?'

'No,' said Beth. She'd never forgotten a single one.

Somewhere in the dark of the city, the bells of St Mary-le-Bow tolled eleven.

'You think on stitching your crew together. You mind that.'

Beth jumped at the chance – anything to take her mind off all those jostling questions. She ran through the Family in her head, shuffling them about like a hand of cards. It'd be a wet job, so they'd want a couple of water-pads to handle the boat, a knapper to keep watch, and a miller if it came to violence. A darksman would lie handy for sure too; they always did.

By the time they'd turned onto Thames Street, she thought she had the crew worked out.

'So, Grampers, I was thinking Longfinger, Will Gist, Ram Cat Peprah . . .' Beth noticed something was wrong even as she started speaking. 'Maybe Argent Liz, for milling . . .'

Sharkwell wasn't even listening.

'Grampers?'

'Don't worry at me now, girl,' Sharkwell snapped.

'But what about—?'

His eyes slammed up to meet her, hard as an iron door. 'Script it yourself. Go on, now. You decide.' He stalked onward.

Beth stared after him, astonished. He never let her plan tricky lays like this by herself. It was the Fifth Law. It was his gizzard-deep way.

They didn't say another word till they slunk out onto Three Cranes Wharf. The moon was still shining bright,

348

its big round face scattered on the river, slivers of moon wriggling this way and that like crazy sea-snakes.

Sharkwell's boatman was waiting to carry them across, but before they reached his wherry Sharkwell stopped dead, slapping his forehead. 'Ain't I the stubble-tit,' he chuckled. 'Beth, I've more doings still, this side. Muss be getting old.'

Beth couldn't see his face, but she was sure he wasn't smiling – and she'd never known him forget a piece of business in her life.

That clinched it: there was something murky afoot.

'You cross on ahead, girl. Stitch your crew together – and mind you make the meet. Savoy liberty. Dark o' the moon.'

'I'll make it, Grampers,' said Beth.

'Don' I know you always do.' Sharkwell was already piking off into the shadows.

Beth felt the hair on her arms rise up. It was all crooked. She'd known since this morning – that speech he'd given on the wharf – something was awry, and she'd put off acting on it.

That could change.

'You wait here!' she whispered to the boatman.

Beth counted to twenty, then followed her grampers back into the dark.

'And so,' said Kit, as soon as Sharkwell and Beth were

gone, 'are we really putting our trust in Cedric Sharkwell?'

'Do we have a choice?' murmured Dee. He already had *The Diabolon* open, and was rifling through the pages.

Kit laughed, a short humourless bark. 'Even if it's true about the books, he's cutting our profit in half. And can we trust him that far, even?' He was stalking around the room, chewing his lip. 'Jack, speak up! You know his ways.'

'I ain't sure,' said Jack. He was remembering all the times Sharkwell had got his shilling – aye, a shilling for every penny that Jack ever saw. And there was more than that. The way Sharkwell had forgiven him, brought him back on board without so much as a cross word . . .

No, it didn't figure.

'It won't be square,' he said. 'Never is with him.'

'Right then,' said Kit. 'We don't trust him – so: we stick to the first plan. Tell your imp to get back to Bygott House. If we've missed Jonson . . .'

'It will matter not a jot if Sharkwell speaks true,' said Dee, still poring over the book. 'And I don't see how he could have guessed—'

'It is the things we don't see that undo us, Doctor,' said Kit. 'I've played this game before. The first rule is trust no one; the second rule is assume nothing. You're suggesting we do both . . .'

'Assume?' the imp chirruped, flashing a violent lemon yellow. It took off from its place on Jack's shoulder, and turned a couple of cartwheels in the air in front of him.

'No assumpt, magic boy. You command I tell you best actions, nei? Not only wait upon orders?'

'Yes,' said Jack.

'And so. Best plan is: I go now, burrow mecktick into river-house, see if toothman story be true.'

'No, you need to go to Bygott House—' Kit began, before the imp cut him off with a pulse of bright white light and a noise like a gunshot.

'Lokmok not master of me!' it said. 'Magic boy commands. I makes as he say what!'

'You could really find that place Sharkwell was talking about?' said Jack.

'Beside river, back of St Mary Rounceval boneyard. Yes, I find house, kiln, I can look – yes.' The imp gave off a brief golden glow of pleasure. 'All is possible, very quick time.'

'Right,' said Jack. 'Go, then.'

In a flash, the imp was gone.

Kit tried to call after it, but the front door was already banging shut behind it. 'Christ, but that thing's quick,' he said. 'Jack, I thought we agreed.'

'We did,' said Jack. 'That's why I think we should scope it. It's too good to just leave.'

'Aye! It's too good,' said Kit. 'Listen. Three choices. First: Sharkwell's lying and plans to cheat us, and most probably kill us.' He spoke rapidly, rapping his forefinger in the air with each sentence. 'Second: he's telling the truth

351

about the books but plans to cheat us, kill us, as you like
. . . Third: he's completely honest. He knew you were
deceiving him all along, but has decided to forgive you
because . . . he likes your face? His heart has grown fond
with age? Which of those do you find . . . probable?'

Before Jack could answer, Dee bolted to his feet as if
he'd been stung by a dozen bees. 'Lud's Blood!' he cried.
'It ain't your first, Kit!'

He reached across to the windowsill, grabbed his own
copy of *The Diabolon*, and laid it open beside the other.

'Sharkwell's telling the truth about one thing – Kit, do
you see it?' Dee's eyes were wild, his nostrils flaring like a
warhorse about to charge. His hand jabbed first at one
book, then at the other.

Kit was frowning down at the two books. Jack peered
round the side of him, squinting at the densely packed
pages. He saw complicated symbols, twisty shapes twining
around each other, and strange cramped writing that he
couldn't read anyway.

'Do you spy the difference?' said Dee.

Kit was shaking his head. 'One is written, one printed
. . . but I don't see . . .'

'You don't – hah! The things we don't see, Kit . . . Aye,
well said!' Dee was almost singing. 'Oh, this clinches all.
Sharkwell is proven, oh yes . . .' He clasped his hands and
shook them over his head. 'Oho! He will be triple-damned
for this, my lads!'

'Who?' said Kit. 'Sharkwell?'

'Webb! Oh come, Kit: look at the books – then look here.' Dee walked to the centre of the room, where his chalk markings were scribbled on the paving. They were all blurred now. He waved his arm at the markings and looked up at Kit. 'Come – do you not see?'

Kit looked at the markings, then at the books, then back again. Then he smiled a small sour smile.

'Oh,' he said, nodding. 'Oh. Aha. Very foul. I see.'

'I don't,' said Jack.

'Forgive me, Jack – let me be plainer.' Dee bent over, snatched up a piece of chalk and began drawing on the floor. He sketched with big, confident strokes.

'You see, there have always been two kinds of devil, Jack, and one is much more dangerous than the other. That is what Webb and his preachers will never tell you. Take your servant, there . . . Where's he gone to?'

'The river house, remember?' said Kit.

'Of course, of course,' said Dee. 'On your command too, Jack. The imp is bound to your service – he would never harm you. He serves you – just like poor old Lady Midnight. She served quite happily at the Vixen's Hole for more than a thousand years, without causing any Horrors.'

'Served?' Jack remembered the young girl with the ancient eyes – she hadn't looked anything like a servant.

'In her way. Someone, in some dark, forgotten age,

bound her to that place to arouse the appetites' – Dee coughed – 'of men.'

'Aye.' Kit nodded. 'She did that.'

'London is old, Jack,' continued the doctor as his chalk traced a big circle on the ground. 'Men have had commerce with the hidden world for a long, long time. Any old city, over the years, collects its share of . . . spirits, devils, call them what you will. They are the magic in the stones, the ghosts that shape our lives.'

'What, there's others?' said Jack.

'Many others.' Dee peered at him under his brows. 'I suspect your – ah – *accident* may have attuned you to their presence, no? Have you seen things, felt things, around the city?'

'Maybe,' said Jack cautiously. But his mouth was dry as he remembered all the times his hand had prickled or his eye throbbed; as he remembered Old Pol's Stump, and the figure he'd seen. 'How many are there?'

'Lord knows. Far too many for Webb to get rid of. Far too many to count,' said Dee. 'Well, perhaps *you* might . . .' He cocked his head to one side. 'But that will keep. My point is that no matter how lively or potent these bound devils are, they are held by the terms of their binding. They cannot get out; and besides, most of them have been bound for so long that they have forgotten their original nature.'

Dee got to his feet, revealing what he'd been drawing.

Actually he'd been more restoring, filling in the scuffed bits of what was there before – a large circle with a five-pointed star drawn very neatly inside it.

'And mark this well, Jack,' he said. 'Their original nature is savage. And whenever a magician summons a devil from Hell – whether to bind it or merely to consult with it – well, there we have my second kind of devil. Savage, wild, direct from their native heath.'

Dee nudged one of the dead mice with his toe. 'First you need a sacrifice, to summon them here.' Now his foot tapped at the five points where the star met the circle. 'And then you need a pentagram, to keep them caged. Even I, calling little Machiel and his friends . . . I took care to draw my pentagram right. The symmetry must be exact. All five points evenly placed. If a line be broken, a point disturbed, the results are catastrophic.'

'What does that mean?' asked Jack.

'Loose devils. Horror and death, Jack. They are mighty, and they will have blood.'

Again, Dee's foot tapped five times around the circle. 'Now, why don't you have another look at this book that Sharkwell has brought us?'

Jack leaned in over *The Diabolon*. The stain on his hand gave a little twinge.

'Do you see it now?'

It was obvious when you knew how to look, Jack realized. 'The star's wrong,' he said. 'Only four points to it.'

'Four! Four!' Dee snatched up the book and began to turn the pages. Each time he came across the pentagram picture, he stopped and tapped it and shouted out, 'Four!' Finally he came out of his frenzy, and flopped back down in his chair. 'Four every time, you see? These poor fool magicians! They were damned before they even began. I'd wondered, before – why so many accidents? It's a dangerous book, to be sure, but . . .' He shook his head. 'Webb needed Horrors, and he made sure he got them! This book is death to the user.'

So Udolpho had never stood a chance. Jack remembered the spider fingers creeping through the flat white hole in the air, and shivered.

'Yes, all very unpleasant,' said Kit. 'And almost as unpleasant as what will happen to you, Jack, when Sharkwell betrays us. Do you really think—'

'Kit, does that matter?' Dee interrupted. 'This book was made by Webb. Can you doubt it?'

Jack agreed: Sharkwell had never had any truck with books, and specially not magic ones. In fact, as soon as he'd understood the four-pointed star, a queer certainty had come over him. It was just the nasty, tricky way Webb would do business. It had his stink.

'It wasn't Sharkwell did this,' he said. 'It was him, Webb.'

'Aye, that's not what I doubt,' said Kit. 'I doubt Sharkwell.'

'Your caution commends you, Kit,' said Dee, 'but now we are sure of the book, at least—'

'I am sure of nothing,' said Kit. 'Enough: I'm for Bygott House.'

He stalked out into the hall as he spoke, and laid his hand on the front door-handle. He began to open it – and then he was stumbling over backwards as a golden streak of chittering glee shot through the door, through the hall and into the library.

'Hooroosh, hoorare, hooricktish!' crowed the imp. 'All is well. Gold, Nickless Webb, all are there! I see with eyes! Old saltyman speaks homely tomely. I tell you, all is true!'

For a moment the only sound was the whirring of the imp's wings as it hovered in the air in front of Jack. Then Dee sprang to his feet and started tearing through the papers on his desk.

'Phoo! Enough! Now we must act!' he muttered. 'Now it is upon us, now the Reckoning comes in truth!'

He snatched up a piece of paper and looked at Jack, and his eyes were shining like the eyes of a much younger man. 'Time to whistle up our witnesses. Never fear, I still have a few lords up my sleeve . . . Hah! Webb's disgrace will be witnessed by men of unimpeachable breeding and integrity.'

He snatched up his cloak from under the desk, flung it about his shoulders and strode out into the hall. Kit was still sitting where he'd fallen, looking winded. Dee clapped him on the shoulder as he passed. He stopped just outside and looked back in, his smile flashing white in the darkness.

'With God's grace, I'll see you at dawn.'

Chapter 29

Kit clambered slowly to his feet. He went over to the door and eased it shut. Then he came into the library and stood there glowering at the imp.

'Well done, you little devil,' he said.

'You welcomes, lokmok!'

'No,' said Kit. 'What I meant was, well done for putting our heads in the trap. Well done for ramming the hook into my mouth, worm and all.'

The imp's shell turned a frosty blue. 'Lokmok not mean well. Why not say as he means? Is wildering.'

'Aye, it's stupid,' said Jack, who felt a duty to defend his servant. Anyway, the imp had done well. 'What's wrong? We've got exactly what we wanted, thanks to him!'

'Aye, exactly what we wanted. Down to the very last detail.' Kit wrinkled his nose. 'I thought you were sharper than this, Jack.'

'But if the books are there, and Webb's there, then it's going to work, ain't it?'

Kit didn't reply to that – he just let it hang in the air; and already Jack could feel the weakness in what he was saying.

The imp went an offended shade of purple. 'Magic boy doubting me, I spry it!'

'No, not you, Imp,' said Jack. Not the imp. But Kit was right, it was all too perfect. Webb, the gold, the books all lined up. It was too perfect to be trusted.

The trouble was, there was no way Jack could turn it down. Because even if they were putting a hook in their mouth, even if Sharkwell was planning to scrag them, Webb would still hang. Just so long as they planted the books in time.

Kit was staring at the open book on the table and chewing his knuckles. For a minute he didn't say a word. Then he nodded once – a private little nod that Jack didn't like the look of.

'I won't do it,' said Kit, and him saying it made Jack all the more certain. They *had* to do it. He'd do it alone if need be, but it would be better to have Kit along too. In a dark business like this, with treachery on the lurk, an intelligencer at your side was just what you wanted. Even if you didn't quite trust him. *Especially* if you didn't quite trust him.

'How much gold was there, Imp?' asked Jack suddenly.

'Much, much,' said the imp. 'Boxes, stackwise, mayhap one hundred cratings.'

Kit's eyes narrowed at that, and took on a dark inner gleam.

'How big?' said Jack.

In reply, the imp lit up a bright golden colour and zigzagged through the air so fast that it left streaks of light behind it – so fast and close that the streaks joined together to form the outline of a box, one foot long, and half as high.

One hundred boxes like that, filled with gold . . .

Jack looked over at Kit. He was staring at the fading outlines with a hungry look.

He was ripe.

Jack gathered up the bundle of books, turned and walked to the library door. 'Come on.'

'Where?' said Kit. 'Dark of the moon's hours off, and besides, I said—'

'No,' said Jack from the corridor. 'Forget the dark of the moon.'

He flung open the front door, glanced up at the moon, then turned back to Kit. The intelligencer had made it as far as the corridor.

'Where are you going?' asked Kit.

'Puddle Wharf.'

'Why?'

'To steal a boat.'

'But . . . Beth's bringing one,' said Kit. 'Why . . . ? No, enough, this is madness, Sharkwell's playing us false, and—'

'That's why we play *him*,' said Jack. 'We're going to play him false as a langret, and he won't have no chance to betray us.' He checked the moon again. 'But we have to leave now. I'll explain on the way.'

He looked back. Kit was halfway out into the hall.

'It'll mean we take more than half the gold. Much more – like seventy, eighty chests if we want it.'

That did it. Kit was striding towards him, shaking his head. 'Explain, then,' he said. 'And if I don't like it, this is over, finished, faster than *snap*, understand?'

'You'll like it.' Jack grinned, and led the way out into the night. The imp clung to his collar, keeping its shell dark. 'You'll like it just fine, Kit Morely.'

Sharkwell scuttled a fair distance – all the way back up to Thames Street, into an alley by Vintners Hall. Beth couldn't stay too close with the night so moon-bright, but she watched from the shadows across the street as he rapped at a door. A moment later it swung open and Sharkwell ducked inside.

Beth scampered over and put her ear to the wood. She heard faint voices, but nothing clear. Deeper into the alley, she spotted a window. She tiptoed over and stretched herself to her fullest height, putting her eye to the crack between the shutters.

It gave an excellent view.

Inside the house, Sharkwell was talking to two dour-faced coves, all dressed up in long black robes. Beth didn't like their sour, pinchpoke look. Sharkwell was doing all the talking; he looked eager too, grinning like a hound. The others weren't smiling. Beth still couldn't make out what was being said.

The palaver ended suddenly, and then they were heading for the door. Beth shrank back into the darkness of the alley. The door slipped open, flooding the opposite wall with light. She crouched down, holding her breath.

As Sharkwell came out, he turned back to look inside, his face lit up. He ducked his head and gave a little bow. He simpered, like a dog craving a pat. Beth suddenly realized he was scared. Her pulse began to thud hard and fast in her throat.

'Dark of the moon,' said an unseen voice. 'Time enough. You shall have your reward once they are taken.'

Sharkwell held out his hand. The fingers that shook it were dyed red.

Beth only half noticed, because mostly she was watching her grampers' face, watching the relief wash over it. The door slammed shut, and he stood there for a moment, blinking. Then he turned and shuffled off into the street like a broken puppet.

Maybe it was because Beth was so shocked at seeing Sharkwell turn ancient right there before her eyes; maybe it was because she couldn't quite get a grip on her suspicions; whatever it was, she fouled up the tail. They'd barely gone twenty paces down Thames Street before Sharkwell whipped round with a dagger in his hand.

'Who's there?' he snarled – and now he didn't sound old at all.

Beth stepped out into the moonlight. She knew better than to risk a Darksman's Jab in the shadows. 'It's me, Grampers,' she said.

'What's this? Why you dangling after me? I told you—'

'I didn't like it.'

'You didn't like *what?*' Sharkwell's voice was deadly soft, but he'd slipped the dagger back into his belt.

Beth wasn't sure how to answer. She was afraid of what would happen. She took a long, shaky breath. 'Any of it. You . . . hunting Jack down, then letting him free. Changing your mind. Splicing in with the wizard . . . And then with those gentles back there. Who are they?'

'Don't you foul this up, Beth.'

'You going to tell Jack about them?'

She saw the fear crackle in Sharkwell's face. There was no way back now.

'I told you the plan,' he snapped. He turned away, heading for the boat. 'I don't give a rat's arse if you like it.'

'But—'

'Mayhap you're waxing above yourself, girl. You need to come along with me now.'

'No, Grampers.' Beth couldn't believe herself. She'd never spoken up like that to him. No one spoke back to Sharkwell – it was the Law.

He couldn't believe it, either. She watched his back stiffen. Watched him turn round, slowly. Watched his hand twitch for the dagger, draw back an inch.

'Better stash that tongue of yours. Best batten it down, Biscay-fashion. Else I'll—'

'Else you'll what?' Beth spoke with a strange sensation of falling.

'Don't make it hard, girl. You know the Law. Do what I say, as you should.'

'What – or else you'll sell me out?' Beth's mind was filled with tumbling thoughts. She saw her grandfather dandling her on his knee, telling her the Law. Teaching her how the most important Law – the only one that really mattered – was that you never, ever turned on your own.

'Now what could you mean by that?' Sharkwell was walking towards her.

It couldn't have taken Beth more than a heartbeat to speak again, but it seemed much longer. She was still falling, very slowly, like a feather.

'How much they paying you for Jack?'

Sharkwell was breathing hard, watching her close, his

fingers playing on the hilt of his dagger. He wasn't denying it.

And now Beth realized what she'd done. Sharkwell had played them all. He'd played her. Jack was bought and sold – and she had put him on the block.

The fall stopped. Now she was back, and the world was very bright and vivid. The brightness was anger. Pure and righteous rage, like she'd never felt before.

'How *could* you?' she said. 'Of all the false, *craven* . . . How could you do it, Grampers?'

He was smiling. Just another crafty, gummy Sharkwell grin. It made her want to kill him.

'Now, Beth,' he said. 'Easy does it.'

'Easy?' She couldn't kill him, so she punched the wall instead. Crazy pain flared in her knuckles. 'Easy, when you've turned traitor? When you've broke the first Law you ever taught me to bide . . .'

Sharkwell took two quick steps and grabbed her by the wrist.

His grip was like stone. He wasn't smiling now. For the first time in her life, Beth was afraid of him.

'You'd best watch that kind of talk, my girl,' he said. '*Traitor*, and such.'

'You sold Jack out,' said Beth.

Sharkwell shook his head. 'No, Beth. When a darksman spurns the Family and throws in with Queen's men, that is a traitor. That is selling out.'

'He ain't. You said it yourself, back there. He's just getting a job done. He ain't spurning nothing.'

It wasn't the whole truth, and Beth knew it. She didn't care. She couldn't let this happen. She was shocked by how terrible she felt, thinking of him going to his death, betrayed.

Betrayed by her – that's how it would seem to him.

She needed to stop it.

'You can't do it, Grampers,' she said. 'You can't do this to him – it ain't his fault—'

'*Can't?*' Sharkwell spat. 'I told him, first time we ever spoke: cross me and you'll be sorry. He'll be sorry now, delivered up into the 'ands of his ma's killer. I done him like I said I would, fearful bad, Sharkie's justice.' He gave her hand another jerk. 'Who are you to question it?'

'You tricked me too,' said Beth. Her hand was buzzing with pain, but that wasn't what was making the tears start. 'You made me part of it. You made me play him false.'

'So that's it.' Sharkwell grinned. 'Knew you were sweet on him. This ain't like you, Beth. You always had a tight little head on you . . . Well, I've got news. Your little sweetling ain't going to make it. He's done. I done him.

'And you helped.' He gripped tighter. 'And now you'll watch him hang. And you're going to like it, Beth Sharkwell. You're going to like it, and you're going to work it. That's who you are. That's your blood.'

Beth looked her grandfather right in the eyes. It took

all her courage, but she knew what she had to do now. She had to warn Jack. But first she had to get free. And to do that, she had to make a coney out of her grampers, the scaliest man she'd ever known. She had to turn him stupid.

She had to make him angry.

'You don't know who I am,' she said. 'You don't know. I never turned Judas. Nor did Jack. You're the Judas. You're frighted! You broke the Laws!'

'Beth!'

'You sold yourself.' She spoke up loud and clear, packing as much venom into it as she could. 'You won't say how much 'cos you're shamed how cheap it was. You sold yourself easy as a tuppenny trug—'

There. That did it. His face was darkening, twisting, and then—

'Watch your filthy mouth!' Sharkwell slapped her face and wrenched her hand, just as hard as she'd hoped he would.

She screamed. 'Let go, you're hurting me!' She made the blood drain from her face. She made her eyes roll back in her head. She slumped, beginning to fall. If he only believed she was badly hurt . . .

He let go. Beth moved fast, coming out of the fall into a sprint. She heard Sharkwell shout, heard him start running himself – but he could never catch her, and he knew it. His chase only lasted a few paces. Then he was bawling after her, words echoing along the street.

'*Oi!* You *come back* here, Beth Sharkwell! Don't you run from me! I'm your grampers! I'm your Family!'

She was nearly at the crossroads up Garlick Hill.

'Don't you go down there, girl! You turn, you're out! You're dead to me!'

Beth turned the corner, but she could still hear him shouting.

'Dead! You're never coming back! Never! Never! Never . . .'

Beth ran on, and there was quiet. She was alone. She was never going back. She'd lost her Family, she'd betrayed Jack, doubted him and scorned him every chance she got: *You're nothing, you stay that way, you stay out of my sight.* That noise she could hear was her own ragged sobbing.

She pounded through the dark, empty streets. The running helped: little by little, with every step, she remembered who she was.

She wasn't a sniveller – or a gull – or a Judas.

She was Beth Sharkwell, the Destroying Angel.

She had to pull herself together.

Jack should still be at the wizard's. Everything depended on getting there before he left. Then he'd be warned. Then the debt would be paid.

After that . . . She wondered if Jack would realize what she'd done for him. She wondered if she could stay in the city.

369

Probably not.

Never mind afterwards, anyway.

She ran on, fast as she could, breath coming in gasps now.

The moon was a little lower when she panted up Milk Street. She banged on the door and shouted for Jack. She went to the windows, which were dark, and rattled at the shutters. Then she went back to the door and banged again – well past the point when she knew they weren't there.

They were gone. Beth turned her back on the locked-up house and slumped on the step. She gritted her teeth, fighting back the howl that was growing inside her.

This was all her fault. Jack had been right all along, and she'd been too proud to listen. He'd saved her life, and she'd paid him back with scorn and betrayal. She put her head on her knees and started rocking. She hissed every curse she knew, and not one of them helped.

She looked up at the moon. She had never seen it loom so large. So unfriendly, crouched over the rooftops like a demon. Low in the sky . . .

Still a long way from setting, though . . .

Beth sat up straight, and cursed herself one last time for a mewling mizzler.

Stay sharp. Reason it through . . . They were supposed to meet at Savoy Steps, at the dark of the moon. But that was hours away. They'd left – aye – but too early for the meet.

Beth started walking, trying to pace out her thoughts. Where had they gone? Jack was no gull, except when it came to his ma. So: say he'd figured Sharkwell's play . . .

Beth was at the end of her strength, but she started running, because there was only one way to be sure. They'd left early: she clung to that thought. Webb might be expecting them at the dark of the moon – lying in wait – but that was hours away. She could still stop them. Long as Sharkwell didn't get there first . . .

She ran West.

The city slept. The moonlight spread over steeples and palaces, splendid gardens and livery stables, dingy courts and ancient trees. It smattered the river with silver, and smothered the dreaming houses in dim, silky shadows.

The city was still – so far as a city like London is ever still. On the ramparts of the Tower, the sentries paced to and fro. In Alsatia and Savoy, night-fires burned; mayhem and merriment were made. And here and there, in the dark places between, the moonlight picked out flashes of movement – cats on the rooftops, watchmen in the streets, dogs and revellers gone astray; darksmen and broggers and all the creeping creatures of the night.

And on the Thames: a little boat crawling upstream on muffled oars.

And at Fleet Ditch: a slim silent figure slipping through

371

the thief-gate, breaking into a run as soon as it was clear of the wall.

And west of the city, in a house by the river, with a kiln at the bottom of the garden, a horseman reined in his steed and dismounted.

He hurried over to the door and began to knock.

His fist was dyed red, but in the moonlight it looked black.

Chapter 30

'Here we are,' said Kit. He eased the boat in against the steps.

The bank was topped by a low stone wall. Beyond it, Jack could see the dark bulk of the kiln, and looming further back from the river was the house itself. No light showed.

He lifted his patch. The two worlds swam together and cleared. Nothing seemed different.

'Imp,' Jack whispered. 'Fly and check the house. See if Webb's there.'

The imp flew off into the night.

So far everything was going to plan – Jack's plan. It was simple: get in early and steal as much gold as they could carry, then sink it in the river to fish up later. They'd be back at Savoy Steps in good time to link with Beth, and then they'd go through with the other plan – Sharkwell's plan. If Sharkwell planned to rook them, he was welcome. They'd already have the lion's share stashed away. Kit's teeth had flashed white at that part.

Kit liked the plan. He liked it so much that he'd started to add to it, gaining enthusiasm as he went on. The way Kit had it figured, Sharkwell wouldn't move against them till the hanging was safely done. By that time, Kit proposed, they should be on their way to France, along with more gold than they could piss at. He even had a friend, a Breton smuggler, who would spirit them across.

Kit chuckled in the darkness as he conjured visions of sun-kissed wine and dark-eyed beauties. They'd be safe from Sharkwell, free to live like kings for the rest of their days.

It was a beautiful picture. Too beautiful, Jack thought. There was no reason why Sharkwell shouldn't do for him tonight, as soon as Webb was taken. Kit was talking like he'd just had the idea of crossing to France, but Jack had seen him go to Smart's Quay secretly to arrange it. Kit didn't want to share the gold – not with Sharkwell, not with Jack, not with anyone. That was one thing he knew for sure, in this whole mess. That was why he'd spent most of their journey up the river trying to tease out a picture of his own.

He'd failed. It was too hard to think on what would happen after tomorrow. Tomorrow, Webb would be on his way to the gallows; what happened afterwards didn't matter so much, if only that part came out right. If only tonight's work went smooth.

Jack found himself praying, silently and furiously, staring at the moon in the water. Kit kept the boat steady with one oar, and scanned the riverbank. They waited and watched until the imp whirled back and alighted on Jack's shoulder.

'Crubshuck,' it said, with obvious relish. 'I see in window: Webb still dreamy, snorty-snort. Two others in house. Sleeping also. One horse in stables, waking.'

Webb was here. Jack hardly dared breathe. He was teetering on the edge of it now. He could feel the blood pulsing in his throat, each heartbeat like a striking serpent.

'What about the gold?' said Kit.

'Gold still there. Where it go in one night, eh? Kraal!'

'Right, Imp,' said Kit. 'You fly back and keep an eye on Webb, let us know if he wakes.'

The imp made a crackling sound of disapproval. 'No orderings from you, scurvy lokmok,' it said. 'Only boymaster Jack. What is commanding, master?'

'Do it,' said Jack. 'Watch him close. He looks like he's waking, or you see any flies, you come straight to us.'

The imp flew off, its shell dark. Jack lost sight of it before it was over the wall.

Kit sprang up the bank and paused beneath the wall. Jack followed him up, and crouched down beside him.

'The books?' Kit whispered.

'Leave them in the boat?' said Jack. 'Later, when we come back . . .'

Kit nodded, then stiffened, finger to his lips.

Jack heard a scratching sound – then a low clucking.

'Chickens,' said Kit.

Jack lifted his head an inch, and then another, till he could see over the wall: a cobbled yard, filled with long shadows by the lowering moon. Here, in front of Jack, stacked against the wall, was a row of hencoops, ending at the kiln. After that was another low wall, with the grave-yard of St Mary Rounceval beyond. Across the yard was the house where Webb was sleeping. The thought of him right there, sleeping or no, filled Jack with a queasy mix of eagerness and dread. For a shuddering moment he thought he felt a fly crawling up his arm.

Kit glided over the wall and along to the kiln. He cursed softly.

Jack joined him, moving soft so as not to disturb the chickens. 'What?' he whispered.

Kit nodded down at the door. 'No keyhole. Bolted from the inside.' He glared about. 'Must be a way in from the house. We'll have to—'

'Wait,' said Jack. He was looking up at the top of the kiln, at the chimney. 'I reckon . . .'

The chimney looked just about wide enough. The wall itself was villainous, all close-set bricks, neatly mortared, and twenty feet high.

'Shouldn't have sent the imp away,' Kit muttered.

'Can't call out now,' said Jack.

He paced around the kiln. The side facing the river had a sparse coating of ivy and moss – a little weathering, a few places where the mortar had crumbled. Fingers and toes: it wasn't much, but it was possible.

'Want a leg-up?' Kit squatted down on his heels.

Jack wasn't quite happy with his route, but he'd planned all he could of it. He took off his shoes and climbed on. Kit rose, wobbling, clutching Jack's ankles.

The first holds were easy enough. Jack hadn't climbed since his Trials, but he felt his muscles remembering how it was done – quick, no hesitation.

Hold to hold, fast and smooth . . .

He pushed off a little too hard and tore a toenail. The pain made him hiss. His feet had grown soft, wearing shoes all this time. He mustn't stop, though. That was the first thing you learned: you rested at the top, not before.

The blood from his torn nail made his left foot slippery. That didn't really matter for this next bit – he was relying on the ivy alone. He swarmed up it, not giving himself time to think, not giving the ivy time to tear. At the last moment it began to come away from the wall. He scrambled up and wedged his fingers into a crack less than four feet from the top.

He paused for just a moment, panting and sweating.

A long way below him, he heard the chickens clucking

softly in their sleep, and the quiet waves of the river. It would be a proper fall if he dropped now.

Jack's fingers trembled, fatigue setting in.

He reached up, missed, and grabbed again. His arms were shaking, but he forced himself to the next hold – and the next – and then he was hauling himself up over the lip of the roof. His arms felt like jelly. He managed to flop them over the edge of the chimney, and now he could rest.

He breathed out.

Everything was working out perfectly – so why was it that, with each piece that fell into place, he felt more afraid?

His arms were still weak, but Jack reckoned he'd had enough of a rest. Enough pondering too. Beth would call it moping, and the best cure for that was moving. Chimneying didn't use your arms, anyway; it was all in the back and the legs.

The chimney was about the right size – a little narrow maybe, but that was better than too wide. Jack braced his back against one wall, his feet against the other, and began to shuffle his way down.

It was pitch dark inside, and he hadn't descended more than a yard before he realized something was wrong. The chimney was broadening fast. Too fast. He wouldn't stay wedged much longer if it carried on like this – and then his blooded foot slipped on the bricks, and he was falling.

A short fall. Jack landed on something that wasn't

stone; something that flew apart under him with a loud crash. His back hurt, and the breath was knocked out of him, but . . . yes, he could stand, though he almost slipped up again.

He waited, and gradually his eyes adjusted to whatever feeble light was coming in through the chimney.

He could see chests. He'd landed on them: dozens and dozens of them, scattered all over the floor. He kicked the nearest one. Heavy enough to be gold.

There was a faint tap at the door, and he heard Kit whispering. 'Jack? All well in there? I heard a noise.'

'I'm fine,' said Jack. 'Wait, I need to . . .'

He wiped the blood from his foot. He groped his way over to the wall, and felt his way round it till he found the door. There were the hinges. There was the bolt . . .

He eased it open. Kit was in the doorway, black against the moonlight flooding in from outside. He took one look at the scattered boxes, and nodded. Then he heaved up the nearest one, carried it outside and set it down on the ground. 'Behold your future, Jack.'

Kit pried the box open with his dagger and scooped up a handful of coins. He turned to look at Jack, eyes wide with delight. 'A hundred of these little beauties, ha ha! I say we take them all – imagine the look on Sharkwell's face! And imagine all the lovely French things we can buy . . .'

Kit poured the coins back into the box. In the

moonlight, the gold glinted silver. He sprang upright and clapped Jack on the shoulder.

'Better load up,' said Jack. He grinned back at Kit. Now that the intelligencer was changing the plan on the fly, Jack was more sure than ever that the whole thing was false.

'Well, Jack?' said Kit. 'You said it: let's get to work!'

Jack blinked. He'd been gathering wool there. Mustn't let on that he suspected anything. He stooped down and picked up the first box.

Together they set about their task, carrying the boxes to the river one by one. They were too heavy to throw very far, but that didn't matter: the river flowed deep here, right up to the bank. The boxes sank with a quick heavy *splosh*.

They'd disposed of eight boxes and were just lifting the ninth and tenth when Jack heard a crashing sound from the house. Kit froze mid-stoop.

Something skittered over the cobbles. Jack snapped round to look.

It was the imp. Its shell was cracked, and its head looked wrong. It came to a stop on its back in front of Jack, legs waving in the air.

'What . . . ?' said Kit.

'S-s-sorry, m-master,' said the imp.

Jack heard another crash, and the door from the house burst open. Men with torches streamed into the yard.

More appeared in the churchyard, clambering over the wall.

Shock left him cold, empty. Quickly he flipped the imp right-side up with his toe. Then he drew his dagger.

Kit had his sword out. 'The river,' he hissed. Jack started that way – then stopped as more men came clattering into the courtyard; men with swords and staves and crossbows.

One of them levelled his weapon at Kit, and another aimed at Jack. More were crowding into the yard, at least twenty now. Everything came very sharp and clear – the sweaty, grinning faces; Jack's own panting breath; Kit beginning to laugh . . .

Jack found himself staring at the sharp end of a crossbow bolt pointed straight at his heart. The tip was trembling ever so slightly.

'No fight now, Jack. They have us.' Kit let his sword fall to the cobbles. Jack let go of his dagger.

'Here you are, so,' said a voice like slim cold steel. 'Good boy.'

Jack whipped round just as Nicholas Webb stepped out of the house, smiling. He was flanked by two fleshy men, big fish by the looks of their velvet robes, their gold chains of office.

'Search their boat.' Webb clicked his fingers, and immediately two of his torchbearers hurried over to the jetty.

'A pretty piece of theatre.' Kit grinned.

'Ah.' Webb sighed and cleared his throat. 'Come, come, Mr Morely. The truth. That is all I want. You are a notorious heretic. The boy is a witch-child, a consorter with demons. This is your secret sin, and now you have been found out. Do you deny this?'

Kit spat. 'Why waste the breath?'

Webb laughed. Jack felt a surge of hatred at the unfairness of it. 'Perhaps you are right. The evidence speaks . . . most damningly.'

One of the searchers came clambering over the wall from the jetty. He was brandishing a book. 'Found this in the boat, sir. More of 'em in there, my lords,' he said. 'Plenty of 'em!'

Kit chuckled softly.

'Bring it here,' ordered Webb. He took the book, and rifled through it. Jack watched his nostrils flare with false indignation.

'See? See, my lords? Hell's writ clear on every page.' Webb's lords leaned in, greedy for it. 'It is plain. This is the fountain-head, the source of all our troubles.'

The lords nodded at one another – grim, certain nods, like merchants concluding a neat piece of business. 'Certainly, I am satisfied,' said one.

'Their guilt is plain,' said the other, and clapped his hands. 'Bind them!'

Soldiers stepped forward, manacles at the ready. Webb

cleared his throat, and the second lord raised his hand. The soldiers stopped.

'If you will allow me . . .' Webb came towards Jack and Kit, holding his red right hand before him. 'The boy is a witch, and may yet have some Hell-craft about him.'

Jack glanced down at the ground in front of him. The imp was gone. Webb caught him looking, and smiled.

'Escaped, has it?' He spoke in a low voice, so that only Jack and Kit could hear, running his hand softly over Jack's clothes. 'Did you think to escape me too, turning up before your appointed time? Tut tut, boy. Your Mr Sharkwell owes me an explanation . . .'

He finished his search, patting Jack on the head. The tip of his tongue slipped out between his teeth, as if he wanted to taste their fear. Jack glared his hatred straight back at him.

'Such a burning rage.' Webb cocked his head to one side. 'Save it for your friends, Jack. Save it for the ones who betrayed you.' He raised his voice loud enough for everyone to hear. 'The witch is disarmed.'

Betrayed. The word tolled in Jack's head.

Webb stepped away, motioning the guards forward.

The ones who betrayed you. He could barely take it in: Webb, arresting them for his own crime . . . And Jack had thought himself so deep, seeing through Sharkwell, seeing through Kit, making his own plans. Webb was deeper than the lot of them. Kit was his coney, Sharkwell his tool . . .

And Beth . . .

Betrayed.

Jack barely felt the chains. He screwed his eyes tightly shut. Webb's voice sounded very far away.

'The venom is drawn, the viper's-nest laid bare. Now, my lords – now for the Reckoning!'

Chapter 31

Beth was still running. By now, it felt more like flying. There was only the moon on the road and the sleeping houses to either side.

Her legs were bone-deep weary, and each breath tore bloody through her lungs, but she didn't feel a thing. It was very simple. She had to get to the kiln-house. She had to warn Jack.

She wasn't afraid, because if she allowed herself to worry, she might stumble, and then she might never get up. She was nearly at the end of her strength – and if she gave in . . .

You're never coming back. Never. Never. Never.

She'd run all the way through the City. She'd run all the way from the Wall. She'd run all the way down the Strand – past the fine palaces, past the flaming brands and the swill-tub mob at Savoy liberty.

She knew that Jack wasn't waiting there.

Beth wondered if she could just keep running. The fine floaty feeling tingled through her – from her toes to the roots of her hair. If she carried on going she'd never have to feel anything else, ever again.

Up ahead she saw the spire of St Mary Rounceval, and behind it the moon. It had sunk a little more now. Nearly touching the horizon. She still had time.

As she came alongside the church wall she slowed to a trot, then a walk. She bent over and almost retched. Her breath came in strange, savage gasps; and now she felt the agony stabbing up her calves.

She still had time, all might yet be well – only now she heard the sound of marching feet. Soldiers. Never a good sign, that. She just managed to dive into the ditch beside the road before the column of liveried men-at-arms came round the corner, marching at the double.

Three Elect preachers swung along ahead of them, burning torches held high, singing a psalm. Beth's heart stopped dead. Jack was there, ringed in by the soldiers. His hands were manacled, his feet hobbled with rope. The intelligencer stumbled along beside him.

Signs hung around their necks. A single word was painted on each, in red letters: WITCH.

She'd failed him. First she'd scorned him, then she'd betrayed him; then, when she was the only one who could put it right, she'd failed. She wanted to scream. He

shouldn't have been taken, not like this, not yet: the moon
was still up. For a mad moment she thought of hurling herself at the soldiers. She wanted to grab hold of Jack, rip
him free, run away with him.

Beth forced the scream down, deep down inside. She
waited till the column had passed, then crept after them
up the Strand.

As they came up on the Savoy, the liberty was in its
usual state of riot. Beth thought of all the doxies, the pug-
gards and punks at their fires, the dabbers and swindlers
spilling out of the taverns, drinking and cross-biting.
Maybe she could rouse them: rile up the mob, and they
were capable of anything. Even attacking Queen's Men.

She jumped down into the ditch and scurried on ahead
of the column. 'Constables!' she bellowed as she came up
towards the tavern yards. 'Comin' up the road! Two of our
own, falsely taken! Save 'em, lads! You can—'

'Witch!' shouted another voice. 'Sorcerer! Devil-
grope!' Beth looked up: it was a drunken man in a
feathered hat, leaning out of a window to take in the view.
He was pointing down the Strand – at the soldiers. At
Jack.

People were getting up from the fires, drifting over to
look.

'Newgate ho!' Other voices joined in.

'Witches!'

'Burn 'em!'

387

'Witch! Witch! Witch!'

'Falsely taken!' screamed Beth, but there was no point. More revellers were streaming out of the taverns, taking up the cry.

'Witch! Witch!' The column slowed, the guards spreading out to push back the crowd.

Beth looked around, desperate. The mob was heaving with pleasure. There was nothing here she could use. They wanted blood. Some of them had started throwing stones.

'Jack!' shouted Beth.

Jack's eyes lifted from the ground. His face was white. His mouth set grim.

Beth pushed herself forward, right to the front. A guard stepped out to block her.

'Jack!' She'd been meaning to tell him it wasn't her fault, or something like it, but the look on his face made the words die in her throat.

His eyes found hers and turned to stone.

The guard shoved her back into the crowd. When she looked again, Jack had turned away.

By the time they reached Ludgate, Jack was covered in mud and bleeding from three places where stones had hit him. His ankles were bleeding too, from the rope, and it was all he could do to keep walking. They stopped for a while at the gate, and Jack thought they might pass through. Instead, they turned north, skirting the outside of the Wall. Jack could guess where they were bound: next up was Newgate.

The whole of Savoy liberty had turned out to follow them. Beth too. Of course Beth. She'd even roused them against him.

'Witch! Witch!' chanted the mob.

Jack wondered if Beth's voice was still amongst them, or if she'd gone back to make her report: *All's well, Jack's taken, Jack's as good as dead.*

'Witch! Hellbride! Burn 'em!'

The first grey light of dawn was creeping over the horizon as they reached Newgate, but the stone walls of the prison looked as dark as ever, crouched above the gate to the City. The gate they would not be entering.

Jack and Kit were bundled forward to the little postern that led into the gaol. A snarling dog's head was carved into the lintel. Jack felt the fear curdling inside him. He knew about this gate. Black Dog's Gullet, they called it. Once it had swallowed you, there were only two ways out. They did for you inside, or they shat you out the other end, took you off to Tyburn and strung you up.

The little gate opened. Inside, the turnkeys were waiting, ready. Torchlight flickered. The steps led down, underground, like a secret way into Hell.

Jack was pushed through, then Kit, and then the gate slammed shut. The Newgate turnkeys closed smoothly around them. Jack heard whispered instructions, then he was being marched on, downstairs to places where the dawn did not reach.

The stairs levelled out into a passage. The stench of rot and filth filled Jack's nostrils. Mould scabbed the walls corpse-white.

They passed over a grille in the floor. Filthy hands reached up through the bars, grabbing at Jack's heels. The turnkeys kicked the hands away.

'Witches, witches,' moaned a voice. 'I'll see you soon.'

'It's true, you know,' said Kit. 'I am a darksome sorcerer.' He was talking to the guard who walked beside him. 'If you don't free me, I'll whistle up Black Dog to suck out your heart.'

'Quiet,' said the guard. 'Or I'll have the skin off your back – aye, and the devil-boy too.'

'The boy is nothing. I am the summoner of demons, I am the nigromancer . . . and I tell you, my servants are still at large.'

Jack wondered numbly what Kit was playing at. If it was a bid to take the blame off him, it surely wouldn't work. Besides, taking all the blame on himself didn't seem like Kit.

'The Horror will come for you in the night. Remember what happened to the last ones? Nothing was left but their privy parts, nailed to the door.'

The guard glowered straight ahead, pretending to ignore him.

'I may yet burn, but you will suffer more. Who will protect you, little man? Who will be there, in the night, when Black Dog comes? Do you have a family, I wonder?'

'Stow it!' The guard rounded on Kit and struck him hard across the mouth. Kit grinned, licking blood, then reached up and smeared it all over his face.

'Laga-laga-laga!' He waggled his tongue. 'Get thee to Tophet, the Roasting Place, where the children burn! I curse you!' A string of pinkish spittle flew out and hit the guard in the face. 'With my blood I curse you!'

'God's mercy!' The turnkey stumbled back, plucking at his face. The rearguard collided with him, and there was a moment of confusion – was that what Kit was aiming for? – but he didn't make a move. Jack couldn't see what move there was to make, the two of them hobbled, men to their front and rear. There was a side-passage branching off here, but that would only lead deeper into the prison.

'Order!' said the guard at the front. 'Here's where we split 'em – let's do it neat.'

The guards regrouped, three around Kit, two with Jack. The one who'd got the spittle in his face fought to be with Jack – none of them were keen to accompany the Great Devil Summoner, in fact. Jack heard Kit start up on his new guards as they marched him off down the side-passage:

'Do you have children?'

'You be quiet,' said the man beside him. He was flinching away from Kit as he walked. Jack tried to catch Kit's eye, to get some clue to what he was about – but Kit was fixed on the guards.

Something hard hit Jack on the back of his knees, and he stumbled forward.

'That's right. On we go. Yer bum-daddy's gentry, gets a tower cell. You, though . . . her her her . . .' The turnkey chuckled like a gurgling drain.

Jack went on, guards to either side. Kit's voice faded quickly, and now Jack was alone. They clattered down a long winding staircase and came out into a low passage, little better than a sewer, with an iron door at the far end. Behind him, a single torch glimmered in a bracket in the wall.

Up ahead, all was dark.

'Welcome to the Limbo,' said the guard. One hand shoved Jack through the door, the other slammed it shut.

Jack stumbled into the murk. At once the rasping privy-reek snagged the back of his throat and he gagged. He tried to get his bearings. It was hard – like opening your eyes in murky water.

The only light came from grilles set in the ceiling – dim shafts of grey, discouraged light. Jack watched knots of prisoners shoaling about them. He heard their restless, uneasy muttering. Under one grille a game of dice was in progress; under another someone had established a kind of tavern – two barrels with a board spanning between them. The bigger crowd was gathered there. Jack couldn't imagine what kind of brew they served down here – or how you paid.

The floor was banked so that the filth trickled down to an open sewer in the middle. The stink hollowed out every part of him. Chains were fastened to the walls here and there. A few shackled unfortunates sprawled on the floor, tethered like swine.

The further depths of the dungeon faded into obscure, ominous shadows. For all he knew, the Limbo might be as boundless as the ocean.

Jack heard a howl cut brutally short. The dice game had turned nasty: a circle of ragged shadows were tearing into something on the ground.

Jack backed away. Lice crackled under his feet with every step.

He found a spot against the wall. All he wanted was to hide. To be alone. Jack remembered a cat he'd once known, one summer when he was small. A barrel, the flies buzzing about the entrance . . .

He shook his head. He didn't have to think about the barrel. There were plenty of other memories from that summer: hot afternoons picking hops; his ma bounding about like a badger – this before she'd had her accident – the first time he'd gone scrumping. And, of course, the day the ancient, battle-scarred tom decided to move in with them. Jack had named him King Blacknose. Sometimes they'd hunted rats together.

But the King was old, and spent most of his time purring himself asleep on Jack's blanket. Then, towards the end of summer, just before the first frost, he disappeared. Jack found the cat two days later, tucked inside the barrel where he'd crawled to die; and he'd been wrong about this – he *did* have to think about the barrel. It all came back to the barrel, because the memory of the barrel was clearer than all the others, complete with the sweet death-smell just starting, and the flies – not too many, not yet – crawling on King Blacknose's face.

Jack had cried, and his ma told him that Blacknose must have known his time was up. That he'd gone off to meet with death, as brave as when he'd faced down all those other ram cats in his day.

Jack didn't feel brave. Tomorrow he was going to die. Hundreds, thousands would watch and scream and cheer. The weight of it made him want to curl up in a ball. He wondered if Rob had felt the same. He wondered if Rob had felt angry with him.

Beth would be there tomorrow too, working the crowd. She'd played him all along, her and her grampers. Of course she had. He'd crossed the Sharkwells; now he was going to die, with everyone watching.

He wished it could be alone.

He wrapped himself up, arms round his shins, forehead

pressed tight to his knees, as if he could squeeze all the bad thoughts out.

'So this is our witch-boy, hnrgh hnr . . .'

Jack looked up.

Stupid. He'd been aware of the prisoners closing in for some time. He could hear their snuffly breaths. He could smell the gaol-stench on them. He hadn't looked up till now because he'd hoped they might go away if he ignored them.

Gullish hope. They were strung out around him in a semicircle, blocking any chance of escape. One of them was shuffling closer – the same one who'd spoken.

'So wicked, and so young.' A woman's voice. 'And so much talk about you already in my dungeon. Did you think you could hide?'

Jack jumped to his feet, swayed, and fell over – he'd forgotten the hobbling ropes. The woman was on him in a streak, quick as a rat. Her hair was matted with filth. Sores bubbled over her lips and across her cheeks.

One wiry arm was wrapped around his shoulder. The woman reached out her other hand. Her fingernails were two inches long, grown thick and yellow like claws. 'What were they thinking? Throwing a nice pretty boy in here?' Her plague breath slimed across him. 'You must have been very, very naughty.'

Jack twisted free and threw her off him; then he was away, crawling rapidly across the floor.

'Jenks,' said the woman.

A great pale maggot of a man loomed over Jack. He was half naked. Where his skin showed beneath the grime it was mottled blue, like cheese. He bent down and grabbed Jack by the neck, holding him tight. Jack twisted, kicked him in the shins. The man didn't move, but his grip hardened, pinching till Jack couldn't breathe.

'Be still, boy,' said the woman. Jack twisted again, tried to bite the arm clinched around his neck. He couldn't reach. His chest was bursting for air, and now an enormous pale thumb pressed into the corner of his good eye, squashing it in its socket. The thumb pressed harder, and Jack would have gasped with the pain if he'd been able to breathe at all.

'Be still, or Jenks'll pop you like a plum!'

Jack went limp.

'That's better.' The thumb went away. Jenks still held him in a choking-grip, but he'd eased off so that Jack could take a thin, whistling breath.

The woman leaned in. Her eyes were blood-red, crazed. 'Now let Moll have a look at you. You're awful sweet for a witch.'

'I'm not,' said Jack. Other faces were leering in. Shambling, hungry skeletons.

'Very pretty. Very little,' Jenks murmured. He ran his other hand through Jack's hair.

Jack still wasn't getting enough air. He felt weak,

fragile, as if his head was about to pop off his shoulders and float away. Someone was tearing at his shoes. Another was pulling at his breeches.

Moll slipped her hand under his shirt and he felt one of her claw-nails trace a line across his chest.

'Smooth as a baby,' she said. 'Now, are you going to make your Auntie Moll happy?'

Jack shook his head. It would be better to die. He spat in Moll's face.

'Oh dearie me,' said Moll. Her mouth twisted down, eyes narrowing into a horrible bitter-sweet leer. 'You'd best not have done that, baby boy.' Her hand came out from his shirt, the claws reaching for his eyes. Jack tried to twist away, but Jenks held him tight by the neck. The tips of Moll's finger-nails were a crusty yellow-brown, and very sharp.

There was a whirring buzz in the air. Moll's face blossomed with blood. She fell away, shrieking.

With a low wet cough, Jenks let go of Jack's neck.

Other voices were swearing, howling, roaring. Jack hunkered down. There was a scrabbling of feet, and a sound like a butcher's knife. Something landed on his back.

Jack opened his eye. There were dark spatters of blood all around him. The thing on his back flopped to the floor. It looked like an ear.

'Master?' the imp whispered. It was hovering above his head, lagging to one side on its damaged wing.

'Imp!' Jack had never been so thankful for anything in his entire life.

'So you *are* a prick-tarred witch,' said Moll, spitting blood. The tip of her nose was sliced neatly open down the middle. Behind her, Jenks's corpse was being dragged away. People were already fighting over his clothes.

'I'll shank your guts for this, whoreson,' said Moll. 'This is my dungeon.'

'If you come close, I will kill you, dead.' Jack spoke as loud as he dared. Around Moll, her cronies had already started backing away. Jack watched the whites of their eyes – wide, staring at the imp.

'Y're brave now, witch – but you have to sleep,' snarled Moll; but she was trembling too. Her face was black with blood from the nose down, pale as bone above it. She spat once and hobbled away.

'Tcha! Pox-buss speaks flimpenkripp,' said the imp, landing on Jack's shoulder.

'You came back!' said Jack.

'Naturals I come. But hushub now.' The imp's antennae twitched this way and that, tasting the air. 'Big Shuk. Close. Watching.'

The imp hobbled down his arm and onto his knee. As well as the missing wing-case, it had lost half its horn and two of its legs. Jack reached down and touched its shell. It was warm to the touch, smooth and grooved like varnished wood.

His head was clearing, fizzing with ideas. The imp could unlock doors. The imp could kill gaolers. The imp could get him out of here! Jack felt hope rising like gorge, so intense that it hurt.

'Imp,' he said, forcing his voice down. 'Listen.' He had to think straight now, straight and true. The imp could open doors, but first he had to know how many doors there were between him and freedom, and then the routes between them, and where the guards were . . .

The imp could scout out the trail. It would mean staying here alone for a while. Jack crouched down with his back to the wall. The Limbo was still in uproar. Vague shadows were tussling over Jenks's body; more were screaming in a pack near the door, crying out about sorcery. No one was coming anywhere near Jack. The Limbo had grown chary of witches.

'What is wishing to say?'

'Right, aye, listen. I need you to—'

'Aark!' went the imp.

The light was sudden, and dazzling bright. The crowd around the door stumbled back. Jack heard a confusion of footsteps. Shouts, a desperate cry, the thud of a body hitting the floor. A band of gaolers burst into the Limbo, swinging their cudgels about. Prisoners went down and didn't get up.

'Little witchy's over 'ere!' Moll shouted, and pointed – all of the Limbo seemed to be looking at Jack. Half the gaolers moved in a mass towards him. The other half guarded the door.

'Can you take them?' said Jack.

'Shhht!' The imp tensed, its remaining legs digging into Jack's knee.

'Can you?' said Jack. 'You cut those others—'

'Now changed,' said the imp. 'Big Shuk is close. Not allowing . . .'

'Who's Big Shuk?' said Jack.

'Black Dog, you name it . . .'

The imp went silent and its shell went dark. Jack scrambled to his feet – darted forward – but there was nowhere to go. The gaolers drew in close, surrounding him.

'Here's little witch-boy,' snarled the biggest and baldest of the gaolers. 'Little runt, making trouble.' He took a step closer, and smacked his cudgel against his thigh.

'Shouldn't have upset the cattle,' sneered another. 'Now we have to take you away.'

'Big mistake, I'd say,' said Baldy. 'You'll be lonely, all on yer own.'

There was a quick step behind Jack. He felt a star explode in the back of his head.

Everything went black.

Chapter 32

The sunlight woke him.

Sharkwell had always been an early riser. Ever since he was a nipper he'd woken before the dawn, and he took great pride in this wolfish habit. Anyone he called friend had heard many times how the sun never once caught Sharkwell napping.

'Hell! What's this!' he growled, astonished at the morning's front. The sun was streaming through the window, bold as anything, as if it had a right to be there.

'Pox on ye,' he cursed it. 'Busy old fool . . .'

His head was buzzing, as if he'd been on a drunk the night before. Which he hadn't – only a few settlers after Beth ran off, and then a few more to douse his fears she'd foul it all up. Besides, he always woke up prompt, even when he'd sunk a brewery. Something was wrong.

'Meatface!' he bawled. 'Get your swinish lump—'

Sharkwell blinked. There was a heavy, solid weight at the foot of his bed. Through the sheets, he prodded the object with his toe. It felt like wood.

This was peculiar. This was strange.

It felt like a wooden box.

Sharkwell pulled back the sheets, and understood. Burned into the top of the box was a crude outline of a fly.

The buzzing in his head seemed to get louder.

For a heartbeat, pure rage flamed through his veins. That fly-blown villain! He'd come in here – come into Sharkwell's own, private chambers – sorcelled him in his sleep . . .

Left the box . . .

A fly bumbled across the bed. Sharkwell flinched.

'Brought it here, did you?' He calmed down, looking at the box. He always respected a man who paid his debts prompt. He licked his lips.

The box looked heavy.

Pig Varsey was afraid.

The word had spread through Newgate like wind in the grass: the sorcerer was here. Not just any sorcerer, but the one the preachers had been talking up – the big one; the one who was to blame for all the Horrors, the Master of Devils. He'd already cursed three of the turnkeys who brought him in. Now the word was that he'd been talking to Black Dog, striking a bargain with the very Devil of Newgate.

He might be an abominable nigromancer, but he was gentry, so someone had to bring the bastard his bread and water. The argument amongst the turnkeys was settled quickly, over breakfast: Pig Varsey would be the one to do it. Pig Varsey was the smallest, most craven turnkey in Newgate, and he always ended up with the arse-end of the work, and so now it was Pig who was climbing the stairs to the Tower Cell.

His bunch of keys jangled at his hip. In his right hand he carried a Bible. He'd refused to do it without a Bible, and they'd found one eventually – a nice Latin Bible, taken from some Popish prisoner, and supposed to be better against magicians than the new sort. That was what they told him, anyway.

Pig gathered up the tatters of his courage, and opened the door.

The cell was very dark. Pig edged in one step.

'S-Sir Magus?'

The door slammed shut behind him, and light streamed in as something was whipped away from the window.

Pig screamed. His Bible slipped to the floor.

The walls of the cell were covered in blood. Smeared blood, lines dribbling down the stone in patterns that made Pig's eyes hurt. Stars and circles, devil-faces scowling and snarling, unimaginable words written in Hell's own script. Pig looked down, and screamed again. He was standing in the centre of a bloody triangle. At each corner was the drained corpse of a fat gaol-rat.

'Turn round,' said a voice behind him.

The voice was soft as cobwebs, strong as steel wire. Pig didn't want to turn, but the voice compelled him.

Standing in front of the door was the sorcerer. The upper part of his face was hooded with white linen. The mouth was exposed, lips reddened with blood. His chest was bare, and more blood was smeared across it, in the shape of a star. His hands hung below his waist, relaxed, still bound by their manacles – though from this last fact Pig took no comfort whatsoever.

'I have expected you,' said the magician. 'Now you are mine.'

Pig couldn't make a sound – not even a whimper.

'What is your name?'

Pig made a choking noise.

'Tell me, or your torment begins now. Black Dog is hungry.'

'P-Per-P-Pig!' He could feel tears streaming down his cheeks now.

'Pig. Men will speak your name in whispers, Pig, hundreds of years hence. The manner of your dying will strike terror and pity into the hearts of torturers. Your ghost will scream its agony through these walls for all eternity.'

Pig knew about agony. In his years as a turnkey, he had seen men put to the question, tortured beyond endurance, and so he knew: no one ever expected it to be as bad as it was; they were always surprised – and that was just ordinary torture. Whatever Black Dog had in store for him, it was bound to be worse than anything he'd seen in the lower dungeons.

'Please,' Pig blubbed. 'P-p-please, sir, I never—'

'Silence.' The magician's voice hardened. Pig shut his mouth, forced his sobs down.

'I had not finished,' said the magician. 'All these things will come to pass, unless you do exactly what I say.'

Pig couldn't stop the sobs now. They were not quite sobs of relief.

The magician leaned forward and spat something greenish brown and spicy-smelling onto the floor. His face was still hidden by his linen hood (his shirt, Pig would realize later – it was his shirt, and the thing that had fallen from the window was his cloak, and the devil-writing on the walls was all sixteen verses of the bawdy ballad 'O Parson, Your Parsnip', written upside down . . .).

The magician held out his hands. 'You will begin by undoing these manacles.'

There was a pain in Jack's head, and a coppery taste of

blood in his mouth. They had been there for as long as he could remember.

He shivered. He was lying on his side in freezing water. His clothes were soaked.

All he could hear around him was a steady *drip, drip, drip* – heavy drops splashing in shallow pools. From the smell, he wasn't sure if it was water.

He opened one eye. Cautiously he swivelled it this way and that. The pain in his head got worse. So did the sinking feeling that had been growing inside him.

At first he could not make sense of what he saw. Everything was black. Everything except for a small bright circle hanging above him. It looked like a green moon. He reached out to touch it.

His fingers sank through thick, slimy moss to stone. The stain in his hand began to itch. Jack swivelled his head to the left, ignoring the stab of pain that shot through his skull. More darkness – maybe not quite so black – and a pinprick shaft of light falling from the ceiling. The light hit the slime on the wall and made the little green moon.

It was the only light he had.

He stood up, and his wet clothes clung to him, stinking like the dead. His arms reached out into the darkness. He could feel the slime and moss on both sides. He ran his hands over the wall.

Five steps and he found the hatchway. Five steps back

and he hit the wall again. He remembered the riot, the guards, the cudgel. They had thrown him down here to rot.

He was buried alive.

The seconds dripped by. He watched the little moon crawl across the moss. Tiny white things squirmed down in the roots, surprised by the brightness. The moon moved very slowly. Jack remembered the Spanish admiral's table in his old gaff. This light was just the same, marking time – except instead of a crack in the wood it was sliding across ragged scratch marks, gouged into the moss.

Someone had tried to claw their way out.

Jack wondered how long you had to be down here before you tried that. Not very long, he thought. This was a very dark place. He could feel it in his stained hand, every time he touched the walls. He could feel it in his eye, throbbing beneath the patch.

And now, behind him, he could feel something else. Something very cold, creeping up his spine. He heard a clattering, whirring noise. It sounded like—

'Imp?'

It was a faint hope. Jack peered into the blackness, trying to see. There was no reply.

His hand stabbed again. Whatever it was, it was very close now. Something watching him. Something big. Something that couldn't be seen with ordinary eyes.

Jack raised his patch, and everything went quiet. No drips, no splashes.

Now he could see. The moss on the walls glowed, faint and ruddy. His cell was bigger than he'd thought, widening out in front of him, the walls irregular. It didn't look much like a prison. It looked more like a cave.

The imp hung in the air before him, frozen and motionless.

'Imp?'

Everything had stopped. All sounds, all movement. Behind the imp a drop of water from the ceiling was suspended in mid-air, gleaming like a dark polished jewel.

THIS IS YOUR CREATURE. The voice came from behind him.

Jack tried to turn, and found he couldn't.

And then he didn't have to.

Moving with velvet grace, a giant black shape glided round in front of him. Everything else was stained with red light, but the beast sliced smooth and black through the frozen space of the dungeon. Around it, against all reason, drops of water hung suspended like liquid stars.

It was Black Dog. Jack knew this was true with a slow, crawling horror. The devil's strength curled and tensed beneath its skin. It had a heavy head, and a big undershot jaw – nothing like a wolf – more like a fighting dog, a big brutal bear-mastiff. The kind you sent in if the bear was a fighter and tore all the smaller dogs apart. The kind you sent in for the kill.

The cold came off it in waves. Jack felt his body

turning numb – his legs iced up, his chest frozen tight. Only his weird eye burned, an itching heat like fiery ants crawling around inside it – his eye, and the stain on his hand. He could feel the twin burns spreading – up his arm, down across his face – fighting the cold.

YOU THOUGHT TO ESCAPE ME. The devil didn't open its mouth to speak; the words rippled soft and silent, straight into Jack's head.

Black Dog bared its teeth. Jack watched them come closer and closer. They were white as bone.

YOU WERE MISTAKEN.

The cold was worse now, but the burn was still fighting it. Jack tried to inch a half-step backwards, but his feet would not move. Black Dog sat down on its haunches in front of him. Even sitting, it was half a head taller than Jack. He watched – trapped, unblinking – as the devil bent forward and sniffed him up and down. Then it looked him in the face. Its eyes were yellow, ancient, hard as marble.

Jack had the terrible feeling that every part of him was being weighed up and judged. Not just him, but everything he had ever done. Every memory. All the things he was proud of, and all the things that made him ashamed.

Black Dog gathered up all of Jack in an instant, and examined him. The awful thing was that it did not care.

This was death. Jack understood.

YOU ARE AFRAID, said Black Dog.

Jack tried to concentrate on the heat in his hand, urging it up his arm and into his chest. Black Dog circled behind him. He still couldn't turn, but his finger twitched. The heat was spreading. Slowly.

MANY FACE DEATH HERE, said the devil. SOME CRUSHED. SOME MAD. SOME WITHOUT HOPE. Black Dog leaned in close to his neck, and he felt its breath, cold, like a draught from a tomb. It took another long, lingering sniff. YOU ARE NONE OF THESE.

With a surge of triumph, Jack managed to raise his hand an inch. It felt like it was moving through treacle.

YOU ARE FIGHTING.

The devil circled round in front of Jack. It cocked its head to one side.

IT WILL MAKE NO DIFFERENCE.

Jack hurled his anger and his fear at his frozen body, gritting his teeth, forcing heat into his iced-up muscles. He felt his sinews creaking, warming . . .

'Dah!' Jack's tongue came loose. His hand lurched upwards.

Black Dog stared at him, unblinking.

Jack reached forward. His hand crept up, agonizingly slow, past frozen specks of dust. It was on fire. He could feel the stain – feel its edges, and the veins glowing red-hot.

Black Dog watched the hand come closer. It didn't draw back.

What was it Webb had said? Jack hauled out the words – past the ice, past the horror of the place, past the fear – till they were there on his thick, heavy tongue.

'I name you, Black Dog.' Jack touched his burning hand to the fur between the devil's eyes. It felt cold and dead. 'I cast you out! Out!'

His hand flamed with heat. Something leaped out of him, into Black Dog.

'Out!'

Black Dog laughed. It sounded like gravel sliding in a dark place miles below the earth. Jack felt the energy that had come out of him returning, only now it was changed – cold and dark and soft as death. He tried to step away but he was held there, his hand clutching at the black fur, out of his control.

YOU HAVE POWER.

Jack stumbled back, gasping and sobbing. It felt as if every tiniest part of him had been gripped, twisted, then let go at once.

The yellow eyes bored into him. Again, Jack had the uncomfortable sensation of being peeled apart and tasted.

KNOWLEDGE ALSO, said the devil. YOU HAVE FOR-GOTTEN. Black Dog stared down at Jack. TOMORROW YOU GO TO THE TREE. TOMORROW YOU MUST REMEMBER.

'But . . .'

NO. TOMORROW COMES THE RECKONING. Black Dog turned and stalked away. The dust glowed bright. Somewhere behind it, the imp fell to the floor with a clatter.

The devil vanished, its final word suspended in the air.

REMEMBER.

Chapter 33

The sun was riding high in a pure blue sky when Beth finally stepped ashore at the Privy Wharf. The wharf was deserted, which was unusual for this time of day. The warehouse too was strangely quiet. A couple of broggers turned from examining some piglets in the corner sty; one of them started to say something, but the face she turned on him made him swallow it fast.

The news about her exile would be out by now. But that didn't mean she had to take high words from some crufty little brogger. She'd spent all morning trying to shape out what to do. She still didn't know. All she knew was that she had to face her grampers at least one more time.

'Where's Himself?' she said.

The brogger's squinty eyes darted back to the piglets. His mate nudged him, but he still didn't answer.

'What? What's wrong with you?'

'D-don't know.' The brogger gulped. 'I only heard . . .'

'What?'

'He ain't coming out, miss. He's in his rooms, and he ain't come out all morn'n.'

Beth glowered at the brogger for a moment, just to let him know that next time she expected her answers prompt; then she carried on through the warehouse.

The way the broggers were acting, she'd have wagered a spanker they didn't know she was banished. That was queer. When her grampers made a decision, he told all the Family, even the broggers. There was something queer about the deserted wharf too, and the abandoned, echoey warehouse.

By the time she reached the Crooked Walnut, Beth was moving at a hungry, wolfish lope.

The taproom was empty, apart from Meatface behind the bar. He tried to mutter something to her, but she charged straight past him, banging through the door and up the stairs to the third floor.

Now she could see why there was no one in the warehouse, or on the wharf, or in the taproom. All the Family was here. The corridor reeked of fear and man-sweat. Beth spotted Mr Smiles lurking by the door to Sharkwell's bedroom: he looked relieved to see her. She heard whispered conversations die off fast as she appeared.

Black Pod was nearest the stair-head, surrounded by a

knot of waterpads. He spoke into the silence: 'She should do it.'

A low swell of agreement rose, starting with the water-pads and spreading through the jam. Beth stared into Black Pod's mud-coloured eyes. He stared back, thrusting out his sharp, bristly chin.

'Do what?' she said.

Something in the question, or something in Beth's face, made him look down. Beth made a small disgusted clicking noise in the back of her throat. 'Where's Sharkwell?' she said. 'What're you all doing shuffling about here? Smiles, what's up?' Mr Smiles looked like he was about to cry. Beth didn't have the patience for this. 'Spit it out, Smiles. What's up with Sharkwell?'

She could see his Adam's apple bobble up and down. 'Obscuration,' he said. 'Door's locked, and all morning passed sans word . . . sans everything, except . . .' He swallowed again.

'Devilry,' said Black Pod. 'Come home to roost, and no wonder. Your little friend, Miss Bethany. Your nigromancer.'

Beth rounded on him, suddenly furious. 'Don't call me that. And don't you talk of Jack, neither. What do you know about it?'

'I know there was noises coming from in there. Wrong noises. I know devilry—'

'Aye, or you're too craven to wake up Himself. Frighted

little kids, you are – flock of bantams, the lot of you!' She pushed past Black Pod, pushed her way to the door. Still furious, but now starting to feel scared herself too.

'It's locked, Beth,' said Smiles. His eyes were moist and miserable.

'Did you hear any noise?'

'No, not I, but—'

'Right then, who wants to gilk the lock?'

No one did. She had to borrow Smiles' tools and do it herself. Something had scared them, that was sure. Something more than their ordinary, everyday fear of Sharkwell.

She hadn't practised the Black Art in a while, but it was the sort of trick that stayed with you. A fiddle and a click, and it was open. There was a swaying in the corridor, a jostle of cravens trying to get away from the door.

Beth went in. The first thing to hit her was the smell – an eye-watering, hot-metal stink like an alchemist's work-shop. The smell was coming from the bed. The bed was a mess, blanket thrashed and tangled, like Sharkwell had been having some terrible nightmare. On the floor beside the headboard was a wooden box. The box was empty. A symbol, a little crooked fly, was burned into the lid. Beth recognized the mark: she'd seen it many times on the coins Jack used to bring in from Webb's preachers.

Her grampers was not here. That was obvious.

Sharkwell was not here, no one had seen him all day, the door was locked, the windows bolted from the inside . . .

Beth was standing over the bed now, and there was a noise coming from under the blanket. A low buzzing noise that set her teeth on edge.

She reached forward and tugged the blanket away. The hot-metal stink rose up to meet her, knifing through her skull.

The entire bed was covered with dead flies. Thousands of them, lying in drifts like foul black ashes. Not quite all dead: a few flies stirred, sputtered into feeble flight – and Beth was throwing the blanket back into place with panicky fingers, trying to blot out the horror. She could still hear them, see the blanket twitching.

She stood there for a moment, staring blankly ahead, until her eyes snagged on the wall above the headboard.

A rapid pulse began to beat in her temple. It felt like being hit over and over with a very small hammer. She was looking at the wall above the headboard, and what she saw was a line of parallel scratch marks, gouged deep. In and all around the scratches, dead flies were smeared over the plaster.

Someone had lain on this bed, belly-down. Someone had reached up and clawed at the wall with hands covered in flies.

Her eyes travelled down to the headboard itself. The hammer in her temples grew to three, four times its former size. Behind her, from the door, she heard Mr Smiles' voice.

'Perchance . . . perchance he moused abroad in the night?' he said. 'Beth? He might have . . . ?'

Beth shook her head. She couldn't speak for the moment. She couldn't take her eyes off the headboard.

Embedded in the wood, thrust in all the way to their blood-crusted roots, were two long brown teeth.

Beth Sharkwell emerged from her grandfather's room, her face composed and utterly unreadable. It made Mr Smiles, who was the only one left near the door, fall back a step.

'He's gone,' she said. 'It was devilry all right.'

From his place at the head of the stairs, Black Pod made a choking, triumphant sound and clutched his pike's-tooth charm. 'The nigromancer! We'll make him pay—'

'No,' said Beth. 'You know nothing, Black Pod. You don't even dare go in there and look. He was my grampers, and *I* say who pays.'

She tilted her head back a fraction. No one would have known that she had come here this morning a traitor and an exile. She had forgotten it herself. In that moment she wasn't even acting; she was the Queen of Thieves.

'All right?' she said. Her voice was very quiet.

No one dared meet her eye.

'There's been dark business. My grampers was in it, and

it brought him to his death. Jack Patch was in it too, and today he's due to swing.'

A low murmur ran through the thieves. This was news to them, Beth thought. No wonder: of course Sharkwell had kept the whole business quiet. Now he was dead, there was no reason to bring up his crooked part in it.

Aye, let them think he died honest.

'Two of us betrayed,' she said, speaking louder over the noise. 'Your leader done in, what you swore to protect. And I won't have it.'

A few eyes were coming up to meet her now – Mr Smiles, Ram Cat Peprah, some of the older nippers. She had them. One more push, and she'd have the lot of them.

'I won't have it, no more than my grampers would have. No more than the Law would. There's payment due, my lads. Payment due by rights and by the Law. My grampers is dead. We're going to make his killers sorry. Are we not, my brave villains?'

No one spoke. Beth smiled at them. It was the bleakest, grimmest smile that any of them had ever seen.

'All right then.'

Chapter 34

Aswing-day was normally a quiet one in The Pomgranatt. It was an obscure wharfside tavern behind Smart's Quay, the customary haunt of masterless men, needy shifters, and a smattering of idle 'prentices – the kind of crowd that would rather take a brick to the head than miss the fun of a hanging.

Crabfoot Flagg, the inkeep, was luxuriating in the calm. The morning had seen no beatings, no stabbings – not so much as a dandyprat. He'd a thirsty patron to serve, and yards of Essex oak to polish. All was right with the world.

The patron was a gentry cove. Crabfoot, who had as fine an eye for a drunkard as any inkeep in London, was passing the time by spying on the man with his good eye, trying to figure him out.

He was about three parts sure the gent was a drowner.

All longtopers drank for a reason, and normally Crabfoot could sniff out the cause just by the manner they called for their first drink. This one was more of a mystery. He wasn't a love-loon or a skitbird – too quiet for that. He shaped well for a lantern-jaw because his legs were hollow – but lantern-jaws were carefree folk on the whole, and this fellow had cares all right, if Crabfoot was any judge. He was busy trying to drown them. Not succeeding, either, by the look of it. He drank in grim silence, ignoring the other customers – French mariners out of the *Occitane* – even though it was plain he was taking passage with them. Crabfoot could see his billet right there on the table in front of him.

A drowner, then – except that sooner or later, all drowners would come out and bemoan their sorrows. Usually to the inkeep, and always at great length. All this gent did was drink enough to drown the ocean, and spin a golden coin, over and over, calling the toss.

'Heads . . . tails . . . heads . . .'

Neither side cheered him up. Crabfoot reckoned the only way he'd be happy would be if the coin somehow landed on its edge.

A few travellers trailed into the tavern and negotiated passage with the Frenchies. Meanwhile the gent downed three stoups of Crabfoot's best stingo. He kept his coin spinning all the time.

'Tails . . . tails . . .'

The Frenchies got up to leave. One of them told the gent to join them – it was time to go. The gent spat out a stream of brownish-green liquid (missing the bartop, much to Crabfoot's relief) and cursed the Frenchie good and round. Proper English cursing: Crabfoot admired it. Apart from 'heads' and 'tails' they were the first words the gent had spoken.

'And I'll board when I choose, you villainous, onion-eyed puttock!' he finished. The Frenchie shrugged, and left with his other passengers. The gent spat again, muttered something to himself, then settled down to the serious drinking – first the humming liquor, and when that bottle ran dry, he called for a snout of Dutch ragwater.

'Heads . . . tails . . .'

Crabfoot was impressed. There was no embarrassing maudling here. Such dedication to the toper's task made an inkeep proud to serve. Hard and steady, just how it should be. Maybe the gent wasn't a drowner after all; maybe he was a whole new sort of animal.

He poured the snout and slid it over.

The man tossed it back, and spun his coin. 'Tails. Another.'

Crabfoot poured again. This time the gent didn't drink it straight, but twisted the mug between his fingers, watching the liquor swill about.

Here we go, thought Crabfoot.

'Tell me, inkeep,' said the gent. 'Tell me – d'you ever save a man's life?'

'Been times.' Crabfoot shrugged modestly.

'Were they grateful?'

'Not mostly.'

The man spat again, hard and true, into the empty mug. A faint smell of spices rose up around him.

Crabfoot waited for the rest of it. But the tale never came. The gent's mouth was corked. To words, at least; to drink it was ever open.

He held out the coin. 'You'll have this, if you keep them coming.' The gent drained the mug, and three more to follow it. His hand stayed steady, even as his eyes grew dark. All the while, he stared at the coin, flicking it in complicated patterns over his fingers.

Nine bells sounded from St Magnus's.

Crabfoot cleared his throat. 'There's the tide to think of, sir.'

From the wharf outside came sailor's shouts as the *Occitane* prepared to slip its moorings and sail away for France.

The gent frowned down at his billet of passage, and finished his drink. He slid the coin across the gleaming bartop. 'Inkeep. You, this time. Toss for me.'

Crabfoot flicked the coin high in the air. They both watched it tumble end over end, till Crabfoot caught it neatly, and slapped it down on his palm.

He held out his hand. A golden fly caught the light.

'Tails.' The gent nodded once. 'God damn you, inkeep!'

The gent jumped to his feet and strode from the room. He left his billet behind. Five minutes later, his ship swept out into the ebbing tide, and sailed for France without him.

Jack spent his last night on earth alone, in complete darkness.

The imp was dead. Black Dog had killed it. The beetle-shell was empty and dark: no help there.

Soon Jack would be dead as well.

His eyes were shut, but he did not sleep. He'd heard once how drowning sailors saw their lives played out, start to finish, before they sank to the bottom. He'd always wondered how that worked – if time slowed down, or stopped even. Maybe those last few moments were so precious that your mind stretched them out into days, years, and you lived your life again.

Jack saw his ma stomping through the Shambles with a curb over one shoulder. He saw boys he'd fought, and coneys he'd caught. He saw devils in the stones, and spider-fingers grasping through a door of flat light. He saw Dr Dee pacing in frantic circles.

Jack wasn't drowning, and time didn't stop. He could feel every moment slipping through his fingers like sand. There were so few left.

You must remember, Black Dog said, and Jack was trying, and it was driving him mad because he didn't know where to begin.

They came for Jack in strength. Newgate Prison wasn't taking any more chances with magicians. They dragged him from his hole, and marched him blind and filthy up into the light.

The turnkeys cuffed him, blinking and stumbling, into the courtyard before the postern gate. The others were already there: cunning-men, piss prophets, a wrinkled crone or two. All of them would face the Reckoning. All of them were falsely accused.

They waited in the courtyard, standing wretched in their bonds. Jack couldn't see Kit. Maybe the intelligencer would be marched out separate at the end, the chief nigromancer getting his own proper entrance. The dark walls of the prison rose up all around. Overhead, a patch of pale, cloudless sky gave promise of a beautiful day.

It could be the last he'd ever see, Jack realized. The clear light made everything seem fresh: the moss clumping between cobbles; a shaving scratch on a turnkey's chin; horse dung and woodsmoke, the London smell.

'I en't a witch! I'm Anne Haddock. I'mma finger-smith!' shouted an old lady.

'You behave, and eat yer slap,' said the guard. 'Finish it,

I would. They don't serve pannum this tasty where you're 'eaded, dearie.'

The porridge was served piping hot in wooden bowls. Jack couldn't stomach it. His tongue was dry and scratchy. His clothes and hair were matted with filth, and he was pretty sure he'd picked up a dose of lice. It seemed stupid to care, but it made him feel worse. To die lousy.

An Elect preacher came into the yard to address them. 'Direful sinners! Do you wish to repent?'

'Repent what?' The old lady shook her fist. 'All I did was bring on babies. You ask in Portsoken Ward. I hulled every babe for twenty years . . .'

A chorus of shouts rose up, drowning her out.

The preacher stepped forward and slapped the old lady hard across the mouth. She collapsed to the ground, sobbing.

'You lie, witch!' The red-hand stood over her. 'We know you trafficked with infernal agents. You have forspoken the godly; you have bound unholy creatures to your wicked will. You are condemned—'

'No I ain't!' shouted a man at the back. 'I'm a baker!' All of them were shouting again.

'Lies! And why lie now? You are fools! You will die unshriven!' The preacher stalked away, disgusted.

'The Parting Cup!' A man was coming down the line carrying a tray of tankards. 'If you won't take repentance when it's offered, then take a drink!'

The prisoners grabbed the ale eagerly, drank it down in big straining gulps.

'The cup will ease the drop.' The man waited in front of Jack. 'Believe it, lad.'

Jack wanted to ignore him, but there was sense in what the man said. He took a tankard. The ale was strong and cold. He drained it in three swallows.

The drop. He still couldn't believe that it was really going to happen. *You must remember* – Black Dog wouldn't have said that unless there was something for Jack to do before the end. Something more than just dying.

It was almost funny – pinning all his hopes on Black Dog, whose job it was to stifle all hope, make sure no one ever escaped the Tree.

You must remember. But what could he possibly remember that would save him now? The imp could have helped him maybe, but Black Dog had put a stop to that. He'd hidden it in his sleeve before they came for him; but it was dead weight, all its lights gone out.

He wondered what a rope would feel like around his neck. He wondered if it hurt when you dropped. He didn't want to think those thoughts – they made him feel half dead already, each breath weighing him down, as if he could count how few were left.

You must remember, you must remember.

He wanted to scream, *Remember what?*

* * *

The carts were pulling into the courtyard. Jack took another cup when it was offered. Still no sign of Kit.

A new set of guards arrived with the carts. They bound Jack's wrists, checked the ropes around his ankles, then bundled him up into a cart between Anne Haddock, the midwife, and a grim red-faced man. The others were loaded up, three to a cart and three carts in all; and then they were rolling out of the gaol-yard.

No Kit. Had he got away? If so, he hadn't troubled himself over Jack.

Sixth Law: Save your own skin.

Good luck to him. Jack looked inside himself and couldn't find any anger. Not at Kit, anyway. It was too late for anger. The sun was smiling down on a lovely May morning, and Jack was going to be dead by noon.

Unless he could remember.

He went over every dodge he'd ever learned from his ma and Mr Smiles. But no one had ever taught him a way of escaping a heavily guarded death-cart with his hands and feet out of play. He'd have to be able to fly, or do magic. Maybe that was what Black Dog had meant – except the list of magic spells Jack knew could be counted on the fingers of one foot. He might as well try to escape by astrology. Maybe, with the imp to help him . . . but the imp was gone, its body a dead weight in his sleeve pocket.

As they rolled out through Newgate onto High Holborn, Jack heard an enormous sigh go up, and felt the eyes – hundreds, thousands of them – crawling over his skin. It made him want to disappear, or die right now and get it over with. His escape thoughts shrivelled up like a salted slug. He could feel the hunger of the crowd; he'd known it before (and thinking of that, Jack had a bright flash of memory – Rob jerking on the end of his rope – and had to swallow hard to avoid spewing up his ale), but this felt different. This had been building for months. All of London had turned out. All of Itchy Town, and now that the time had come to scratch, there was something missing.

The crowd was silent.

Jack lifted his head, and flinched.

He saw an old man in a sheepskin cap glaring like he wanted to chew him up, his mouth working silently. There, a girl Beth's age, her hand resting lightly at her throat. Was she wishing him dead?

Her hand was dyed red.

Jack glanced again at the old man, and saw that his hand was red too – and now another, and another – the crowd was full of them. Elect preachers stood out like crows in their black garb. They too were silent. Waiting.

A single voice went up. One of the preachers, further back in the crowd: 'Behold! Brothers and sisters, today we are cleansed! Today we scour off the corruption, we scour it out!'

Another sigh, soft and soughing.

'This is the word of God, my brothers: if thy hand offendeth thee, cut it off! If thine eye offendeth thee, put it out! And did not wise King Solomon say, *Thou shalt not suffer a witch to live?* The canker is brought to light, and now – now we cut it out! Out! Out!'

The storm broke.

The silence was bad, but this was worse; this was so much worse than Jack could have imagined, because it was pointed all at him.

'Out! Out! OUT!' shouted the crowd, raising their fists in time to it, and the punching fists were punching straight at him. The faces were twisted with hatred of him. He was innocent and it made no difference, because there were so many of them and they knew in their hearts that he was guilty as Hell.

Under the hammer blows of 'OUT! OUT! OUT!' Jack couldn't help but feel guilty himself. The fear was strong on him now, in his throat, in his bowels, in his neck.

'OUT! OUT! OUT!' It pounded away at him. He tried to resist, tried to tell himself there was still a way to escape if only he could remember it. It was no good. The shouting ground him down, flooded him out.

'Silly buggers,' muttered the man to his left. His face was brick-red, heavy dark brows beetling down over his eyes. He was fumbling with a pouch at his belt. He looked up at Jack. 'Stand up straight, sonny. Look the mumping sods in the eye.'

The man got his pouch open, deft-handed in spite of the ropes binding his wrists. He pulled out pipe and tobacco. Jack saw that his hands were shaking.

'You're a mite young for a witch, ain't you, sonny?' said the man.

'I'm not one.'

'Course not. No more'n I am.' The man let out a short, hacking laugh. 'Harry the horse-cope, me. Only magic I know is the likes of this here.' He nodded down at the twist of tobacco in his hand. 'Best Caribbee Strongweed. Shove a wad of this up a spavined nag's arse, he'll prance like a palfrey.'

Jack tried to smile. The man gave him a short nod, then bent over his firebox. Soon a wreath of blue smoke rose and wafted about his head. 'Like a puff?'

Jack hadn't smoked since the early prosperous days with Rob – had never taken to it – but now he nodded and accepted the pipe. The Strongweed was very strong indeed. He coughed, mouth watering, head buzzing.

'Aye,' said Harry. 'Best Caribbee.'

'Give me some o' that,' said Anne Haddock. Jack passed the pipe along. The midwife took a deep drag, then bent double. Jack thought she might be about to choke.

'God's . . . Blood . . .' she gasped. She passed the pipe back, eyes watering all the way down her cheeks. 'Always wondered about tobaccer. Jesus!'

'Aye,' said Harry.

The horses plodded on. The crowd pressed hard about them, and the guards struggled to keep them back. Jack stood taller. The feeling of guilt, the feeling that so many people shouting all at once must be in the right . . . Somehow, passing the pipe back and forth with Anne and Harry made that feeling go away.

Jack smoked, and stared, and realized something amazing was happening. He was staring them down. His gaze roved across the crowd, and one by one, the eyes dropped.

'That's better, sonny,' said Harry. Jack wanted to hug him. He was still terrified – more and more, with every plodding step that took them closer to the scaffold – but he was staring them down, the mumping sods, and it felt good. Even through the terror, it felt good.

Harry passed him the pipe. Jack puffed, and coughed, and glared; and the voice of the devil started whispering through his head again. *You must remember, you must remember* – quicker and quicker, like his heart, the closer he got to the place marked out for his death.

It was very close now. The last stretch was fenced off, a straight empty path with the crowds packed on either side. Jack didn't look down once, not even when he saw the scaffold up ahead and heard the roaring of the biggest crowd he'd ever known. The Tree stood out black against the blue sky. He watched it coming closer, until he could see the loops in the nooses hanging down.

The cart was passing a viewing gallery opposite the Tree, prime seats packed with courtiers. In between the gallery and the gallows platform was a sort of pit, crammed full of angry, expectant Londoners. The pit was encircled by another fence, this one painted red and white. The gallery and the gallows platform lay just outside it. Five raised pulpits stood at regular intervals along the red and white fence, each one occupied by an Elect preacher.

Yesterday – was it really only yesterday? – he'd been standing right here, right on this spot, standing with Kit, watching Jonson. The five pulpits, perfectly spaced – Jonson fussing over them, making sure the placing was just right—

The red and white fence, a perfect circle.

There. There in the fifth pulpit, directly in front of the viewing gallery, was Webb. He was not preaching, not speaking at all; he gazed out over the heads of the crowd, and for a moment Jack felt his gaze brush over his face.

And he remembered.

Everything turned, and fell into place. It was like picking a lock – pushing the door open – and finding the Horror on the other side.

That was when he saw Mr Smiles.

Chapter 35

'Lady Vambrace, how delightful. If you will permit . . .'

'. . . so enjoy a good hanging . . .'

'. . . you believe, two hours from Whitehall Stairs! These awful people. I am fair exhausted.'

In the royal gallery, the Court settled and preened, twittering to each other like brightly jewelled birds. The gallery stood well above the seething mass of Londoners. Higher still, the Elect had laid on a private curtained box for Her Majesty's benefit, raised above the seats of the lesser Court. The Queen had arrived early, and was now safely screened out of sight. Once, Dr Dee would have sat up there with her as his right. Not now.

Even from the lowest level of the gallery, Dee had a perfect view of the gallows. In fact he'd have had a perfect view from anywhere on Red Lion Fields: the gallows were mounted on stilts, ten feet high, towering over the crowd. The cross-bar on its two heavy supports formed a rectangle above the platform. Framed within it, nine nooses hung ready.

Dee's eyes travelled away from the gallows, across the fenced-in herd of Londoners, to rest on his enemy. Webb's pulpit was right in front of the gallery, centre stage; from where he was sitting, well off to one side, the doctor could just see his profile. Webb was concentrating on looking humble. A sea of red hands reached up to him, voices shouting his name, begging for his blessing – but Webb was quiet. For the moment, thought Dee. Webb had worked too hard for this day to let it pass without a speech.

The shouting swelled to a dreadful throbbing roar – 'OUT! OUT! OUT!' mixed in with '*Webb! Webb! Webb!*' – and then stopped, as if a heavy blanket had been dropped over all. Webb had raised his red right hand for silence, and such was his power today that the whole crowd obeyed at once.

'Friends!' Webb's voice rang out pure and clear. His audience roared in answer. He waited for it to die down before carrying on.

'Friends. Brothers. Good Christian folk. Today is a great day. For today we make a Reckoning to God, for our errors. For too long we have suffered evil to walk among us. It is time to root it out.'

A few cheers went up, quickly shushed.

435

'Today is a great day – and yet, my friends, this morn-ing I wept.'

Webb paused, let the silence hang till Dee heard a hum from the crowd – then cut across it.

'I wept. Yes. And not for the errors of the past, my friends. I wept for the future. I wept for the news that was brought me in the night, while I slept. A warning, brought me by an Angel of the Lord sent from Heaven.'

Here it comes, thought Dee. He did not know what form it would take – only that Webb was about to make his play. The listening silence was absolute. Webb had them in the palm of his hand.

'My friends, the evil is still among us. The sorcerers lay their schemes even as I speak. Even now, oh, very now – on this our holy day of Reckoning – our enemies plot their foulest Horror of all! "Beware!" was the Angel's warning. Beware, my brothers – for the sorcerers, in league with Satan himself, today plot treason! Regicide! The death of our beloved Queen!'

Screams of outrage, and this time Webb did nothing to calm the crowd. He stood there, leaning slightly forward in his pulpit, scanning his audience with a look of deep approval. When he'd had his fill – when the rage had reached its high-tide mark and was just beginning to ebb – he raised his left hand high above his head. In it he held a small black-bound Bible.

'Yes!' he shouted, and again the crowd hushed for him.

'Yes, we are angry, my brothers. Yes, we must take up arms. Yes, I will lead you in this fight! That is why I have come here today . . . bearing a sword!' With a swift steely swish, Webb drew his rapier and held it aloft beside the Bible. 'On the Holy Gospel I swear: this sword shall not be sheathed until the evil is vanquished!'

He turned his back on the crowd, and faced the gallery. 'I dedicate this sword to the realm's service, and to the Queen's protection.'

Webb knelt in his pulpit, one hand holding his Bible to his heart, the other clasping his sword-hilt.

'Sweet Majesty, I beg you: accept my loyal service.'

The crowd erupted in the loudest cheers Dee had ever heard. The preachers in their pulpits were in full cry too, but the cheering drowned them out. Someone had lit braziers beside each of the five pulpits. The flames sent up a thick, pungent smoke.

Now the din of the crowd took on a new note, as the death-carts rounded the side of the gallery. Dee could clearly make out the smaller figure on the leading wagon. He glanced back at the gallows, and mouthed a silent prayer. The game was not over yet. Not while the boy still lived.

A gust of wind carried the smoke from the braziers curling towards the gallery. It smelled like bitter onions. It smelled . . . familiar.

Dee sniffed again, and stiffened.

There was no mistaking it: he'd smelled it at divinations, invocations, summonings – at a thousand rituals.

Squill.

He gripped the bench so hard he scratched the wood. His eyes darted about, settled on Webb, still kneeling in his pulpit . . .

. . . and returned to the gallows.

With an oath, Dee sprang to his feet and began pushing his way through the courtiers. There were laughs, grumblings, cries of protest. He ignored them all.

At the steps up to the royal enclosure, a man of the Elect barred his way. Pale hair, pale skin, mad, pale eyes: Jack's man – Spitting-with-rage Jonson or whatever his name was.

'Where do you think you're going, wizard?'

Dee did not have time to spare. 'I am indeed a wizard,' he said. 'I talk with devils and conjure storms. I coped with the Spanish fleet. I can cope with you, you funny little man.'

He grasped the amulet at his throat. The devil bound within it stirred, then unfurled, its power coursing through him. 'Dance aside, fool.'

Jonson gave a little squawk like a rabbit's death-cry. His eyes rolled, then crossed, and his mouth spread wide in a crazy grin. The squawk came again, only this time it sounded more like a bird. His arms twitched – and then he was dancing round in circles, squawking and flapping like a chicken. From somewhere behind him, Dee heard a titter of laughter.

He pushed the capering preacher aside, and started up the stairs.

Mr Smiles was staring at Jack, making some sort of sign with his eyes. Jack wanted to stare right back, show him he wasn't afraid, but he couldn't, because inside his head he was still reeling. Still remembering.

No one could see it but Jack. No one would believe him.

He remembered Dee in the library, foot tapping out the five points of his pentagram.

Evenly spaced.

He saw Webb and the preachers in the five pulpits – and Jonson, yesterday, fussing over their placement. He saw the gallows looming over them all. *First you need a sacrifice, to summon them here.* Dee had used mice. And here was Jack, along with Anne and Harry and the others, going to their deaths.

They were the sacrifice. Webb was going to summon up a devil.

He heard Black Dog's laughter ringing in his ears.

Jack forced himself to look at Mr Smiles. He wanted to shout at him, warn him – *there's a devil on the way* – only Smiles wouldn't believe it, and for certain it wouldn't stop

Webb. There must be something else; *must* be, else why would Black Dog have spoken?

Smiles kept darting his eyes down and to the left, and Jack couldn't help himself: his own eyes went that way too, away from Smiles . . .

. . . and there was Jill Proper, the youngest of the nippers, nestling up behind a reedy man with a red-dyed hand. She had her claw on, and was reaching for his purse-strings.

They'd come. Of course they had – it was the Law. Jack would swing, and Sharkwell would get a little bit richer.

Now that Jack had seen one, he could see nippers everywhere, trickling through the crowd like ants in pine straw. Not just nippers, either; there was Argent Liz over by the scaffold, and Ram Cat Peprah lounging by the viewing gallery. He sloped off into the crowd as Jack watched. And there – on the far side of the ground – there was the hot-pie wagon, doing a brisk trade.

All the fun of the fair.

'Webb! Webb! Webb!' shouted the crowd.

'Here, sonny. Have another puff.'

Jack shook his head. He couldn't look at Harry. The gallows were drawing closer, and although the carts were moving slow, they were moving. If he was going to do something, it had to be now. Otherwise he'd be hanging from the noose, with the Family watching him swing and twitch and kick. Maybe Beth would watch and be sorry.

No, he thought, she wouldn't even look. She'd be too busy minding the Law and lining Sharkwell's pockets.

Except – he realized with a strange slow horror – she wouldn't. None of them would. The devil would come, and then . . . what?

Death and horror.

He looked back at little Jill Proper, just in time to see her make her nip. The purse fell into her hand – and then she looked up at Jack, looked him right in the eye, and winked.

Jack heard a shout from behind him. He was still watching Jill as she quite deliberately bumped into the man she'd just robbed, waved the purse in his face and dodged away. The man cried, 'Thief!' and gave chase.

She did it on purpose, Jack thought. And that wink . . .

'Webb! Webb . . .'

'THIEF! STOP HIM!'

'. . . Webb . . .'

The crowd's chanting faltered. Another shout of 'Thief!', this time over to Jack's right, and now the hue and cry was coming from all around. Jack saw Ram Cat Peprah barging along at the head of a knot of angry citizens, all shouting, 'Stop, thief!' Nippers were streaking through the crowd from every direction, all of them pursued, all of them heading for Jack's cart. A wiry-thin old lady was waving a cane, spitting with fury as she tried to get at Liz Argent – who was also heading straight for Jack.

Six nippers vaulted the fence, slid past the guards and ducked under the cart. The guards turned to grab them, but then the waves of pursuers reached the fence and broke over it, crashing into the guards.

Jack felt light-headed. This didn't make sense.

What were they about?

Chaos. The people who'd had their purses stolen fought to get at the nippers; the guards fought to keep them back. The old lady appeared again, borne forward by the howling mob, crushed against the nearest guard. She shrieked, and fainted into the guard's arms. Another guard went down – and there was Liz Argent's enormous beefy arm, reaching up.

It happened faster than thought. Jack's shinbone scraped against the edge of the cart with a bright stab of pain, then he was in the scrum. One of the guards was shouting after them. Ram Cat appeared in front of him, clearing a path – Liz Argent bundled him along – and suddenly the old lady was there beside them, leading the way, and it wasn't an old lady now; something had changed in her face . . .

'Beth?'

She was panting, and sweat was washing runnels through her old lady make-up. Her wig had come askew, and a wisp of dark hair was stuck to her brow. She took his hand and squeezed it hard, dragging him on through the crowd.

'Lucky Jack,' she said. She was grinning like a crazy person. 'Fancy a pie?'

By the time Jack reached the hot-pie wagon, the idea that he might be safe was starting to settle in and make itself at home. It felt like a mad jester dancing in his head. *You're alive*, it sang. *Alive, and like to stay so.* Meanwhile his body was floating in a dream, as Ram Cat and Liz propelled him along, further and further from the death-carts. He couldn't feel his feet touch the ground.

Mr Smiles had fallen in with them, cut the ropes around Jack's wrists and ankles and rammed a big floppy hat onto his head. No one would recognize him as the witch-boy who was meant to hang.

'Sleek and spritely, ladderoon.' Smiles grinned.

Jack was too astonished to speak.

'Right,' said Beth. 'Smiles, you keep stirring havoc. Ram Cat, Liz, go and find the nippers, get them out safe.' She scanned the surroundings and nodded. 'Jack, in the wagon, now.'

Jack climbed up into the wagon. Beth followed, pulling down the covers behind her. They were alone in the dim grease-stink, the noise outside muffled now. Jack sat down in a clatter of empty pie-trays, from the little penny dishes to the enormous platter of Sharkie's Special. His head was whirling – maybe he understood he was safe, but nothing else made any sense at all – and before he could think of anything to say, Beth was hugging him tight, her warm cheek pressed against his ear. Jack hugged her back. She felt good, something flowing between them, and now he was shaking with relief, the relief not just in his head but in his throat and belly and bones.

'Aye, Jack. Aye . . .'

'Thanks, Beth.'

His voice sounded thick and choky. Beth drew back and looked at him. Jack realized his hands were still clasped around her neck. Suddenly he was very aware of her skin. He took his hands away double-quick.

Beth looked away. Jack felt his face going red. His dizzy wits wouldn't settle.

'Why?' he said.

'Why what?'

'Why'd you do it?'

Beth looked up, startled. 'What?'

'Why'd you save me, after . . .'

'After what?'

'I thought . . . Webb knew we were coming, he knew. He said it was you told him.'

'And you believed him.' Beth's voice sounded dangerous now. 'Just like that.'

Jack didn't know what to say. He *had* believed it, no question. He still half believed it now. 'Someone must have told him . . .'

'Aye.' Beth shook her head, blew out a breath. 'It was

my grampers. I didn't know. No one knew. And now he's dead.'

'Who's dead?'

'Grampers.'

'What, Sharkwell?' That didn't sound right either. Sharkwell was never meant to die: he was too old and awkward.

Beth held up her hand. 'Wait. Listen. This is important. Webb killed him—'

Jack tried to speak, but Beth shook her head. 'No, wait. See, now I'm in charge of making him pay. Ninth Law, ain't it? So once we're out of here, you've got to find a way of doing for Webb. I told everyone you'd know how so you'd better think of one.'

'But . . .' Webb was going to summon a devil. Jack had to stop it. Now he was free, he had to do something.

Outside, the crowd had gone quiet. The silence hummed.

'It's about to happen.'

'What?' said Beth.

Jack reached for the curtains over the pie counter and twitched them back.

Over a sea of heads he saw the gallows. The three carts stood empty beside them. On the raised platform, eight figures stood with their heads in the nooses. The ninth noose hung empty. Jack could see Anne Haddock and Harry the horse-cope standing straight and tall.

And it came to him – the way to stop Webb.

'A knife. Gimme a knife,' he said. Beth dived back into the wagon.

Jack could hear someone on the gallows crying, begging for mercy. From one of the pulpits, an Elect preacher was still shouting something; then he too went silent. Up on the gallows, the hangman stepped forward, and Jack felt his stomach drop away.

It was happening now. Jack knew how to stop it, but he was too late. There was no way of getting to the gallows in the time he had – the crowd in the pit was too thick. He'd have to be able to fly. He was too late.

In his sleeve, something stirred. Jack nearly fell off the wagon.

'Crukmuk,' said the imp, crawling out onto his wrist.

'*What?*' said Jack. 'Imp? I thought you were dead.'

'Not deathly. Big Shuk freeze, make to not help in scapings.'

Beth was back, staring at the imp with her mouth wide open, holding up a large pie-knife forgotten in one hand.

'Right . . . fine,' said Jack. 'Now – you're back – yes! Quickly, Imp, the gallows, you've got to cut the ropes!'

'No can. Big Shuk freeze, I tell you. No scapings.'

'But . . .'

'Magic boy command, Imp telling always when is more mecktick plan to do.'

'Yes. Yes, I did – so, what . . . you've got – a plan?'

446

The imp flourished its single remaining jaw. 'Bestest plan. Flying now to save days.'

'But you said you can't.'

'Not me. You flying, just as wisht.'

The imp whirred up into the air, and alighted on the two-foot tray that had recently held the grease, gravy and gristle of Sharkie's Special.

'You can. With reverse bind.'

Chapter 36

They blasted straight into the air. The imp shot up so fast that most of the pit didn't notice. Those that did shaded their eyes and peered up at the perfect empty blue of the sky, wondering if they'd drunk too much stingo.

A moment later, the same folk were wishing they'd drunk the whole bottle. The pie-dish plummeted out of the sun like a stooping falcon. Everyone in Red Lion Fields noticed it then, and saw the small figure who clung to it, black as a peppercorn against the sky.

'Aho! A divvil! There! Divvils a-flyin'!'

The fear rushed through the crowd like flames feasting on dry tinder.

'Down – down – down! Left!' Jack yelled.

The pie-dish rose and tipped to the right. Jack nearly

toppled out. His knuckles gripped white on the dish's greasy rim. A few flakes of pastry tumbled into the void. 'No! Left!'

'Ferrrkp't! Whid lef!' The imp's new voice was tinny and muffled, like a broken trumpet. The pie-dish had no eyes: Jack was doing the steering. It wasn't going well.

'There!' he said, and leaned left. The pie-dish swung into a heart-bursting dive. Far below him, but rushing closer fast, were thousands of tiny faces. They all stared up at him open-mouthed, arms pointing.

'Devilry! Sorcery!' The pie-dish arrowed into a sea of terror. The faces were screaming, fighting to get out of the way.

'Up! Up!' Jack begged, pulling back on the rim of the dish.

''P,' mumbled the imp.

They skimmed over the crowd like a stone skipping on a pond. A pulpit whipped past. Out of the corner of his eye, Jack saw Webb's face contorted with rage – and now the gallows were galloping closer.

'Right a bit – right, yes!' He pinched with his fingers and the dish jerked to the right. 'Slower!'

''Iff-cult,' growled the imp. The pie-dish began to slow.

'Slower!' said Jack. They were slowing, but not near fast enough. They hammered over the front of the gallows platform. The guards dived out of their way, jumping off the edge. Only the hangman stood his ground, stepping smartly to one side to let them pass.

'Slow *down*!' Jack gripped the rim of the dish and pulled hard.

The pie-dish swerved up in a fierce, teeth-rattling arc. 'GgggggGGGHHGK!' moaned the imp.

Jack closed his eyes.

When he opened them again, the cross-bar of the gallows was coming straight at his head. There was no time to make a decision.

He jumped.

The beam thumped into Jack's ribs, knocking the breath from him. His arms groped and gripped. His legs kicked over thin air. His foot twisted in one of the hang-ropes.

'Aark!' someone shouted from below.

'Sorry,' Jack gasped, untwisting his foot. He threw himself up over the cross-beam. He was perched high and vulnerable, twenty feet above the ground. He hurt all over. Close by, the pie-dish hovered in mid-air.

From up here, the perfect circle of the red and white fence and the pulpits was very clear. Inside it, the pit was a crush, a scrimmage of fear and fury. Beneath Jack's feet he could see eight shocked white faces looking up at him. He pulled the knife from his belt and slashed at the first rope.

'See the devil-child! Come to free his own!' Webb's voice soared above all the others.

'I ain't no devil!' shouted Jack. 'You are! You killed my ma!'

Howls and catcalls from the crowd.

'Lies! Witches' plots! *Hang them!*' Webb commanded.

The hangman! He was standing, hooded and motionless, beside the enormous lever that operated the gallows. He was staring up at Jack – too frighted to move.

'Do it, man!' shouted Webb. The crowd roared its agreement.

Still the hangman did nothing except sway on his feet. He looked drunk.

A firm final cut and the first rope parted. Jack looked down into Anne Haddock's face. She gaped up at him, eyes wide, then started scrabbling at the noose about her neck.

The roaring from the crowd stuttered and died.

Out of the corner of his eye Jack saw a flash of light. He looked across the pit.

Standing tall in his pulpit, Nicholas Webb held a sword high above his head. The sword was made of light. The light flared white, dazzling bright.

'God is with me!' Webb shouted, and flung the sword at Jack. It wheeled twice, end over end, then levelled out, coming on dead straight.

'*Imp!*'

'*Grrrp!*'

The pie-dish lurched wide. Jack grabbed it as it passed,

turned it up like a shield. The sword slammed straight into it, hammering an inch-deep dent in the pewter right in front of Jack's nose. The impact knocked him off balance, and he was falling, clinging to the tumbling dish.

The sword swerved, murderous quick, chasing him down. He rolled as he landed. Pain sliced sharp down one side of his face. He scrambled away, and the pain roared hot and red in his ear.

The sword was embedded, quivering, in the gallows platform. The blade had slid down Jack's cheekbone and torn off his patch, and part of his earlobe. The blood ran down his neck in a thick hot stream.

The devil-sword twitched like an angry snake. The light had gone out of it. Through his weird eye, Jack could see whispering shapes like insects moving beneath the surface of the blade.

'Up, lad!' said Harry the horse-cope.

The boards of the platform squealed as the sword strained to free itself. Away across the crowd, Jack saw Webb clench his right hand into a fist.

Jack grabbed the pie-dish. The crowd was hushed with excitement. Thousands of people, watching – and only one of Jack. He looked out across the space at Webb, and at the sea of goggling faces in between.

'Can't you see?' Jack screamed at them. 'He's lying to you! It's magic – he's a sorcerer!'

The sword came free. It sprang up out of the platform, shook itself and arrowed straight for Jack's heart.

Jack raised the dish just in time. The devil-sword shrieked across the pewter. It glanced away in a tight curve and swept back in – going for Jack's head. He threw up the dish again.

The sword drove up hard, and Jack couldn't hold on. The dish fell from his fingers – rolled with a slow dying grumble across the platform. Jack heard the crowd cheering.

'Imp!'

The pie-dish flew off in the wrong direction, away from Jack.

There was nothing to use as a shield, nowhere to hide. The sword was coming fast. Coming down like lightning from on high.

Something kicked Jack's legs out from under him.

Jack fell to the platform, and the hangman stepped over him. Drew a long dagger from his belt. Turned aside the sword.

An expert flurry of blows. The hangman's blade moved faster than thought, driving the devil-sword back.

Jack lay there, too surprised to move. Each block and parry drew a gasp from the pit. Jack saw wide-eyed faces lit up with excitement. The crowd was enjoying the show.

Beyond and above them, Webb swept his arm to the right, trying a new attack.

With a flick of the wrist the hangman thrust the sword aside. Webb snarled. It wasn't so easy for him, Jack realized – not like with the knife in the courtyard. He was fifty yards away, locked at blades with a master swordsman who'd appeared from nowhere. It must be taking all his concentration.

' 'K'swuick, nei!' The imp was back.

Jack was no swordsman, but he was Southwark through and through. He knew the dirty fight; that the blow landed best when it came unexpected.

'Here, Imp,' said Jack. 'Remember your old master?'

'Ack!' mumbled the imp. ' 'Mell his reek.'

'Good.'

Jack drew back his arm and threw the dish as hard as he could. '*Seek blood!*'

Screaming like a banshee, the imp spun over the heads of the crowd, slicing through the air towards the pulpit. Jack just had time to imagine it cutting Webb in half before it reached its target.

There was a bright flash of red light, and a crack like thunder. The speed the dish was going, it should have sliced through Webb's throat, or at least broken all his fingers. Instead he caught it neatly with one hand.

The sword stopped dead mid-thrust, dropped out of the air, and clattered to the gallows platform.

Webb held the pie-dish aloft. 'I am the Lord's servant!' he shouted. A few cheers from the crowd, but there was a muttering mixed in too. Dark red light pulsed in his stained hand.

'Mebbe he *is* a bloody wizard!' someone shouted. The pit was shifting, twitching like the skin of a fly-pricked animal – unsure which way to turn.

'I do the Lord's will!' Webb held the dish out in front of him. The light burned brighter. Jack felt the imp's beetle-body twitch in his sleeve, then go still.

'Imp?' he said.

Nothing. Webb tossed the dish aside and raised his right arm.

The sword rose up in the air.

The hangman stepped forward, tangled his feet together, and fell over. Jack caught a waft of a familiar spicy smell, tinged with booze. He twisted, desperate, expecting to see the sword swooping down on him.

Instead he watched it slam hilt-first into the gallows lever.

The front of the platform dropped away with a loud *clunk*. The prisoners fell. Jack, the hangman and Anne Haddock tumbled to the ground; the rest came up short with a jerk and a wet crunch as their necks broke. Fourteen feet twitched and kicked above Jack's head.

A great cheer went up from further back in the crowd. Down beneath the gallows it was all confusion – half the people surging forward, reaching through the red and white fence to grab Jack; the other half fighting to get away. A hand twisted in his collar – the hangman. He fought against it, and now another hand was closing on his wrist: someone had managed to climb over the fence, and was dragging him the other way.

The hangman pulled Jack to him, and floored the other man with a neat kick to the cods. He hissed and fell to one knee, clutching his ankle. He kept a good hold on Jack.

'All's well, gents!' he bawled. 'I have him!' He pulled Jack closer, arm closing round his neck. He was tugging at his hood, lifting it up – and it was Kit's face underneath, sweaty and bloodshot and, yes, definitely drunk.

'Saved again, Jack,' he said. 'That makes three.'

A sharp hot-metal smell stabbed at Jack's nostrils, making his head swim.

'Not saved,' he said, staring up at the twisting, dangling bodies. The sacrifice. 'Not save—'

A thunderclap rolled out across Red Lion Fields.

It rang in Jack's ears like Satan's own anvil.

All noise stopped all together.

Chapter 37

The first burst of white light was so bright it was like a new sun.

Oof, went the crowd. It was almost funny – the sound of a thousand pairs of lungs emptying in the same instant.

The mob before the gallows turned away from Jack and Kit. Turned as one to watch the light that was growing in the middle of the pit. Jack heard a child begin to cry.

'What is this?' Kit stared at the light, transfixed.

'Webb,' said Jack.

'More devilwork! O foulest sorcery!' The triumphant shout rang out across the pit. Beyond the light, rising above it like a beacon tower, Webb stood straight and tall in his pulpit. His face blazed. His right arm was outstretched. 'Fear not, my brothers! The Lord is with me! The Lord gives me strength!'

'Save us!' shouted someone in the crowd.

'Save us! Save us!' others took up the cry.

The light ate up everything it touched. Jack saw one man turn to run, waving his arms – too slow. For a crazy moment the upraised arms hung free, cut off clean at the elbow; then they toppled into the light and were gone.

Panic broke like a thunderstorm. Men and women were screaming. Some were trampled underfoot. The crowd shrank away from the light, surged against the five pulpits, crushed itself bloody on the red and white fence. Jack saw people straining, weeping, trying to hold their children above the press. The hot-metal smell was eye-watering, choking, stabbing sharp.

'Time to go, Jack,' said Kit. He'd caught the panic – his voice wavering out of control.

The light vanished. All at once, people began to fall. It looked like an invisible scythe, sweeping round in a swift circle. They fell without a sound. The nearest ones were close enough that Jack could reach out and touch them – but it would do no good. There was something so heavy about the way they fell, he knew that they would never get up.

Hundreds of them. Their bodies lay like cut corn, in a neat circle bounded by the fence and the five pulpits. Above them, a great shadow was simmering and stirring, twitching and puckering. It gathered itself together and became solid. Up in their pulpits, the men of the Elect were chanting, holding out wooden crosses like swords. They looked very brave, or very foolish.

The devil unfolded itself over the carpet of corpses. Jack saw its enormous size; its writhing pale skin; its soft, shuffling limbs. It reached down and snuffled over the dead – dabbing here and there, as if selecting from a plate of dainties.

As it fed, it began to take form. Two pale limbs tangled together to form a tail. Others sprouted where arms should be. They reached up and wrenched out a head, forming the flesh like warm wax. A gaping snout was dragged up across the face; two pointed ears were plucked out; the slug-skin clenched and bubbled like bad milk.

'Devil!' Webb's commanding shout cut across the screams and moans of the crowd.

Silence. Webb looked strong and good, scarlet robes billowing out around him, his red hand outstretched, his other hand clutching his Bible.

All lies, thought Jack.

'Devil!'

The devil's head swung round. For a moment it faced Webb, sightless; then a cluster of yellow eyes glommed up from inside its head.

'Devil! I conjure you to me!'

The devil took a single shambling step towards him.

'What's he doing?' said Kit.

With every step the devil was growing clearer. Strange

organs throbbed beneath its skin. Now its arms sprouted hands, with long spiny fingers. Teeth wriggled up like worms from its pulpy gums.

Webb never flinched. 'You were summoned forth by our enemies,' he said. 'Yet the Lord is with me.'

The devil towered over him. Its tail lashed from side to side. With frightening, unnatural speed its head snapped forward.

'Halt!' cried Webb.

And the devil stopped dead – just like it was meant to, at the border of the circle. Its jaws slopped shut inches from Webb's outstretched hand. He eyed the devil. The devil eyed him back.

The preachers in the pulpits roared with triumph.

'We should leave,' said Kit. 'Now. Before that thing breaks loose.'

'It won't,' said Jack. 'Don't you see? It's a trick . . .'

Webb was holding out his hand to the devil, fingers spread like talons. The devil strained to get at him, but it could not cross the line of the red and white fence. It was nothing more than a baited bear – chained, plucked of its claws.

Webb was the monster.

'Foul sorcery!' he cried. 'Black treason! But see how faith defeats it!'

His preachers believed. Their faces shone with it, like a madness. The nearest one, to Jack's left, was weeping for joy. The crowd believed too. Outside the death-circle, the survivors were falling on their knees, praying. Some fools were even coming back to see the show.

'We're leaving,' said Kit, grabbing Jack by the arm. 'Now.'

'No,' said Jack. He felt bile rising in his throat. It hurt. It burned white-hot, the helpless rage of it. Webb's trick was working. After today, he would be the devil-slayer – the holy saviour of the Queen. He'd be able to do whatever he wanted.

'No,' muttered Jack.

Kit's hand was still clenched around his arm. He had to struggle to get free.

'What are you doing?' asked Kit.

'Goodbye. Thanks. I can't let him . . .' Jack waved over at Webb.

He wasn't saying it right. It didn't matter. He shook off Kit's hand, and ran for the nearest pulpit. Kit started after him, but his ankle buckled beneath him. He fell, cursing.

The stampede had emptied this part of the fields. Jack was alone, but for a few trampled bodies, and one of the guards from the carts – crawling away, his half-pike abandoned. To his right was the devil, in its ring of death. Ahead was the weeping preacher, high in his pulpit. No imp to help Jack now. Just Jack – scrunty Jack – Anne's piglet.

And now he knew exactly what to do.

Jack scooped up the half-pike without breaking stride, and raced on for the pulpit.

'Doing it, Ma,' he said. His hands were slick with sweat. 'Doing for him now.'

The pulpit was very close. Beyond it, the devil was huge. No one was watching Jack. All eyes were on the other side of the circle, on Webb, as he reached forward.

'I name you, Astirpel!'

The devil twisted and struck. Webb moved faster, his red right hand flashing out. He gripped it by the snout. The devil screamed – a terrible unearthly shriek like a mountain of broken glass grating together. Jack kept running. He was almost there.

'The power of faith is my shield! I name you, Astirpel – Duke of the Seventh Circle – and as I trust in the Lord my God, I cast you out!'

Jack reached the pulpit. He looked up. The preacher was gazing out across the circle at Webb: Jack might as well have been invisible.

His robe was cinched round his waist by a leather belt.

'Out!' Webb shouted.

One chance. Jack could hear his ma's voice, from those long days before the testing, the endless practice she'd put him through – *Curbing, lad – it runs in the family. I've the knack for it and so have you. Easy now . . .*

He hefted the half-pike and hooked it under the preacher's belt. It caught first time. The preacher yelped –

462

Jack hauled, levering back with all his might – and then the man in the pulpit was toppling . . .

'Out!'

The preacher hit the ground with a thud.

And now there were four. The circle was broken. On the far side, the devil broke free. It shook itself; its head lashed forwards, snapped at Webb . . .

And disappeared into a buzzing black cloud of flies.

The devil reeled back, bellowing. The flies swarmed up over its head and onto its shoulders. They gathered there, massing together into the shape of a man. As Jack stared, the cloud thickened and he caught a flash of red.

'No . . .' he whispered.

The cloud burst apart, and there was Webb, riding on the devil's shoulders, clear for all to see.

The devil's roars turned to howls as Webb thrust his right hand into the soft flesh behind its ear. An angry red light flashed out, deep inside. His legs gripped tight on its neck. His flies swarmed about his head in a filthy halo.

The devil twisted its head and snapped its jaws at him; Webb tensed his arm, and the red light burned brighter. The devil roared and thrashed. Webb's eyes burst. He thrust his hand deeper, and snarled.

Webb was changing all over. His skin was flaking and blistering, sloughing off in patches, as if something inside could no longer stand the touch of human flesh. His eyes shone pale and bright through wells of blood.

'He's a demon himself!' someone shouted from the royal gallery. 'He's—'

The speaker broke off as the devil whirled round to face him. In the lower gallery, someone screamed. The devil lunged in at the royal box. The curtains whipped open, and Jack saw Dr Dee, standing gaunt and steady, clutching the amulet at his throat. Sparks crackled all around him – flew out and burst over Webb. The devil twisted away; stumbled back into the centre of the pit; reared up its snout and screamed at the sky.

The light from Webb's red hand blazed up. The devil lowered its head, shuddered, and stood still, flanks heaving. Jack looked up past the slavering mouth, past the swollen neck, straight into Webb's pale, glowing eyes.

YOU. BOY. It was Webb's voice – except it was inside his head; just like Black Dog; only Black Dog had spoken softly, and this voice trembled with rage and hate.

The devil took a step towards Jack. Mounted on its shoulders, Webb was in full control. And another step. Slow purposeful strides, belly low to the ground. Stalking him. There was nowhere to run – no safe place, now that Jack had broken the circle. Even if there had been, he couldn't move. Webb's eyes rooted him to the spot.

'Oi!'

The devil's head swung round, away from Jack.

'Aye, over here!'

The voice was coming from over to Jack's right, where

the hot-pie wagon stood – where a skinny figure was leaping down from the wagon, ducking under the red and white fence, dashing out into the circle.

'That's right! It's me! Come on, you big craven!'

The devil squinted down at Beth. It looked confused. Up on its shoulders, Webb yanked his arm. The devil sidestepped.

'Go, Jack! Get away!'

Beth was stumbling through the field of corpses, straight towards the devil. Now it turned to face her head on. It opened its mouth, and Jack felt a slow sick sensation yawn open in his stomach.

It was happening again. First his ma, then Rob, now Beth.

'No!' Jack heard himself shout, and then he was running.

He ran to cut across Beth's path. It was hard going, dead limbs tangling round his legs. He staggered through them in clumsy, giant steps. Beth stopped and screamed at him to go the other way. Jack shook his head, stumbled and sprawled, landing with his face in a dead man's belly. He clambered to his feet, and raised his red right hand.

What did Webb say?

'Devil!' His voice sounded shrill and stupid. 'I . . . I conjure you to me!'

The devil reared up. Webb bore down on it, wrenched

its head round to face Jack. Its tail whisked over Beth's head.

'To me!'

The devil came at him. No more confusion. Webb spurred it on, his glowing eyes fixed on Jack. Time thickened and clotted like blood.

You must remember . . .

'I call you – Ast – Astirpon . . .' What was it? What came next? But Jack couldn't remember.

He took a step back and looked about. There behind him was the empty pulpit, and there was Kit clambering up into it, trying to restore the circle. No good. The three remaining preachers were still in their places, shocked rigid; but Webb's pulpit stood empty. '*Four,*' he heard Dee shout; saw his finger jabbing at the book. *Four and four and four – damned before they began.*

The devil loomed over him. A gurgling sound rose up from its throat. A dreadful deep sloshing sound, like some vast wineskin full of black, poisonous liquid. Jack looked the devil in the eye, and knew in that moment that he was going to die.

The devil was laughing at him.

STUPID BOY. Webb's voice was calm – curious, almost. The devil's bulk blocked out the sun. Jack could smell its breath, sickly sweet like spoiled meat. See the way the soft skin shifted, cracking, bubbling up and leaking. And there, leaning out over its shoulder in triumph, was Webb – eyes shining like ice in winter sun, grin stretching wider and wider as his lips peeled away from his skull.

'Run, Jack!'

That was Kit. Up in the pulpit now. Everyone telling him to run – but Jack wasn't going to. Even if it was stupid.

Jack was going to fight.

The devil's mouth plunged towards him, wide open. The teeth filled the whole mouth, wriggling and swarming. There was no tongue.

Jack threw up his right arm, spreading his hand. The stain burned.

'I name you . . .' Jack couldn't remember any of it. He screamed in frustration. '*Sod off!*'

The devil bit down on his hand, sucking with its wormy mouth. The slime-teeth writhed and gripped like eels, hauling him in. The head reared up. Jack felt his stomach fall away as he was borne up, high in the air.

The world wheeled below him. There was the gallows – the hot-pie wagon – the gallery; and there in front of it stood Dr Dee, a figure of golden light blazing forth from Webb's pulpit.

The fifth.

The wriggling teeth gripped harder, and Jack's arm slid down the devil's gullet to the shoulder.

'Sod *off!*' he screamed. Pain swirled through him, a blazing white heat. Lightning in his heart, and thunder in his blood. His hand was made of fire – buzzing, tingling, crackling out through his fingertips. Jack was laughing, a hoarse mad cackle that had nothing to do with mirth. The devil tried to spit him out. Jack grabbed a clump of writhing flesh and clung on.

NO. Webb's voice again, but no longer calm.

Five lines of white light shot out from the pulpits, joined to form a star.

NO. Webb's voice rising in sudden fear. NO NO NO!

Flat.

White.

Light.

It sucked the devil down, just as Dee's trap had sucked at the imp; but this was much bigger, much faster. It dragged Jack in too – his hand stuck, seared into the devil's flesh.

The devil opened its mouth to scream. Jack wrenched his arm free. He tumbled to the ground. A hot hand gripped his wrist – Beth, hauling him back, away from the light. The devil went under, and now it was Webb floundering in the flat white light. He reached out for Jack, struggled for the space of two heartbeats, his face wide open like a baby crying at its first breath – and then he was gone.

The light rippled once, settled, and blinked out.

Chapter 38

Mist snaked along the river. It slithered through the streets like a wet rat's belly. London's revels were not yet ended, but the mist dampened them, muffling the blooms and booms of the fireworks.

Slack-water, and the Thames flowed soft. The oars splashed as Kit sculled in towards the bank. Jack and Beth sat together in the back of the boat, beads of moisture forming on their faces.

Up ahead, ghostly merriment floated down the river from Westminster. The mist played strange tricks with the sounds of the drums and trumpets, so Jack could not tell if they were near or far.

'Royal barge'll be out soon,' said Kit. 'That would be embarrassing, if they came upon us...' He laughed. 'Covered in mud and carrying a boatload of stolen gold.'

'We ain't raised it yet,' said Beth.

'True enough,' said Kit. 'But this . . . Yes, this is certainly the place.'

Jack nodded. The kiln tower loomed clear through the mist now, as they edged in towards the bank beside Webb's garden door. At this time of the tide the boxes would be under several feet of water and probably a good depth of ooze as well. Kit had wanted to come and pick them up at low tide, but Jack had talked him out of it: at low tide, there'd be mudlarks all over the flats, and mudlarks paid close attention to strangers salvaging small, heavy boxes. Better to do it now, secretly, even if it meant a long, wet evening.

If only they had the imp, he thought. The imp would sniff up the boxes easy. Jack had woken after his battle with Webb to find the beetle gone from his sleeve. Eventually they'd found the pie-dish, but the imp was gone from there too. In the three days since what people were now calling the Deliverance (but what Jack still thought of as the Reckoning), he had woken hoping that it had somehow survived, that it would come back today. It hadn't.

Those three days had been gloomy ones for Jack. Everyone else was happy. All of London – only knowing the story that Dee had chosen to tell. Dee had saved the Queen, it was said, and so his version of events pretty much stood as the truth; and it was true too, as far as it went.

It was true that Webb had deliberately brought about

the Horrors, and summoned the devil Astirpel in order to put on his cozening show. Not just true, but the perfect story too: the honey-tongued prophet revealed as a servant of Satan, one of Hell's own. Everyone claimed they'd seen it all along.

That was natural enough – Jack guessed there were a lot of red hands being scrubbed around London. What was giving him trouble was the bit about the boy hero who'd assisted the daredevil Kit Morely in dispatching the Duke of Hell. It was the high point of the story, the bit the balladeers lingered over, and whenever he heard it Jack felt sick.

Webb was dead. Jack kept on trying to feel triumph, or satisfaction, or something . . . but all he felt was hollow. His ma was just as dead as before. More dead, now that he'd kept his vow and there was nothing left to do for her. And the way Webb had looked at the end, Jack wasn't sure what it was he'd killed – or even if it was dead at all.

The boat nosed into the riverbank, and Beth stepped ashore with the mooring rope, tied up and surveyed the waters with a frown.

Kit levered himself up on his crutch. 'Well, they're in there somewhere,' he said. 'I name myself prodder. You two can fight it out to see who wades.' He leaned over and thrust his crutch into the river, feeling for the bottom. 'Hm. Mud . . . Mud . . . Yes, deep mud – I suppose gravel would have been too much to hope for.'

Beth looked over at Jack and rolled her eyes. 'Perky as a perch,' she muttered. 'Imagine how he'll be once he's got his gold.'

'I heard that,' said Kit. 'And it's *our* gold, my dear, as you never tire of reminding me . . .'

'I ain't your dear.' Beth sniffed. 'And I think it should be you goes in. Take off your pretty jerkin – stop shamming about on your ankle . . .'

'I'll do it,' said Jack.

'Good lad,' said Kit.

The boxes of gold – the thought of them lying there safely tucked away in the river had burned like a little candle-flame in the three days of gloom. Maybe it was wrong that gold could do that, but it was true. Jack wanted to feel the boxes, feel them hard and solid, to be the first one to lay hands on them.

'Mud . . .' said Kit. 'Mud . . . Mud— Ah! What have we here? Jack?'

Jack clambered over the side. The water was cold. He felt his privies shrivel up.

He grasped the crutch and slid his hand down it, realized he wasn't going to reach the bottom without a ducking, held his breath and plunged under. Now his hand was burrowing into muck, still following the crutch-pole – and now he had it, something hard, but it didn't feel like wood . . .

He came up gasping and spluttering, with slime clinging to his head. 'It's a stone.'

'Bad luck,' said Kit.

'There's a snail in your hair,' said Beth. 'Come here – I'll . . .'

Jack waded up to the bank, and she drew off a thick skein of water weed from his hair. There were three snails, it turned out. She flung the whole mess into the water.

'I filched some stingo for the damp,' she said. 'Here.'

She passed Jack a flask from under her coat. The liquid went down burning strong, and Jack was glad of it. Wet from head to toe, on a day like this, a little stingo was just fine.

Jack plunged for one more stone, six clay jars and a cow's skull before he found the first box. By this time he was exhausted, juddering cold. Kit bedded the crutch in deep under one side and levered up, Jack squeezed the ropes underneath and fastened them, and they hauled it up together from its sucking, oozy bed.

The box came out dripping black, trailing weed, small and heavy and exciting. Kit pried up the lid, and they all looked at it for a moment in silence, the gold untouched by the mud, perfectly stacked in gleaming rows all the way to the top.

Somewhere upriver, a mighty firework boomed and crackled.

'Seven more . . .' said Kit. He looked west along the river. Away beyond the mist, the sun was sinking. 'Seven more, but not today, I think. Now's for a warm fire, and coins to count.'

The mist was thickening, lowering, tenting over the river as they slipped out into midstream. The tide had turned, and Kit let them drift, occasionally dipping an oar to keep them from spinning out of control.

The sounds of the celebration upriver had been blowing in and out of hearing all evening. Now, all of a sudden, they were close at hand. Trumpets and pipes, drums and squibs, shouts, songs and laughter; a glow of coloured lanterns, green, red and blue; ghost-lights in the mist.

'Stone me, they're going to run us down,' said Kit, hauling on the oars as the outlines of the leading boat appeared. It was coming on fast.

It missed them, but not by much. The procession passed within six feet.

The first boat was a sturdy wherry packed with hard-rowing oarsmen. The tow-rope bent out behind. Looming after it came the royal barge.

Lit by strings of coloured lanterns, wafting through the mist, it looked like a magical ship from a tale. Beneath a canopy of green, gold-blossomed silk, its glass windows flashed, now glinting back the light of the lanterns, now allowing a glimpse of the rout inside.

'Strike my eyes,' muttered Beth. Their boat bobbed and tipped in the swell.

Some of the lords and ladies wore masks. Jack thought

he spotted Dee's beard bristling out beneath a grinning harlequin face. The barge seemed in another world, set apart from Jack and his companions in their muddy little skiff.

Even as this thought occurred to Jack, the barge began to fade.

A woman was leaning out of a window, trailing her hand in the water. She looked straight at Jack – he couldn't have been more than ten feet away – but she didn't see him, and as he watched she became thin; thin all the way through so that Jack could see straight into the cabin behind her.

Jack shivered, and it was more than just the cold.

A man on the stern was juggling fireworks, a fizzing whirl of dazzling white sparks. He faded to nothing as he passed, and for a moment the lights were spinning by themselves in mid-air. Then they too were gone. The lanterns seemed to blink out all at once, and in the same instant the music stopped. All gone, as if they'd never existed.

The barge vanished. Jack had the sudden haunted feeling that the whole of London might have disappeared along with it.

Kit laughed, but there was a tremor in his voice.

'Feels like a goose just walked over my grave,' said Beth.

'It's just the mist,' said Jack. 'Just a trick.'

She shook her head. Jack knew she was right. They should be passing the palaces on the Strand by now; but he was not at all sure what they would find if they steered for the bank. The silence was the silence of deep, dark forests – a listening silence, of hunters and prey straining their ears, of cruel beasts and savage men crouched in ambush, of birds and small things in the undergrowth, hushed and waiting.

'Keep out in midstream,' Jack heard himself say.

'Aye,' said Kit.

The words fell into the quiet like stones into a well, and were swallowed up.

Jack listened. The silence was not quite complete: he could hear the water bubbling under the boat's prow, and the dip of the oars. And something else, close at hand.

The creak of a branch (*branches that shouldn't be there*, thought Jack). A sighing sound, wind in leaves . . .

A fallen, swamped tree trunk scraped along the side of the boat, twisting its course.

'I said keep out—' said Jack.

'I know, damn it!'

'What are you—?'

Kit was scuffling at the oars; there was a splash as he dropped one in the water, and then they were aground with a jolt.

To either side, brownish-grey sand stretched out for a few paces before vanishing into the mist.

No palaces. No people. No sound but the wind in the trees.

'This ain't the Strand,' said Beth.

'Heh,' said Kit. 'No. But we *are* stranded.'

'Let's get out into the stream again,' said Jack. He jumped over the bows, bare feet sinking into cold damp sand. 'Come on.'

Beth followed him. Kit picked his way over the side, stumbled in knee-deep water and cursed. Jack put his shoulder against the bows and shoved. The boat shifted a fraction, then Kit splashed round to join him and it shifted a bit more.

'Come on, Beth,' said Kit. 'Let's be gone from here.'

Beth was just standing there, up to her ankles in water, staring past them into the mist.

'Beth?' said Jack.

'Look.' She pointed.

Through the mist, coming from inland, a muffled ghostly light was dancing. It shifted through different colours – gold and green and purple, white and blue and green again. It twirled and looped merrily up and down.

It was coming towards them.

'What manner of wraith . . . ?' said Kit. 'Jack, I think we should—'

'Wait,' said Jack. 'Listen.'

There was music coming from the light – a rasping, chirping whistle, something between a march and a battle-song, harsh and strange. And now, under the whistling, came another sound. A whirring sound.

A familiar sound.

'Imp!' said Jack.

The imp whirred straight at his face, changed course at the last moment, circled a triple halo about his head and landed on his shoulder.

'Master, I return,' it said.

Jack could feel a grin spreading across his face. Beth was staring at him like he'd suddenly grown a third eyeball.

The imp clacked its jaws together and glowed gleeful white. Jack twisted his neck to look at the shining little creature on his shoulder. He couldn't believe how happy he was to see it.

'What about Webb? I thought—'

'Ack, what very big Shuk that is.' One of the imp's gleaming blue eyes winked out for a second. Its voice dropped, became sly. 'Tasking to be done here, before you . . . ah . . . scape this place, master . . .' It trailed off.

'What, Imp?' Jack shivered. The mist brushed cold and clammy against his skin. 'What is this place?'

'Place of Shuk. Big and bigger. You must command tasking, then we make scape.'

'Command you what?'

'Command to lead to Shuks. You, lovey-dove and lokmok too.'

478

Jack heard Beth take a little hissing breath. 'What did you call me?' she said.

'You are Master's dearling, no?' said the imp.

'Shut up, Imp,' said Jack. Instantly the imp's jaws clacked shut, and its shell went dark. 'Sorry, Beth.' He couldn't quite look at her.

'Always been an impudent little brute,' said Kit. He was eyeing the imp suspiciously.

'Well, go on then,' said Beth. 'Command it.'

'All right,' said Jack. 'Imp, lead us to the . . .'

'The Shuks,' said Kit.

'The Shuks.'

Without a word, the imp flew up off Jack's shoulder. Its shell took on a soft golden glow like a candle-lantern, and it led the way through the mist.

The three of them followed, Kit floundering through the sand on his crutch.

'Heavy going,' he muttered.

Soon the sand gave way to firm, dark grey mud, then marsh grasses, then solid ground. They were walking through a wood, with gentle slopes to either side of them. A trail had been hacked through the undergrowth, and this was the path they followed. They did not speak. The imp was never more than a couple of paces ahead, and it had started humming again – a cheerful tune – but Jack felt afraid. More than ever, the silence seemed like it was listening.

Listening, waiting, and watching.

When they arrived at the grove, the mists rolled back like curtains. Jack stopped dead. Behind him, he heard Beth gasp, then breathe out very slowly.

Ringing the clearing were nine pale lights. When he looked closer, Jack saw that each one was a ghost – a hanging corpse made of light, swaying gently back and forth. There were men and women and one child, a girl. They were dead, but their eyes were open. Aware. Watching Jack, and Beth and Kit.

Watching the centre of the grove.

There was a stone there, half buried in the ground. It was smooth and black, except where a single seam of pure white gold cut through it.

A flicker of light gleamed through the stone. From the trees beyond the grove came a wild cry, something like the scream of a fox. A clatter of birds burst from the branches, and a rustling sound rushed across the clearing, like wind in dead reeds.

And then they were there.

Three figures, standing before them.

On the right was Black Dog, slouched on its haunches, its brutal, heavy head bent low over its chest.

On the left stood a bent old man made of weeds and wet leaves, silt and gravel, and bleached, wind-scoured wood. He watched Jack with eyes the colour of Thames mud.

Between them stood the thing that Jack had seen at

Old Pol's Stump. Towering over the others, glossy black –
and now it was facing him, and he could see that its head
was the head of a raven, and its eyes were twin pools of
white gold.

The head turned from side to side, observing them first
through one eye, then through the other. The eyes held
Jack fast. He heard a wheezing sound from behind him. He
couldn't tell if it was Beth or Kit.

'Here, master, they show,' said the imp. Its voice was
grave, with none of its usual bounce and play. 'First is
Black Dog of your already knowing. Second is the Old
Father, the River-Shuk. And here is the Great One of this
place, First of the City, the one you name King Lud.'

The black beak opened and clacked shut. No words. A
tremor ran through the trees, setting the ghosts
a-swinging.

The beak opened once again, and King Lud croaked.

The words came then, whispered into the centre of
Jack's head.

You have done us good service, you three.

Jack thought that was it; but the croaking came again,
a dry ancient voice that set his bones on edge.

I grant you the freedom that is within my power.
I grant you the freedom that is within my gift.
In the dark places.
In the thin places.
The Freedom of the City of Lud.

Something small and hard was pressing against Jack's chest. He looked down and saw that it was a key. A key of copper or bronze, very old, crusted and cankered with lumpy green tarnish.

When he looked up, he was standing back on the river-bank, with Beth and Kit to either side. The greyish sand was gone; instead, their boat was tied up to a little stone jetty in what looked to Jack like some great lord's deer park. A trim box hedge bordered the jetty on three sides, and a nicely coppiced willow tree swayed overhead. The grove, the hanging corpses, the three devils might never have existed.

But the key was still there, cold against his chest; and on his shoulder he felt the prickly pressure of the imp's claws.

The mist unravelled, the river's tent was broken, and Jack could see the waters rolling past the banks; shadows dark under the trees; the last of the day's light shattered into spears by the branches. There to the west was the kiln tower, and there beyond it the spire of St Mary Rounceval.

The waters rolled on to the east, past the palaces of the Strand, round the bend into the city. The tatters of the mist hung about the streets, and the sunset light painted the walls and the towers rosy gold.

In the thin places, the voice of King Lud echoed in his head; and it seemed to Jack that the city was nothing more than a painted lantern, glowing against the gathering night beyond.

In the dark places.

Jack fingered the key around his neck. Later he would wonder long and hard about the key, but in that moment he didn't have to. Everything was very clear.

Kit and Beth stood beside him. The imp sat on his shoulder. Away downstream Jack could see the royal barge, beetling along like a tiny magnificent toy.

The chest full of gold lay forgotten in the bottom of the skiff.

Jack stood very quietly, and gazed upon the city of Lud.

Acknowledgements

Thanks to Simon Mason, our editor, who found us dismasted in the doldrums and piloted us safely home. Thanks to Catherine Clarke, our formidable agent, for making lots of people (including us) believe we could do this. Thanks to Hannah, David and all at DFB – for unwavering support, and making us take the time to get it right.

For encouragement and acute criticism, thanks to our wonderful parents, and all the other family and friends who read the book in its many different drafts. Above all, our dearest thanks to our wives, Issy and Sarah, for their patience, wisdom and love.